Betty Walker lives in Cornwall with her large family, where she enjoys gardening and coastal walks. She loves discovering curious historical facts, and devotes much time to investigating her family tree. She also writes bestselling contemporary thrillers as Jane Holland.

The Cornish Girls Before the Storm is the ninth novel in Betty Walker's heart-warming series.

The Cornish Girls series:

Wartime with the Cornish Girls
Christmas with the Cornish Girls
Courage for the Cornish Girls
A Mother's Hope for the Cornish Girls
A Wedding for the Cornish Girls
Victory for the Cornish Girls
A New Hope for the Cornish Girls
Brighter Days for the Cornish Girls

Readers have fallen for the Cornish Girls

'A fascinating story, beautifully written, with interesting characters I really liked. A most enjoyable read!'
Kitty Neale

'A warm-hearted story – at times I laughed and at others I held my breath ... I loved the characters and I'm delighted it is the first in a series'
Pam Weaver

'Much loved characters that will stay with you, due to their courage, determination and patriotic spirit'
***** **Reader Review**

'Beautifully written and totally draws you in from the beginning'
***** **Reader Review**

'A poignant and all-round heart-warming saga'
***** **Reader Review**

'Truly beautiful historical fiction. What a wonderful cast of characters to meet!'
***** **Reader Review**

The Cornish Girls
Before the Storm

BETTY WALKER

avon.

Published by AVON
A division of HarperCollins*Publishers*
1 London Bridge Street
London SE1 9GF

www.harpercollins.co.uk

HarperCollins*Publishers*
Macken House, 39/40 Mayor Street Upper
Dublin 1
D01 C9W8

A Paperback Original 2026
1
First published in Great Britain by HarperCollins*Publishers* 2026

Copyright © Jane Holland 2026

Jane Holland asserts the moral right to be identified as the author of this work.

A catalogue copy of this book is available from the British Library.

ISBN: 978-0-00-871517-5

This novel is entirely a work of fiction. The names, characters and incidents portrayed in it are the work of the author's imagination. Any resemblance to actual persons, living or dead, events or localities is entirely coincidental.

Typeset in Minion Pro by Palimpsest Book Production Limited, Falkirk, Stirlingshire

Printed and bound in UK using 100% Renewable Electricity at CPI Group (UK) Ltd

All rights reserved. No part of this text may be reproduced, transmitted, down-loaded, decompiled, reverse engineered, or stored in or introduced into any information storage and retrieval system, in any form or by any means, whether electronic or mechanical, without the express written permission of the publishers.

Without limiting the exclusive rights of any author, contributor or the publisher of this publication, any unauthorized use of this publication to train generative artificial intelligence (AI) technologies is expressly prohibited. HarperCollins also exercise their rights under Article 4(3) of the Digital Single Market Directive 2019/790 and expressly reserve this publication from the text and data mining exception.

This book contains FSC™ certified paper and other controlled sources to ensure responsible forest management.

For more information visit: www.harpercollins.co.uk/green

CHAPTER ONE

Dagenham, England, February 1939

'Happy Valentine's Day, my darling,' Henry said, halting in front of a posh teashop with a triumphant gesture. He grinned at her baffled expression. 'I thought you might like to be the one ordering the cakes for once, not serving them.'

So that was why he'd dragged her all the way to Ilford on their afternoon off. 'Goodness me, are you going to buy us tea and cakes?' Sheila was astonished. 'That's very good of you. But the Regal Tearooms? Ain't it a bit dear?' She peered through the glass at the ladies on the nearest table. They were dressed in posh hats and nibbling on dainty sandwiches, nothing like the folk that came into the caff where she worked. She deserved a treat; that was for certain. But she worried she might feel out of place here.

'We can afford it,' her husband insisted stubbornly.

Lovingly, she studied her husband's reflection in the teashop window. He was sixty-six now, yet still as handsome as on their wedding day. His hair was silver these days, and his best waistcoat had recently needed to be let out another inch, but he still turned heads, just as he'd turned hers the first time they'd met. Beside Henry's smart figure, she looked a little portly and pink-cheeked, though her new hairstyle made her feel ten years younger. Still, she could scarcely believe she was fifty-eight now.

Where had the years gone?

Still, they had two grown-up daughters to show for it, her lovely Violet and Betsy, and two adorable granddaughters as well. Betsy and her husband, Ernest, were justifiably proud of their girls. Dear Lily was a capable fifteen-year-old and almost ready to leave school, while Alice, an incorrigible bookworm, was eagerly looking forward to her fourteenth birthday in April.

Sheila would have liked a grandson to fuss over too, but you couldn't have everything, and they were the sweetest girls in the world.

'Shall we go in, then?' Henry was holding the door open for her.

'To tell you the truth, Mr Hopkins, I've been so blooming busy this week, I clean forgot about Valentine's,' she hurried on, feeling embarrassed. She had not bought him a present and perhaps she ought to have done. She didn't want him to think she didn't care. 'Ron's got some bee in his bonnet about moving all the tables about and repainting the walls to match the new red-check tablecloths he bought. I can tell you, we've been at sixes and sevens for days, since Ron refuses to close the caff while all that's going on, and Betsy and I . . . Oh!'

Her explanation was abruptly cut off as he dragged her into the quiet opulence of the teashop, where a smiling platinum-blonde waitress in a smart uniform was waiting to escort them to a table, menus already in hand.

'Are you sure, Henry?' she whispered urgently in his ear. 'You know we're still saving up for Betsy and Ernest's wedding anniversary bash. Won't this put a dent in the fund?'

'Not by so much as a sixpence, my love,' her husband assured her smoothly.

He held out her seat for her, waiting until she'd sat down. The blonde waitress bustled away to fetch them a pot of tea, while they looked at the menu. Henry nodded across to the photograph of the branch manager, framed and on proud display behind the cashier's counter. 'That's Phil Potts . . . I done him a favour the other week, and he offered me free afternoon tea for two in return, should I wish to bring the missus in for a special Valentine's celebration.' He pulled a card from his wallet and placed it on the table. 'So here we are. Fill your boots.'

Sheila eyed him and the card suspiciously. 'What sort of favour?'

'I wrangled a knockdown price for one of our fancy new Ford Prefects just coming off the production line. We're not meant to give out discounts except for family, but what the eye doesn't see, the heart can't grieve over, eh?' Henry handed her a menu before opening his own and raising a brow at the contents. 'Cucumber sandwiches. Strawberry cheesecake. Buttered slices of walnut and date bread. Well, my word . . . This is the life.'

'Ain't it just?' Sheila could have wished he'd thought to bring her here without the offer of free grub. But she wouldn't have it any other way. Henry Hopkins was still the silver-tongued salesman she'd married, always with a sharp eye for a deal.

'I'm fair parched too, so I hope they're not slow with the teapot.'

Thankfully, they weren't. The manager had spotted Henry and came over with the tea tray himself.

'Mr Hopkins, a pleasure to see you.' Mr Potts extended his arm and they shook hands warmly.

'How's the Ford Prefect doing?' Henry asked.

'Even better than expected – runs like a dream,' said Mr Potts.

Sheila studied their surroundings covertly while the two men talked cars, wondering if Ron would ever make them wear a starched uniform at the caff, rather than just a frilly pinny, and if he'd ever invest in printed menus, not just their tatty drinks list and the chalkboard they wrote up each morning with specials.

The waitress returned with dainty cakes and sandwich triangles displayed elegantly on a three-tier willow-pattern cake stand, and at last Mr Potts took the hint and left them to it.

'He could chat for Britain, that one,' Sheila muttered.

For all the bread was wafer-thin, the sarnies were still delicious, and the cakes rich and achingly soft, laced with oodles of whipped cream. The tea was pale and fragrant compared to the mugs of strong, mud-brown workmen's brew they served at the caff.

As they tucked into a tasty spread, courtesy of Phil Potts, they talked of the coal bunker at their back door, which needed a new door, the old one having rotted. This interesting topic having been exhausted, Henry raised the spectre of troubles in Europe, insisting that war was on the cards if Mr Hitler didn't stop messing about with Germany's neighbours.

Sheila, left deeply uncomfortable by this, decided to change the subject to something lighter.

'Talking of messing about,' she interrupted, pretending not to notice his offended stare, 'I need to stop faffing and finish my letter to Maggie tomorrow so I can post it.'

Her older sister Margaret still lived back in Cornwall where they'd both been born. Sheila had left there almost half a century before, moving to Dagenham with her parents, but her sister had remained behind to get married. Sheila still held fond memories of blackberrying in Cornwall's green lanes with a certain lad whom she'd tried and failed to forget over the years. All that was in the distant past, of course, but she and Maggie were still in touch. More or less, anyway.

'Gawd knows why it's taking me so long to write it,' she went on hurriedly. 'I suppose I'm not in the habit anymore of putting thoughts together on paper.'

Henry looked at her from under dark brows. 'Writing to your sister? That's not like you, Shee.'

'Didn't I just say that?' She took a sip of tea. For all its delicacy, she decided she preferred the brew at the caff. This was weak as dishwater. She took a spoon to the silver pot, vigorously stirring it. 'Well, Maggie's still my flesh and blood, however much she turns her nose up at us. And I'd like her to come upcountry for Betsy and Ernest's anniversary this year. I know Cornwall's a fair distance but there's a train, ain't there? And it's not too far to come for her own niece, is it?'

'No,' he agreed, selecting a beef paste sandwich and biting into it, 'and it's not as though she has any kids of her own.'

Sheila clucked her tongue. 'Henry, don't. That ain't her fault. Gawd knows she tried hard enough with that awful good-for-nothing bloke she married straight out of school. And by the time he'd shuffled off, and she married Stanley, there weren't much chance of children anymore, not at her age. Poor Maggie.' She gave him a direct look. 'We had a few problems in that line ourselves, if you recall.'

'I haven't forgotten.' He reached across and squeezed her hand, his look earnest. 'And never will.'

'Me neither.' Sheila's eyes turned misty as she recalled an early lost pregnancy that had left her down for months, barely able to get up in the morning some days. But they'd got through that tough time together – and all the tough times that had followed – and the future was looking bright for them at last, if they ignored the troubles brewing on the Continent. 'I do love you, Henry.'

'I love you too, Sheila.' He raised his cup in a salute, a twinkle in his eyes. 'To us, Mrs Hopkins.'

'To us,' she echoed with a tremor in her voice, tears in her eyes, and sipped from her own cup only to shake her head in disapproval. 'Oh, this tea ... Whatever do they make it with? Acorns?'

And they both laughed.

After getting off the bus in Dagenham, they popped into the Corner Caff on their way home to see if Betsy had finished her shift and wanted to walk some of the way back with her parents.

Betsy and her husband lived only a few streets away from them, in a recently built three-bedroom home on the Becontree Estate, so they were often in and out of each other's houses, while young Lily and Alice sometimes came to their gran's for tea on the way home from school. Betsy had started working two afternoons a week at the caff, earning a little extra housekeeping money while giving Sheila a day off and more time at home for all the jobs that needed doing.

It wasn't easy for a married woman to hold down even a part-time job, what with all the cooking and cleaning she had to get through each week at home. Sheila's late mum had frequently pointed out how much harder it had been for *her* generation, keeping house while old Queen Vic was still on the throne, without all the labour-saving devices modern housewives enjoyed. But, as Sheila had just as often retorted, many housewives in those days hadn't been expected to work outside the home.

It wasn't that Sheila had wanted to take work for the money. Henry brought home a good salary, even if it did leave them short every now and then. But once her two daughters had grown up and no longer needed looking after, she'd been bored stiff. True, her younger daughter, Violet, was unmarried and still lived at home, kept busy by a cleaning job at a nearby factory. Though twenty-seven now, Violet was an attractive blonde with plenty of admirers, and could leave to get married at any moment if she would ever agree to go courting again. Her fiancé had sadly died not long before they were due to marry. Ever since then, she had behaved like a nun, staying home every weekend as though still pining for poor Leonard.

Anyway, Henry had disapproved of her taking a job at first. He'd felt it was a slight on his ability to bring home a good enough paycheque. But she'd soon set him straight. 'I ain't cut out to sit moping about at home all day. I'd rather be out and about, making meself useful.' And indeed, a few days' work every week gave her a renewed sense of purpose.

Sheila loved Ron's busy caff and enjoyed nothing better than a cosy chat with his regulars.

When Ronald had eventually wanted her to work longer hours, Betsy had offered to take on two shifts. This left Sheila with more time to ensure the housework was still looked after. Between that and the extra money she brought in, her husband really had nothing to complain about.

Betsy was just taking off her apron as they walked in the door. She was tall, like her father, and wore her long fair hair in soft rolls that sat prettily under a headscarf during work hours.

'Hello, Mum,' she said cheerfully, and nodded to a lidded tin on the counter. 'Ron said we might as well help ourselves to the last of that sponge cake with the coconut icing, as it'll be too dry to eat by the morning. I've taken a few slices for me, Ernest and the girls; the rest is for you.'

Ron, who'd been busy with a customer, now turned with a ready smile at the sound of his name. 'Hello, Sheila,' he said, and nodded to her husband, holding out a hand. 'Mr Hopkins, how are you?'

Henry's reply was a little stiff, though he shook the owner's hand. He didn't much like Ronald and never bothered to hide it, suspecting him of flirting with his wife. Which was just ridiculous, given that Ron was over seventy now. 'Well, thank you, Mr Coates. I hope your arthritis is improved?'

Wrapping up their cake slices in greaseproof paper, Sheila threw her husband a resentful look. She'd told him confidentially about Ronald's arthritis. Her boss was a proud man and might not take kindly to his employees gossiping about his various ailments behind his back.

Thankfully though, Ron didn't blink. 'Much better,' he

said. 'Have you dropped in for a cuppa? It's nearly closing time, but I can bring a tray over if you care to take a seat.'

'No thanks,' Henry said shortly. 'We've just come from afternoon tea at the Regal Tearooms, as it happens. They do a tasty seedcake, don't they, Sheila?'

'But not as nice as our own Victoria sponge, which always goes down a treat with a mug of tea,' Sheila insisted, grabbing an astonished Betsy by the arm and marching her to the door. 'I'll see you tomorrow, Ron. Tatty bye!' She was seething but waited until they were out of sight of the caff before whirling on Henry, hands on her hips. 'Henry Hopkins, what do you mean by embarrassing me in front of my boss like that? There was no call to tell 'im we'd just had tea at the Regal. Now he'll think we're too stuck-up to have a cuppa and a slice of cake at his caff.'

'I'm sure Mr Coates won't think anything of the sort,' Betsy told her, but shook her head, glancing fondly from one parent to the other. 'You two . . . You're not happy unless you're arguing.'

'I don't know what you're talking about,' Henry grumbled, but Sheila noted how he didn't quite dare catch her eye for fear of another scolding.

Carrying the cake tin, Betsy walked on with a chuckle. Sheila thought her eldest daughter was looking a little pensive but made no comment, linking arms with Henry instead as they followed behind. She knew Betsy wouldn't like her nosing around her business, and besides, she'd found it was always best to talk to her daughters on their own when things weren't going well.

'So Dad took you to the Regal Tearooms for a Valentine's treat, did he?' Betsy gave a sigh. 'I wish Ernest would take me somewhere posh like that. But you know how hard up we've been lately; it wouldn't be fair to ask him to spend more.'

'Do you need any help with money, love?' Henry offered, though Sheila wasn't sure they were in much of a better position themselves. They paused outside Betsy's new home.

'Oh no, Dad, though thanks. We'll sort things out eventually. The rent on this place is so much more than our old digs, and although the job at Ron's is useful for housekeeping money, it ain't enough to put more than an extra few sausages on the table each week.' Betsy looked wistfully at her house, which was south-facing with a smartly scrubbed front step and pretty front garden. 'I'd dearly love some good fabric to make up a pair of new curtains for the front bedroom. Them ones there are so thin, they let in all the light.'

'Your dad and I were just the same when we started out,' Sheila told her with a wink. 'But we made do, didn't we, Henry?'

'That's right,' he agreed, fiddling with his pipe.

The door opened and Ernest came down the garden path still in his work clothes, oil-stained overalls with *Ford* on the front pocket, wiping his dirty hands on a clean cloth.

Ernest Fisher was tall and fair-haired, and still exceptionally handsome even in his forties. Sheila remembered having been rather impressed by her daughter's clever, well-read suitor when Betsy had first brought him home to meet the parents. Ernest had worn well since then, with only a few lines here and there to show his age.

'Mother, Father, it's good to see you,' he said with a smile, inclining his head in his very correct way, with the merest hint of a German accent giving away his heritage, though in truth he was half English too. His given name was Ernst, but in recent years, a growing anti-German feeling had intensified, and he'd begun insisting that everyone refer to him as Ernest instead. Sheila reckoned that was a wise decision. She knew from the last war how quickly things could turn violent, even among usually sensible people.

'And my dearest Betsy . . .'

His eyes softened, resting on his wife's face as she pushed open the garden gate. Sheila was always happy to see how deep in love he was still after all these years. Not that he had any reason not to be. Betsy was thirty-five now, yet still as pretty and golden-haired as she'd been the day he'd married her, even after raising two girls. She was a good wife and mother too, always looking out for her daughters. And they'd done so well for themselves, getting this smart new house – it fair made her heart burst with pride.

'I was just coming to escort you home from work, my love,' he went on. 'But I see I'm too late.'

'I wasn't expecting you home so early, love,' Betsy exclaimed, kissing her husband on the cheek. Then her gaze narrowed on his face. 'You ain't been given the push at the Ford plant, have you?'

'On the contrary,' Ernest told them all, pushing his blond, floppy hair back with a smile, 'I've been given *a promotion*.'

Betsy's jaw dropped open. 'Now you're pulling my leg.'

'No leg-pulling, I assure you. I put in an application last week and had my interview this morning.' Ernest was looking very pleased with himself.

'I say, well done.' Henry shook his son-in-law's hand over the low fence. 'Better money?'

'Much better, yes. And it's office-based too, so I can finally wear a suit to work, as you do, instead of these dirty overalls.' Ernest glanced down at himself with a wry grin.

'Good show!'

'That's excellent news, Ernest,' Sheila said warmly, pleased for the younger couple. 'But what kind of office work will you be doing? Sales, like Henry?'

Ernest nodded. 'Similar, yes. European sales and export negotiations. I already speak German, of course, but my French and Italian are also pretty good. Our previous negotiator just left for a job in America, so I jumped at the opportunity. I may know how to put an engine together, but I prefer the idea of using a typewriter or a telephone to make my living,' he added with a wink. 'There's some suggestion that if I do a good enough job and impress the bosses, I might get sent to the big showrooms in Regent Street.'

'Central London?' Henry's brows rose.

'My clever husband,' Betsy said, smiling proudly.

Ernest grinned.

'Well, more money sounds good to me,' Sheila told him. 'Betsy was just saying as how she'd love a new pair of curtains in your front bedroom.' She nodded to her daughter. 'I'll lend you my Singer, if that'll help.' The Singer wasn't new but it would be quicker than sewing curtains by hand.

'Yes thanks, Mum.' Betsy looked delighted. 'I've a few dressmaking projects that could do with some help from your Singer too.'

'Ah, more of Ron's leftover cakes?' Ernest took the cake tin from Betsy with a sardonic smile. 'I wonder, perhaps you would like to go to the pictures tonight to celebrate my promotion? And a fish-and-chip supper afterwards?' He laughed when she flew into his arms. 'It is Valentine's Day, after all.'

'Oh, Ernie . . . Yes, please!'

'Well, we'll leave you lovebirds to have a nice evening,' Sheila said with a cough as they kissed, pulling Henry away discreetly. 'Come along, Mr Hopkins. I've got that letter to write, remember? And Violet will be wondering where on earth we've got to.'

Sheila and Henry let themselves into Number 27, the cosy two-up, two-down terraced house where they'd been living since their first years as a young married couple. It might not be as fancy as the houses on the new estate, with their indoor lavs and big gardens out the back, but it was still Home Sweet Home, as her own framed embroidery that hung above the hall mirror agreed. It was blooming chilly though.

Sheila bustled into the front room to turn on the gas fire and startled her daughter, Violet, who'd been sitting under a blanket with her back to the door, huddled over the photograph album.

'Oh, Mum, Dad . . . I didn't hear you come in!' Violet jumped to her feet, closing the album. Her eyes were red, and she was trying to hide a crumpled handkerchief in one fist, her cheeks suspiciously damp.

'You all right, love?' Sheila asked, her heart welling with pity. She knew precisely what Violet had been doing: weeping over the only two photographs she owned of poor Leonard. He had died of influenza only a few short months before their planned wedding day. How long had it been since Leonard had passed away? More than two years, she thought with an inward sigh. Yet Violet was still pining for her lost beau.

Leonard had been a lovely lad, of course, and he and Violet had been head over heels in love. But surely time ought to have healed that wound by now?

Looking embarrassed, Violet rubbed the back of her hand across wet eyes. 'I'm fine, Mum, don't fuss,' she mumbled, putting away the photograph album. 'Look at the time . . . I'd better get the tea on.'

'I'll be right in to help you,' Sheila promised her.

Henry hung up his hat and coat in the hall, watching their daughter go into the kitchen, then turned to Sheila.

'I keep wishing she'd meet someone new,' he said in a low voice. 'But when she barely leaves this house except for work . . .' He sighed, leaving the rest unsaid.

'I know. But least said, soonest mended, eh?' Sheila didn't quite believe that, but what else could she say? She gave him a brave smile instead. 'Now, before I write that letter to Maggie, how about we eat them slices of leftover cake from the caff with a glass or two of my home-made wine? To finish off Valentine's Day in style?' She turned towards the cupboard under the stairs where her wine bottles were stored. 'My elderberry should be about ready to drink by now.'

Her husband hesitated. 'Oh, erm, your elderberry wine? I wouldn't say no. But maybe just a small glass for me.'

Sheila stopped and narrowed her eyes at him. 'What are you trying to say, Henry Hopkins? I thought you liked my home-made wine?'

'I do . . . Nothing more delicious, love. It's what it does to my head afterwards that worries me.' He grinned. 'I've got work in the morning, remember.'

'Maybe an early night might be the answer, then,' she suggested with a cheeky wink, and smiled happily when he put an arm about her waist, bending to kiss her. 'Oh, Henry...'

CHAPTER TWO

Betsy Fisher rethreaded the needle, though it was devilishly tricky, and checked her fabric was properly aligned. Satisfied, she pressed down on the foot pedal, smiling as the Singer hummed happily along. Her mum's old sewing machine was looking its age now, but it still worked a treat. And as it was better than the alternative – stitching by hand – she had accepted the loan gladly. Ernest had promised her a second-hand Singer of her own once his next paycheque arrived, but this job couldn't wait. As soon as they had decided to throw an anniversary party, she knew which frock she was going to wear. It had to be the same dress she'd worn on the day he'd asked her to marry him, all those years ago, after they'd attended a friend's birthday party together. The dress held huge sentimental value for her, and she knew Ernest would recognise it immediately. He was a clever, thoughtful man, and very little escaped him. It was a wonderful quality, even though that meant she often found it hard to keep secrets from him . . .

Since her pre-marriage days though, she'd had two

children, and her figure had changed significantly. Ernest might find no issue with her larger bust and hips, or the curve of her belly, but she had struggled to get into the old frock, despite its loose-fitting style.

Thankfully, she'd managed to find similar material at the haberdashery with which to add two discreet but stylish side vents, permitting the knee-length dress to fit her more mature figure. Perhaps she wouldn't look exactly the same as she'd done at nineteen. But it was the sentiment that counted, and she knew that Ernest would understand. Besides which, they couldn't afford for her to buy a new dress off-the-peg or some lengths of fabric to make one up herself on the Singer, so this was also the most economical choice.

Betsy held the half-finished frock up against herself and smiled. Yes, once the second side vent had been added, it would fit nicely. The anniversary party was right around the corner, thank goodness. Because she'd started having a queasy feeling in the pit of her stomach, and that strange tingling sensation she used to get in the early days of pregnancy. Could she be expecting again at last?

She draped her frock over the back of her sewing chair and slipped into the hall to check her figure in the mirror under the hat stand. There was nothing to see yet, not even a rounded tummy. But she had missed her last monthly, and she knew the signs . . .

Should she tell Ernest about this new pregnancy yet? They had been trying to have another child, off and on, since Alice had reached the age of five. Years had gone by, and she'd almost given up hope.

She knew that Ernest would dearly love a son as well as

his two daughters. But he'd not put her under pressure to produce one, of course, and she loved him all the more for that. However, she was eager for another child herself, and if she could manage to bring a boy into the world at last . . . Well, she would be the happiest woman alive.

But she'd learnt not to get her hopes up too soon. Or Ernest's. She'd already lost three pregnancies at an early stage of pregnancy, once before the doctor had even confirmed that she was expecting.

Those losses had been so painful. She'd wept bitterly for days afterwards, finding it hard to get out of bed in the mornings or concentrate on her daily tasks, inconsolable with grief. Ernest had tried his best to cheer her up, but she'd seen how unhappy the grief had left him too. They had tacitly decided not to try again after the last traumatic time.

Somehow, they must have been careless though, for here she was again, with that odd butterflies-in-the-stomach sensation.

She was biting her lip, gazing into her own wide eyes in the mirror, when a loud noise made her jump. Somebody had banged with their fist on the front door, only a few feet away. Her hand flew to her mouth, and she stared at the closed door in shock. Who on earth could that be? It was still early afternoon and she wasn't expecting Ernest back for ages. Though he had a key and would never bang on the door in such an aggressive manner. Nor would her mother.

Tentatively, she crept to the door and listened. The loud hammering came again, close to her head, and she started, gasping. Whoever it was had said nothing, but their knock sounded so angry.

Did Ernest owe somebody money? Surely he would have

told her. He'd never leave her in the awkward position of having to deal with some embarrassing demand for money on the doorstep.

Her heart thudding, she unlocked the door and jerked it open. But the perpetrator had already fled.

She looked out at the sunlit street. There was a group of boys milling around. School had just finished for the day and often the older children messed about outside, kicking a ball about and shouting, before heading home for tea. She recognised some of the faces with a sinking feeling. They were unpleasant young men who often sneered at her in the street when Ernest wasn't there.

They had turned to stare now, and two of them were openly laughing. One lad yelled something she didn't catch.

How dare they come and bang on her door, frightening her like that?

Furious now, she demanded, 'All right, who knocked on my door? Was it one of you lot? Don't you have any manners?'

'Not for Hun-loving scum, we don't!' one boy shouted back and pushed past his friends to confront her. His hands thrust into his trouser pockets, his shirt hanging loose, she recognised him as Peter Short, the son of a local troublemaker. He was in his last year in school and he'd be heading off to an apprenticeship at Ford in the summer, she suspected. Until then, Lily had told them he was doing as little schoolwork as he could get away with. There was a jeering expression on his face. 'We all know what your husband is. Tell him to go back to Germany where he belongs.'

He threw up a hand stiffly, in what was undoubtedly supposed to be a Nazi salute.

The other boys all laughed, watching her with malicious excitement.

'You horrible, vile boys . . .' she started in a choking voice, and then abruptly stopped.

Peter Short was a nasty bully, but his dad had worked alongside her own husband at the plant until recently. Now Ernest had been promoted into a sales and negotiations department, away from the mechanics, because he spoke several European languages. Ford management had thought he might do better in an office-based job than on the production line.

Perhaps some of the workers had thought his promotion was unfair and were looking for revenge. It went against the grain, but it might be better to ignore the boy and not get into a scrap that could only end badly and jeopardise Ernest's career.

Betsy stalked back inside, her head held high. But once inside, her composure crumbled. She leant back against the closed door, breathless and fighting off panic.

What could she do? Not very much. But she ought to tell Ernest when he got home. He knew Mr Short, and some of those other boys' parents, and would want to go round and have words with them. It wasn't right, allowing young lads to rampage about the streets like that, banging on people's doors and throwing unpleasant and untrue accusations at them. And that brutal, distressing gesture that everyone knew meant one thing only.

She couldn't believe how bold he'd been, behaving so rudely towards her in public. Though she knew why he'd done it. Everyone was saying there would be a war soon, and with all the anti-German sentiments swirling around, no doubt nasty bullies like Peter Short and his dad felt emboldened to behave like savages. So few people seemed to understand that being German and being a Nazi were not the same thing.

Betsy pushed away from the door and glanced at herself in the mirror again. A single tear was rolling down her cheek and her lip was trembling. Trying to do what was best for her husband, she wiped damp eyes and took a deep breath. It was getting late. If those boys were already playing out in the streets, that meant the girls would be home from school soon too.

Her party frock forgotten, she hurried into the kitchen where she began to prepare vegetables for the evening's meal, her hands shaking, her movements uncoordinated.

Hun-loving scum . . .

No, she decided. She wouldn't tell Ernest. What good would it do, after all? It would only make him angry to know that such insults had been thrown at his wife, and she didn't want him to get into a row over it.

It was so unfair though, she thought bitterly, fetching a colander to wash the vegetables. Ernest was a good man; he didn't deserve all that hatred. He worked hard to provide for his family, like everyone else. He'd lived in Britain for as long as he could remember – he more or less *was* British – yet a few of their neighbours still seemed to hate him, simply because of his parentage.

Soon, she heard light, running footsteps, and then the back door flew open, letting in the welcome sunshine. Alice tumbled into the kitchen, giggling. 'I got top marks in reading again,' she exclaimed, holding up a schoolbook. She dashed to the biscuit tin, dragging off the top, and thrust a hand in.

'Well done . . . But you still only get one chocolate biscuit, I'm afraid, so put those other ones back,' Betsy told her, ignoring the girl's disappointed protests. She turned instead to smile at her eldest daughter, Lily, who had trailed into the house after Alice in a less excitable fashion. 'Hello, love. How was your day?'

'Not too bad, thanks,' Lily told her with a carefully neutral expression, also heading for the biscuit barrel. 'What's for supper?'

'Bangers and mash with greens, and trifle for dessert.'

'Super! Smashing!' Alice cried indistinctly, with a mouth full of biscuit. An avid reader, she was prone to devouring *Boys' Own Annuals* instead of the nice stories about kittens and puppies that the school librarian always tried to point out to her, and had taken to adopting its slang.

Betsy took Lily's school blazer and hung it over a chair back. She didn't like the strained look on her eldest daughter's face. 'What is it, love? You don't look well.'

Lily hesitated.

'They're bullying her at school again,' Alice blurted out. 'Kenny and Bobby, the dastardly duo. In the playground at home time, they snatched her schoolbag and threw it up into a tree, calling her names. Me too, I suppose. I never paid any attention to them though, because boys are just stupid squirts, but Lily . . .' She tailed off, no doubt catching Lily's furious shake of her head. 'Well, I'd better go upstairs. I made one tiny mistake in arithmetic today and now I've been press-ganged into doing a whole extra sheet of trigonometry problems,' she added darkly and flounced out of the kitchen, slinging her school satchel over one shoulder. 'I swear that Miss Nicholson hates me, horrid old bag!'

Alone with Lily, Betsy put a hand on her shoulder. Her daughter was trembling, she realised. She felt a surge of sympathy. But she was careful not to make matters worse by forcing the issue. 'Do you want to tell me about it, love?'

Lily shook her head. 'It's nothing,' she whispered, and averted her gaze.

'Because I can let your father know, and he—'

'No!' Lily said emphatically.

Their eyes met.

'I got my bag back, all right?' Lily's chin lifted stubbornly. 'One of the other boys fetched it for me. Everything's fine.'

'Very well,' Betsy murmured and let her go. 'You'd best change out of your uniform before supper. Hang that dress up, mind. No dropping it on the floor.'

'I'm not Alice, Mum,' Lily pointed out, but her smile had returned, even if it struck Betsy as a little fragile. She took one biscuit with careful economy and replaced the lid on the tin. 'Bangers and mash . . . That sounds tasty. With gravy too?'

'Of course.'

Betsy watched her go, and then sank down onto a kitchen chair, potato peeler in hand, fighting back tears. Bad enough that she'd been insulted by those bullying young men outside the house today. But now it was happening to her daughters, and at school too, where they should be safe. Why should her daughters suffer because of who their father was, his blood giving them partial German heritage themselves? Worst of all, she didn't think it would be a good idea to share any of this with her husband.

More than ever, with rumours flying everywhere about war with Germany being all but inevitable, they needed to be seen as model citizens. And if Ernest knew there had been cruelty and name-calling, he would be rightly furious and defend his family, potentially making everything far worse . . .

Much to Betsy's satisfaction, all her hard work over the adjustments to her old frock were vindicated when their anniversary came around the following week. The evening of the party, she saw Ernest's eyes widen as she came downstairs wearing the dress, and grinned back at him. 'Yes, it's the same frock . . . What do you think?'

'I think you haven't changed one jot since the day I asked you to marry me,' her husband murmured, bending over her hand to kiss it as though she were royalty. 'Mrs Fisher, *Liebling*, I love you madly.'

Betsy blushed, thrilled by this response to her choice of frock, and kissed him on the lips. 'I love you too.'

The two girls had already gone straight to the caff after school that Friday to help their gran lay the tables and put up decorations. Mr Coates had kindly agreed to let them hold the celebration there after closing time, with no charge except for food and refreshments, which her mum had insisted she would mostly prepare on her own.

Ernest drove her to the party and then went looking for a parking place, as the streets were quite narrow around the caff. She had intended to walk in with him, but it was drizzling with rain when they pulled up and she was worried about her hairdo being spoiled, even though she'd kept it covered with a headscarf since leaving the salon that afternoon.

'I won't be long,' Ernest promised her as she clambered

out. 'You get in out of the rain, love. Pour me a drink. Rum punch, if there is any . . . None of your mother's strange, home-made concoctions, all right?'

Laughing, she hurried inside and found her family waiting impatiently for her.

'Where's Ernest?' her mother demanded, helping her out of her jacket. 'Gawd . . . You don't 'alf look a treat in that blue frock, love. Done yourself proud there. Ain't she, Henry?'

'My little girl,' Henry said proudly, and kissed her on the forehead. 'I remember that dress from when you were young. Too young to be courting, we thought! But you proved us wrong.'

'I had to let it out a bit,' Betsy admitted, hugging her girls as they too clustered about her. 'Otherwise, I'd have bust a seam as soon as I sat down!'

Betsy gave a twirl for Violet.

'Not bad, sis,' Violet told her with a wink. 'But you might want to take the headscarf off . . . You look like you're going shopping.'

'I'd almost forgotten that!' They all laughed as Betsy carefully unknotted her headscarf.

'Happy anniversary,' said Ronald Coates, holding out a present wrapped in garish red paper. Betsy took it in surprise, stammering a few words of thanks. 'But where is *Mr* Fisher?' he added.

'Yes, why didn't Ernest escort you in?' her mum demanded, hands on hips.

'He's just parking the car,' she told them, quickly unwrapping the present and gaping down at a dainty china milk jug. Turning it over, she saw it was an expensive piece made in Dresden, Germany. 'Oh, Mr Coates, thank you . . . But this is too much. You really oughtn't have.'

'Nonsense. I saw it on a market stall and thought you might like it, given that your husband's German . . .' An awkward silence followed this, and Ronald cleared his throat, looking embarrassed. 'Well, we'd better check on those sausage rolls before they burn, Sheila.' He smiled round at Lily. 'Give us a hand in the kitchen, there's a good girl.'

Betsy looked at her daughter. Lily had changed out of her school uniform into a demure green woollen dress with two big front pockets. She thought proudly that she'd never seen her eldest daughter looking so grown up.

Ron and Lily disappeared into the kitchen together, leaving Betsy unsure what to do with the caff owner's expensive gift.

'Give that to me, love,' her dad muttered, holding out a hand. 'I'll put it in your mum's handbag for safekeeping. Lord knows that bag's big enough to hold the *Titanic* . . . Yes, and all its deckchairs.' And he too hurried away.

The door jangled, and Betsy turned in relief, expecting to see Ernest. But it was a group of their neighbours, smiling and also holding out small gifts.

'Oh, you shouldn't have!' she exclaimed, thanking them warmly. She hadn't even considered that people might bring them anniversary presents. She caught her father's eye as he returned. 'Dad, maybe we could find a box to put gifts in?'

Soon, the busy caff was packed with party guests, milling about with glasses of sweet wine and plates of Sheila's thick ham and cheese sandwiches in hand. Many complimented Betsy on her lovely frock, and almost as many asked where Ernest was, especially his friends and fellow workers from the Ford plant. His new boss even made an appearance, introducing himself with a beaming smile, and she felt embarrassed and confused that her husband had still not returned from parking the car. It surely oughtn't have taken so much time?

'Where on earth has Ernest got to?' Violet whispered in her ear.

Betsy hugged herself, trying to keep smiling. 'I wish I knew,' she told her sister.

Ronald had set up a gramophone player in the corner and put on some lively dance music. The tables were pushed back and a few couples started to dance. Betsy watched them with a forced smile on her face, her thoughts whirling. Where could he be? Whatever could have happened?

Finally, the bell over the door jangled again and she spun around, exclaiming in horror.

It was Ernest at last.

But . . . oh! Her husband looked very different now. His smart suit had a torn lapel, his fair hair flopped wildly over his forehead, and he had a bruise swelling on his left cheek. Despite all this, he quickly smoothed his hair into place as he came limping slightly to shake his boss's hand, throwing an apologetic smile at Betsy and his in-laws.

'So glad you could make it, Mr Rogers,' he told his boss, rather breathlessly, and slipped an arm about Betsy's shaking shoulders. 'You've met my wife, I see. I'll get us both a drink in a tick. Sorry I was delayed, darling,' he added, kissing Betsy on the cheek. 'I ran into some trouble.'

Her dad had come up, listening to this. 'Trouble, Ernie?' he demanded in his deep, rumbling voice. He was frowning. 'What kind of trouble? Looks like you've been in a fight.'

'Oh, it was nothing. A bit of rough and tumble in the

street. Some young idiots . . .' Ernest brushed aside whatever had happened with his usual calm, but Betsy couldn't help staring at him in consternation. Had he really been in a *fight*? It seemed impossible. And yet there was that bruise on his face, and his torn clothes . . .

After he and his boss had exchanged a few smiling words, she dragged Ernest aside. 'What happened? And I want the truth.'

'I told you the truth.' His brows drew together, and he kissed her soothingly. 'Please, *Liebling* . . . There's no need to fret. They were just a few kids making a nuisance of themselves, that's all. You know how high tensions have been running lately. It was nothing I couldn't handle.'

'You need to tell the police,' Betsy insisted.

But Ernest smiled and shook his head. 'And spoil our anniversary party? I've wasted enough time on those little twerps already tonight.' He tapped his foot to the popular tune playing on the gramophone, then seized her hand, winking. 'Come on, let's dance!'

And he whirled her away to join the other dancing couples, with only the occasional wince for his injuries. Betsy laughed, caught up in his arms, but there was still doubt at the back of her mind. Who exactly had attacked him tonight, and why? It wasn't like her lovely, polite Ernest to be fighting in the street like a ruffian. What if it happened again, only worse next time? Her monthlies still hadn't arrived, and she might really be expecting another baby at last. More than ever, she needed her husband safe and by her side . . .

CHAPTER THREE

Weighed down by her bulging suitcase, Edith trudged around the corner in the gloom of an April early morning and stopped, studying the row of small shops and houses opposite. Her heart lifted at last. She had half expected the Dagenham address she'd been given to have gone and been replaced by a hairdressing salon or a butcher's shop. That would have been just her luck . . .

Yet there it was, on the corner, exactly as advertised in faded lettering on the board above the door.

RON'S CORNER CAFF

Through the steamed-up windows she could see a handful of customers tucking cheerfully into cooked breakfasts and hot mugs of tea, just as she'd like to be doing. Not that she could really afford to splash out on a cooked breakfast. Besides, it was a job she was after, not something to eat.

Her tummy rumbled at this fib. She sucked in a shaky breath, squaring her shoulders and drawing herself up. For a fleeting moment, she wished she was taller than a mere five feet, but height wasn't what counted when it came to waiting tables and scrubbing floors. It was friendliness and elbow grease most employers were after, and she had both in spades.

Traffic was a mite busier here in Dagenham than in the quiet Cornish village she'd left at dawn yesterday. She looked carefully both ways before crossing the road, footsore from all the unaccustomed walking. The handle of her heavy case slipped in her hand, and she cursed under her breath, pausing to adjust her grip. Just a few more yards, she promised her weary bones . . .

The door jangled as she shouldered her way inside the caff, hampered by a capacious handbag as well as her suitcase, but nobody looked around. In her tiny village, a stranger would have been the object of instant curiosity and speculation. Here, nobody cared.

The place was cosy though, and the smell of coffee and fried bacon made her empty tummy rumble again in protest.

'Grab a table, love, I'll be with you in a tick,' the middle-aged waitress told her with a kindly smile, nodding towards a spare table against the wall as she bustled past, carrying plates of hot food across the caff.

Edith took the indicated seat, tucking her bags carefully under the table, and studied her surroundings with discreet fascination. There was a small crew of labourers in overalls devouring bacon and eggs and laughing over mugs of steaming tea, a large black lady in a bright flowery dress chatting with an elderly gentleman in a smart cook's uniform – the owner, perhaps? – plus three other tables of bleary-eyed men in jackets and ties, glancing rapidly through newspapers as they wolfed down a full English breakfast.

The buzz of conversation, added to the noisy clatter of

chinaware and cutlery in the kitchen, was exhilarating for someone more used to the peace of the countryside. It was also unnerving.

'Now, love, what can I do you for?' The waitress had arrived, an order pad in hand, looking down at her sympathetically. 'You look a bit peaky. But we'll soon put that right with a nice cuppa and some buttered toast, and maybe a plate of Ron's world-famous bacon and scrambled eggs.' Her glance strayed curiously to the suitcase under the table. 'Come a long way, have you?'

The waitress's hair was silvered, her face fallen into deep-etched smile lines, and she was comfortably built, reminding Edith of her gran, always ready with a warm hug and a few words of wisdom.

'Yes, I have . . . From Cornwall.'

The woman's eyes widened. 'Cornwall?' Her smile grew broader too. 'Gawd bless you, that's where I come from too . . . Oh, years ago now. I left the duchy when I was only a few years younger than you, I'd guess. Whereabouts do you live?'

'P-Penmarrey,' Edith stammered, watching her face.

Sure enough, the woman blinked. 'Penmarrey?' she repeated blankly, and took a step back, looking her up and down. 'Is this one of Ron's silly jokes? Go on with you, girl . . . You must be pulling me bloomin' leg!'

'I'm not, I swear.'

'Penmarrey?' She paused, sucking in a sharp breath. 'Little place just outside Penzance? Not much more than a few houses, a pub and a church?'

'That's the one. Though we have a village shop now. And a bakery.'

'Gawd... Well, I never.' The waitress dropped her order pad and stooped to pick it up, looking flustered. 'Penmarrey... That's only where I come from too.'

'I know.'

The woman was staring now, her mouth open. Ignoring a shout from the kitchen, she dragged out the chair opposite Edith and sat down heavily. 'You *know* I'm from Penmarrey?' She looked intrigued now. 'Sorry, love, but what does that mean? Because I don't know *you* at all.'

'You're Mrs Sheila Hopkins, aren't you?' Edith whispered, her cheeks flaring with heat.

'Blow me, yes, I am.'

'I came here to find you, Mrs Hopkins.' Her shaking voice tailed off as her nerve failed.

Several heads had turned in their direction, and Edith wished she could just sink into the ground. That she had never left Cornwall in the first place, in fact. But she'd had no choice, had she? It had been flight or goodness knows what. And now she was here, if she made a dreadful mess of things yet again... If this woman turned her away too...

'Is that right?' Mrs Hopkins' encouraging smile put new heart in her. 'Well, you've found me. So go on, love.'

'I brought you this letter.' Edith pulled the folded brown envelope from her jacket pocket and handed it over. 'It's from my grandmother.'

'Bless me...' Sheila Hopkins took the envelope and turned it over, staring down at her name written across the front in a bold hand. 'And who's your granny when she's at home?'

'Rosalyn Treloar. Though you will have known her as Rosalyn Penhaligon.'

Sheila looked astonished, her jaw dropping. '*Rosalyn*? You

don't mean it . . . Me dear old mate from school days? Well, I never.'

She turned in abrupt irritation as her name was called again from the kitchen, and called, 'Give me a bloomin' minute, would you?'

Then she seemed to catch the elderly gentleman's stern look from behind the counter and pulled a mutinous face. 'Hang on a tick, love,' she muttered to Edith and jumped up, thrusting the envelope into the capacious pocket of her apron. 'Don't go anywhere. I'll be back in a minute.'

Mrs Hopkins hurried away to serve the plates of food waiting on the counter but was soon back, breathless and smiling. She sat opposite her again, opening the envelope. 'Right, let's see what Rosalyn has to say, shall we? I'll need to be quick though,' she added in a mutter, 'or Ron there will have my guts for garters. He's the boss, you see.'

Edith blushed and peered down at her hands while Mrs Hopkins read the letter. Edith had not read it herself, of course, but she knew what it contained: a request for her grandmother's old friend Sheila to help Edith find work and lodgings in Dagenham.

It was awful, having to beg for a stranger's help like this. Yet what other choice did she have? She couldn't have stayed in their little village a moment longer. It had seemed best to start again somewhere like this – far enough away from anybody who knew of her disgrace.

She'd suggested London at first, but her grandmother had been worried. 'You don't know anyone there. And cities are such dangerous places.' Then she'd mentioned Mrs Hopkins, and Edith had decided to take a chance on Dagenham instead, which wasn't as busy and built up as nearby London, but with new factories and industrial plants springing up about the town should still have plenty of jobs available for a hardworking young woman like her.

At the time, it had felt more important to get away and less vital where she ended up. Only now did the full embarrassment of her position strike her. She wondered miserably what this lady must be thinking . . . That Edith was running away from some dreadful mistake, no doubt. And she would be right.

Mrs Hopkins finished reading and lowered the letter to her lap, whistling under her breath as she studied Edith across the table. 'Blow me,' she muttered, a lively curiosity in her face. 'So you're looking for a job and a place to stay. Do you need a bed for tonight?'

Edith nodded. 'I'm ever so sorry to be a nuisance.'

'Bless you, never mind that. Rosalyn and me . . . Well, we were thick as thieves at school. The Inseparables, they called us. And you have a strong look of her too. That chin . . .' Mrs Hopkins chuckled. 'This your first time away from Cornwall, love?'

'Yes,' Edith admitted.

'It can be a shock, all the noise and traffic . . . But you soon get used to it,' Mrs Hopkins told her kindly. 'A pity your gran couldn't have written ahead of your coming, as it'll be hard work finding you digs at such short notice. But I daresay we'll manage. The weather's improving now we're into spring, but we still can't have you sleeping on the streets.' Seeing Edith's downcast face, Mrs Hopkins beamed encouragingly. 'Now, don't look like that, love. You leave everything to me.'

'Thank you, you've very kind.'

'What kind of work are you looking for? There's usually something going in one of the warehouses along the river. Or there's factory work. My daughter Violet works in a factory as a cleaner. It don't pay well, but it's steady.'

'I've never worked in a factory before. Or a warehouse.' Edith's gaze drifted towards the kitchen. 'In fact, I've only ever worked in a shop.'

'Oh aye?'

'My father's the village baker,' Edith confided. 'He's taught me how to make bread and cakes and pastries since I was little. But I daresay you already have someone to do all that.' She bit her lip. 'I can clean though. I'm handy with a mop and a duster.'

Mrs Hopkins' brow was furrowed. 'If you know your way around an oven so well, couldn't your dad have given you a job?'

Edith blushed. 'He . . . He did,' she admitted. 'But I needed a change. To . . . To get away.'

Mrs Hopkins glanced down at her grandmother's letter again, then folded it back into the envelope. 'Of course you did,' she said firmly, pocketing the envelope. 'Cornwall's a lovely place. But there's a big world outside the duchy, and a young person often needs to see more of it before settling down.'

Edith had been perfectly happy in the Cornish village of Penmarrey; leaving it had been an awful wrench. But this didn't seem like the right time to contradict her grandmother's old friend.

The elderly man in the cook's outfit came over to their table, wiping his hands on a tea towel. He gave Edith a quick look, then turned his stern eye on Mrs Hopkins. 'Sorry to interrupt your chat, Sheila, but we need you serving. The order for table three is almost ready to take out.'

Mrs Hopkins had jumped up at his approach, though she didn't seem particularly remorseful as she introduced them. 'This is Edith Treloar, the granddaughter of an old friend of mine from my school days in Cornwall. Edith, this is my boss, Mr Coates. He owns this place, so you'd best be polite.' Despite this warning, the waitress winked at Edith before addressing her boss. 'She's looking for a job. Ain't you, love?'

Mr Coates turned back to Edith, his gaze assessing. 'Is that right?'

Edith got to her feet and thrust a hand boldly towards the café owner, keen to make a good impression. 'Pleased to meet you, Mr Coates. I'm not afraid of hard work, and I'm a good baker, if you need one.'

'A good baker, eh?' His bright eyes, crinkling at the edges, sharpened on her face. 'Good enough for my customers though?'

'People say my Cornish pasties are delicious.'

'We don't sell pasties here.'

'But we could do,' Mrs Hopkins remarked slyly.

'I can bake bread, rolls and cakes too.' Hurriedly, Edith explained how she'd spent the past two years since leaving school in her dad's village bakery, working several shifts a week. 'It's not a caff like this, it's true. But I'm used to dealing with the public. Yes, and getting things right first time, so nobody goes away disappointed. My dad's ever such a stickler for high standards.'

'I'm glad to hear it.' Mr Coates looked her up and down again, then pulled a face. 'Trouble is, I'd like to help you, young lady, but I've all the staff I need. I can't take anyone else on right now, and that's the honest truth.'

Edith's heart sank but she kept smiling. 'Of course. Thank you anyway. I'll try somewhere else.'

'There's a good bakery on the high street.' Mr Coates rubbed his chin thoughtfully. 'They might have an opening there, if you're as skilled as you say.'

With a quick nod to Mrs Hopkins to return to her work, the owner turned to speak to a customer who'd just come in.

Edith sat down again, feeling despondent. She hadn't thought much beyond bringing her gran's letter to Mrs Hopkins and hoping for the best. But she could hardly expect the poor lady to go round with her, trying to help her get work.

Whatever was she going to do? She'd spent a large proportion of her meagre funds on last night's bed and breakfast place after leaving the noisy, overcrowded concourse at Paddington Station. She'd felt so lost in the big city. Then she'd had to pay for the lengthy bus ride required to bring her out to Dagenham.

Panic swelled inside her and she could hardly breathe. If she didn't get a job soon . . .

But Mrs Hopkins bent down with a smile. 'Don't you fret, love,' she insisted. 'And no disappearing before I've had a chance to think, do you hear? I haven't forgotten that you still need lodgings.'

'Th-Thank you,' Edith said, forcing a shaky smile back to her lips. But it was hard not to let her misery show. She'd always been fiercely independent. Now she would need to rely on other people if she didn't want to end up on the streets of the city, doing goodness knows what work to survive from day to day.

'Though it's probably for the best if you come and stay with us tonight,' Mrs Hopkins went on, looking thoughtful.

'I beg your pardon?' Edith looked up into the kindly face with shock. 'Stay with . . . with you?'

'Me, my husband and my daughter Violet. Maybe for a few nights. Just until you get yourself sorted out, love. We've a spare room and I'm sure you won't be any trouble. Now, let me bring you a cuppa and something hot to eat, and I'll ask Ronald if I can take you back to our place during my break.' She beamed at Edith's speechless expression. 'I told you, don't worry. It ain't far to walk, and you'll be very welcome.'

With that, Mrs Hopkins bustled away to answer the imperious summons of the kitchen counter bell.

Edith sat in shock, staring after her. Stay with her grandmother's old friend? She was sure that wasn't what Gran had intended when she suggested Dagenham as a possible bolthole. Whatever had she put in her letter?

She ought to say no, of course, and that she was very grateful but could organise her own lodgings. But the truth was, with so little money at her disposal and no job yet, it would be foolhardy not to swallow her pride and accept Mrs Hopkins' charitable offer.

As soon as she got a job, she would be sure to pay the kind lady back for breakfast and board out of her first pay packet.

Outside the caff, people walked past in a near-constant stream as the working day began, while traffic lurched along. There were so many cars and vans, more than she'd see in a whole year passing through their remote Cornish village. Across the street, a newspaper boy had set up his stall and was yelling out front-page headlines to passers-by, something about Germany and the prime minister.

The desperate troubles in Europe had seemed so far away back in Cornwall. Now it felt as though they were right on the doorstep. She wanted to put on a brave face like everyone else. But the prospect of war with Germany frightened her, and that was the plain truth of it.

Her empty tummy growled again, and she stifled a sob. Why on earth was she fretting about the world's problems when she could barely solve her own? She'd always known that leaving her family behind in Penmarrey and starting again so far from home would be difficult. But the reality of that drastic change was only now beginning to sink in.

Part of her blamed Susan Teague for what had happened. They'd been good friends once, living close together in Penmarrey, always in and out of each other's houses, even after they'd both left school. But then Susan had abruptly turned on her, spreading gossip that had made it impossible for Edith to stay in the village she loved even one more day . . .

But she couldn't blame Susan completely. While it had been wicked to ruin her reputation like that, and had left Edith's father and grandmother horribly uncomfortable, the gossip had been based on truth, not lies.

In other words, Edith had no one to blame but herself.

Mrs Hopkins lived in a neat, terraced house with thick nets at the windows and a well-scrubbed front step. 'Nobody's home,' she assured Edith, letting herself into the house. 'My husband works at the Ford plant, and my daughter Violet cleans at a factory close to the plant. I'll show you upstairs first so you can unpack and wash up, make yourself nice and comfy.'

'I'm ever so grateful,' Edith began but her new friend merely tutted, waving her inside the house.

'It's the least I can do for Rosalyn's granddaughter. Besides, truth be told, you'll be good company for my Violet. She's had a tough time of it lately, poor lamb, and could do with cheering up.'

Edith wondered what Violet was like and what had happened to her but was too polite to ask. She followed Mrs Hopkins inside and struggled off with her coat in the narrow hallway. The walls were cream and beige, with an oval mirror next to the coat stand and a smart brown hall runner.

'Sitting room's there,' Mrs Hopkins said, pointing along the hall, 'and the dining room's at the back, next door to the kitchen.'

'Should I take my shoes off?' Edith asked, eyeing a pair of dirty boots tucked under the coat stand.

'Gawd, no. Those are Violet's. She does love her long walks but comes back muddy when it's been wet. I'm sure yours are clean enough, love. Come on . . .' Smiling, Mrs Hopkins led the way upstairs. 'You'll be in the back bedroom. It used to be Vi's room when she was little. But when our Betsy left to get married, Violet moved across the hall because Betsy's room was bigger. I daresay there'll be some of her old stuff lying about, but I can ask her to move it when she gets home.'

'I don't want to put your daughter out.'

'Nonsense, it's no trouble.' Mrs Hopkins paused at the top of the stairs, seeing her stop and glance up in surprise at framed black and white photographs on the wall. 'Yes, that was Penmarrey back in the day. My dad was a keen photographer. I think we still have his old camera somewhere.' She smiled. 'That's me and my parents on the village green near the church. Must be nearly forty years ago now. Has it changed much?'

'Those two houses are now the village shop and my dad's bakery . . . But otherwise, not much.' Edith felt a tug of longing, studying the pretty Cornish village with its village green and duckpond, and the squat Norman tower of the church in the background. Then her gaze wandered to the other photographs, which were of elderly Victorians, out walking somewhere less familiar. 'Goodness . . . Who are they?'

'Henry's gran Thomasina. Long dead, bless her. That one was taken in Valentine's Park over in Ilford. What some used to call Cranbrook Park, back in them days.' Mrs Hopkins chuckled. 'They look hot in all that heavy clothing, don't you think? Rather them than me. Come on, then. The room's this way.'

The spare bedroom at the back of the house was a dimly lit space with curtains shutting out the light, and a slight smell of damp. Mrs Hopkins bustled across to rattle back the curtains and throw open the window. 'There,' she muttered, pulling a face, 'that's a bit better. It'll smell fresher once it's been properly aired.'

Outside, a small yard held an ancient coal bunker, a washing line and a dusty-looking lilac bush huddled in one corner. The backs of the houses on the next street faced them directly, and Edith, peering out, could see a young woman rather optimistically pegging up damp nappies and linen despite the cloudy skies. The whole house shook as a heavy vehicle rumbled past on the street, but Mrs Hopkins didn't even notice. Edith winced, but she supposed that she too would soon grow so used to the noise of traffic that she barely minded it.

Her grandmother's friend must have spotted her expression and misunderstood it. 'I know it's not the Ritz,' Mrs Hopkins began defensively, shifting a box of bric-a-brac from the dresser to the doorway.

'It's lovely,' Edith told her firmly. She put down her suitcase, looking around with a determined smile. 'What gorgeous wallpaper! Little rosebuds . . . My favourite flowers.' She hesitated. 'What will you be charging for the room, Mrs Hopkins?'

'Charging?' Mrs Hopkins looked flustered. 'Well, we can discuss all that after supper. I'll have to get back to the caff now, but I'll make up your bed with fresh linen as soon as I'm home.'

'Please, let me do that.'

'Oh, very well.' Reluctantly, Mrs Hopkins showed her the landing closet where the clean linen was kept before hurrying back downstairs and dragging on her coat and hat. 'Make yourself at home, love. I clock off at two today, so I'll be back before you know it.'

The front door closed and realising she was all alone in the house, Edith wandered back into the bedroom with an armful of fresh-smelling linen, her head spinning at the rapid changes in her life.

Was it only yesterday that she'd woken up in her bedroom in Penmarrey, listening to birds twittering in the pre-dawn glimmering? Now here she was, in a strange house in a strange town, with traffic rumbling past outside and city smog still in her lungs.

And this town was going to be her home from now on. Dagenham.

But she could hardly trespass on Mrs Hopkins' hospitality forever. Gran's friend or not, it wouldn't be right. No, she needed to find a job sharpish and start earning, so she could get her own room or bedsit somewhere in town. Then, perhaps, she could finally put the past behind her and begin to forget.

She tidied the room and made up her bed, tucking the sheet under neatly at each corner, just as her gran had taught her, feeling pleased with herself for her home-making skills. But when she lifted her heavy suitcase onto the bed, meaning to unpack before exploring the house, a familiar spasm hit her and she sucked in a breath, feeling awfully unwell for a moment.

'Oh Lord,' she groaned, wincing.

Rigid, her gaze fixed straight ahead as she counted slowly to ten in her head, Edith stood holding her breath. By the time she'd reached ten, her muscles had relaxed, the impulse to retch had faded, and she was able to breathe again, as though nothing untoward had happened.

'Must be nerves,' she told herself, shaking her head at her own silly weakness. 'Oh, do try to buck up, Edith Treloar. You're on your own now, so enough of these ridiculous fits and starts.' And, with a determined glare, she bent to unpack her case.

Yes, Percy had left her and England less than two weeks ago. But this was her chance to start again, in a place where nobody knew anything about her or what she'd done with the handsome young visitor from Canada, and she refused to allow what was likely to be a bout of nervous indigestion to get in her way.

At supper, coming down in response to Mrs Hopkins' summons, she met both Mr Henry Hopkins and Miss Violet Hopkins for the first time, father and daughter chatting and laughing as they helped lay the table. They stopped to stare at her as she came in, their eyes wide . . .

Before she could say anything, Sheila had bustled in with a dripping ladle in hand to introduce them. 'Tea tray's ready for you to bring in, Henry,' she said briskly. 'And this is the granddaughter of my old mate Rosalyn Penhaligon, though she's Rosalyn Treloar now. Her name's Edith and she'll be staying with us for a while.'

'Only for a few days though,' Edith added hurriedly, but her new friend had already vanished again, uttering mild shrieks over something that had bubbled over on the stove in her brief absence.

'Hello there, Miss Treloar, pleased to meet you.' Mr Hopkins was a wiry gentleman with silver hair and a friendly smile. He shook Edith's hand with surprising enthusiasm, given that she'd just been thrust unannounced on his household. He even pulled out a dinner chair for her. 'Do sit down. Since this seems like a special occasion, can I perhaps pour you a glass of sherry?'

'Edith, please . . . And thank you, I'll be fine with tea.'

He looked disappointed but slipped away into the kitchen to fetch the tea tray.

Violet, who looked to be in her mid-twenties, sat down opposite. She was slim and startlingly tall for a woman, with sleek blonde hair that hung past her shoulders and a cool, slightly distant look in her eyes. What had Mrs Hopkins said of her youngest daughter? *She's had a tough time of it lately and could do with cheering up* . . .

Edith gave her as warm a smile as she could muster, thinking of her own recent 'tough times', and received a few fingertips to shake and an answering smile that didn't quite reach Violet's eyes. But of course the daughter of the house wasn't feeling very hospitable. She didn't know Edith from Adam, and now here they were, sitting opposite each other at supper.

It was hard not to feel a little unwelcome though . . .

Mr Hopkins came back and poured them cups of tea to drink with their supper, then helped himself to a small glass of sherry, which he knocked back in one gulp. 'Have I met Rosalyn?' Henry asked his wife as she came back in, flushed and bearing dishes in both hands.

'No, love. Before your time. Old school friend from my Cornwall days.' Sheila Hopkins placed the dishes on the central table runner and beamed down at Edith. There was a heap of mashed potato shining with butter, a platter crammed with juicy lamb cutlets, and another dish of steaming peas and carrots. 'There now . . . Help yourself, love. We don't stand on ceremony here.' Then she headed back into the kitchen.

'Erm, gravy, dear?' Mr Hopkins called after his wife.

'Gawd, give us a chance! It's coming.'

'Veg, Edith?' Politely, Violet passed across the dish after taking a meagre spoonful for herself. 'Cornwall, eh? You're a long way from home. You look young to be setting up on your own.'

'I'm twenty,' Edith said defensively.

'*Twenty*? You pulling my leg? Well, I'd never have guessed it.' Violet's assessing blue gaze narrowed on her face. 'So, Edith, what brought you to the big city?'

'The train,' Sheila told her daughter sharply, returning with a large, brown-lipped jug which she dumped heavily on the table. 'And that's enough questions at the meal table, Vi. Leave the poor girl to eat her supper in peace. Gravy, anyone?' And she gave Edith a comfortable wink before taking her place at the head of the table. 'Will you say grace, Henry?'

CHAPTER FOUR

Sheila was wiping down the counter when the door to the caff opened, and her friend Judith Campbell came in, her small grandson on one hip and a pineapple cradled in her other hand.

'Look what I found at the market this morning,' she called in her rich Jamaican accent. 'Only a pineapple . . . A pineapple! Here in Dagenham. Can you believe it? I shall make a delicious fruit salad with this tonight. My grandson was born here and says he's never seen a fresh pineapple. *Never* seen one! Ha, wait until he tastes it.'

Sheila had seen a pineapple before, of course, and even eaten canned pineapple sometimes, but not often, since exotic fruits had never been to Henry's taste. But she remembered how sweet and unusual they tasted, so smiled broadly. 'It looks marvellous, love. And I'm sure little Jimmy can't wait to taste his gran's fruit salad.'

Judith was a little older than Sheila, a lively widow from Jamaica in her early sixties who lived a few doors down from the caff with her daughter Evie and son-in-law Charles, and their three young children. She wore bright, colourful clothes, and was always smiling, even when it was wet and miserable outside. 'You're a proper ray of sunshine, Mrs Campbell,' Ron always said approvingly whenever Judith came into the caff. And it was true, she was a cheerful soul, never complaining, despite constantly having to run around after her grandchildren while her daughter and son-in-law both worked at one of the nearby factories.

'There's nobody in today,' Sheila went on. 'So you're in luck. Your favourite table by the window is free.' She hurried over with an order pad as they sat down. 'Right, what can I get for you today, Judith? And how about you, Jimmy?' She gave the boy a winning smile as he squirmed on the seat, clutching a metal toy car to his chest. 'That's a smashin' brum-brum, ain't it? Tell you what, I've just taken a fresh batch of strawberry tarts out of the oven. You'd enjoy one of them, I dare say. And a nice cup of squash too.' She winked at Judith. 'Your usual, love?'

'That sounds perfect, Sheila, thank you. I must say, you do know how to put people at their ease. But when will you start running a café of your own? Ron's a nice man but you're *wasted* on this place,' Judith murmured, one eye on the door to the street, which had been left propped open while Ron came and went with rags and a bucket of soapy water, undertaking his weekly clean of the outside windows. 'You should have a nice café of your own, someplace you can really put your mark on.'

'Me? Run me own caff?' Sheila laughed, shaking her head. 'I wouldn't know where to start. All that paperwork? And talking to suppliers, and finding the capital? I swear it makes Ron look twenty years older, dealing with all that nonsense, day in, day out. No, love, I'm happy enough being a waitress. I take the orders and bring the food out, and I have a nice chat while I'm serving. That suits me down to the ground.'

Judith folded her arms over an ample bosom, chuckling. 'You make it sound so easy. But you know it isn't.' Her brows rose. 'Let's face it, not all your customers are as nice as *me*.'

'Ain't that the truth?' Sheila agreed, and they both laughed.

'You try out that recipe yet? The one I gave you last week?'

'I did.' Sheila bit her lip. 'I thought it was the best thing I've ever tasted, even though I couldn't quite find all them fancy ingredients, especially all the spices. But I made do, and it turned out fine . . .' She hesitated, not wanting to offend her friend.

'Henry hated it, didn't he?'

'A mite too hot for his taste buds,' Sheila admitted, grinning. 'But Violet loved it, and we haven't given up yet. Next time, we'll try it with more tomatoes and not so much chilli powder. See how that goes.'

The bell over the door jangled again noisily, and she turned, frowning at the group of young men shouldering their way inside. She vaguely recognised one of them as the son of a local thug, though she disliked the word. But he'd made himself unpleasant in the area and even done a spell in prison a while back for some petty crime. The son – Ben Fletcher, that was his name – was shaping up to be no better than his father, people said, though he was barely nineteen. The youths were all clad in similar black shirts and black ties, neatly buttoned up and tucked into tight grey trousers that looked like riding breeches, with great big jackboots on their feet. Some of them were wearing black jackets too, and a few sported peaked caps that wouldn't have looked out of place in the RAF, though they were careful to display no badges. They looked sinister rather than smart, but Sheila imagined that was the point.

'What's this then?' she muttered to Judith, her gaze on the young men. 'They off to a funeral?'

'*Blackshirts*,' her friend whispered. Her habitual smile had faded on seeing the lads troop into the caff. She looked almost frightened, in fact. 'I'd heard there were a few in Dagenham,' she whispered. 'But this is the first time I've ever seen them up close. I do hope they're not going to start coming in here on the regular.'

Sheila didn't know what to say. *Blackshirts*?

She'd heard about them, of course. Horrid news stories in the papers and on the wireless of inciting violence and causing trouble. They supported that Hitler fellow in Germany. Fascists, Henry called them. Well, she didn't follow politics very closely. But although they had no insignia, their outfits did look suspiciously like a military uniform, which was no longer allowed for political organisations, and she couldn't blame Judith for being fearful. She felt a little afraid of them herself.

There was a clang outside the shop, and Ron descended laboriously from his ladder, threw his sopping wash rag into a bucket, and headed back inside. He'd been taking advantage of the sunshine and the quiet lull between breakfast and lunch to do the window cleaning. But the sight of those boys in black shirts had brought him back inside.

'Morning, lads,' he said warily, addressing the young men who had taken a large table near the counter. He didn't smile though, and his look was far from welcoming. 'What can I do you for?'

The young men ordered teas and coffees, and Ben Fletcher asked for a ham sandwich.

'Coming right up,' Ron said flatly, but Sheila could tell that he didn't like having them in his caff and would have dearly liked to send them packing. The lads had mean faces though, and she suspected they'd come here deliberately looking for a row. Several had already glanced in her direction too, whispering among themselves in a way that left her feeling nervous and unsure of herself, which was most unlike her. Though Sheila might have been uneasy around certain men when she was younger, these days she rarely let folk make her uncomfortable and would usually have come straight out and asked what they were staring at. Yet with these young men she didn't quite dare . . .

She headed into the kitchen to prepare Judith's usual order, which was simply buttered toast and a large mug of tea. Ron was setting out cups for their order. There was a thunderous look on his face. Sheila prepared the squash for young Jimmy while the toast was under the grill, glancing at her boss sideways.

'You all right, Ron?'

'Blackshirts,' he muttered, his mouth barely moving. 'In my own bleedin' caff. But I can't refuse to serve 'em. They've done nothing wrong, though they shouldn't all be wearing the same gear . . . Uniforms were banned in '36, weren't they, for groups like theirs? Still, they're just young lads, even if they are following that Mosley fella.' Ron pulled a face. 'I don't much like seeing them in here though. I heard they were in the Chequers the other night. Left the landlord with a black eye and a broken arm. The police had to be called.'

Sheila was scandalised. 'These same lads? Are you sure?'

His mouth tightened. 'I don't know for certain. But I'm willing to bet. Still, if they drink up sharpish and get out, no harm done, eh? I don't want no trouble in my caff.'

On the other side of the counter, Sheila glanced up just as one of the youths noticed Judith and her grandson. He stared round at them with open hostility. He said something that Sheila didn't catch, and the lads all laughed. Something about her pineapple, it sounded like. Judith sat tense, not replying but staring resolutely down at the table; it was plain that the young men had said something at her expense.

Sheila hurried out carrying Jimmy's cup of squash. The lad who'd spoken stood, half turned towards her, his chair legs scraping. Judith jumped up. Thrusting the prized pineapple into her shopping basket, she took little Jimmy by the hand and hurried to the door as though the devil were after her.

'You all right, love?' Sheila called after her friend.

Judith paused, glancing back at her guiltily. 'I'm sorry, Sheila, truly I am,' she stammered. 'I don't mean to be messing you and Mr Coates about. But I've just remembered that I . . . I left something on the stove. We'll come back later for that strawberry tart.'

'Good riddance!' one of the lads called after her, and it was clear that poor Judith heard him, for she stiffened in the doorway but didn't look back.

Outraged, Sheila glared at the young man who'd shouted, and stepped forward to give the little terror a piece of her mind. But Ron put a warning hand on her arm.

'Not now,' he murmured, and she knew he was probably right.

She stamped back to the kitchen and set the squash aside

in case Judith really was planning to come back later. Though she doubted it. She knew Judith had just said that to avoid a row. Horrible boys, she thought furiously, grabbing up a large knife to cut the ham sandwich into neat triangles. If she had her way . . .

Ron carried across the tray of hot drinks. 'I'll thank you not to make a ruckus in my place,' he told them gruffly, avoiding their eyes as he set down the tray. 'I run a respectable caff. You're welcome here, but only so long as you mind your manners.'

'What manners would those be, old man?' one of the lads snapped back.

But Ben Fletcher, the one Sheila had recognised, who seemed to be the ringleader, angrily told his friend to shut up. 'We're not here to make trouble, Mr Coates,' he insisted, leaning his elbows on the table, his face intent. 'So long as you respect us, we'll respect you. But if you disrespect us . . . Well, then you get what you deserve.'

Ron looked at them helplessly, then turned back to the counter. 'Your sandwich is on its way,' was his only reply.

The sandwich was ready on a plate. But Sheila didn't fancy having to carry it out to them and was relieved when Ron took it from her hand, his face understanding.

The door jangled again, and Sheila jumped, fearing it might be more troublemakers. But it was only her eldest daughter, Betsy. She often called into the caff on her way back from the market to have a quick chat with Sheila and sometimes a cup of tea. Today though, Betsy was looking troubled. She squeezed past the young men with an anxious glance at their shirts, and leant over the counter to whisper, 'Can I have a word, Mum? When you're free, that is.'

'Of course, love.'

Ron rounded the counter with the ham sandwich, strain showing in his face. But he still nodded politely at her daughter. 'Morning, Betsy.' He jerked his head at Sheila, indicating the empty tables on the other side of the caff. 'There's not many in. Why don't you take your break early today?'

'Thanks, Ron.' Sheila made a quick pot of tea, tossed some fancy biscuits onto a cake plate, and sat down with Betsy at one of the wall tables, far enough away from the young men that they wouldn't be overheard. Though the lads seemed to be deep in conversation among themselves now. Plotting something dreadful, no doubt.

'So, what's the matter?' she asked her daughter, careful to keep her voice low. 'You look bloomin' miserable. I'm sorry I've not been around to see you and the kids in a few days. But like I told you, I've had this girl staying with us . . . young Edith. I'm not saying she's hard work, but gawd knows I've been busier than usual.' She hesitated, studying her daughter's averted face. 'Oh, love . . . You're not having trouble with Ernest, surely?'

Though she knew the answer would be no. Betsy had never had any trouble with her husband. He wasn't the type to mistreat a woman.

Betsy shook her head. 'No, Ernie's a sweetie . . . Always has been, always will be.' She glanced briefly at the young men, then lowered her gaze to stare into her tea mug. 'Though I wish folk would lay off 'im. Yes, he's half German. But he don't like what Hitler's doing any more than us Brits do. And it don't make him a wrong'un either, whatever people may say, calling him Hun and all them other filthy names.

His family may come from Germany but that don't mean he's a Nazi!'

'I know, love. It ain't right and that's a fact.' Sheila wished she could wave a magic wand and make all her daughter's troubles disappear. But of course that was impossible. 'But if you're not here about that—'

'The thing is, Mum,' Betsy interrupted her in a rush, 'I think maybe . . . That is to say, it's possible that—'

But before she could finish, one of the young men called out, 'Hey, Mr Coates . . . Put this poster up for us,' and Betsy fell silent, glancing his way again. The ringleader took a sheet of printed paper from his pocket and unfolded it. 'On your noticeboard over there.'

Ron came out from behind the counter, drying his hands on his apron. 'The noticeboard? That's for lost and found, odd-job men, community stuff . . .' He hesitated. 'What's it about, your poster?'

'A good cause. We're holding a rally next week. Meeting outside Ilford Town Hall. Everyone welcome. Bring your own placards.' Grinning, the young man held out the poster to him.

'*We?*' Ron hadn't moved.

'Supporters of Oswald Mosley.' All the other young men banged the table with their fists at this name, nodding ardently. 'Mosley's going to save this country, Mr Coates. Go on, take that poster and stick it on your noticeboard. You'll thank me later.' The young man took a large bite of his sandwich, adding indistinctly, 'Or ain't you a patriot?'

Ron flushed angrily. 'Of course I am.'

'If we don't stop this government in their tracks, they'll take us to war with Germany. Hitler's got the most powerful army, tanks, weapons in Europe . . . Thousands of British men will lose their lives. Is that what you want, Mr Coates?'

'Don't be daft.' Ron took the poster and studied it. 'Nobody wants that.'

'Ah, but you're wrong there. There's plenty as want it. Agitating for war in Europe, that's what they're doing. When we should be stopping and thinking what's best for us, for the Brits.' The lad turned to look directly at Betsy, as though he knew exactly who she was. 'Your husband's welcome to join us too, and you'll tell him that, if you know what's best for you. German-born, ain't he?'

Betsy was trembling, barely looking at him. 'Yes,' she muttered, 'but he's no friend to Hitler. Nor your bleedin' Oswald Mosley neither.'

The young men fell silent, staring at each other as though wondering how to answer this. Eventually, Ben Fletcher said angrily, 'Then he's a traitor and deserves what's coming to him.' The ringleader sat back in his seat, folding his arms across his chest as he smirked across at Betsy. 'Though I heard he already got a taste of that. Someone showed him the error of his ways . . . Eh, lads?'

Several of the young men slapped each other's backs, nodding and jeering. It gave Sheila a cold shiver down her spine, watching them. Across the table, Betsy bowed her head, her shoulders quivering, and reached in her bag for a hanky. Sheila could tell that she was crying.

Ron took a sharp step forward. 'That's enough! I'll have no talk like that in 'ere.'

The ringleader jumped to his feet, his sandwich forgotten. 'Is that so?' he asked, his air menacing. 'If you don't like it, pin that poster on your board and we'll be on our way.'

The others sat waiting while Ron dithered. One of the lads stirred a lump of sugar into his tea, then banged the spoon rhythmically against the mug in the silence, a sinister sound. Sheila's heart drummed hard in her chest; she sat tense and still, unsure what might happen if her boss refused to do their bidding. Yes, they were only kids, but . . .

She kept remembering how Ernest had turned up late to his own anniversary do, looking like he'd been given a thumping. Could it have been these boys? Gawd, some of them weren't even old enough to shave yet. But in a group . . .

Her son-in-law had laughed it off at the time as a 'bit of rough and tumble,' and Betsy hadn't said a peep about it afterwards either. But it wasn't hard to see that Ernest being German, even if only *half* German, and these lads being supporters of Mosley, had made him a target.

To her relief, at that moment the local bobby came wandering past the caff on his usual beat. He peered through the window and stopped dead, seeing the young men inside. Ron raised a quick hand in greeting, or maybe warning, and the policeman frowned. He pushed the door open and put his head in.

'Everything all right, Mr Coates?' PC Hobbs asked, his eyes on the Blackshirts.

'It is now, Constable Hobbs.' Ron crumpled up the poster and tossed it back at the ringleader. 'This lot are just about to pay their bill and leave. Ain't you, lads?'

PC Hobbs stood waiting in the doorway while the boys threw a few coins on the table and shuffled out past him.

'How's your dad, Fletcher?' he asked the ringleader, who was last out of the shop, his hands deep in his trouser pockets, his expression hostile. 'It's always hard to come home after a stretch inside. Dad coping all right, is he?'

The ringleader said nothing to this query but spat on the pavement outside before sauntering away, his friends gathered about him in a tight group.

As soon as they were out of earshot, Betsy slumped forward, moaning into her hands. 'Oh, Mum . . . Why do they have to torment me and Ernest like this?'

'Don't fret, love.' Sheila reached for her daughter's hand, squeezing it comfortingly. 'That silly lot ain't much more than snot-nosed kids, when all's said and done. Oswald Mosley, indeed! Anyway, they've gone now.'

But she was thinking how lads even younger than that nasty lot had died for their country two decades back in the Great War. Now it seemed like it was all about to happen again. It was only last month that Hitler, despite having been given part of Czechoslovakia to keep him quiet, had ignored the blooming agreement he'd signed at Munich and invaded the rest of the country anyway. Now these young men were going around in their silly black outfits, thinking joining Hitler would be enough to stop him invading Britain. Fools, she thought, bristling with outrage. Hitler would grab the rest of Europe if he could, and Britain too, no matter what Oswald Mosley and those boys said. Anyway, if the rumours were to be believed, war was all but inevitable now.

'Got time for a quick cuppa, Toby?' Ron asked the constable, snapping Sheila out of her thoughts. The young police officer was still staring out of the window after the vanishing Blackshirts. 'On the house, of course.'

'That's very kind, Mr Coates. Yes, I've got time.'

The constable removed his helmet and smoothed down

his thick wavy hair. He was a friendly man, if with a slightly nervous disposition. Sheila guessed him to be about Violet's age, in his late twenties. She knew his sergeant by sight, a burly man with a generous moustache, and imagined he didn't think much of his constable. Though he'd handled those lads without much trouble, she thought, watching him with approval.

'I was in half a mind to threaten them with arrest, wearing all that black clobber. Bit too close to a uniform to be lawful, if you ask me. But lads will be lads, eh? Still, they'll be called up for military training once they hit twenty, under the new regulations. That should sort them out.' PC Hobbs took a seat near the door, nodding towards Sheila and Betsy agreeably. 'Morning, ladies.'

While Ron and the constable were deep in conversation, Sheila fetched a milky coffee for old Mrs Timothy, who'd come in as the lads were leaving, and then hurried back to her daughter.

'Go on, love,' she said, nibbling on a biscuit. 'You said you wanted a word. Now them nasty lads have gone, what's up?'

Betsy was dabbing her wet eyes, her face miserable. 'I . . . I should be happy, I know. But I can't help worrying.'

'Happy about what?' Sheila was confused.

'I've missed my monthlies,' Betsy whispered, gripping the damp hanky in her fist. 'Twice now, for sure.'

Sheila blinked. Then realised what she was saying. Her daughter was expecting another baby. 'Oh gawd . . . Congratulations, love. Though it's still early days, ain't it?' She hesitated, unsure what to say for the best. 'Does Ernest know?'

Betsy shook her head unhappily. 'How can I tell him? After what happened the last few times? If I lose this one too, he'll be in pieces.'

Sheila's heart went out to her. Her daughter had lost the last two babies she'd carried, after only three or four months, and maybe more, if just one missed monthly period meant a pregnancy had begun but not continued. Betsy had stopped telling her in the end when she was expecting, though the signs had usually been there – pale cheeks, a tendency to burst into tears over nothing in particular, being careful not to carry anything too heavy . . .

Betsy had kept her secret well this time. But perhaps Sheila had been so busy lately with her work at the caff, and this new lodger they'd taken in, young Edith, that she'd not had time to notice the changes in her daughter.

'Well,' she said uncertainly, 'you must be at least ten weeks along by now. That's something to celebrate.'

Her daughter nodded. 'But I'm worried about Ernest, Mum.'

'Why?'

'This awful situation with Germany . . . He's getting it from all sides now. Blokes at work calling him bad names, and now these Blackshirts are everywhere. You say they're only kids, but it was them what gave him a kicking the night of our anniversary. Ernest swore me to secrecy, said it would only cause more trouble if folk knew. But how can I keep quiet? It's so unfair.'

'Oh, love.' Sheila got up and hugged her close. 'One problem at a time, yes? I'm glad you told me about the baby. And of course I can help with the shopping and housework, if you like, so you can get plenty of rest.' Sitting down again, she chewed on her lip, anxious for her daughter. 'But what about your job here at the caff?'

'Ron will be furious if I quit,' Betsy moaned, with a guilty glance in his direction. 'But now I'm in the family way, I dare not take on too much. If I was to lose this baby too . . . and all over a few extra quid a month . . .' Tears sprang readily into her eyes again.

'Hush, love, don't worry. I'll square it with Ron, I promise.'

'But how?'

'Hmm.' Sheila considered the problem, and then beamed with sudden inspiration, remembering her new lodger. 'Young Edith . . . She's looking for work, ain't she? They didn't have no jobs going at the bakery in the high street, but maybe she can take on your shifts here.' She shrugged. 'It won't be much money for her, poor lamb. But at least Ron won't be left short-handed, eh?'

CHAPTER FIVE

Betsy had been dreading giving in her notice to Ron. But to her surprise, when she approached him a few days later, he took her resignation very well. Though he rather spoilt the effect by admitting he'd been thinking he might need to let her go soon anyway. 'Because of them lads,' he'd said with a jerk of his head, not meeting her eyes. 'I can't risk the trouble, see?'

'Trouble?' She had stared at him, bewildered.

'With them bleedin' Blackshirts, if you'll pardon my language. Oh, not on account of *you*, Betsy. You've been a lifesaver, and no mistake.' Ron had scratched his white stubbly chin, glancing nervously at the door to the caff as though expecting those vile lads to march in there at any moment. 'But your husband.'

'Ernest?'

'Him being German.' He opened his eyes wide, seeing her furious glare. 'I ain't got no problem with him personally. Nice man, very likeable. But with things the way they are, politically speaking . . . Well, you being married to him, and them Blackshirts coming into the caff more often these days . . .' He grimaced. 'I don't want no trouble.'

Coming home after her last day at work, she told Ernest about their encounter with the Blackshirts, and that she was giving up her job at the caff. Not surprisingly, he put two and two together, and made five, a spark of fury in his ordinarily cheerful blue eyes.

'This isn't right. You shouldn't be forced out of a job because your husband's not one hundred per cent British.' Ernest jumped up from his armchair and paced about the room, which took him all of two strides, given his height and how small their sitting room was. 'I'll speak to Ronald about it. I'll make him give you back your job.'

Despairingly, Betsy seized his hand and dragged him to a halt. 'No, love, no . . . I don't want the job.'

'But you were happy there. I know you were.' He was frowning.

'For a while, yes. But things have changed.' Betsy knew she couldn't hide the truth from him any longer. It was time. 'Well, one thing has changed, at least.'

'*Ach so*?' He sank down on the sofa next to her, his clever eyes sharpening on her face. 'What one thing? Tell me, *Liebling*, please.'

So she admitted what she'd been hiding from him for weeks . . . That she was expecting a baby again, and was too afraid to keep working, in case it caused her to suffer another miscarriage, like every time she'd tried to conceive since Alice had been born. Her fears poured out as he listened without speaking, his hands joined firmly with both of hers, his gaze steady. Tears came again, and she let them fall, uncaring, until he finally released her hands to hunt for a clean hanky in his pocket.

'Here,' he murmured, and dried her tears with the white handkerchief.

'I know we agreed not to try again, but honestly . . . It just happened.'

A smile flickered across his face. 'Accidents do happen. And I'm certain that part of the blame must be laid at my door. Perhaps all the blame.'

'Oh no!'

Ernest laughed. 'Yes, I fear it must.' He kissed her, and for a while there was no sound in the little room except for the ticking of the clock. He did not seem angry about the pregnancy. If anything, she thought he looked happy. 'So, we are having another child.'

'Please, Ernest, don't jinx it.' Betsy shuddered.

'You know I'm not a superstitious man. But since you wish it . . .' He stood and paced the room again, more slowly now, hands clasped behind his back. 'Who else knows?'

'Only Mum.'

'Not the girls? Or Ronald?'

'I would never tell anyone else before you,' she exclaimed.

'Except your mother.'

She bit her lip, watching him nervously. Ernest was always scrupulously polite to his mother-in-law, but she knew he secretly thought Sheila loud and foolish. His own parents had passed away long before they'd met, but he had always revered them as intelligent progressives, keeping a treasured photograph of them in his wallet and sometimes telling fantastical tales of his childhood adventures with them. He had never confirmed this, but she suspected his father had been quite high up in German diplomatic circles before emigrating to England. Beside them, her own mum and dad must seem rather dull and ordinary.

Indeed, she often wondered why Ernest – or Ernst, as he'd called himself when they first met – had married someone like her. She wasn't unintelligent, but she was nothing special, that was for sure. She had longish blonde hair, with similar looks to his mother, she guessed, though beyond that . . .

She'd asked him once in the early years of their marriage, needing some reassurance, but he'd merely laughed and said something nonsensical about her dancing skills. 'As soon as I looked across the room,' he'd murmured in her ear, referring to the dance where they'd first been introduced, 'and saw your foxtrot and quick step, I knew you were the girl for me.' She had been in London with some friends, and he'd been there with the sister of a friend, though only as an escort, not her boyfriend. She often wondered how her life might have turned out if she hadn't gone dancing in London that night, for they had moved in very different circles, and it had been quite a wrench for Ernest to leave his London friends and get lodgings in Dagenham while they were courting. But he'd never complained, merely adjusting to his new life with his usual calm efficiency and common sense. And she'd never questioned it, fearing how she might feel if he admitted to missing more intellectual company.

'I want us to be married,' he had told her after only a few months, 'so wherever you are, there I must be too.' And she'd been so bowled over by his loving gestures and excellent manners, she had quickly said yes.

'I needed to ask her advice first, that's all.' Betsy shrugged. 'She's my mum, ain't she? Besides, I still wasn't sure at that stage.'

'But you're sure now?'

'I saw the doctor a few days ago,' she admitted, blushing. 'He examined me and seemed certain too. But he made me take a test, just in case. I called into the surgery this morning, and it was positive. I'm pregnant.'

His smile reassured her. 'That is the most marvellous news, darling. I could wish you'd told me sooner, but . . .' He studied her face before kneeling before her and kissing her hand like he used to do back when they were first walking out together. 'I love you, Betsy,' he told her, his blue gaze locked with hers. 'I can see you're worried in case something goes wrong. But whatever happens, we will deal with it together. Yes?'

She swallowed, tears in her eyes again. 'Yes,' she stammered, and closed her eyes in relief as he hugged her.

He was such a lovely husband. The very best she could imagine, in fact. But she couldn't dismiss the nagging suspicion that his life had not lived up to all the promise of his youth. That would be her fault, of course, for insisting when they got married that she needed to live close to her mum and dad, not with him in London. He had agreed and willingly given up his job there to move out to Dagenham, though he'd never confirmed what that job had been. Something in translation, he'd told her once, rather vaguely. She'd often wondered if in fact he could have done far better for himself than working at the Ford plant, for all that he was so clever with engines and machinery, not to mention languages. His recent promotion might signal a change in his fortunes though.

'Everything's going to be all right,' he insisted.

Betsy badly wanted to believe him. 'But with everything in the newspapers lately, and the whispers flying around . . . And the Blackshirts?'

His expression hardened. 'Boys like that make me despair. They can't seem to think for themselves. But it's a free country, and I'd like to keep it that way. Even if that means we must allow men like Mosley and his followers to have their say.' He kissed her tenderly. 'But I won't let any of this touch you, my love. I swear it on my life.'

She tried to feel reassured, nodding.

'Besides, there are men in the British government right now who plan to stop Herr Hitler and his sympathisers in their tracks.' He hesitated, a frown returning to his face. 'Though it may mean another war, unfortunately. But with any luck, it'll be a short one this time, if Germany sees sense.'

'And if they don't?'

Ernest put his arms about her, and she laid her head on his strong chest, wishing she could always feel so safe as she did now, held close in his arms.

'Let's not dwell on that possibility, *Liebling*. The only thing that matters right now is you . . . and the new life growing inside you.'

After she'd seen their two girls off to school first thing next morning, Betsy pulled on a jacket against the stiff spring breeze, and a head scarf to prevent her blonde hair blowing about, and set out to her mother's house. There, she found her sister Violet and her mother's new lodger, Edith, on the doorstep, about to leave. She'd offered to walk with Violet to the cemetery today, for it would have been Vi's late fiancé's birthday, and she knew that Violet hated going alone to the grave.

Edith was a pretty little thing with vibrant red hair and warm chestnut-brown eyes, though her face was rather pale.

She was on her way to work, she told them, for she'd taken on Betsy's shifts at Ron's Corner Caff and was settling in well, according to their mum.

'Hello, Vi,' Betsy said with forced cheeriness, linking arms with her. 'You ready, little sis?'

'As I'll ever be,' Violet murmured but stuck her chin in the air when Betsy glanced at her sharply, a brave smile on her face. 'I told Edith we'd walk with her to the caff before catching the bus. That all right?'

'Of course.' Betsy studied the younger woman dubiously though. 'Don't you know the way yet?'

'No,' Violet said quickly for Edith, 'it's because of them horrible lads again – those Blackshirts. They came by the caff the other day and one of them yelled at Edith for no reason at all. Ron came out to have a word with them, but they'd run off by then. Disgraceful behaviour.'

'But why did they shout at you? Surely not because of . . . of me and Ernest?' Betsy was horrified when Edith bit her lip, looking away without a word. 'Gawd, I'm ever so sorry.'

'It's not your fault,' Edith insisted.

But Betsy couldn't help feeling guilty.

'It's nothing. Just a bunch of idiots,' Violet whispered in her ear. 'They know she's staying with us, that's all, and that Ernie's my brother-in-law. Nasty little toads, they are.'

'Have a nice day at work.' Violet gave Edith a cheery wave as they reached Ron's Corner Caff. 'Don't pay too much attention to Ron moaning at you. He's always complaining about something. See you at dinner.'

Betsy watched Edith slip inside, the younger woman already taking off her hat and coat ready for her shift. She felt a pang of nostalgia; she'd enjoyed chatting to customers and getting out of the house for a few precious hours every week, even if the job hadn't paid very well. It was a shame she'd had to give it up.

Still, she was never lonely for long with young Alice and Lily about the house after school, and her own husband to keep her company in the evenings. Besides, this new pregnancy was more important than a job, and she'd feared for her safety after the way those lads had spoken to her, so malicious and threatening. She'd hoped they would stop giving Ron a hard time after he'd refused to put up that fascist poster for them, but it seemed like they hadn't backed down. She only hoped that Ernest was right and the government would sort everything out in time. It was just a matter of being patient.

'Seems like you and Edith are making friends,' she remarked, shooting her sister a curious glance, for Violet had never made friends easily.

'She's good company,' Violet agreed. 'I love hearing about her life back in Cornwall too. I'd like to go there myself one day. Not a quick visit to Aunty Maggie but for a proper holiday. It sounds like a marvellous place.' She hugged herself, peering up into grey suburban skies. 'She says there's open countryside where she lives, for as far as the eye can see, and a beautiful coastline too down at Penzance. Oh, Betsy, do you remember them day trips to Southend-on-Sea when we was little? Mum used to make us paste sarnies for a picnic lunch on the beach, only we'd get sand in them, so she'd laugh and say—'

Betsy chorused with her, 'Well, they're called sandwiches, ain't they?' and they both chuckled at the memory.

'I did love making sandcastles and watching the waves come rolling in,' Violet admitted.

'Good times.' Betsy nodded, smiling. But there was sadness in her heart too. 'It's a long while since we saw the sea though.'

Violet nodded without saying anything, but Betsy saw tears in her eyes. They'd had a carefree childhood after the Great War. But times had grown darker and tougher in recent years, and all that fun and laughter seemed a long way off.

They caught the next bus that went past the cemetery where Leonard, once Violet's beau, had been buried. The clouds had finally drifted away under a brisk wind, and it soon became warm and sunny enough that Betsy began to regret wearing her coat. A woman in the seat in front was remonstrating with her small child, telling him not to eat his bag of sweets on the bus but to save them for home. Betsy recalled similar conversations with her daughters when they were younger, especially Alice, who had a sweet tooth. But they were both well-behaved girls and had never given her much trouble, even as little kiddies. Cheekily, the little boy stuck his tongue out at his mum, though only when the poor woman was looking the other way.

When it was their stop, she followed Violet off the bus and across the road to the large, wrought-iron gates to the cemetery. 'I sometimes wish I'd had a boy as well as my two girls,' she admitted, glancing back wistfully as the bus trundled on.

Violet threw her a shrewd look. 'Feeling broody again, are you?' Then she seemed to catch something in Betsy's face, for she stopped dead, her eyes widening as she turned to stare. 'Oh my word . . . You're never pregnant again, are you?'

Betsy blushed.

'Why, you dark horse. You've kept that quiet. How far

along are you?' When Betsy told her, she whistled. 'Well, no wonder you gave up your job at the caff. I couldn't understand it at the time, but now . . .' Her sister grinned, giving Betsy a hug. 'Congratulations!'

'Thanks. Though we're keeping it secret for now. Just in case . . .'

Violet sobered. 'Understood.'

Betsy had told her about one of the early pregnancies she'd lost, though not in much detail. It had been too painful a loss. But her sister had clearly not forgotten.

They walked through the neat, green rows of headstones in the cemetery. A man with shirtsleeves rolled to his elbows was pushing a mower between the graves. He stopped under the shade of a gnarled old yew tree as they passed and touched his hat. 'Ladies.'

Betsy smiled at him and murmured a greeting in return. But Violet seemed not to have even noticed the man, her expression abstracted. Lost in the past, no doubt, as she so often was when they visited her beloved's grave.

Leonard was buried a long way back in the churchyard, in the new section where they were still expanding, knocking down walls to make room for new graves. It was quieter there, with trees for patchy shade and a few wildflowers allowed to run riot in the long grasses where the mower had not yet been.

'Happy birthday, Leonard.' Violet had brought a simple posy of flowers wrapped up in brown paper, mostly marguerites picked from an obliging neighbour's garden, with a fan of soft white petals surrounding each egg-yellow centre. She stooped to place these daisy-like flowers on Leonard's grave and then stepped back, head bowed as she murmured a few words under her breath.

Betsy kept a respectful distance until her sister looked up again. She breathed a sigh of relief, thankful to see that Violet was not crying this time. Last year, on Leonard's birthday, she'd wept at his graveside for over an hour, inconsolable. But time moved on, didn't it?

It was some years now since Leonard had slipped away in a hospital bed, his mother holding one limp hand, Violet the other. It was clear that his death had left a deep scar, for her sister rarely went out socialising these days, and by all accounts had turned down more than one invitation to dinner from nice blokes she knew from the factory. But she knew that one day Violet would emerge from under that dark cloud and start her life anew. She just hoped it would be soon.

'I can't imagine how it would feel to lose my Ernest,' Betsy admitted, linking her arm with Violet's. When her sister didn't reply, she feared having been inconsiderate, and added awkwardly, 'I'm sorry that you lost Leonard when he was still so young and the two of you had barely got to know each other.'

Her sister stirred at last. 'I do wonder sometimes what kind of man he would have become, given more time. It's so cruel and pointless, having someone snatched away like that, barely any warning. He caught influenza and that was it. Even the nurses at the hospital couldn't believe how quickly he succumbed. But I suppose he had a weakness of the lungs.' Violet had lifted a hanky to her face, her voice muffled. 'It's his parents I pity most. Their only child . . . I see his mother around town now and then, but she hurries away whenever she catches sight of me. I suppose I'm a reminder of what happened to her boy.' Violet looked down sorrowfully at his grave. 'I can't say I blame her.'

'It wasn't your fault he caught the flu,' Betsy exclaimed, feeling aggrieved for her sister.

'I know that. But you can't expect her to be happy to see me. Leonard spent so much time with me just before he died . . . Perhaps if we hadn't been in love, he might have spent those final days with his parents.'

Betsy pulled a face but didn't say anything. Violet had funny ideas and it was no good arguing over them. 'He's at peace now though,' was all she said, 'and the rest of us have to get on with being alive.' She hugged her sister close. 'I just wish the world wasn't so dark right now.'

'What do you mean?' Violet gave her a puzzled look.

'Come on, Vi . . . Mum told you about them lads in the caff, didn't she? The Blackshirts.'

Violet shrugged. 'What about them?'

'Gawd, don't you care what's going on in Europe, or even in this blessed country?' Betsy frowned, wondering if her sister ever bothered reading the newspaper or listening to the wireless. 'There's something wrong when lads like that can support Mosley and his fascists, and walk around Dagenham like they own the place, being rude to their elders and betters, threatening law-abiding folk . . . It ain't right, Vi.'

'But they're just idiots. And as for what's happening in Europe . . . It seems so far away, that's all.' Violet sighed, turning away from her beloved's grave with one last longing glance at his headstone. 'You don't really think there's going to be another war with Germany, do you? It doesn't seem possible. What does Ernest say about it?'

'He says there'll be a war before the end of the year. But he doesn't think it will last long.'

'Ain't that what they said about the Great War?' Violet was looking worried at last. 'Home by Christmas?'

'But maybe they'll remember how disastrous that war was for Germany, so it'll help cut things shorter this time,' Betsy said practically. 'You know, it's strange. I used to think how lucky we were to have been so young during the Great War. Four years of hell, but I can barely remember it, except for all the soldiers on the streets and the celebrations when it was finally over. But if there was to be another war like that now . . .' She shivered, unable to complete that thought.

'I know what you mean.' Her sister hugged her close. 'But what can *we* do to stop Britain going to war? Not bloomin' much. So we might as well try not to fret.' Violet hesitated. 'Though, if there is a war, I think we'll win. I mean, Britain *has* to win if we go to war. It don't bear thinking about otherwise.'

They began to walk along the road outside the cemetery, heading for the bus stop and home.

'But Germany's so strong.' Betsy felt cold in the sharp wind, thinking unhappily of her daughters and her unborn child. 'The Nazis have all these tanks and aeroplanes and huge guns. And they're taking over most of Europe, if the news reels at the cinema are to be believed. Gawd, I couldn't bear to see them marching into London in their great big black boots. Can't imagine it either. It seems absurd. Impossible, too.'

'Well, even if they somehow managed to overrun London, I doubt they'd get much further.' Violet gave her a rueful smile. 'I reckon there are some Scots up in Glasgow who'd give them one hell of a fight.'

'Haggis at dawn!'

The two sisters glanced at each other and chuckled.

'Let's look on the bright side,' Betsy told her firmly. 'Things will likely work out for the best. Ernest says the German government is bound to see sense in the end, even if it takes a bit of resistance to show them all we're not asleep over here. Because nobody wants a repeat of the Great War, do they?' She tried to comfort Violet as well as herself, pushing away her fears with a brave smile. 'And my Ernie ain't never wrong.'

CHAPTER SIX

Edith loved her small back bedroom in Sheila's comfortable but often chaotic house. The place wasn't quiet but after a few weeks it already felt like home. To Edith, forced to leave Cornwall and her friends behind, anything that felt like home was welcome. Maybe there wasn't sweeping green countryside to be seen out of her bedroom window. And yes, she was woken by traffic every morning rather than the gentle lowing of cattle and the occasional rumble of a milk truck in a distant lane, navigating potholes and mud ruts. And she didn't know any of the people she passed on her way to work, except for a few faces she was beginning to recognise from the local area. Back at home she knew everybody, from the smallest child to the white-whiskered old gents who sat smoking their pipes outside the pub on a summer's evening. But this was home to her now, a place where nobody judged her, and nobody knew what she'd done.

But it seemed that guilt still haunted her, leaving her sometimes feeling physically sick with it. For several days over the past week, she'd stumbled out of bed to pull back the curtains and let in the daylight, and had felt almost queasy. Like she needed food in her empty tummy, and quickly, else she was going to be sick.

Each time, she'd racked her brains to think what she could have eaten the night before to upset her stomach. Maybe the milk in her tea had been off. Or the fish on Friday had not been as fresh as it might have been. Of course, she might just be suffering from nerves. After all, she'd heard nothing from Cornwall since that first letter from her grandmother had arrived, in response to her own letter home to say she was staying with Mrs Hopkins.

She couldn't help wondering if her grandmother was still furious with her, or if perhaps she'd written again but the letter had gone astray. Edith herself was still writing home every week, letting her gran know how the new job was going and what it was like living in Dagenham, and how much she missed Cornwall with every breath in her body. But the longer there was no response, the more her nerves churned inside her. That would certainly explain why she kept waking up queasy and unsettled.

Or perhaps it was because she missed *him*.

The very thought of Percy made her catch her breath, her eyes shut tight. She had promised herself – had sworn an oath, in fact – that she would not think of him. That his name wouldn't cross her mind or her lips, however much she missed him.

But it was so hard. Percy had come into her life like a whirlwind, she'd loved him to bits, given herself to him, and now to simply forget that he'd even existed . . . ? No, she couldn't do it. Yet another reason why her tummy was all over the place.

One day, she would be over him. And when that day finally came, she would feel strong again and able to face each new challenge without shrinking.

It was a lazy Saturday evening, after an early supper, when Violet knocked at her bedroom door and then burst in without waiting for permission. She was breathless and a little flushed. 'Edith . . . Gawd, what are you doing? Reading a book? On a Saturday night?' Violet shook her head in amusement. 'Each to their own, I suppose.'

Edith laid aside the library book she'd been reading, half lying on her bed on her stomach. Her nerves were causing merry hell again, probably caused by such a busy week.

'What on earth's going on?' She looked her new friend up and down in surprise. 'Watch out, your stocking's got a ladder.'

'No, has it?' Violet shook her head in exasperation, peering down at her left leg. 'Bloomin' hell, that's the last thing I need. Still, at least I'm not still wearing my uniform,' she added, studying her significantly.

Edith laughed, plucking at her plain black skirt and white work blouse with its high, buttoned neck. 'Yes, sorry, I couldn't be bothered changing after supper. I was just too exhausted. Do you need something?'

'Only a little favour.'

Curious now, Edith sat up. 'Go on, I'm listening.'

'There's this lad at work, you see,' Violet told her, blowing on freshly painted nails as she leant on the doorframe. 'Everyone calls him Nobby. He's got a Welsh cousin who's come to stay. Aled, his name is. Anyway, Nobby asked if I'd like to go the pictures with him and Aled, and did I know anyone else who'd go along with us? Another girl, I mean.'

Violet bit her lip. 'As far as I'm concerned, Nobby's just a friend, so it's not a serious date. But I did feel sorry for his cousin, coming all the way from Wales, only to get stuck home on a Saturday night. So I said yes.'

Edith's heart beat hard. 'And you've volunteered *me* to go to the pictures with you and these two lads?'

'To make up a foursome, yes.' Violet looked guilty at last. 'Gawd, did I do the wrong thing? You never go out except to work at the caff, so I thought you'd be keen.'

'Well, I'm not sure . . . But I thought you never went out socialising either?'

'Oh!' Violet looked taken aback. She came into the room properly and sank onto the bed next to Edith. 'You're right, of course. I do prefer staying in. In fact, I only said yes this time because . . .' She gave a heavy sigh, turning the silver engagement ring she still wore. 'Betsy says I can't mourn forever. And I suppose she's right. Leonard and I weren't even married, and it's been two years now since he passed. High time I snapped out of it, Betsy says.' She looked up, her eyes shiny with tears. 'What do *you* think? If I was the one who'd died, I'd be miserable if Leonard had forgotten about *me* after only a few years. Wouldn't you be the same?'

'I . . . I don't know.' Edith chewed on her lip, not sure what to say. She'd heard plenty about Leonard from Mrs Hopkins. He'd caught influenza and passed away before he and Violet could marry, and she'd been pining for him ever since, refusing to date anyone else.

Now here she was, encouraging her friend to stay in on a Saturday night, when Violet was finally beginning to come out of the doldrums.

'Look, maybe it *would* be nice to go to the pictures.' She

pretended to be interested, though she wasn't remotely. 'What's he like, this Welsh boy?'

'You interested, then?' Violet straightened, a spark in her eyes. 'Aled's all right. Nineteen and a bit wet behind the ears, perhaps. But I bet he'd spring for an ice cream at the interval, if you smiled at him nicely.' And they both fell about giggling.

'What time are we supposed to be leaving, then?'

'Nobby said he'd call at the house for six-thirty.' Violet's gaze flew to the clock on the mantelpiece, and she jumped up, gasping. 'Blimey, will you look at the time? I'd better change my stockings and put some lippy on. And you can't go out looking like a waitress, love. Meet you downstairs in twenty minutes?' And she dashed out of the room.

Not entirely sure what she'd let herself in for, Edith checked her reflection in the mirror and groaned. She'd accepted an extra shift at the caff that afternoon and hadn't yet tidied her hair since coming home from work. Not only that, but her normally rosy cheeks were pale, and the queasiness that she hadn't been able to shake over the past week had left her looking gaunt. She'd been skipping meals to avoid feeling unwell.

Hurriedly, she changed out of her work uniform into her favourite green skirt with a cream blouse, then grabbed a brush and began wrenching it through her bright red hair, wishing there was time to take a bath before going out. But a few clips should hold the style in place.

She had a lipstick on her dressing table, which she applied lightly most days before heading out to work. She'd never worn make-up in the country. But here in Dagenham most women wore powder and lipstick, and she didn't want to feel out of place or old-fashioned. And for a trip to the cinema with a date – for what else was this but a date? – surely make-up was required.

Feeling rather daring, she applied her lipstick more liberally than usual, checking in the mirror to make sure she didn't make a mess of it. It seemed to clash with her red hair, but what could she do about that?

She pinched her cheeks to make it look like she was wearing blusher, and pulled on a cardigan over her blouse, for the evenings were still a little nippy. Maybe it wasn't the most alluring outfit, but she wasn't interested in getting herself a boyfriend. She was doing her friend a favour, that was all, so that Violet wouldn't have to go to the cinema on her own with two boys, one of them a stranger.

She found Violet waiting downstairs, looking considerably smarter than her. Her arched brows rose as she looked Edith up and down. 'Must you wear that old cardi?'

'I don't want to get cold,' Edith protested.

'It's May now . . . Hardly midwinter!' Violet shrugged. 'But I suppose you'll do.'

She herself had changed into a summer frock with impressive black heels, and was wearing a striking scarlet lipstick, her lashes thick with mascara. Edith glanced at her dubiously but said nothing. Violet had to be a good six or seven years older than her and no doubt knew what she was doing.

There was a brisk knock at the door.

'Who's that?' Mrs Hopkins appeared in the hallway, staring in consternation. 'Violet, love?' She seemed astonished by her daughter's glamorous appearance, very different from her usual humdrum work outfit. 'You look very, erm, nice . . . You and Edith going out somewhere?'

They'd had their evening meal earlier that day, since Mr Hopkins didn't go to work on a Saturday. Traditionally, Mr Hopkins washed up the dinner plates at the weekend, and the splash of water and him whistling could be heard through the half-open kitchen door.

'We're off out to the pictures, Mum.' Violet yanked open the door to reveal two young men on the doorstep, both looking embarrassed, their hands in their pockets.

'Who are they?' Mrs Hopkins demanded.

'Oh, just some friends,' Violet replied carelessly. 'Well, we'd better get a move on. Don't want to miss the start of the main feature. It's an Alfred Hitchcock film . . . *Jamaica Inn*.'

'Gosh,' Edith exclaimed, 'that's set in Cornwall.'

'I know, that's why I thought you'd like to see it.' She dragged Edith outside before she'd even had a chance to fasten her jacket. 'We might be back late, Mum. But I've got my latchkey, so don't wait up, eh?'

Without waiting for an answer from Mrs Hopkins, they hurried off down the street together. Violet introduced Edith to the two young men as they walked. Nobby looked to be about Violet's age, tall and broad-shouldered with short fair hair and a constant jeering grin, while his cousin Aled was more slightly built, his dark hair curling almost to his collar. It was coming on to rain as they reached the pictures, and Aled had brought an umbrella, which he used to shield the two girls from the rain while Nobby queued at the box office to buy their tickets.

'Our treat,' Nobby insisted gallantly when Violet took out her purse.

They found their seats and settled in to watch *Jamaica Inn*. It felt so odd to be watching a film set on Bodmin Moor in Cornwall, not that far from where she herself had lived with her dad and grandmother. Edith watched with rapt attention, her heart beating fast at times, for it was quite a thrilling story. It didn't look much like Cornwall to her, but the music was dramatic and carried her along.

They were nearly an hour into the film when Nobby put his arm around Violet's shoulders and tried to kiss her. There was some kind of scuffle, then Violet jumped up and stormed out, with everyone staring. Nobby swore and didn't move from his seat, but Aled looked after her, clearly dismayed.

'I'd better go after her,' Edith whispered, and gave Aled an embarrassed smile. 'Sorry about this. Nice to meet you.'

Outside the picture house, she found Violet in tears.

'Are you all right?' Edith asked, not sure whether she would welcome a hug or push her away. 'Whatever happened?'

'Horrid beast,' Violet hissed, shuddering. 'He kissed me, and then . . .' She described what else Nobby had done, and Edith was horrified. 'I'm sorry to have dragged you out of the film though; I could see you were enjoying it. You should go back in. Do you have your ticket stub? It's still light . . . I can walk home on my own.'

'Don't be silly,' said Edith firmly. 'In any case, I don't mind leaving. The film didn't look anything like the real Cornwall anyway, except some moments when they were on the moor.' Edith could still hear the shake in her friend's voice and risked a quick hug. 'And please don't cry. You were quite right to leave. He shouldn't have done that. Nasty creep.'

'But you and Aled—'

'He was a nice enough lad, but nothing special.' Edith took her arm. 'Come on, let's go home. I think the chip shop might still be open. We could grab some chips and eat them on the corner before going home. So your mum won't ask any awkward questions about why we're back so early.'

Violet smiled through her tears, nodding, but gave her an odd look as they headed for the chip shop. 'Tell me to mind my own business, Edith, but did you leave someone special behind in Cornwall?'

'Why do you ask?'

'Aled's not a bad looker. If I was five years younger . . . And he had eyes only for you. But you barely glanced at the poor lad.' Violet dried her tears with a hankie. 'I just thought maybe you were already involved with someone back home.'

Edith struggled against the desire to tell her new friend everything. She'd had nobody to confide in, and hadn't even dared tell her grandmother the whole story. But after the way Susan Teague back home had betrayed her confidence, after years of being one of her closest friends, she felt so uncertain about trusting again.

'There was a boy,' she admitted shyly, picking her words with care. 'But he went away. So that was the end of that.'

'Went away?' Violet echoed blankly.

'Back to Canada.'

Her friend peered at her, amazed. 'He was Canadian? What's his name? However did you meet him?'

'Oh, it's a long story.'

'I can keep up.'

Edith hesitated, then decided to take a risk and hope that Violet wouldn't turn out to be as untrustworthy as Susan. 'His name is Percy . . . Percy Grigg.' She swallowed against a lump in her throat, trying to explain without showing too much emotion. Whenever she thought about Percy, she always came perilously close to tears, and she didn't want her new friend to think her a wet blanket. 'Originally, the Grigg family were from our little village in Cornwall, where your mum was born, but they emigrated to Alberta in Canada about fifteen years ago when Percy was still a little boy, so I never knew him when I was younger. Only last year his uncle in Cornwall died and left everything to his dad. A big farmhouse and all the land.'

'Go on.'

'When they heard about the will, the Griggs decided to come back for a visit and view the estate. They have a successful business in Alberta selling animal feed, you see, and are happy there. They didn't want to return to Cornwall for good. But they thought it would be prudent to look at their inheritance first.' Edith smiled wistfully. 'That was when I first got to know Percy. I met him out walking one day. I showed him around the village and took the bus into Penzance with him a few times to visit St Michael's Mount and go to the pictures. But then his dad finalised his arrangements to sell the estate, so they sailed back to Canada again.'

'And you and Percy?'

Edith couldn't reply at first, her chest tightening with emotion. At last she said shakily, 'We . . . We said goodbye, and that was it. I wrote to him early on but . . . Well, maybe my letter got lost.'

'Or he hasn't got it yet,' Violet said practically. 'The sailing to Canada must take a while. And letters take ages to arrive too. Maybe he's already written back and there's a letter waiting for you at home in Cornwall.'

'Gran would have sent it on,' Edith mumbled, and shook her head. 'I know what's happened. Percy's gone back to

Canada and forgotten all about me, so that's that.' She thrust her chin in the air. 'Anyway, I destroyed his address when I decided to come to Dagenham. I didn't want to spend my life pining for someone I'd never see again.' Only after she'd said that did she realise how it sounded . . . Violet had lost her fiancé and was still pining for him, wasn't she?

Thankfully, her new friend didn't seem offended. Instead, there was a terrible sadness in her face. 'Oh, Edith.' She stretched out a hand. 'I'm so sorry.'

'I'll survive.' She took Violet's hand, smiling with an effort. 'Plenty more fish in the sea, eh?' But her voice was hollow. She was lying and Violet knew it. Percy had been her soulmate and she would never get over him, not even if she lived to one hundred.

'That's the spirit,' Violet told her. 'Tell you what, love . . . Betsy's invited me to Sunday lunch at her house tomorrow. Would you like to come too?'

'Oh, but—'

'They won't mind another guest, trust me. The more the merrier.' Violet gave her a shrewd look. 'Besides, you need cheering up. And nobody's better at making people laugh than Ernie.' She pulled a face. 'Except possibly my mother. Though I'm not sure Mum's funny on purpose, if you see what I mean.'

Sure enough, Sunday lunch at Betsy and Ernest's house was good fun, and Edith soon forgot her troubles as she playfully arm-wrestled with young Alice and then helped Betsy carry out the dessert bowls for washing. Lily and Alice were already outside in the garden, competing with each other to do handstands against the shed door, their long Sunday best frocks tucked modestly into the tops of their socks on their mother's strict orders, so as not to alarm the neighbours.

Ernest followed them into the kitchen, rolling up his shirtsleeves ready to attack the washing-up, but Betsy shooed him out.

'We can do the dishes this time,' she told her husband, nodding to the two girls messing about in the garden. 'You promised them you'd put up that hammock between the tree and the shed, don't you remember? They'll be disappointed if you don't keep your word.'

'Ah, yes.' Ernest hesitated, then shot Edith a quick smile. 'Would you care to help me with the hammock, Miss Treloar? I may need an assistant.'

Edith hesitated, wanting to be helpful after having enjoyed the Fishers' kind hospitality, but unsure it would be wise to go outside into full May sunshine. She'd been feeling fragile again after another night spent tossing and turning, her body full of unfamiliar aches and pains, and strange tinglings . . .

'I'll do it,' Violet volunteered promptly, steering her brother-in-law outside. But she paused in the doorway, peering round at Edith. 'You all right, love?'

'Perfectly, yes,' Edith insisted with a forced smile. But she caught the swift glance between Violet and Betsy and knew more was required to explain her lack of appetite at lunch. It was worrying and she wished she could explain it to herself. But despite these odd, queasy flutterings in her tummy, she couldn't bear the thought of others fretting over her health. It was probably nothing important. Her easily upset nerves again, most likely.

'My t-time of the month, that's all,' she added feebly, once Ernest was safely out of earshot.

Though that was a fib too, wasn't it? For she'd not had her monthlies in a while. It wasn't unusual for her to skip the odd period. But perhaps it had been rather a long time . . .

'Oh, you poor love,' Violet exclaimed, her eyes instantly sympathetic, before whisking herself out into the garden.

Edith drew herself up, shaking off the silly notions whirling about in her head. This was no time to be dreaming up yet more trouble for herself.

'Where shall I start?' she asked her hostess, who was now busy scraping plates. 'Washing or drying?'

'Drying is fine, thank you. My hands are permanently wrinkly these days. No point us both looking pruny.' Betsy set the plates to soak while Edith located the stack of clean tea towels. She bent to retrieve a dropped fork and winced. 'Oh my gawd . . .' Clutching her tummy, she blenched, then fled the kitchen, muttering, 'Excuse me.'

Bewildered, Edith hesitated, then followed her hostess to the lavatory, where she could hear Betsy being violently unwell. Hovering outside the door, she waited a decent interval, then said quietly, 'Can . . . Can I help?' Though, in truth, the sounds alone had made her feel horribly sick too. But she swallowed, holding herself stiffly as the door opened to reveal a pale, wan-faced Betsy. 'Can I fetch you some water? Or call for your sister, perhaps?'

Betsy gave her an unhappy smile but shook her head. 'I'm feeling much better.' She ran a hand over a gently swelling belly. 'The truth is, and please keep this to yourself,' she added in a whisper, 'since the girls don't know yet . . . But I'm expecting another baby. I'm always a bit unwell in the early stages. Funny aches and tinglings, and this awful nausea, especially in the mornings, though at any time of day, really . . . Nothing to be done, I'm afraid. Though my mum swears by a strong ginger tea to start the day.'

Betsy was expecting a baby?

Then the rest hit her.

Always a bit unwell in the early stages . . . Funny aches and tinglings, and this awful nausea, especially in the mornings . . .

Edith was staring like a fool, her mouth open.

'I . . . I . .' She couldn't finish, her mind a frightful blank, but she hurried back to the kitchen instead where she stood staring out into the sunny garden at the two kids, now squabbling over a doll. Under the shade of a young tree, Ernest and Violet were struggling with the folds of a vast cloth hammock, both laughing, not a care in the world.

'What is it, love? Are you sure you're all right?' Betsy had followed her and now put a gentle hand on her shoulder. 'If you need someone to talk to, you can always—'

Panicked, Edith shook her head. Guilt flared inside her, hot and cold at the same time. She felt as though Betsy already knew what she was thinking. As though everyone must have been able to see the truth for days . . . Ever since she'd arrived, in fact.

Everyone except her.

'I'm sorry,' she whispered, turning with an anguished look. 'But you're right, I'm not feeling very well at all. Would you think me terribly rude if I went home early? It was a lovely lunch, and I said I would help with the washing-up, I know, but . . .'

'Gawd, don't be silly, love. Of course I don't mind. And the girls can help with drying the dishes. But there are no buses back your way on a Sunday and I can't let you walk. Not in the state you're in. Ernest will drive you home. Now go and sit down while I fetch him.' Edith made a weak protest, though her head was spinning and she had to lean against the wall to support herself. Betsy tutted loudly. 'No, I insist . . . Trust me, Ernie won't mind a jot. It will give him a good excuse not to finish putting up that hammock.'

'Thank you. You're both very kind.'

'Don't worry about that. Just promise me you'll go and see a doctor as soon as possible.' Betsy gave her a concerned look. 'Will you?'

Edith had no intention of going to a doctor. But she nodded meekly, knowing it would lay her friend's fears to rest. 'Of course,' she agreed.

Betsy went to the back door to call her husband while Edith sank onto a kitchen stool, her cheeks flaming at the lie.

This was not something she could take to a doctor.

Only one person could solve the mess she was in . . . and he would be thousands of miles away by now, back home in Canada.

CHAPTER SEVEN

Sheila stood at the counter in the caff, arranging dainty fairy cakes on a doily. She was minding the caff while Ron nipped out for more sausage meat after a particularly busy morning, and was enjoying the unfamiliar experience of being in charge.

The entrance door jangled and in came Mrs Peabody, the dairyman's loud wife, who often popped in for a bite to eat and a cuppa between chores. Today, she threaded her way slowly between the front tables with a large, well-sprung pram, its spoked wheels gleaming, barely glancing at customers on either side as they shifted aside for her, and almost ran over Mr Archer's ancient terrier, who'd been sprawled at his master's feet as usual while the old man read the newspaper.

'Oi, watch out!' Mrs Peabody complained, stopping. 'Your bloomin' dog's in the way of my pram. I can't get through.'

Mr Archer muttered something under his breath and moved to another table, newspaper and coffee mug in hand. The terrier got up and slowly ambled after him, man and beast both wearing the same mournful expression . . .

Mrs Peabody threw the old man a disdainful look, but settled at the table he'd just vacated.

'Sorry, love,' she told Sheila without any real hint of apology. 'I'm looking after Shirley's youngest today. You don't mind me bringing this bleedin' great thing in here, do you? I didn't want to leave little Donald out in the street, not in this sunshine.' She shrugged out of her jacket and draped it over the pram handle. 'Not that I'm complaining about this nice weather, mind. Not after the drenching we had last month. Nice to see the sun out at last, ain't it?'

'Gawd yes, the weather's turned lovely now.' Sheila beamed, bending over the pram to admire Mrs Peabody's sleeping grandson. 'And he's lovely too. Hello, darlin'.'

'Five pound, three ounces, he was.'

'Oh, what a good weight. Your Shirley must be proud as Punch. Her third, ain't it?'

'That's right. And all boys.' Mrs Peabody shot her a sly look. 'You've only the two granddaughters, am I right?'

'Lily and Alice, yes. Such nice girls. They never give us any trouble. Though I'd love a grandson like this little chap. Henry would too.' Sheila chuckled. 'He's given up waiting, so he's been teaching young Alice to kick a football. Lily ain't interested in any of that carry-on, of course.'

'She must be quite grown up now, your Lily.'

'Oh yes . . . She's fifteen.'

Sheila turned to Edith, who was hovering behind her uncertainly with an order pad. 'Mrs Peabody always has a pot of tea with a large bacon sandwich, crusts cut off the bread. Can you sort that out, love?'

'Yes, Mrs Hopkins.' Edith hurried away, but Sheila thought she seemed distracted. She had been all morning.

Mrs Peabody watched her go. 'That new girl looks a bit pasty-faced. She not well?' Her voice was suspicious, almost as though she feared Edith might spread some dreadful disease to all the customers, including herself and her grandson.

Sheila shrugged, though she had to admit that Edith hadn't been as bright and alert recently as she'd seemed on first arriving from Cornwall. She'd had lunch at Betsy's on Sunday last though, so perhaps Betsy or Violet would know if anything was wrong. 'Still getting used to not being in the country, I suppose . . . Dagenham's a big change from Cornwall.'

'Yes, it can't be easy.' The baby began to mewl. Mrs Peabody lifted her wriggling grandson out of the pram, cradling him with an indulgent smile as she sat back down again. 'There, there, poppet. I'll be taking you home to Mummy as soon as I've had a nice cuppa.' She winked up at Sheila, whispering, 'I promised my Shirley I'd take him out the house for an hour while she bakes a birthday cake for her eldest. He'll be six tomorrow, bless his soul.'

'Boys are a treat at that age.' Sheila sighed, wishing again for a grandson of her own.

Edith, hurrying back with the tea tray, her gaze fixed on the street outside instead of where she was going, somehow managed to trip over Mr Archer's dog, whose large dirty paws were protruding from under his table. She gave a despairing wail as she stumbled, and the tray went flying. The china cup and saucer smashed to pieces as they hit the floor, hot water jug and teapot splattering their contents all over the table and chairbacks.

Mrs Peabody leapt up with her tiny grandson hugged tight

to her chest, shrieking furiously, 'You stupid girl!' Frantically, she checked the baby, who was now red-faced and wailing, for signs that he'd been scalded, though Sheila felt sure no hot liquids had gone anywhere near either of them. 'You could have killed my grandson. There, there, my poor little lamb, Granny's got you safe.'

'It was just an accident,' Sheila said hurriedly, grabbing the tea towel over her shoulder and using it to mop up the spilt tea on the table. 'Edith, fetch the dustpan and brush. Once you've cleared up the broken crockery, you can mop the floor.'

'Accident, my eye,' Mrs Peabody complained. 'She's not well, that girl. I told you as much . . . She shouldn't be in work.'

'I'll fetch you a fresh cuppa,' Sheila told her soothingly.

'I'd rather not risk it, thanks.' Her colour heightened, Mrs Peabody had popped her grandson back in the pram and was dragging her jacket on again. 'I don't want to be rude but I'll try that new teashop in the high street instead. Shirley says they're very good. Though thanks all the same,' she finished in a mutter, not meeting Sheila's eye. She wheeled her pram about so abruptly, she knocked over one of the chairs with a clatter. 'Sorry.'

Sheila stared after the disappearing customer in dismay. So much for enjoying being in charge . . .

'Blimey, Edith . . . Be careful!' The girl had returned too fast with the dustpan and brush, skidding on the spilt tea and colliding with her. Sheila staggered backwards, glaring down at her. 'Gawd, what's wrong with you today? You're buzzing around like a mad fly.'

'I'm sorry, Mrs Hopkins. I didn't mean to be so clumsy.'

Edith sounded tearful as she knelt to sweep up the fragments of smashed crockery. 'I thought I saw those boys outside again, and it scared me, that's all.'

Sheila was mystified. 'What boys?'

'The ones you called . . . erm . . . Oh, I can't remember the name. But you said they were troublemakers.'

'You mean the Blackshirts?'

'That's right.' Edith pointed, her face miserable and apprehensive. 'Look!'

Sheila turned, following her finger. Sure enough, she could see a group of lads in dark clothing gathered on the street corner, heads bent together conspiratorially. 'Blow me, they're persistent,' she said, replacing the fallen hot water jug, thankfully made of metal, on the wet tray. 'I thought we'd seen the last of them young idiots after the constable chased them away.'

Ron came back in, a roll of sausage meat wrapped in paper under one arm, and a container of eggs in his hand. He was frowning back over his shoulder at the Blackshirts. 'Sheila, I just met Mrs Peabody heading for the high street. She said something about an accident?' He stared as Edith emerged from the kitchen with a mop. 'Do you ladies mind telling me what happened? I've never seen her so upset.'

Edith flushed scarlet and threw an anxious, pleading look at Sheila.

Oh, for goodness' sake . . .

'Erm, yes, sorry about that,' Sheila said through gritted teeth, picking up the tray still dripping with tea. 'My fault,' she lied, not wanting the girl to get the sack. 'I wasn't looking where I was going, see? Nearly threw a pot of tea over Mrs Peabody and her baby grandson. I'm not surprised she was upset. I'll make it up to her next time though. A nice fat slice of Victoria sponge to follow her usual bacon sarnie, and a pot of tea on the house too. How's that, eh?'

'On the house?' Ron's silvery eyebrows shot up.

'Out of my wages,' Sheila corrected herself, and cast Edith a fulminating look behind his back. 'The least I can do. Sorry, Ron. I don't know how it happened.'

'Hmm,' was all her boss said, but to her surprise he didn't press the matter, disappearing into the kitchen with his roll of sausage meat instead. He seemed distracted too. But she rather thought that was down to the Blackshirts gathering in the street outside the caff rather than his forgiving nature, though it was true he was a fair man and rarely reprimanded his staff for 'accidents' – just docked their wages for broken items or spoilt food if those accidents happened too often.

Edith gave her a wan smile. 'Thanks for not landing me in hot water, Mrs Hopkins,' she whispered as Sheila went past.

'Well, there was enough hot water going around as it was.'

'I owe you one.'

'You certainly do, young lady,' Sheila told her sharply, but relented at Edith's wide-eyed look. 'Oh, it don't matter, love. Though if you're not well, maybe you should ask Mr Coates if you can go home early. Ron won't mind, not now we're past the breakfast rush.' There was a noisy commotion outside the caff and she turned in alarm, tutting as some of the lads started scuffling with each other. 'In fact, he'll probably be closing early tonight, looking at that 'orrible lot right outside the door.'

'They're fascists.' Grimly, Mr Archer tapped the newspaper he'd been reading. 'They want us to invite Herr Hitler and his army to Britain.' The headline shouted something about war being imminent, above an alarming image of German soldiers marching along in jackboots and black uniforms. 'And they'll shoot us in the head if we resist.' His querulous voice rose above the sound of shouting from outside. 'You mark my words . . . I've seen this before . . . It's like 1914 all over again.'

Edith stared at him, speechless and clearly terrified.

'Pay no attention, love. Mr Archer don't mean it. Nobody's going to invite Hitler into this country, and as for that lot out there . . . Blackshirts? Huh! They're just silly little boys itching for a fight,' Sheila told her firmly, shooing her back to work. 'Look, there's a lady over there still waiting to be served. Go and take her order before she walks out; there's a good girl.'

But she knew she didn't believe a word she was saying. The Blackshirts had her scared too, and she knew they'd put the wind up Betsy, and even done for poor Ernie on the night of their anniversary party.

The old man and his newspaper were right. War with Germany might be coming any day now, and she didn't have a blessed clue what would happen when it did, not with the enemy's supporters brazenly walking British streets and terrorising ordinary people.

A crash behind her made Sheila wheel in alarm. 'What in gawd's name . . . ?' She nearly dropped the tray she was carrying. 'Oh good Lord.'

Someone had lobbed a brick through one of the caff windows. It lay on the floor in the sunshine, surrounded by shards of glinting broken glass.

Outside, a lad stood triumphant, grinning evilly through

the shattered window at them, his mates behind him, their faces alive with wicked glee. Sheila recognised him as one of Ben Fletcher's cronies, but didn't know his name. Miss Haines had leapt up, sobbing and shaking glass from her hair. Mr Archer called his old dog to heel as it set up barking ferociously. A middle-aged couple who'd been seated near the broken window hurried away to the back of the caff, holding hands and staring out at their attackers in baffled fear. They seemed shaken but thankfully unhurt.

'What on earth . . . ?' Ron came out from behind the counter, his mouth agape as he stared from the brick on the caff floor to the jeering boys outside, one of them waving a flag that depicted what looked like a white streak of lightning against a blue background. 'Not them again? They've gone too far this time. I . . . I . . . I'll ruddy kill 'em!'

Ron started for the door, flushed with rage, the lads scattering like the wind at the sight of him.

'Ron, don't!' Sheila ran after him and grabbed his sleeve. He tried to pull free. She shook her head urgently. 'No, love, listen to me. You should leave it to the police. Going after them . . . That's what them nasty thugs want. You out of this caff, somewhere on your own, with no witnesses.'

The flush faded from her boss's face as he considered that. Then he gave a jerk of his silvery head. 'I suppose you're right. No point getting meself beat up over some broken glass.' He took a deep breath, shot her a quick, grateful smile, then headed for his panicked customers. 'Anyone hurt? You all right, Miss Haines? They've gone now, no need to worry.'

Ron righted a fallen chair and called for Edith, who'd sensibly taken shelter behind the counter at the sound of breaking glass. 'Fetch the broom, girl. We'll soon get this mess swept up, eh? And a glazier called for the window.' He came back to Sheila, muttering under his breath, 'Thanks for that. I'll go for Constable Hobbs once I'm sure it's safe.'

Sheila gave him a reassuring smile in return, though she felt far from reassured herself. Them loud-mouthed boys weren't just an idle threat anymore. The more serious the rumours of war, the more lawless they became. And she'd read something in the newspapers recently about that flag . . . It belonged to Oswald Mosley's group, the British Union of Fascists. So they weren't messing about, playing at soldier boys; they were getting organised. She doubted that young Constable Hobbs would be able to deal with them on his own again. Where would it all end?

'Time I got shot of this place anyway,' Ron added, his mouth turning down at the edges as he watched Edith diligently sweeping up the glass. 'I'm too old for this nonsense.'

'Oh, Ron, no.' She was horrified.

'I'm over seventy now and I've been thinking for a while of retiring. Now all this with the Blackshirts . . . and another war on the cards too? It's helped make my mind up. I'm sorry to be putting you out of a job, Sheila, but . . .' He paused, rubbing his chin. 'You told me once that you and Henry had a tidy nest egg set by. You could use that to buy me out, take this place on yourself.' His mouth cracked in one of his rare smiles. '*Sheila's Caff*. How does that sound?'

'Perfectly daft,' she told him firmly. 'You'll be here forever, Ron, mark my words. Just like I will too.'

Sheila spoke to Henry about the young man who'd thrown a brick through the caff window, and told him what Ron had suggested, secretly taken by the idea of owning her own establishment. But her husband had looked at her, aghast. 'We're not using our savings to buy Ron's caff,' he'd told her, his air one of finality. 'You don't know the first thing about running a caff, Shee. It would be a disaster from day one. Besides, what if them fascists came around again to threaten you? I wouldn't be there to protect you.' He'd shaken his head at her protests. 'Sorry, love, me mind's made up. You stick to what you know and we'll keep that nest egg for a rainy day, eh?'

Sheila had been disappointed but had known better than to insist, not wanting to put Henry's back up. Besides, he was right. Everyone said she made a lovely cup of tea, and she might enjoy a cosy chat with regulars like Judith, but what did she really know about running a business?

Thankfully, Ron didn't mention the idea to her again, as admitting that Henry had put his foot down over it might have been awkward. Though a few times she heard her boss talking to customers about selling up, so she knew he hadn't changed his mind.

She was at home one night in mid-June, standing in the kitchen in her housecoat, heating up some milk for a mug of cocoa, as she waited impatiently for Henry to come home from the pub, when there was a loud knock at the front door.

Sheila jumped, startled, and glanced at the clock. It was almost midnight. The house had been deathly quiet for the past hour, both Violet and Edith having headed up to bed. Sheila hesitated, unsure if she should answer it at first. Ordinarily her husband insisted on opening the door if anyone knocked after dark. It was one of his few rules. Henry was still out though, as he often was on a Friday night, albeit not usually to such a late hour.

The knock came again, even louder, and she stopped dithering and hurried down the unlit hallway to the front door, glad that she hadn't yet put her rag curlers in for the night.

'Who . . . Who is it?' she demanded through the door, her hand on the latch. 'Is that you, Henry? Did you forget your key, love?'

'It's Constable Hobbs, Mrs Hopkins,' came a muffled reply. 'Could I come inside, please?'

Baffled, she opened the door and peered out at him. It was indeed the good-looking young constable, holding his helmet under his arm, his face in shadow.

'Gawd, whatever are you doing here at this time of night? It's gone eleven o'clock.' He said nothing but shuffled his feet on the doorstep. Sheila stood aside, alarmed now and wishing that Henry was home. Her husband would know how to deal with this unexpected intrusion. 'Well, I suppose you'd better come in.'

Constable Hobbs stepped into the hall, smoothing down his thick, brown wavy hair. His gaze rose up the stairs. Violet stood on the stairs in her dressing gown, looking equally surprised by this late-night visitor.

'What is it, Mum?' Violet asked, staring at the policeman.

'Don't ask me,' Sheila muttered.

'I'm sorry to disturb you so late,' Constable Hobbs told them, turning his helmet between his hands now.

Sheila clicked on the light in the hall and saw his expression properly at last. She sucked in a breath, suddenly filled with a terrible sense of foreboding. The young officer looked almost . . . *scared*.

'Come into the sitting room.' Her stomach churning with nerves, she led him through and stood there wringing her hands. Violet came to stand beside her, her fair hair in braids over her shoulders, her blue eyes wide with apprehension. 'If it's bad news,' Sheila went on brusquely, pretending to be braver than she felt, 'you'd better spit it out.'

The constable cleared his throat. 'It's your husband, I'm afraid, Mrs Hopkins,' he admitted.

She blinked. *Henry*?

'You want to speak to my husband?' she asked, not quite understanding. Maybe Henry was a little later getting home than usual, but that didn't mean anything. He often forgot the time when he was out drinking on a Friday night. 'He's still out . . . Down the Chequers, I expect, with his mates from the car plant. Should be back any minute.'

But the constable shook his head. 'No . . . He was in an accident, you see.'

Now Sheila stood speechless and stricken. *An accident*? Instinctively, she refused to believe it. Not her Henry.

'What hospital did they take him to?' Violet demanded.

He swallowed. 'I'm ever so sorry, Mrs Hopkins, Miss Hopkins. But the truth is, he didn't make it. Mr Hopkins died . . . That is, he passed away in the ambulance on the way to hospital. They did everything they could, but he was in such a bad way. A head wound.' There was a short silence, then he added, 'But his son-in-law is being looked after at the hospital. He's in good hands, the sergeant said to tell you.'

'You mean *Ernest*?' Violet's voice tailed off. She gave a gasp, as though she'd only just understood what the police officer had come to tell them. 'Oh my God . . . Dad . . . Dad's dead? And Ernest is in the hospital?'

'I'm ever so sorry,' Constable Hobbs repeated, turning his black helmet around in his hands, no doubt wishing himself a thousand miles away too.

Sheila pulled her flimsy summer housecoat tighter. She felt cold as ice, and wished herself a thousand miles away. Her and Henry.

Maybe she'd fallen asleep while heating the cocoa and was now caught up in a dreadful nightmare. Yes, that had to be it. Because this couldn't be happening. It simply wasn't possible. Any moment now, she'd wake up with a snort to find all this nothing but a bad dream.

She'd throw open the door, and Henry would be waltzing up the street – well, more likely weaving and swaying after a night at the pub – and laughing his bloomin' head off at the very idea that he'd been in an accident, let alone a fatal one. '*Dead*?' he'd say, grinning at her in that lopsided way he had when he'd been drinking. '*Dead*?'

Her dry lips parted. 'I . . . I don't understand, Constable. When did this happen? Where?' She gripped her daughter's hand. 'What . . . What kind of accident was it?'

'Oh, Mum . . .' Violet was weeping, leaning against her.

'I believe there was a car involved, Mrs Hopkins, but I don't know all the particulars—' the constable began awkwardly.

Impatient, Sheila interrupted him. 'Wait. You said Ernest was there as well? With my husband? And he was hurt in this accident too?' She was struggling not to drown. Her darling Henry was dead. She couldn't seem to keep hold of that knowledge though; it kept slipping away and then returning to shock and terrify her all over again. She needed facts, something solid to cling to. Her mind flashed to Betsy, the new life she was carrying. 'Does his wife know? My daughter?'

'I don't think so, Mrs Hopkins. They could only spare one officer. I was going to visit her next.'

She thought achingly of the girls, who doted on their father. Then pushed away the awful realisation that she'd have to tell them they'd lost their grandfather tonight before emotion could overwhelm her and make speech impossible . . .

'Ernest, my son-in-law . . . Was he hurt bad?'

'I don't think so, Mrs Hopkins,' he said, scratching his head. 'Bad bruising but nothing broken, that's what the doctor told us at the hospital. They're keeping him in overnight though. In case of concussion.' He hesitated. 'The ward closes to visitors after six-thirty, but you can visit him in the morning.'

'We'll go and see him right now,' Sheila told him.

'But the rules—'

'*Now*, Constable,' she said with dangerous emphasis. 'Violet, hurry upstairs and change. We'll stop at Betsy's on the way, and you can stay there with the girls while Betsy comes to the hospital with me. She'll want to see Ernest straightaway. And I want to talk to him too, if he's up to it.'

Violet ran upstairs without a word, and Sheila turned to the young policeman without meeting his eyes. She knew she'd cry if there was pity in his face. And she couldn't allow herself to cry tonight or nothing would get done.

'Will I be needed to identify my husband's . . .' She stopped, unable to say the word *body*. 'My husband?'

The young man nodded, putting his helmet back on at last. 'In the morning,' he told her apologetically. 'My sergeant said he'll come to collect you. Probably around ten o'clock.' He tugged nervously on his uniform. 'I'm ever so sorry for your loss, Mrs Hopkins,' he said again.

'Not as sorry as whoever did this is going to be, I promise you,' Sheila hissed, and then struggled into her outside coat, rejecting the young man's help.

A tear trickled down one cheek as she waited for her daughter to return. There had been an *accident*. Ernest was hurt and her beloved Henry was dead. It didn't feel possible.

An *accident*, she told herself wildly, trying to imagine it. Involving a car, the constable had thought.

But where and whose car? Going to the Chequers or coming home from it? Or maybe Henry hadn't been to the pub at all.

What *kind* of accident?

CHAPTER EIGHT

It was almost dawn before Betsy's husband finally stirred, opened his eyes and blinked up at her, confused. Which was not surprising, Betsy thought, given the length of time he'd been unconscious and the thick bandage wrapped securely about his injured head.

'Love?' Ernest struggled to sit up in his hospital bed, but she tutted and nudged him back, rearranging his pillows more comfortably instead. To her relief, he did not protest. 'What . . . What's going on?'

He gazed vaguely about the dimly lit ward with its two rows of stark hospital beds, only half of them occupied. The nurse on duty had not wanted Betsy to sit with her husband all night, but her mother had insisted, giving the young woman some sharp words before heading off with the constable some hours ago.

'*Ach, Gott in Himmel!*' he muttered. 'I remember now. There was a van came out of nowhere. Looked like a Model Y. Probably a blue one, but it was hard to be sure in the dark. I didn't see any signage on the panelling, so most likely a private owner. Not a business.' He tried to sit up again, frowning. 'I don't think I told the police that detail.'

'I'll tell them.'

He nodded slowly, easing back on his pillows. 'We'd just come out of the Chequers and were crossing the road. Henry was a little drunk, and I wasn't much better. The van pulled away from the kerb, accelerating fast, and headed straight for us. I swear the driver saw us, but he just kept going.' His blue eyes narrowed on her face as memory returned. 'Henry . . . How is he?'

'Hush, darling, the other patients are sleeping.' She devoured his handsome face with her eyes, acutely aware how close she had come to losing her husband last night. 'The doctor says you might still have a concussion and need to rest. Try not to speak.'

'But I need to know how Henry is,' he continued in an urgent whisper. 'He looked pretty knocked up when they put him in the ambulance last night. I was able to walk, so I came in with the police. Gave them a statement on the spot, for what it was worth. Then I came over so exhausted, I couldn't get up. And my head was pounding . . .' Wincing, he put a hand to the bandage about his temple. 'The doctor who saw to me insisted that I stay overnight. But he wouldn't tell me how Henry was doing.'

Betsy covered her face with her hands, weeping silently.

After a pause, Ernest reached for her. 'Oh, my love.' There was dread in his voice.

'Dad died in the ambulance.' Her lips felt numb, barely able to form words. 'Mum went to identify the body. She never came back, which can only mean . . .' She gulped. 'The police told her it could wait until morning but she wanted it over and done with. Said she wouldn't be able to sleep a wink until . . .' Betsy broke down in sobs, unable to control herself any longer. 'Poor Mum. Poor *Dad*. And our two girls . . . However will I tell them? That their wonderful grandpa is gone forever?'

'I'll tell them,' he said deeply, and took her hand. 'Betsy, listen to me. Where are the girls now?'

'At home, of course. I left them with Violet.'

'Good.' He winced in pain again, then exhaled slowly, patting her hand. 'You and the girls . . . You're not to leave the house. You can ask Violet to run any errands, do you hear? Or I can go, if they let me out of here today.'

She stared at him, bewildered. 'But why? And how on earth can I keep them at home all day? The girls have school.'

'You'll send Violet to the school with a note. Tell the head teacher anything you like. Say that the girls are sick. That we're all sick. Or that we've gone away for a while. It doesn't matter what you say. Just promise me you won't leave the house, and you won't let those girls out of your sight. Not even for a minute.'

'You're not making any sense, Ernest,' she said, frowning.

'Betsy, it was one of the Blackshirts,' he hissed under his breath, glancing about the quiet ward as though afraid someone might be listening. 'I remember the driver in the van that hit us. And I'm sure I've seen that van before.'

It was a week before Ernest was released from hospital, though he was in no condition to return to work. A few days later, the police turned up in force to the Becontree Estate and arrested two men for suspected murder, a father and son living on the very same street as them. The blue

Model Y van that was often parked outside their home was taken away too, presumably to be checked for damage.

With the kids safely playing in the back bedroom, Betsy and Ernest watched through an upstairs window as the officers knocked at a door further down the road before dragging the two men out, both protesting loudly that they were *not* Blackshirts.

Betsy knew there was no mistake though. It wasn't only down to the blue van. The son was not only one of the lads who'd come into the caff, making trouble for Ron, but she also recognised him as one of the young thugs who'd shouted unpleasant things at her and the girls in the street. Ben Fletcher, whose father had a string of convictions for assault, kept a poster of Oswald Mosley in his front window, for goodness' sake.

She felt sorry for his wife though. The poor woman was left sobbing on the doorstep in her dressing gown as both husband and son were taken away on a murder charge, the neighbours watching everything, some openly in their front gardens, others more discreetly from behind their curtains like her and Ernest. The Fletchers had not been the most popular family on the estate, many whispering that having an ex-con there brought the neighbourhood down, even if he had been the sort of man nobody dared cross. It was likely that Mrs Fletcher would lose her home over this too.

Betsy turned away from the window as the men were being bundled into a police wagon, and pressed her face into Ernest's chest. She was trembling and felt sick and off-balance again. Only this time it was not the sickness of early pregnancy but the awful, gut-wrenching horror of knowing that their own neighbours hated them so much, they had killed her dad and attempted to kill her husband. And for what? To punish him for not siding with their anti-British movement? For refusing to support Hitler and his vile fascists? It was too horrible.

'It's all right, love, they've gone now,' Ernest murmured after a while, stroking her hair. His voice was deep with worry. 'Don't take it so personally. I know what you're thinking but you're wrong. That man and his son . . . They're following a cause, that's all. It was never about me or you. It was about their beliefs, about ideology.'

'You make them sound almost reasonable.'

'That was not my intention.' He sighed. 'Men like that, they are fanatics. They don't understand why someone who is German, or at least half German, wouldn't support Hitler in his drive to conquer half the world. But that's their problem, not mine. And now the police will question them and discover if my testimony was correct and they were the ones who deliberately ran Henry down.'

'And if they are, they'll be hanged for murder?'

'Probably.'

Betsy shuddered.

'I don't make the laws,' he pointed out mildly. 'But I don't break them either.'

'That poor woman—'

'I believe it was her husband who was driving, so the lad may merely get a prison sentence. He might even be home again after a few months, given a good lawyer.'

Betsy closed her eyes. 'They're not the only ones who believe in what Hitler's doing though. It makes me feel sick to think we're surrounded by such hatred . . . Hatred that's left Dad dead and you covered in bruises. I can't bear it!'

'No, we're not surrounded. It's just a few rotten apples,' he told her soothingly. 'And in a big barrel too, don't forget. We were unlucky to live so close to several people of that ilk. But that's all it was. Bad luck.'

She raised her head, tears running down her face, and gazed up at him in despair. 'And if our luck doesn't change?'

'*Liebchen* . . . Don't cry, there's no need. I won't let any of this danger touch you. The police have arrested them, so that's an end to it. Let's leave them to do their job.' He took out a handkerchief and dried her eyes with it, then kissed her gently. 'How is your mother coping with her loss? I feel so guilty about your father.'

This perplexed her. 'Why?'

'Because those men were aiming for me.' He looked troubled. 'To have lost her husband over this, when Henry wasn't even the target . . . She must blame me for his death.'

'Don't be daft. I'm sure that's not even crossed Mum's mind. Besides, you can't be held accountable for what them vicious animals did. Nobody forced them to run you and Dad over.' Betsy took a deep breath, trying not to worry that one of the other Mosley supporters might come back and try to finish the job. 'Anyway, she's putting on a brave face. Keeping busy and not admitting to how she's feeling. But I know Mum. Behind her smile, she'll be struggling. And I don't know how to help her.'

'You don't need to. Your place is here with the girls. They're upset and need you too,' he reminded her. 'Besides, Violet is still living at home, so I'm sure she will be on hand to help your mother with whatever needs doing.' His arms came about her, holding her warm and close. 'Now, how are *you* feeling today, darling? And how is the . . . the baby?'

His tone was delicate, for he knew she didn't like talking about the pregnancy. She was scared that getting used to the idea of having another baby would jinx things. She might have safely passed the dangerous first three months. But she knew from bitter experience that a baby could be lost at any stage of pregnancy.

'I'm much better these days,' she told him, and it wasn't entirely a fib. Her morning sickness had eased, but she felt uncomfortable in the summer heat and found it difficult to sleep at night. But she was a lot older now than when she'd been carrying Alice and Lily. Perhaps it was always harder on the body when you were expecting a baby in your thirties instead of your twenties. The doctor had warned her it might not be easy, but she'd been so pleased and amazed at simply having *conceived* that she hadn't thought much about what the later stages might bring.

Ernest seemed relieved. 'The weather is fine. Perhaps we could go into town on Saturday and make a day of it, since the police have arrested those two. Lunch and shopping, and maybe a walk in the park afterwards. It should be safe enough to go out again now.'

'Oh, love, I can't.' She bit her lip, feeling guilty. 'I know you think Violet will be doing everything that's needed, and you're probably right. But I already promised Mum that I'd visit her Saturday morning with the girls, to keep her company and help with the funeral arrangements.' She looked at him defiantly. 'I must go. I can't let her down.'

'Of course you must help your mother. But how about afterwards?' He smiled indulgently as she sagged in his arms, relieved that he wasn't going to forbid her from visiting her mum. He was a dutiful son-in-law, but he did love his family days-out with just the two of them and the girls. 'Lily has been pestering for a new summer frock, hasn't she? Since my promotion, we have more money left over at the end of every month. It would be nice to see a smile on her face again. She and Alice have been so quiet and unhappy since your father's death.'

Her heart lightened at this suggestion. 'What a smashing idea, Ernie . . . You are a love. And yes, Lily will be over the moon to get a new frock. Though Alice will be bored stiff, dress shopping. She'll want to visit the library instead while we're in town.'

'I'll take her,' he promised.

'Thank you. Ever since Alice got her library ticket, she's been devouring books like sweeties. Though you'll have to watch her closely. She keeps trying to swipe my adult ticket, so she's not stuck only choosing books from the children's section.'

'That's my clever Alice.' Her husband laughed and bent to kiss her forehead. His own head was still bandaged, and his body was badly bruised from hip to foot, but the doctor had promised there would be no visible scarring. 'I love you, Betsy,' he told her with a smile.

'I love you too, Ernest,' she whispered back. She hoped fervently that he was right and there was no longer any need to be worried about the Blackshirts.

As promised, Ernest drove her and the girls over to her mum's house on Saturday morning to spend a few hours there, even though they could easily have walked. 'Given everything that's happened, I prefer to keep an eye on you all,' her husband had insisted, ignoring her protests. 'Anyway, it's no bother.' He wasn't alone in being concerned either. The news that two local Blackshirts had been arrested for Henry's murder had hit Sheila hard. She feared that she and Violet might be targets for the gang now. Ernest had not helped matters by warning her to keep her front door locked and to watch out for anyone suspicious loitering about the street. Her mum was clearly devastated by the loss of her husband. However, to Betsy's relief, she didn't seem to blame Ernest for Dad's death as they'd feared she might.

Betsy hated seeing her mother so wretched and withdrawn, though she seemed to pull herself together at the sight of her granddaughters. Alice and Lily had been left distraught by the news of their grandad's death. As soon as they came in looking pale and unhappy, their grandmother forced a smile and suggested the girls bake a cake together.

'Me and your mum need to talk about the funeral, and you don't want to hear about that,' she'd insisted, nodding to Violet to help them. 'Your Aunty Vi will show you how to measure out and mix the ingredients. That's it, off you go. Good girls.' But after shutting the door on them, she'd sunk back onto the sofa with a faint moan. 'Oh, Betsy, whatever am I going to do without your dad? It's been such a terrible shock, losing him so suddenly . . . And them poor girls. I can't bear their sad faces.' She wept noisily into her hanky.

Betsy jumped up to comfort her, though there wasn't much to say except, 'I know, Mum, it's awful. I miss Dad dreadfully too. But we'll get through it as a family, won't we?'

'I suppose you're right,' her mum said thickly, and blew her nose. 'And it's just what your father would have said too, God rest his soul.' Her tearful gaze moved to the wedding photograph that had taken pride of place on their mantelpiece for as long as Betsy could remember. 'My darling Henry . . . He weren't always the best husband in the world, no point lying about it. But he was mine and I was his, and we were happy together. And he was so proud of you and Violet. But what am I meant to do now? I'm a bloomin' widow before my time.'

'Don't, Mum.' Betsy put an arm about her mother and held her close. Her heart was breaking but she recalled from Ernest's account of the dark days when he'd lost both his parents in quick succession that it was important to stay practical. 'Hush, please don't cry. The girls are only in the kitchen and will hear you.' At this reminder, her mother nodded, stifling her sobs. 'Now, did you draw up that list of people who ought to be notified?'

Her mum pointed to a sheet of paper on the sideboard. 'I've done my best with it, love. Not that many people won't already know by now,' she added. 'It was in all the local papers, and even a few of the nationals, according to Mrs Timms, the newsagent. "Dagenham man killed in hit-and-run." You read about 'orrible stuff like that all the time, don't you? You never think it will happen to you.'

Getting up from the sofa, Sheila crossed to the window and twitched the net curtains aside to peer up and down the street. 'I expect it's all the neighbours can talk about. Not that I blame them. I'd be the same if one of my neighbours had been run down and left for dead by those bleedin' Blackshirts . . . I don't like going out to the shops now. Folks look at me funny, and nobody wants to say anything except how sorry they are.' She sighed. 'I feel like a bloomin' leper.'

'I expect they don't know what to say, Mum. But if you'd rather stay home, no one will think the worst of you.'

'Ron said I should stay home until after the funeral has taken place.' Her mum looked pained. 'He means well, bless him. But working at the caff would take my mind off everything that's happened. I don't like being at home, Betsy, love. I sit down with a cuppa, and all I can think about is Henry, and then . . .' Her voice tailed off, tears in her eyes.

Betsy secretly agreed with Ronald Coates. If people didn't know what to say to Sheila out on the street, it would be even worse in the caff. And besides, what if Blackshirts came in and saw her mum in there? They might make trouble about Ben and Mr Fletcher having been arrested over her dad's death. That would be awful. But she didn't want to alarm her mum, so gave her hand a reassuring squeeze instead.

'If you want something to do,' Betsy told her mum, 'you can come round to ours for the day. I'll be cleaning out the girls' room this week. Lily's forever complaining about having to share with Alice, and how much mess her little sister makes. So Ernest has agreed to clear his parents' books and belongings out of the box room and let Alice have that as a bedroom.' Seeing her mother unconvinced, she added hurriedly, 'You would not believe how many toys those two rascals have shoved into their drawers and under their beds. They're too old for them now, so most can be got rid of. But I could do with a hand sorting the room out, if you're free over the next few days.'

Her mum smiled without any real enthusiasm. 'I'm happy to help, love. I know you . . . You'll be throwing out things that could be kept with a quick stitch or a nail in the right place, and donated to the church jumble sale. Make do and mend, that's what my old mum used to say.'

'I remember,' Betsy said drily, hoping her mum wouldn't try to salvage the girls' old tat rather than disposing of it as planned.

'How about I come over for Monday lunchtime? That way, you and I can sort out a few piles of bric-a-brac in time for the girls to squabble over them when they come home from school. They are back at school now, aren't they?'

Her mother picked up her knitting bag and rummaged through it absentmindedly before putting it back under her armchair, her expression troubled.

Betsy realised that she hadn't seen her mum knitting since before her dad's death. But perhaps that chore was almost as bad for her mum as sitting alone with a cup of tea. Sheila tended to knit automatically, her mind busily whirring while she worked, and right now she probably preferred not to think too deeply.

'They go back Monday.'

'Oh, that's good to hear. I know you and Ernie have been keeping the poor lambs home since they lost their grandpa. But girls that age . . . Well, they need their friends,' she finished, turning her head as though to listen to the young, high-pitched voices in her kitchen, a wistful look on her face. 'We all need someone to tell our troubles to, don't we?'

That afternoon, leaving her worn-out mum to take a nap, Ernest drove them into Ilford town centre where they went shopping for a new summer frock for Lily. Afterwards, they all strolled together to Valentine's Park, a green, wide-open space that seemed to connect the town to the countryside.

Lily was looking more cheerful, having chosen a pretty, knee-length blue cotton dress picked out with embroidered daisies along the bodice, the colour complementing her corn-fair hair perfectly. And Alice had been thrilled when Ernest took her to the library, and spent a quiet half hour looking at detective novels, his favourite reads, while she scoured the titles on the shelves in the children's area.

'I've read most of the ones worth reading,' Alice told her mother afterwards, 'but I did manage to find a few good'uns.'

Glancing at the African adventure novel under his arm, Betsy suspected that Alice must have asked her father to take it out on his library ticket. Though she wasn't too worried by how fast Alice's reading tastes were progressing; Ernest wouldn't have agreed to take out a novel unless he thought it appropriate for a girl that age to read. Besides, what did it matter, so long as it kept her happy at such a difficult time for the family?

It was a sunny Saturday afternoon in late June. The park was busy. After walking around the large boating lake and listening to the brass band entertaining the crowds gathered about the beautiful old bandstand, Betsy felt the most overwhelming fatigue.

'Ernie, I . . . I need to sit down for a bit,' she told him.

Alice ran eagerly ahead to claim an unoccupied bench under a beech tree, situated on the main path not far from the entrance gates. They followed her more slowly, Lily swinging her shopping bag and making quacking sounds at a family of ducks waddling along on the grass verge.

Studying Betsy with concern, Ernest put her arm through his. 'You're so pale. Are you feeling unwell again, darling?'

'No, I . . .' A spasm of pain gripped her, low down in her belly. She bit her lip, her whole body tensing. But she said with an effort, not wanting to worry him or the kids, 'I'm just a bit tired. Perhaps I overdid it, tramping around all them shops in the heat.' Her smile was forced. 'I need a few minutes off my feet, that's all.'

'Then that's precisely what you shall have,' he told her fondly, then gave Lily a wink. 'And perhaps an ice cream for everyone? I spotted a small booth near the bandstand where they're selling ices.'

'Yes please, Daddy!' Lily agreed, grinning.

'Alice, you can come with me to help carry the ice creams. Lily, stay with your mum, all right?'

While her husband and Alice walked back to the bandstand for their ice creams, Lily sat with Betsy in the shade, chattering on about missing her friends at school and how glad she was to be going back to school on Monday. Betsy thought of what her mum had said about the girls needing someone their own age to talk to and was startled by how right she'd been, about Lily at least. She wasn't sure that Alice had many close friends at school, being more of a loner and a bookworm than her big sister.

She felt nervous about sending her daughters back out into the world so soon after their grandfather's death. They were still vulnerable children in her eyes, even if Lily was growing up so fast . . . But now that the men who'd attacked Ernest and her dad were locked up, being questioned by police, it ought to be safe enough.

The family of ducks who had settled on the grass suddenly flapped their wings in panic and flew back to the water. A dog nearby began to bark too, dragging on his lead. There was a loud commotion behind them, deep angry voices and marching feet.

Lily turned, staring. 'What on earth . . . ?'

It was a large gathering of men dressed in black, twenty or maybe even thirty of them, striding through the entrance gates into the park, placards in hand, chanting pro-Nazi slogans that sent a shudder rippling down Betsy's spine . . .

'Gawd, it's the Blackshirts,' Betsy whispered in horror, and clutched Lily's hand as they both jumped up at the same time. 'Stay with me, love. Don't look at them. They'll have gone past in a minute.'

But one of the young men at the front of the parade stopped, pointed her way, and then shouted something. Betsy vaguely recognised him and stiffened, alarmed. Was he one of Ben Fletcher's friends? She didn't know what he'd said, but they all abruptly wheeled around and came marching their way instead, faces aggressive, booted feet thumping in unison on the path like soldiers.

Lily gave a little gasp and shrank close to her side. 'Mummy?'

'It's all right, love, they wouldn't dare do anything in a public place,' Betsy insisted with her chin up, though her heart was beating fast and she felt queasy with nerves.

To her relief, Ernest appeared by her side. He too was staring grimly towards the Blackshirts and their placards.

'You and the girls get behind me,' he told her tensely, quickly handing his ice cream to Lily. Alice was there too, a look of fear in her eyes as she studied the marching men in their sinister dark clothes. Some had scarves obscuring their faces, despite the warm weather, as though they didn't want to be recognised. Though given the tougher laws that had come in recently, barring political protests like this, that wouldn't be surprising.

'Betsy, please do as I say,' Ernest said sternly when she

didn't move. 'Take the girls and head for the bandstand. You should be safe there. Look, the police have arrived, thank goodness. No doubt they're coming to arrest this lot for an illegal political rally.'

She was reassured to see a police wagon had drawn up in the gated entrance to the park, and policemen were already spilling out of it. But before she could take the girls to safety, the first of the Blackshirts had reached them. One squared up to Ernest, throwing the word, 'Traitor!' in his face. Another jostled behind him, deliberately knocking into young Alice, who was standing with her mouth open.

Startled, Alice dropped the ice creams she'd been clutching and then stared at the mess melting into the grass, shock in her eyes. 'That . . . That wasn't very nice,' she told the man who'd knocked into her, defiance in her face.

'Get lost,' he snarled.

'No, you g-get lost,' she stuttered bravely. 'And you can leave my dad alone too.'

'Alice, for God's sake!' Ernest sounded frantic as he pushed forward to protect his daughter. 'Get behind me.'

'Come here, love.' Terrified, Betsy reached for Alice. But as her daughter stubbornly evaded her, the young man she'd recognised from the caff stepped between them, shoving Betsy backward.

'I know it was you what got Ben Fletcher banged up for murder,' he shouted. Several passers-by turned to stare, their eyes also accusing. 'Bleedin' snitch! Calling down the law on him and his dad like that. You deserve what you're going to get.'

The police were almost upon them, but he waved the other Blackshirts forward, as though so intent on revenge he didn't care about being arrested. The men swarmed towards their family, chanting slogans in German. Betsy was dimly aware of one of them aiming a punch at her husband.

'Leave him alone!' she screamed. 'Help! Police!'

Recalling what they'd done to her father, Betsy fought her way towards her husband through the tight press of men, but was knocked back again so violently, her hat tumbled off. Somewhere ahead, Alice shrieked, 'Mum!' and Betsy surged forward again on a tide of pure fury, unable to see her daughters now through the crowd of Blackshirts but determined to protect them.

In the chaos that followed, with Alice lost to view and Lily running for help, she whirled around to locate the police, shouting again for help. But a placard pole struck her on the side of the head, leaving her half stunned. Betsy reeled backwards, gasping, and a jeering, pockmarked face swam into view. Rough hands grabbed her. Someone muttered an obscenity in her ear.

'Get . . . off . . . me!' she gasped.

Betsy heard her husband call her name, strain in his voice. Then a booted foot tangled with hers, she lost her footing and stumbled backwards across the wrought-iron bench. Trying to turn in mid-fall, she gave a tremendous grunt as her gently rounded middle slammed into the hard edge of the bench.

'Oh, Ernest,' she cried, and doubled up in agony. 'The baby . . . !'

CHAPTER NINE

Edith didn't know why Mrs Hopkins had left home to stay with her daughter Betsy instead, given how busy the poor woman had been recently with funeral arrangements for her late husband. But she'd heard some gossip at the caff; something about Betsy having met with an accident, and Sheila had moved in to keep the household running while her daughter was laid up in bed. Only when she'd innocently enquired what kind of accident, had the ladies she'd overheard chatting over morning coffee fallen silent. Even Ron had merely shrugged and said he didn't want to get 'involved'. Involved in what? she'd wondered, feeling baffled.

She and Violet had been left to fend for themselves at home. Edith could bake, of course. But she didn't know much about ordinary, everyday cookery. Her gran had always taken care of such things.

Luckily, Violet knew a little more than her, and together they generally managed to prepare an evening meal for themselves, though often it was a flan or a pasty, both of which Edith knew how to make, usually served with mounds of salad, since it was summer now and the evenings were too warm for potatoes and boiled vegetables. Twice though, they spent their hard-earned cash on fish and chips, and ate it straight out of the newspaper wrappings in the backyard, enjoying the last of the sunshine.

Over dinner, Edith would ramble on about her working day and the customers she'd served at the caff. She was pulling double shifts while Mrs Hopkins was off work. She had always liked to share every detail of her day and back in Cornwall would chatter on to her gran in much the same way after a busy day in the bakery. 'My little chatterbox,' Gran had often called her.

Violet rarely said much at all in response, her face glum as she ate, staring at nothing. That was no surprise, Edith considered, given she'd just lost her dad. She was probably feeling awful and needed cheering up.

She'd asked Violet tentatively about the funeral one evening, and her friend replied gloomily that it would take place soon. 'Next week sometime,' was all she'd said. 'The body couldn't be released any earlier, you see, on account of his death being seen as murder.'

Late one afternoon, when they'd both come home from work and were discussing dinner as they washed and dried yesterday's dishes in the kitchen, there was the rattle of a key at the front door and Mrs Hopkins appeared unexpectedly in the kitchen doorway.

'Mum!' Violet exclaimed, staring.

Mrs Hopkins pulled off her brightly patterned headscarf and thrust it into a pocket, saying gustily, 'Hello, Vi, love. Hello, Edith . . . Can you believe it, there's no bloomin' flour to be had in Betsy's house? Not a single blessed ounce. So

I've had to come home for some flour. Yes, and a tin of peaches too. I've promised to make a tasty fruit tart for Ernest and the girls and maybe persuade Betsy to eat a slice too. Poor souls, they've had such a hard time of it lately. Them girls . . . Bawling their eyes out for their old grandad, and now their mum's been taken so ill, she can barely leave her room.'

Mrs Hopkins' eyes were red-rimmed, as though she too had been weeping. But of course she had. The unfortunate lady had just lost her husband. Yet here she was, caring for her family instead of herself. She was certainly made of stern stuff, just like Edith's own gran.

'If you don't mind though, I'll grab a quick cuppa before I walk back,' Mrs Hopkins added, blowing out her cheeks. 'I'm fair puffed out.'

'I'll put the kettle on, Mum,' Violet told her soothingly, and pulled out a chair. 'Take a pew . . . And you should teach those girls to make a fruit tart for themselves. It's high time they learnt how to cook.'

'Hark at you, young lady.' Her mother chuckled, sitting down heavily and leaning her elbows on the table. 'I've tried to teach *you* how to cook often enough. But you always say you're too busy to learn. Talking of which, how have you two been getting on without me around to make your dinner?'

'Perfectly fine,' Violet said loftily.

'It's not been easy,' Edith admitted at precisely the same time, and they both glanced at each other and laughed.

'We're managing,' Violet insisted, and got up to make the tea.

Edith smiled. 'We have missed your cooking, Mrs Hopkins.

We made a big plate of bubble and squeak the other night, following your mum's old recipe; only it didn't turn out nearly as tasty as yours.' She hesitated. 'By the way, how's Betsy? Still poorly?'

She was curious to know what exactly was wrong with Violet's sister, but didn't pry. It was none of her business, anyway. Betsy had been knocked down in some scuffle while out shopping, or she'd had a funny turn in the park, it wasn't clear which, and nobody was talking about it. Except that 'Blackshirts' had been mentioned in a muttered aside by Violet.

Mrs Hopkins gave her a wan smile. 'My Betsy just needs time to . . . Well, to get her head straight. I expect she'll be feeling better soon, and I'll be able to come home. The doctor says she's on the mend, thank goodness. But he also says you can't rush things like this. Besides, I don't want her out of bed too soon, looking after the family when she's not ready yet.' She paused, her smile fading. 'She'll need to be up and about for Thursday, though. That's when the funeral's being held.' She peered across at Edith. 'You'll come, won't you, love?'

'Of course, Mrs Hopkins.'

There was a loud knock at the front door. Violet, pouring hot water into the pot, looked up in surprise. Mrs Hopkins just sighed.

'I'll go and see who it is,' Edith told them helpfully.

She hurried down the hall and pulled open the front door. A tall, thin young man with dark, close-cropped hair and a surly expression was standing outside. He looked her up and down, something unpleasant in his expression.

'Can I help you?' she asked, uneasy at the way he was staring at her.

'I'm looking for Ernest Fisher's family,' the youth told her in a hostile growl. 'Do they live here?'

Edith felt cold inside. She'd heard that two Blackshirts had been arrested for Henry's murder, and she had a suspicion this lad might belong to the same gang. Though why on earth he was looking for more relatives of Mr Fisher, she couldn't imagine. Hadn't they done enough by murdering old Mr Hopkins? And after Violet's muttered suggestion that they'd been involved with Betsy's mysterious illness . . .

'I don't know anyone of that name,' she told him abruptly. 'Now, if you don't mind, I'm busy. Goodbye.' And she shut the door in his face.

Edith stood at the door listening until she'd heard the young man walk away. Facing him down had left her oddly trembly, with butterflies in her tummy. She hoped she'd done the right thing by denying that she knew Mr Fisher. It had been a bold-faced lie. But whatever he'd come here for, she wanted nothing to do with that thug. Those awful Blackshirts had murdered Mr Hopkins and tried to kill Ernest too, and now were hounding a grieving widow, simply because her son-in-law was half German. If fascism was all about violence and intimidation, she couldn't understand why anyone wanted anything to do with it.

Unsure what to tell Mrs Hopkins about the young man, she hesitated in the hallway and inadvertently caught Violet saying in a low voice, and obviously not meant for her ears, 'I feel so sorry for her, Mum. She had her heart set on another baby.'

'I know, poor pet,' Mrs Hopkins replied in a whisper. 'The doctor says she's been in bed long enough and doesn't need to rest anymore. But Betsy simply won't get up. I don't know what to do. I'm putting on a brave face for the girls, but I'm not sure how much longer I can lie to them.' She tutted under her breath. 'It's a crying shame. Another miscarriage, and at her age too . . . I don't think she'll ever get over it.'

This stopped Edith in her tracks.

Betsy didn't have an illness. She'd been laid up in bed for a week because she'd *lost her baby*.

Awkward and off balance, Edith pushed into the kitchen, pretending not to have heard what they'd said. 'That was someone at the door collecting for charity,' she said in a rush, not looking them in the face, 'but I . . . I didn't have any money, so they left.'

She felt awful, lying so shamelessly to her friends. But, after all, how could she tell them the truth? It would scare the widow half to death to know there were still Blackshirts out there, trying to find Ernest's other relatives. And Violet might be tempted to dash after him. With Mr Hopkins' funeral coming up, the last thing the family needed was more fear and upset.

'Here's your cup of tea, Mum,' Violet said warmly, pushing it across the table. 'Fancy a cuppa, Edith? We can finish the washing and drying later, eh?'

'Yes, thank you.' Edith sat down with them, trying to look normal and unconcerned. But her heart was racing and her palms were clammy. And not simply because of that horrid young man at the door . . .

Betsy had lost her baby.

Edith could not imagine what such a calamity must feel like, aware how happy Betsy had seemed to be expecting a child. She herself had often woken early since realising that she was pregnant, alone and unmarried, and half wished the baby could be gone. Yet now, hearing about Betsy's loss, she felt cold and numb inside, and realised something astonishing.

Her breathing stuttered. She *wanted* this baby. She couldn't bear the thought of losing it the way Betsy had. Even if she hadn't wanted it before, she did now. Because this was Percy's baby. She might have lost him, but he had left this new life behind, growing inside her.

How could she wish away such a wonderful thing?

Below the table, her hand slipped down unseen to cradle the soft curve of her belly. *Percy's baby.* It was surely a miracle that she had conceived at all. They had only slept together once, both innocent and inexperienced, yet deeply in love . . .

Before, she had felt panicky, out of her depth with all those unfamiliar physical sensations. She had wished herself not pregnant at all.

Now this baby was the most important thing in her world.

Once Mrs Hopkins had left, walking back to Betsy's house with a bag of provisions, Violet took one look at her face and said bluntly, 'Spit it out, love.'

'Sorry?'

'Whatever's bothering you, tell me now. And don't try to pretend you're fine, not with me. Ever since Mum arrived, you've been looking sick with nerves.' She reached down two glasses from a top shelf, opened a bottle of her mother's home-made gin, and poured a dash of the lethal concoction into both glasses. Then she placed one in front of Edith. 'Go on, get that down you. You look like you need a serious pick-me-up.'

'I . . . I don't want any gin,' Edith stammered. 'Sorry.'

'Just take one sip.' Violet gave her a wink. 'Honestly, it will put heart back in you, I swear it.'

Edith eyed her friend uncertainly but lifted the glass to her lips and took a sip. Instantly, she regretted it, coughing and spluttering. Her lips burned as though they were on fire. 'Good grief, how does anyone drink this . . . and survive?'

Violet chuckled. 'Mum's gin is an acquired taste, that's for sure.' She herself took a cautious sip and put the glass back down, her gaze on Edith's face as she exhaled slowly. 'Now, whatever's bothering you, let's hear it. Who was that at the front door, for starters? And don't tell me it was some charity collector rattling a box, because I won't believe it. They never call at this time of day.'

Edith blushed, though it could have been the home-made gin rushing through her veins. 'You're right, I was lying. But I had a good reason.' Guiltily, she told Violet about the surly, dark-haired youth who had asked after Ernest Fisher's family, and saw her face change. 'You see? I couldn't say anything in front of your mum and upset her. She's having a bad enough time as it is.'

'Them vile Blackshirts . . .' Violet said something very unladylike, and Edith's blush deepened. Though her friend wasn't wrong.

'That's not all that's bothering you though,' Violet said, taking another sip of her gin. She shuddered at the taste. 'Might as well tell me the whole of it.'

'I suppose so,' Edith admitted, pushing her own glass back towards her friend. 'Sorry. I can't drink any more of that. It's disgusting. And it can't be good for the baby.'

'*Baby?*' Violet jumped, staring. 'What baby?'

Edith sat scarlet-faced, unable to say another word. It had

just slipped out without thinking. Now she was in hot water, for sure.

'Are you expecting a baby? You mean, you and that young man you've been missing . . . Percy . . . That you and he . . . ?' Violet came to a stuttering halt, her eyes huge as saucers. 'Edith Treloar, you'd better tell me the truth right now, or else.'

In a faltering whisper, Edith told her what had happened between her and Percy before he left for Canada, and how her strange symptoms had grown worse and worse while she battled to ignore them, until she'd heard Betsy complain about pregnancy sickness and finally admitted to herself what they meant . . .

'Then I overheard you and your mum talking about Betsy, and realised what's wrong with her,' she admitted, hot-cheeked. 'She's not just poorly, is she? She's lost her baby.'

Violet bit her lip. 'Mum's been keeping it a secret, for Betsy's sake. It's private, ain't it? But you were bound to find out sometime. Yes, she's lost her baby . . . and it took her so long to get pregnant again in the first place.'

'I'm so sorry,' Edith whispered.

'Betsy's in pieces about it, poor thing.' Violet sighed. 'And she ain't getting any younger. She reckons that was her last chance to have another child.'

'That's awful. No wonder she's taken to her bed.'

Nodding unhappily, Violet took an ill-advised gulp of gin, and turned a strange colour, choking noisily. When she'd recovered, she asked faintly, 'But what about you? Expecting a baby too and you ain't even married? No wonder you've been looking so peaky.' Violet looked her up and down. 'I thought it strange how you'd put on weight lately.

You won't be able to keep this quiet for much longer. My mum's got sharp eyes, and I'm betting she'd have guessed already if it hadn't been for Dad dying. And once she realises . . .'

Edith buried her face in her hands. 'Oh, Violet, I don't know what to do for the best,' she choked. 'Percy's half a world away in Canada, and you're right, I won't be able to keep my job much longer, not once the baby's showing. But I can't go home. How could I face my gran? It was bad enough when I had to admit that the gossip wasn't . . . wasn't a lie, that Percy and I had slept together the night before he left.' She sobbed. 'I'll never forget her face . . . The disappointment. But telling her I'm *pregnant*?' She swallowed, unable to go on.

Violet reached across, taking her hand. 'Listen, if you can't bring yourself to tell your gran about the baby, at least tell my mum.'

Edith stared. 'Tell Mrs Hopkins that I'm *expecting*?'

'My mum knows a thing or two about young people in love.' Violet gave her a crooked smile. 'She won't be cross, I promise. Besides, she's had two kids herself. Mum will know what to do if you're having problems.'

'I can't.' Edith hung her head. 'I'm too embarrassed.'

'Well, you can't keep it secret forever, love. And you should write to Percy too. He ought to know that he's fathered a child.'

Edith stared dismally at a tea stain on the tablecloth. There was no getting around this by pretending it wasn't happening, was there? So, no more delays. She would write to her gran straightaway and tell her about the baby. And Violet was right. Of course she needed to get Percy's address and tell him. But the plain truth was, she was terrified. Terrified what

Gran would think of her, terrified that Percy would never write back, terrified of her future as a single mother with no money and nowhere to live . . .

It took her hours to compose a short letter to her grandmother, admitting she was pregnant with Percy's baby. The words came painfully, and she went through several drafts, ripping up each one and throwing it in the wastepaper bin, pacing about in turmoil between drafts.

Gran, I feel awful for not telling you this before now . . .

Another inky sheet was crumpled up in an impatient fist before being lobbed across the room.

I should probably have told you as soon as I knew for sure, but . . .

Oh, for goodness' sake, she thought, groaning and touching her forehead to the paper. Just say it straight.

But she still struggled to find legitimate excuses for why she had not written earlier. Because there were no excuses. The fact was that she'd been living in denial as soon as her earliest symptoms had begun, too terrified even to admit to herself what she feared, that deep down inside a new life might be growing.

Taken aback by her queasiness, Edith had assumed at first that it was food poisoning. Then, when it continued, she had pretended not to consider pregnancy as a possibility, firmly telling herself it must be nerves at having left Cornwall to start afresh in a strange place. And when Betsy's similar symptoms had made it impossible to maintain that pretence, forcing her in one terrible moment to face the truth and consider the implications for her future, she had been so frozen in fear and uncertainty, she hadn't felt able to confide in anyone, not even her beloved grandmother.

Rosalyn was a wise and generous woman. But she could also be stern where she saw wrongdoing. Not judgemental, but accusatory. She knew what her grandmother would say . . . *What were you thinking, Edith? How could you have done such a thing? And how on earth are you going to put it right?*

Except this wasn't something that could be 'put right'. She was having a baby, and she had reconciled herself to that now. She felt protective of it.

Finding the strength at last, she wrote a short note telling her grandmother about the baby and asking her advice, firstly on whether she should stay in London to spare their family further shame, and secondly, whether her grandmother would help her discover Percy's address in Canada.

Percy had given her his address overseas and begged her to write as soon as possible. And she had written one letter after he'd left, unable to resist. But then, on the night before she left her beloved Cornish home for London, she'd traced a finger yearningly over the Canadian address he'd scribbled down for her on a spare piece of paper, and then tore it up. She had promised herself a fresh start. There was no point them being in touch if they couldn't be together. Not that his own family would approve of *that*, which was one reason she had shied away from the idea.

It had been clear from his parents' faces whenever they saw her that they didn't think she was good enough for their son. Percy had a bright future ahead of him, according to his family, and no working-class Cornish girl would be permitted to spoil that.

But by now, she felt certain he must have forgotten all about her. Her grandmother had not forwarded any letters from him so far, and he must have got back to Canada long ago. If he felt anything for her, then he would have written. But so far, she had heard nothing.

She also let her grandmother know about Henry Hopkins' death, how it had happened, and when the funeral was taking place. She knew so much bad news all at once would upset her grandmother. But what else could she do? She doubted that Mrs Hopkins would have found time to write and let her know, being so busy with the funeral arrangements and then Betsy's awful miscarriage. Besides, Edith was sure her gran would wish to send a sympathy card, them having been such close friends at school.

She posted the letter home to Cornwall on her way into work the next day, and by the time she reached the Corner Caff had plastered a big, fake smile on her face. Ron was always telling her, *smile more for the customers*. Recently, life had felt rather bleak though, not just for herself but her adopted family too, the Hopkinses and the Fishers. But she was determined to smile through the tough times. Maybe the newspapers were wrong and there wouldn't be a war, after all. And she now realised how much she treasured this little life growing inside her. There were genuine reasons to smile . . .

'Ah, there you are at last,' Ron said brusquely as she hurried behind the counter to pull on a clean white pinny and cap. 'There are two breakfasts ready for table five, and a bacon sandwich to be made for table one. Think you can manage that?'

The question was sarcastic, for she'd been dithering over the order pad and tucking a pencil behind her ear ready for the customers. 'Yes, Mr Coates,' she said with a quick apologetic smile, for she badly needed to keep this job. 'Sorry I was late today, but—'

'I'm not interested in why you're late. Don't let it happen again. Understand?'

'Yes, sir.' She grabbed up the two breakfasts and dashed them over to table five.

Sometimes, when she thought about Percy and the unborn baby inside her, she felt as though she were living through a dream. But this job was her reality, and it might just save her from going mad with worry about the future.

Mrs Hopkins herself dropped into the caff a few days later to speak to Mr Coates about coming back to work again.

'The funeral's tomorrow,' she explained, 'and my Betsy's on the mend now, bless her. She won't need me helping out much longer. I'll go out of my mind at home with nothing much to occupy my time. Besides, don't say you ain't missing me here at the caff, Ron. Because I won't believe it.' There was a twinkle in her eye, but her boss did not respond with an answering smile.

'I think you'd best sit down, Sheila,' Ron told her, pulling out a chair, 'and we'll talk about that.'

'What can I get you, Mrs Hopkins?' Edith asked, pencil poised above her order pad.

'A pot of tea and an extra-thick slice of your ginger cake, love.'

Edith smiled. 'Anything for you, Mr Coates?'

He cast her a sharp look. 'I'm working, ain't I?'

'Sorry, sir.'

Leaving the two to chat at the table nearest the counter, the one staff tended to use when having their break, Edith cut her landlady a double slice of Cornish ginger cake. She'd been making the cake for the caff for several weeks now, using an old recipe of her gran's, and it had proved very popular with the Dagenham locals.

She didn't mean to eavesdrop on their conversation as she stood filling the teapot from the hot water urn, but the caff was almost empty in the post-lunch slump, and they weren't exactly keeping their voices down.

'You're welcome to come back, of course,' Ron was telling Mrs Hopkins in his deep, rasping voice. He stopped to light a cigarette, and Edith guessed he must be nervous, for she'd noticed the boss only ever smoked at work when he was feeling uneasy. 'But the thing is, Sheila, I don't know how much longer you'll have a job here.'

'Eh?' Mrs Hopkins stared at him, perplexed.

'Since you've been away, I've had more visits from them lads what were causing so much trouble before,' he admitted, blowing a smoke ring and watching it drift away. 'After I reported them the first time, Constable Hobbs dropped by, and swore blind the police would be cracking down on these bloomin' Blackshirts, especially after what happened to Betsy. Well, there've been a few other nasty incidents too. But I ain't seen no sign yet of any "cracking down". Them lads are still marching most weekends, bold as brass, terrorising ordinary folk and calling on the government to support Herr Hitler.'

'Oh, it's wicked,' Mrs Hopkins muttered. 'Support Hitler indeed!'

He nodded and coughed, turning to ask Edith for an ashtray, which she brought at once. 'Anyway, how's Ernest bearing up?'

'He's all right,' Mrs Hopkins said stoutly. 'There's more to that fellow than meets the eye. And he's been an angel since Henry's death, helping me with the funeral arrangements while Betsy was too poorly to leave her room.'

'I'm sure,' Ron agreed, rather awkwardly Edith thought. He didn't strike her as a very sentimental man. 'Listen, there's something else you should know.' He leant forward, saying more confidentially, 'I'm thinking of chucking it in forever. No, I'm serious this time . . . Running a caff like this ain't a job for a man of my years. Not the way things have been going lately.'

'Oh, Ron, you can't mean it!'

Edith brought over Mrs Hopkins' cake and tea, prettily arranged on a tray. 'There you go, Mrs H,' she said chattily, loitering in the hope of hearing more, then caught her employer's stern eye and hurried away to wipe down tables ready for closing time.

Outside, the clouds had melted away after a wet morning to leave a damp but sunny July afternoon. In the distance, a thin, angular woman in late middle age was coming along the street towards the caff, leaning heavily on a cane. Edith's wiping slowed to a halt as she watched this woman, her eyes widening.

'Anyway, what would you do if you gave up the caff?' Mrs Hopkins sounded flustered now. 'The Corner Caff has been your life, Ron. I can't imagine this place without you in it.'

'That's as may be. But it's time I retired, Sheila. I knew it as soon as them bully boys came barging in here, demanding I put up posters for them. I was scared to refuse, and I'm not afraid to admit it. But that's no way to run a business.'

'But, Ron—'

'No,' he insisted, shaking his head, 'I've had enough. Someone else can buy the place and take it over.'

'Yes, and likely give me the sack,' Mrs Hopkins pointed out tartly.

'Not if *you* was to buy it—' But he got no further than that extraordinary suggestion, for Edith gave an excited shriek and ran to the door, wiping her hands on her pinny.

He turned to stare, his frown thunderous. 'Stop that racket. What's got into you, girl?'

'I'm sorry, Mr Coates . . . But look, Mrs Hopkins!' Edith pointed, her heart welling up with joy. 'It's my gran . . . She must have got my letter, because she's come all the way from Cornwall to see me.'

She pulled open the door, the bell jangling, just as the lady with the cane reached the caff.

'Well, I never!' Mrs Hopkins pushed back her chair and stood up, staring, open-mouthed. '*Rosalyn*?'

Edith's grandmother limped into the caff, supporting herself on her cane and carrying a leather travelling bag, which Edith rushed forward eagerly to take.

'Edith, my dear. How lovely to see you looking so well.' Her bright gaze studied her figure closely for a moment, then moved to Mrs Hopkins' face. She smiled, though sadly. 'Hello, Sheila, my old friend . . . I was so sorry to hear about your Henry. What can I do to help?'

CHAPTER TEN

Sheila didn't think her poor heart could stand it. She had always expected that she and Henry would spend their old age together, enjoying the company of their daughters and granddaughters, long into their twilight years. Now, here she was, following her beloved husband's coffin from the church where she'd just sobbed her heart out, listening to Ernest's heartfelt eulogy for his father-in-law.

The vicar's white robes flapped just ahead of her, and she focused on them, dabbing at her eyes with a hanky. It had turned out to be a sunny day in the end, but the wind was brisk, and shook the dark, gloomy branches of the churchyard yew trees. So many folk had turned out for Henry's funeral, it was a sea of black suits, hats and dresses. There were so many in attendance, in fact, she doubted that anyone was still working at the Dagenham car plant that day.

Among the mourners, she caught a glimpse of her old friend Rosalyn, Edith's grandmother. She'd been so shocked to see her at the caff yesterday, that dear familiar face she remembered from her school days, yet strangely lined now.

Did she look that old too? Not that either of them was *old*, of course. But she'd remembered Rosalyn as a quick, lithe, smiling girl with smooth skin and glorious hair, and now here she was, silver-headed and leaning on a cane . . .

It had been kind of her to come all that way to pay her respects though, bless her. There hadn't been much time for them to chat yet, but perhaps there'd be a chance at the wake, or afterwards. She looked forward to it, and to hearing about her old haunts back in Cornwall. With both her parents gone, there was only Maggie left in the family who'd known her as a girl, and her sister had not come to pay her last respects to Henry, merely sending a card of condolences. She looked forward to a few hours of catching up with Rosalyn and reminiscing with her about their Cornish upbringing, so many decades ago.

Grief enveloped her once more at that thought. She'd hoped to return to her old stamping grounds with Henry one day, to visit her sister Maggie and paddle in the sea at Penzance, once he'd finally retired and was no longer working all the hours God sent. Now she would have to go down to Cornwall alone, if she went at all . . .

She whimpered, biting her lip against the sound, and a comforting hand crept into hers. Sheila looked round at her youngest daughter with a strained smile.

'Oh, Vi, love,' she muttered, fresh tears springing to her eyes, despite her determination not to keep impersonating a bloomin' watering pot. 'Whatever am I going to do without your dad?'

'We're all here for you, Mum,' Violet whispered. 'You won't be alone.'

Sheila managed to squeeze her hand in return, but weakly.

Her daughter meant well. They all meant well, kind souls, and she loved them for it. But it wasn't true. She would be alone from now on. Alone when she wanted to share a joke or a funny anecdote about her day, alone in their big double bed at night, and alone in her heart.

At the grave, the pallbearers – Ernest among them, uncharacteristically sombre in a smart black suit and tie – lowered Henry to his final resting place.

Sheila stood weeping with her family around her. She could barely hear the vicar's words of comfort and ritual. Her heart stuttered with pain. Her legs could barely support her, and for a few dizzying moments she felt sure they were about to give way, and she would fall in there with him, into the damp earth . . .

At last, it was over. Everyone seem to be gazing her way. There was a long, terrible silence. Sheila knew what to do. But she couldn't bear to turn away, to let him go.

'Oh, Henry.' With a moan, she cast a white lily down into the grave, and it struck the top of her husband's coffin, lying there amidst handfuls of soil. 'Henry . . .'

'Come on, Mother, time to go,' Ernest said firmly in her ear, and she staggered away, supported by him and Violet, Betsy following behind with an arm about each of her girls, Alice wiping away a tear, while Lily walked pale and tight-lipped.

Sheila said goodbye to the last stragglers at the wake, half rising from her armchair to shake the clammy hand of the chief foreman from the car plant. 'Good of you to come and pay your respects,' she said, for about the fiftieth time that afternoon. Her throat was sore from speaking to people, most of whom she only knew very slightly, if at all. 'Henry would have been pleased.' She swallowed against a lump in her throat. 'So very pleased.'

Mr Moss touched the brim of his hat. 'Henry was a good man and an excellent salesman, and what happened to him was a tragedy, Mrs Hopkins. I hope the villains that killed him are speedily brought to justice. You should know, everyone at the plant is very sorry for your loss.' He cleared his throat, adding, 'Management too.'

Sheila nodded. 'I saw the card of condolence from the executives, thank you.'

'We'll be on our way now. No, please don't get up, Mrs Hopkins. We can see ourselves out. Thank you ever so much for your hospitality.'

As he shuffled away, another man bent to shake her hand. She didn't know him, nor the other men with him, but she smiled gratefully up at them, nonetheless.

'It was a lovely service,' the man said in a rough voice, 'and a nice wake, Mrs Hopkins. Them sandwiches were very tasty.'

'Thank you. My daughter Violet made them.'

Violet, standing in the doorway with Edith at her side, gave the men a thin smile. 'Mum, Edith's gran would like a word with you before she goes, if you're up to it?'

Sheila was relieved at the idea of speaking to someone she actually knew. 'Of course I am, love. Show her in.' She smiled past her daughter at Rosalyn, waiting patiently in the hallway.

The men from the plant trailed out one after the other, hats in hand, nodding respectfully to the ladies on their way. 'Goodbye . . . Thank you, goodbye.'

Once the front door had closed behind the last of them, Sheila heaved a sigh of relief. 'Blimey, I feel like a queen on a bloomin' throne here . . . Any more guests left, Vi?'

Violet shook her head thankfully. 'Ernie and Betsy are still in the kitchen though, cleaning up, and the girls are playing in the yard.' Looking rather pale and weary herself, Violet ushered Rosalyn into the living room. 'Can I get you a sherry, Mrs Treloar?'

'I'd prefer a cup of tea,' Rosalyn admitted. 'If you don't mind, that is.'

'It's no trouble, honest.' Violet glanced at Sheila. 'Mum?'

'I'll have a cuppa as well since you're making a fresh pot. Thanks, love, you're a diamond. But then you and Edith should put your feet up and have a proper rest.' Sheila handed her daughter her empty sherry glass, giving Rosalyn an embarrassed grin. 'I'm not a big fan of sherry, to be honest. My home-made gin would have suited me better. But I'd have been fast asleep after a few glasses of that . . .' She glanced around. 'Where is my home-made gin?'

'Just wait, I'll fetch you some tea.' With a disapproving look, Violet hurried away with Edith trailing after her, and the door clicked shut behind them.

Rosalyn limped across to take Sheila's hand. 'Sad days, Shee,' she said gently, using the childhood name for her that only her closest family ever used. There was a familiar Cornish lilt to her voice that reminded Sheila of her childhood, mostly spent in the lanes around Penzance and the rich, green countryside beyond. 'But you'll pull through eventually. When I lost my Edward, I cried for weeks. Thought I'd never get my sparkle back. But you do, given enough time.' She bent and kissed Sheila on the cheek.

'Though you never forget, of course,' she added, smiling. 'And why would you want to? Henry seems to have been very well liked by his colleagues and friends, from that turn-out. And he was clearly loved by his family. An excellent husband and father, by all accounts.'

Sheila gave a tired chuckle. She'd heard Henry's praises sung all day, and it had amused her. While she'd loved him dearly, she hadn't been blind to his faults. 'True enough, but he could be a bugger at times too.'

'Oh, can't they all?' Leaning heavily on her cane, Rosalyn turned to the high-backed armchair opposite, the one Henry had always occupied in the evenings after dinner. For an instant, Sheila almost protested. Then she recalled that he would never sit there again, and fell silent. 'Now,' her old friend went on, leaning her cane up against the side of the chair, 'you know I came to Dagenham as much for my Edith as to see Henry off, don't you? No point pretending otherwise. That girl's got herself in a right pickle, and I've come to take her home to Cornwall.' She pulled a face. 'Not that she wants to leave you and Violet . . . But I can't see any way around it, I'm afraid.'

Sheila was perplexed. 'Take her home?' She wished she'd kept her sherry glass, for there was still a tidy drop left in the bottle at her elbow, and it might have helped her think. 'I don't understand. What kind of pickle is she in?'

'The kind where she won't be able to hold down that job in the café much longer,' Rosalyn said tartly. 'Not once she's showing, anyway.'

Sheila's jaw dropped as she realised what her old friend was saying. At once, the signs she'd noticed but not thought much about came back to her . . . The girl's increasingly heavy-set look, despite barely eating. Her pale cheeks, frequent lack of energy, and the odd bouts of sickness that had kept her off work at times. A tummy bug, she'd claimed. And Sheila had thought nothing of it, too wrapped up in her own troubles to wonder . . .

'Gawd, I don't believe it. Little Miss Butter Wouldn't Melt? Up the bloomin' spout?' Eyes wide, Sheila shook her head. 'How on earth?'

'A young man called Percy, that's how,' Rosalyn said grimly. 'A nice enough lad, I suppose. But he took advantage of my granddaughter, and then upped and left. Now she's in the family way.' She peered at Sheila. 'She didn't tell you?'

'Not a word.' Sheila stared. 'You said in your letter that she'd been having trouble in the village, that she'd been bullied by some of the other girls and needed a fresh start somewhere new. You never said *why*.'

'I said there'd been a young man involved, which was all I knew at the time. Trust me, this baby was as much of a surprise to me as it is for you.'

'Poor girl, she must have been terrified. I wish she'd confided in me. Pulling the wool over my eyes all these weeks . . .' Sheila sat up as Violet bustled back into the room with the tea tray and some biscuits. 'Oh, thanks, love.' She hesitated, then asked delicately, 'Where's Edith, by the way?'

Violet blinked and took her time answering as she poured the tea with a dash of milk each. 'Erm, Edith? She's gone upstairs. She was exhausted, poor thing. Had to work a shift at the caff early this morning, before Ron closed up, then hurry home to change for the funeral. And once we got back here after the service, she helped me hand out the sandwiches and keep the tea urn refreshed.' Her smile was a little too bright. 'After all that scurrying about, she looked puffed out, so . . . so I told her she should have a lie-down.'

'Violet Hopkins,' Sheila said sharply, 'you *know*, don't you?'

'Eh?'

'Don't give me that. You know why she's tired, and it ain't nothing to do with sandwiches and tea urns.'

Violet looked from her to Rosalyn, and blushed furiously. 'Oh.'

'How long have you known she was expecting?' Sheila demanded, sitting up straight. 'And why on earth didn't you tell me?'

'She asked me not to,' Violet said simply, and handed them both a steaming cup of tea. 'Sorry, Mum.' She chewed on her lip, looking contrite. 'Do you want me to fetch her downstairs to talk to you?'

'No,' Rosalyn said quickly. 'Let sleeping Ediths lie. Me and your mum still have plenty to discuss. We can talk to her later.'

Looking relieved, Violet went away again, and Sheila turned to her old friend, burning with curiosity.

'Come on then, spill the beans . . . Why hasn't this young man of Edith's married her yet? I mean, she's carrying his baby, for goodness' sake. Can't you get him to do the decent thing by her?'

Rosalyn sighed. 'I'd love to see them wed. But he's gone to Canada.'

'A fine time to be taking a holiday!'

'No, you don't understand. He lives there . . . His great-uncle died childless and left the boy's father a property in the village. You might remember them. The Grigg family. Wealthy landowners, but Tom Grigg was forever falling out with people. Ended up living on his own and letting the place go to rack and ruin. The land's worth something though, and the farmhouse isn't in bad condition. So they came over as a family to take a look. Spent a few weeks exploring the area and talking to land agents, then Percy's father closed up the house, and they all sailed home again.'

'Leaving a bun in the oven.' Sheila tutted crossly.

'I don't think the boy realised. Edith certainly didn't. Not for a long while. She only wrote to tell me the whole sorry tale last week, and I was horrified, as you can imagine. And saddened to hear about Henry too.' Rosalyn heaved a sigh. 'But I knew what had to be done. So I packed a bag and jumped on a train at Penzance, and I fully intend to take Edith back home with me as soon as she's had a chance to say her goodbyes. In her condition, she needs family around her. And to stay home where her condition can't be gossiped about.'

'You're going to hide the poor girl indoors for the next five or six months, is that it?' Sheila grimaced. 'And what does Edith think of this plan?'

'She's not happy,' Rosalyn admitted cautiously. 'But she has little other choice but to come home. She'll accept it eventually.'

'Hmm.'

Sheila wondered how much her friend really knew of her granddaughter's temperament. Edith was not as meek and biddable as she'd seemed at first glance. Indeed, if she'd been hiding a secret like this for such a long time without breaking down in tears, it pointed to a young woman unlikely to bow down at her grandmother's command.

But she said nothing, merely nodded. It was none of her

business, and the girl would no doubt make up her own mind soon enough.

'Where are you staying while you're in Dagenham, Rosalyn?' Sheila was feeling a little fragile again, but she smiled for her old friend's sake. 'Listen, you're welcome to come and stay with us here. Edith can give up her bed for you and sleep in Violet's room for a few days. It's very comfortable and she won't mind. And you're surely not travelling back to Cornwall without even a rest and a look around Dagenham?'

Rosalyn hesitated, her brow furrowing. 'I had intended to take Edith straight back with me. Or as soon as she can pack her bags and say her goodbyes. I'm in a spartan bed and breakfast near the station, and I barely slept a wink last night. But when you put it like that . . .' Her face softened. 'Shee, are you sure I wouldn't be a nuisance though? At a time like this, when you've just lost your husband, wouldn't you prefer to have family around you?'

Sheila leant forward to pat her hand. 'You *are* family, Rosalyn,' she insisted, and that lump returned to her throat, this time reducing her to tears. 'Or as good as. I may not have seen you since I was a girl, love, but I haven't forgotten your kindness back when things went wrong for me. I think you know what I'm talking about.'

Her friend put down her cup of tea, staring. 'Sorry? You can't mean . . . *Bernard Bailey*?'

'Gawd!' Sheila half laughed, half cried at that name, the strangest emotion welling up out of nowhere. 'Bernard bloomin' Bailey . . . I had such a pash for him when we were young.' She choked on the words. 'I shouldn't be saying that on the day we buried Henry, gawd rest his soul. But the fact is, I have thought about Bernard Bailey a few times over the years, and wondered what happened to him, whether he ever married . . . Oh, I made such a cake of myself over that boy.'

'I quite liked him myself,' Rosalyn admitted with a wink.

'You too, eh?' Sheila dabbed at her wet eyes with a hanky. 'Still, plenty of us girls were mad for him at school, weren't we? I can see him now . . . So young and handsome in his school uniform, with a chiselled jaw and smiling eyes. I always thought he was destined for the music halls, he had such charisma . . .' She chuckled at the memory. 'I expect he's got a head of hair as silvery as ours now.'

'I saw him not so long ago,' Rosalyn admitted, blushing slightly, 'and nearly didn't recognise him.'

'Changed that much, has he?' Sheila couldn't help feeling curious about her old crush. 'Well, we all get old in the end.'

Rosalyn shook her head. 'It's not his looks so much, but his clothes. Bernard Bailey married into money, you see,' she confided. 'A very well-to-do woman, though I can't for the life of me remember her name. They lived up-country for a while, I believe, but he must come home to Cornwall occasionally, for I saw him across the street in Penzance, in a posh pinstriped suit and carrying a briefcase. Black polished shoes and a brolly too. Quite like a city gent, he was.'

'So Bernard did all right for himself in the end. Well, his wife's a lucky lady, that's for certain.' Sheila mused over her long-gone youth for a moment, lost in nostalgia, then gave her friend a grateful smile. 'I'm glad you came today, Rosalyn. I opened my eyes this morning feeling so bloomin' miserable, I didn't want to get out of bed. It took Violet threatening me with all sorts just to get me up and dressed in time for the funeral. But it's made all the difference having you here. All the difference in the world.'

Ron Coates had come to her husband's funeral, but not the wake afterwards, having made his apologetic excuses and hurried back to reopen the caff. So Sheila didn't have a chance to speak to him again about the future until she went round to see him a few days later. She'd been busy showing Rosalyn around Dagenham, and also finding time to have a few quiet words with Edith, poor lamb, who was in a right state over her unexpected pregnancy.

But with Rosalyn and Edith having gone shopping in Ilford with Betsy, who knew the best stores for summer bargains, she was determined to go into work and have it out with Ron.

Ever since his first startling suggestion that she should buy the Corner Caff from him, she'd been by turns amused, astonished and intrigued by the idea, even though she'd firmly turned it down the first time he'd brought it up. Amused because, her, Sheila Hopkins, run a caff? She couldn't imagine being the boss and giving people orders. Astonished because she couldn't understand why he would have asked her, of all people, when he knew she didn't have a blooming clue how to run a business. And intrigued because, the day after Henry's funeral, she'd visited the family solicitor, an elderly gent with spectacles and an unlikely toupee, and discovered two things. One, that Henry had left her every blessed thing he owned in his will, including the nest egg they'd been saving for years towards Henry's retirement. And two, he'd taken out an insurance policy against his death, without ever telling her.

The solicitor had named a sum due on that life insurance policy that had left her faint with disbelief. It was more than enough to keep her comfortably for the rest of her life, along with the savings in their bank account, her widow's pension, and a generous pension due from the plant where Henry had worked for so many years.

But if she wanted to risk some of the capital, the solicitor had said, when she tentatively asked about buying the caff, it would be possible to take over the business without leaving herself entirely broke. 'A risk, Mrs Hopkins,' the old boy had admitted, peering at her over the rim of his spectacles, 'but not out of the question. After all, if you ever got into difficulties, you could always sell the business on. It would be an investment.'

An investment.

Sheila had never made an investment before in her life. The word alone scared her. And there was no Henry to ask for advice. But the idea of running her own business was enticing. Above all things, she did love chatting to the customers, and the only fly in her ointment was Ron, constantly chivvying her away and belly-aching about her chatting when she should be frying bacon or making tea. Sheila, on the other hand, saw chatting to the customers as part of working, an important way to make them feel happy and welcome in the caff, and if she were the boss, there'd be no one to tell her off for doing what she loved best . . .

So she marched into the caff with her handbag clutched to her chest, silvering hair curled neatly under her headscarf, and her best lipstick on.

'I'm not here to work, Ron,' she told her startled boss, and plonked herself down at one of the tables, her heart thumping fit to burst. 'I'm here to talk business. It's about buying this place, like you suggested.' Swallowing down her nerves, she took out a notepad and pen. 'How much, for starters, would you be asking for it?'

CHAPTER ELEVEN

Betsy was out shopping in Ilford town centre with Edith and her grandmother, trying on dresses and shoes in a large department store, and trying to appear happy and normal. Yet how could anyone be happy after what she'd been through?

The world felt so dark now, the whole nation holding its breath, waiting for war. It was hard to imagine there could be any light whatsoever at the end of the long, bleak tunnel they had already entered.

Worse still, not only had she lost a much-wanted baby, but the miscarriage had been caused, to her mind, by the same group whose vile, aggressive members had killed her dad and tried to take Ernest away from her too. Try as she might to stay cheerful, to keep smiling for the sake of her two lovely girls, her mouth stayed stubbornly downturned and her heart ached as it had never done before, not even when she'd heard about her father's shocking death.

Still, one good thing had come of that awful day in the park, she thought, following Edith into the changing rooms with a selection of new frocks. The police had responded by clamping down on any Blackshirts gatherings in the Dagenham area. There were also rumours of young men being arrested for defying the law on political uniforms by turning up at marches dressed, as Ernest scathingly put it, like '*Hitler-Jugend* . . . Hitler Youth'. Not that British rules and regulations seemed to stop the ringleaders doing whatever they liked. Most folk were too scared to interfere when they came marching past their homes and businesses, shouting slogans and waving placards that celebrated Nazi ideals. But she'd heard that Constable Hobbs had told the local fascists' group not to set foot in Ron's caff again, or else. So some people were standing firm, at least.

Their leader, Oswald Mosley, had certainly not been cowed by the British government's new restrictions, however, and was intent on leading a huge rally in Earl's Court that very weekend, with tens of thousands expected to attend.

'How is such a dreadful, unpatriotic thing even legal?' Betsy had cried the morning before, reading the newspaper report aloud to her husband over breakfast.

But Ernest had merely shrugged it off as, 'The price of a free society,' insisting that these gatherings by the so-called British Union of Fascists would not sway the public into sympathising with the Nazis. All the same, she could tell that he too found such open displays of support for Hitler disturbing.

'What do you think, Betsy?' Edith asked, coming out of the cubicle where she'd been changing and twirling around in the green and white summer frock she'd picked out. 'The green's not quite the right shade.' She peered at her reflection in the mirror with a critical frown. 'A bit too strong for my colouring.'

'Yes, and rather tight-fitting,' Betsy said with an apologetic smile, not wanting to make the younger woman self-conscious about her figure, and handed her a pale cream skirt suit instead. 'Try this.'

'Oh no,' Edith's grandmother said at once. 'Sorry, my dear, but it's far too formal for a girl of her age.' And she passed across a much less sophisticated yellow dress with short, capped sleeves and an old-fashioned low waistline. To Betsy's eyes it looked more like a tent than a summer frock. 'This will look nice on you, especially with those pumps we picked out.'

'Gran, I'm not twelve,' Edith protested, and then caught her grandmother's eye and subsided. 'Oh, very well. I'll try it on.' And she disappeared back into the cubicle.

Rosalyn returned the cream suit to the attendant, saying flatly, 'No, thank you.' She glanced at Betsy and said in a low voice, 'Please don't be offended, my dear. But you must allow me to know what is best for my granddaughter.'

Betsy said nothing, and when Edith emerged again, grudgingly admitted that it did fit her rather better than the other dresses she'd tried on. It was only when Edith performed another twirl, then smoothed the yellow fabric over her tummy that the truth hit Betsy like a punch. She gave a sharp gasp, and the other two turned to stare at her.

'Excuse me, I'm just going to . . .' she muttered, her voice tailing off, and hurried out of the changing rooms, heading down the stairs to the next level of the department store.

She didn't know exactly where she was going, only that she needed to be alone. Because she knew that gesture, for she'd made it often enough herself in recent months. It was the secret proud gesture of a woman who was pregnant but hadn't yet told the world.

Edith was expecting a baby.

And *she* wasn't.

Not anymore, Betsy thought, catching a glimpse of her slender outline in one of the shop-floor mirrors and barely able to breathe for the sheer pain and torture of it. She leant over a display case, trying to steady herself.

Not anymore . . .

'Can I help you, madam?' a gentleman in a smart grey waistcoat and grey silk tie asked from a few feet away. Betsy straightened with a start. There was a badge on his waistcoat that read, *Assistant Manager*. He smiled apologetically. 'I can see I've disturbed your train of thought. Forgive me. But you were admiring our range of diamond and pearl earrings.' He gestured to the glass-topped counter beside her. 'Is there a particular pair that caught your eye?'

'Earrings?'

She had stopped in the jewellery section of the department store, which consisted of a few brilliant counters in a sea of perfumes and silk scarves. Everything smelled and looked gorgeous and shiny and expensive. Elsewhere, one woman was helping a customer with a necklace while another polished the fittings assiduously with a cloth. A fancy mirror with gilt surround stood on the counter, no doubt so ladies could admire themselves as they tried on pieces of jewellery, to see what they looked like against their skin tones and hair colour.

About to stammer no and move on, Betsy stopped herself and said, with a flash of defiance, 'Actually, yes . . . That pair on the end. Could I have a closer look at them?'

He raised his brows, as she was pointing at a sparkly pair of sapphire drops with silver mounting.

'Madam has excellent taste,' he murmured, though she saw his quick assessing look, presumably wondering if she could afford them. Which she absolutely could not, judging by the discreet price tag. Not even if Ernest worked flat out for a full year to buy them for her.

Suddenly, she was sick of how dark and depressing everything was. She wanted to see those sapphire earrings up close, to touch them, maybe hold them up to her ears in the fancy mirror and imagine . . .

He bent to unlock the drawer under the counter, and drew the jewellery display out. 'Just a moment, if you please.' Reverently, he placed the rows of earrings, set on a bed of red velvet, on top of the glass. 'This pair?' He unhooked them from the display and held them out on his palm, the jewels glinting invitingly. 'Beautiful, aren't they? And sapphires would look perfect with your hair colouring, if you don't mind my saying so, madam.'

'Yes,' she whispered, and took them, holding them delicately up against her ears and admiring them in the mirror.

A large woman was looking at silk scarves a short distance away. Wearing a wide-brimmed hat and a jacket trimmed with black fur, despite the hot weather, she was pushing a pram and holding a small boy by the hand. The child, three or four years old and dressed in a blue and white sailor suit, was babbling some nursery rhyme and knocking his free hand against every display he passed, leaving mucky handprints. His mouth and chin were smeared with chocolate, as now were the glass cabinets and expensive silk scarves. One of the female store attendants went hurrying after them to remonstrate with his mother, who was looking harassed, wrestling with the pram in that narrow space.

From the pram, Betsy caught the first thin wail of a baby's cry . . . 'Madam, you need to control your son!'

The assistant manager had turned that way to watch them too, concerned and also beginning to protest as the baby's cry intensified. 'Madam, please . . .'

Betsy turned away, her mind elsewhere. She felt lightheaded. The store was so hot and stuffy, and she couldn't stand badly behaved children, that was all. Though she knew the baby's cry had made her think of something else. Or *someone* else, perhaps. Now all she could think was that she needed to get outside and breathe fresh air.

'Betsy?'

She kept going, ignoring her name being called behind her.

'Betsy . . . Where are you going? Wait for us.'

It was Edith.

Betsy did not look around, her heart thumping. She was almost at the large revolving doors to the store when a man's hand gripped her sleeve hard.

'Store detective . . . Stop!'

Gasping in shock, she pulled free, hurrying on, but another man stepped neatly in front of her, blocking her path to the outside world.

It was the assistant manager, a heavy frown on his face. 'I think you'd better come with me, madam.' He gestured towards a side room half hidden behind an elaborate display. 'The manager's office is this way.'

Betsy stared at him. 'The . . . The manager's office? I don't understand.'

'Come along,' he said smoothly, taking her arm. 'Best not make a fuss.'

She went with him numbly, not quite sure what was happening but aware of a sick, leaden feeling in the pit of her stomach.

'Excuse me,' Edith called after them, her voice high-pitched and agitated. 'That's my friend. Where are you taking her? What on earth is going on?'

The assistant manager stopped to take stock of her, his clever gaze moving from Edith to her grandmother, now making her slow way down the staircase from the first floor. 'I'm afraid we're going to need your friend to turn out her pockets, Miss. I believe she may have taken something from the store without paying.'

'Poppycock!' Edith's grandmother exclaimed, limping towards them.

Edith looked embarrassed. 'Erm, what my grandmother means is that you . . . you must've made a mistake.' Edith lowered her voice as a smart-looking couple passed by, glancing at them curiously. 'We can vouch for Mrs Fisher. She's very respectable.'

'Mrs Fisher, eh?' The man who had grabbed her sleeve looked Betsy up and down, contempt in his eyes. '*Respectable*?' And he laughed.

'How dare you?' Betsy demanded of the man, furious now. She hesitated, on the verge of begging Edith and Mrs Treloar to stay and help her, but knew that would be selfish. Clearly, there had been a hideous misunderstanding, and she couldn't work out what or how it had happened. Everything felt so confused. But that didn't mean she wanted Edith's elderly grandmother dragged into this fiasco. 'Thank you, Edith, but I'll be all right,' she added with an effort. 'You should go now. Take your gran home on the bus. I'll see you later.'

And she turned away without waiting to hear more. The assistant manager showed her into the manager's office. As soon as the door had closed behind them, the other man stuck out his hand.

'Until the police arrive, consider yourself arrested for theft, Mrs Fisher. Now give 'em back,' he growled.

'Thanks, Charlie, I'll take it from here.' The assistant manager nodded to the door. 'You can wait outside.'

Betsy stood trembling with anger, her eyes fixed on the man with loathing. There was much she wanted to say, but she couldn't trust herself to speak without being rude.

Once the store detective had slunk off, looking surly, the assistant manager turned to Betsy. 'Now, Mrs Fisher, if that is indeed your name . . . The manager isn't here today so I'll be dealing with this. The earrings, if you please?'

'Earrings?' She didn't know what he was talking about.

'In your pocket.'

'I beg your pardon? The only thing you'll find in there is my hanky.' Furious, keen to prove him wrong, she slapped a hand straight to the pocket he was indicating, and faltered, finding a tell-tale bulge instead. Her fingers crept inside, tentatively exploring. To her horror and astonishment, two small hard objects were nestled in the folds of her hanky. 'Oh!' Slowly, she withdrew the beautiful sapphire earrings she'd been admiring upstairs and stared down at them. Heat flooded her cheeks. 'I . . . I don't know how they got there. This is a mistake.'

He didn't believe her, of course. But it was true. Betsy thought back to how she'd stopped at the jewellery counter and asked to see the sapphire earrings, when the child with the sticky fingers had caused a commotion. Then a baby had started to cry, and after that her memory of events became hazy. Though she could remember hurrying down the stairs, intent on getting out of the store and into the sunshine as quickly as possible.

He took the earrings and placed them carefully on the leather-topped desk. 'Is this your first time being caught shoplifting, Mrs Fisher?' he asked, and pointed her towards a chair.

'But I wasn't.' She sat down heavily, suddenly weak and overwhelmed. 'That is, I didn't mean to take them. I don't know what happened.' She buried her face in her hands and burst into tears. 'I've never taken anything without paying in my life. I'm ever so sorry.'

It was well over an hour later when there was a knock at the door to the manager's office, and there was Ernest. Betsy jumped up and ran into his arms. 'I'm sorry,' she whispered, her eyes sore with weeping. 'I can't remember putting those earrings into my pocket. You have to believe me.'

'Hush, everything's going to be all right.' Ernest held her for a moment, then turned politely to the assistant manager. 'I know what this must look like. But I can assure you my wife doesn't make a habit of forgetting to pay. The thing is, she hasn't been well lately. And she was recently bereaved. Her father, Mr Hopkins, was killed in the street. You may have read about it in the local papers... We only just buried him.'

The assistant manager, who had been waiting with her until Ernest arrived, had stood up to welcome him. 'Yes, so your wife has been telling me. Indeed, as soon as I realised who her father was, I arranged to have you contacted.' He shook Ernest's hand. 'Pleased to meet you. I'm Tony Jackson. I'm so sorry for your loss, Mr Fisher. Henry was a good man. In fact, I've always bought my cars through his recommendation. It was awful, what happened to him. However, this is a serious matter.'

'Of course,' Ernest murmured.

'This is a first offence, and I can see that your wife is very contrite, so I won't be calling the police this time. But there is a condition, I'm afraid.' The assistant manager turned to Betsy. 'You must agree to see a doctor, Mrs Fisher, for your own good.'

'Thank you for being so understanding, Mr Jackson.' Cheeks hot with shame, she took Ernest's hand and hurried out of the store with him before the man could change his mind and summon the police. 'Oh, that was so embarrassing,' she muttered once they were out on the street, still barely able to look her husband in the eye. 'Honestly, I don't know how it happened. One minute I was shopping, the next I . . . I had those sapphire earrings in my pocket.'

'Keep walking, dearest. My car is parked just along here. You know, if you'd wanted more earrings, *Liebchen*, you need only have asked. I would have bought you a pair.' Ernest pulled a face. 'Though maybe not quite as expensive as those ones . . .'

'But I don't want any earrings,' Betsy moaned. They had reached the car, and she climbed into the shady interior, thankful to be out of the public eye at last. He got in beside her but didn't start the engine, turning to study her with a worried expression. 'Ernest, I feel fine, honestly. I just can't explain it. Do I really have to go and see a . . . a doctor?' The thought appalled her.

'I think you must, yes. And not only because Mr Jackson made it a condition of letting you go without calling the police.' Ernest took her hand, his voice concerned. 'Darling, you haven't been yourself for a long time. Even before your father's death, before you . . . you lost the baby, I felt you were struggling to be happy.' He was holding her hand gently, running his thumb over the thin gold band of her wedding ring, his face troubled. 'I want you to be honest with me, Betsy. Is it me? Are you no longer happy being my wife?'

'Of course I am,' she whispered. But she knew deep down that those two horrific losses had left her broken inside . . . She couldn't express it though, not even to Ernest. The wound still felt so raw and bitter. 'Maybe it's all this talk of war,' she stumbled on, trying to convince herself as much as him. 'Everyone's been talking about what will happen if Germany won't back down. People are saying there might be mass conscription. Soldiers on the streets. Kids sent away from their parents into the countryside for safety. Alice and Lily . . . They're not little girls anymore, but I don't want them in harm's way.'

'No more do I,' he said deeply.

'We grew up during the Great War,' she reminded him. 'I can't bear the thought of being plunged back into that darkness. All the death and horror. The young men who would be lost.' Her gaze rose, meeting his in sudden trepidation. 'You wouldn't join up, would you?'

'My dearest love.' Ernest kissed her softly on the lips. 'Do you really need to ask me that? Of course I would. The sooner the better. Apart from anything else, if I didn't—'

'People would say you supported the Nazis.'

'Exactly so.' He chuckled. 'Though I wouldn't join the army

simply to avoid being called a Nazi sympathiser. I would join because I love this country. I may be half German but I am also half English. This is my country too, and I'm no supporter of Hitler and his obsessive desire for power. So I shall fight for Britain.' His smile grew crooked. 'Die for her, if needs be.'

'Don't, please!'

'But that's a conversation for the future,' he assured her, 'not today. For now, you will visit a doctor, and we will take his advice. Yes?'

Betsy sighed, fearing what might be suggested at such a consultation, but unable to see any way around it. 'Yes.'

Late that afternoon, leaving their local GP surgery with a prescription for pills to help her sleep and an order to make a 'clean break' for a month or so from her life in Dagenham, Betsy stood blinking in the golden sunshine, unable to believe what Ernest and the doctor had decided for her between themselves. None of her arguments had held any sway with the two men, and the doctor had merely looked away at her tears, clearly embarrassed. At least Ernest had put a comforting arm about her. But he had refused to change his mind.

'I don't want to go away,' she muttered, looking at her husband in desperation. 'The girls . . . How will they cope without me? And my mother? She's just lost Dad. I can't leave and abandon her when she needs me most.'

'Your mother needs you well again,' Ernest said calmly, 'as do the girls. Besides, Sheila will understand.'

'Why must I spend a month or two in the countryside, though? Just as we're on the brink of war too? It's not right.'

She clung onto his hand. 'Please don't do this, Ernest. I . . . I don't even know where I would go. Or how we would afford such a thing.'

'I've got an idea about that. Your mother could write to her sister, Margaret, in Cornwall. She and her husband have a farm down there, don't they? The perfect place for you to spend a couple of months, recovering from . . .' He pulled a face. 'The stress and strain you've been suffering lately.'

'But Maggie can't stand us . . . And I don't want to spend the summer on a farm in the middle of nowhere!'

'You heard the doctor. You need a clean break from Dagenham. And I'm sure your aunt wouldn't charge you for staying with her.' He hesitated. 'Though I imagine she may ask you to take up some chores around the house and farm in return for your bed and board. But that wouldn't be a bad thing,' he added, smiling at her tenderly. 'You're too pale. Some brisk exercise in the fresh Cornish air will do you good.'

'But why can't I stay here and take the pills he prescribed to help me sleep? I'm sure after a week or two of sleeping properly I'll be right as rain.'

'Not everything can be resolved with medication, love.' When she looked away, on the point of tears again, Ernest sighed. 'You weren't very forthcoming with the doctor, and I understand why. He wasn't particularly sympathetic over what happened at the department store. But I know why you did it, how unhappy you've been lately . . . You can't hide any of that from me.' Ernest stroked her cheek. 'Besides, his overall prognosis was correct. You need a change of scene. Something to take you out of yourself.'

Betsy hugged herself, feeling wretched and misunderstood.

'You're sending me away to cheer me up . . . But I won't be happy without you and the girls. How could I be?'

'The doctor knows best, darling. Let us trust his judgement and give this a try.' Ernest hesitated. 'If Margaret agrees, I will drive down with you and see you settled at the farm myself. We could visit the seaside one day, perhaps. Tour the countryside around the farm, see the sights . . . I'm sure the plant would give me a week or two off work if I explained the situation.' He grimaced. 'Unpaid, of course.'

'You . . . You'd come with me to Cornwall?' Her heart lightened.

'If that's what you need,' he told her, smiling. 'Just until you feel happy there.'

That will never happen, Betsy thought defiantly, but she took a deep breath. 'In that case, I'll go. But under protest.'

'Duly noted.'

CHAPTER TWELVE

It was with a genuine sense of shock that Edith discovered precisely why Mrs Fisher had been taken away for questioning by the assistant manager of the department store. Because she had *stolen* something. Yet it seemed impossible. Why on earth would she steal anything? She was such a nice lady, with lovely daughters and a kind husband. Edith couldn't imagine stealing anything from a shop and could only think that it must have been a mistake. But when she said this, her grandmother shook her head.

'I had it firsthand from Sheila,' she told her quietly, for they were sitting in the sunny backyard with a cup of tea, and the windows were all open in the house behind them, to help dispel the stuffiness of the hot July weather. 'She pocketed a pair of sapphire earrings. Very expensive. Probably worth a year of her husband's salary at the car plant. It was a miracle the management at that store didn't call the police. Though her mother says that was because of Henry.'

'Mr Hopkins?'

Gran nodded. 'The assistant manager knew him,' she went on in a whisper, 'and could see how distraught poor Betsy was. So he let her go with a warning. Though he did insist that she should visit a doctor, as she couldn't remember how the earrings came to be in her pocket in the first place. But it sounds as though her father's death has affected her very badly.' Her grandmother tutted. 'It's all very sad.'

Edith thought of the miscarriage Betsy had suffered too, though it wasn't her place to mention it. 'Goodness,' she murmured instead. 'So the doctor recommended she goes down to her aunt's farm in Cornwall for a spell? It seems an awfully long way to go. And what about her daughters?'

'Sheila and Violet will look after them in her absence,' Gran said confidentially. 'Besides, it's only for a few weeks. Or maybe a few months. I wasn't clear on the details. But, you know, it is an excellent idea. Cornwall is such a tonic... Fresh air, beautiful countryside, and sparkling clean rivers.' She smiled, proud of her home. 'I predict that Betsy will be fit and healthy again by the end of this summer, if she follows her doctor's orders and lets Cornwall work its magic on her. As you would be too, if you'd only listen to reason.'

Edith squirmed under her grandmother's penetrating look. Too late, she realised she'd been led into a trap with this conversation. 'I'm not going back home, Gran,' she said defiantly.

'Well, you can hardly stay here.'

'Oh, can't I?'

'Now, Edith, do be sensible. It's all very well to leave home to pursue a career and earn money. It was very brave and laudable of you. That's why I supported you when you told me you needed to escape the village, even though I thought it would be better simply to confront Susan Teague over her lies.' Her grandmother gave her a stern look. 'Except they weren't lies, were they?'

'No,' Edith admitted miserably.

'Not that Susan had any right to talk about someone else's private business behind their back. A fine friend she was . . . But that aside, it's clear you cannot have a baby here in Dagenham. Not without any family to support you. After all, you can't continue to hold down that job much longer.' Her gaze fell to Edith's gently swelling tummy. 'My dear, you're practically showing. People will talk. And once people start talking, you'll get the sack. Because no employer wants to have an unmarried mother serving their customers, do they?'

'I'll make it work,' Edith insisted, stubbornly gritting her teeth. 'I agree that Susan turned out to be the worst friend in the world . . . But what happened with Percy was *my* fault, so I should be the one to fix it.'

Her grandmother's eyebrows shot up. 'It was hardly your fault alone. Besides, there's no *fixing* an unwanted baby. You're not thinking straight.'

Edith took a deep breath. 'This baby is wanted,' she said. 'Very much wanted.'

'I'm glad to hear that, young lady. Because you'll be having it, either way. Better to be happy about the prospect than cast down. But,' she added more gently, 'you must know that many people will consider it shameful for you to be having a baby when you're not married, and with no hope of you being married any time soon. It's just the way the world is, and we must be practical and face that fact.'

'V-Violet will help me,' Edith stammered. 'And Mrs

Hopkins too, I'm sure. She's such a kind lady. And she didn't take the news of my pregnancy so very hard, did she?'

'It's one thing to be understanding about a silly young girl who's made a dreadful mistake, and another to have her lodging under your roof while she's looking after a baby. And unpaid too. After all, in a short time, you won't be able to earn any more money. How will you keep yourself and this child?'

Edith felt hopeless. 'I don't know,' she whispered.

'Which is why you need to come home with me to Cornwall.' Her grandmother sighed. 'If we had enough money, we could send you away to one of these nice little bed-and-breakfast places on the coast. A place where nobody asks any questions and, at the end of the pregnancy, you can hand over your child for adoption, and that's an end of the matter. But we can't afford that, and besides, I'm sure we'll be able to find a couple in Cornwall willing to adopt without going to such lengths.'

Edith's heart was thundering in her chest. 'A-Adoption? I'm not putting this baby up for adoption. It's my child. Mine and Percy's. How could I ever look him in the face again if I gave his child away to strangers?'

'My dear girl, he must've returned to Canada by now, yet he hasn't written to you. I don't want to hurt your feelings, but it's obvious Percy did not feel the same about you as you did for him. And this baby . . . Well, it was a mistake,' her grandmother said flatly. 'But a mistake that can easily be rectified, so your life won't be ruined.'

Edith jumped to her feet, flushed and tormented. 'This baby is not going to ruin my life. This baby is going to make me a mother, and I'm keeping her. Or him. Is that clear?'

And she stormed off, so blinded by tears that she almost blundered into the back door by accident.

It seemed that the baby had worsened her temper, she thought, feeling calmer once she was out of the heat. Remorse flooded her. She should go back to apologise, but then she remembered her grandmother's suggestion that she should give up her baby.

As she stumbled towards the stairs, desperate to be alone to brood and weep in private, Mrs Hopkins let herself in through the front door.

'Hello, Edith, love. How are you feeling today? Not suffering too much in this heat, I hope?' she called out cheerfully.

Not wanting to be rude to the woman who'd taken her in so kindly and helped her find work, Edith stopped and tried to smile. 'I . . . I'm very well, thank you, Mrs Hopkins.' But her voice shook as she spoke.

'Oh dear, whatever's this? Have you been crying? Come here, love.' Before she could escape, Mrs Hopkins had enfolded her in her matronly arms, giving her a warm hug. She smelled faintly of lavender and roses.

'There, there. It'll all come out in the wash. That's what my mum used to say, and she was usually right. Though not always, I must admit.' Mrs Hopkins caught sight of Edith's grandmother coming along the hallway and pulled a sympathetic face. 'Have you two had a barney? I fall out with Violet and Betsy sometimes too,' she whispered in Edith's ear. 'It don't mean nothing. When you're that close to someone, it's easy to fall out occasionally. But you'll soon be back to best of friends again; mark my words.'

Edith looked at her grandmother, who gave a heavy sigh.

'I'm sorry if you felt I was pressuring you to do something you don't want to do, Edith,' her grandmother said a little stiffly.

'And I'm sorry for speaking to you like that, Gran. I know you meant well. But I'm not going back to Cornwall,' she finished in a rush, 'and I'm not giving up this baby, and that's final.'

Mrs Hopkins, who had listened to their mutual apologies with a beaming smile, looked dismayed at this. 'Gawd . . . Are you not going home with your gran, then? After she came all this way just so she could take you back to Cornwall and look after you properly there?' And then she seemed to understand, her eyes widening as she glanced from Edith to her gran. 'Blimey, you weren't planning to stay here instead? Because I'd like to help you, honest I would. Only I can't look after Betsy's poor girls, and Violet too when she's feeling down, as well as you, with a newborn baby coming this side of Christmas.' Mrs Hopkins bit her lip. 'I don't want to upset you, love. But you'd best go home with your gran and try to be happy.'

Edith's grandmother gave a satisfied nod. 'Thank you, Shee. It's good to know we're of the same mind where my granddaughter's welfare is concerned.'

Edith stood stricken, feeling abandoned.

'I'm sorry to disappoint you, love,' Mrs Hopkins told her huskily, 'but your gran's right. Cornwall's the best place for you now. But listen, it's not all doom and gloom. Ernest is running our Betsy down to her aunt's farm in Cornwall soon, and there should be plenty of room in their big car for you and Rosalyn, and all your luggage too. So much cheaper than two train tickets all the way from London. Ain't that a stroke of luck, eh?' And, with an apologetic smile, she hurried away into the kitchen.

Trembling, Edith lifted a tear-filled gaze to her grandmother's face. 'It seems there's no hope at all. I have to go back to Cornwall with you.' And she burst into tears.

'Oh, Edith . . .' Her grandmother gave her a brusque hug, perhaps intended as both a rebuke and a comfort at the same time. She had never been like Mrs Hopkins, who seemed all heart. And Edith had never minded that before, accepting of her grandmother's logical approach to life. But just now, a little sympathy would have been more welcome. 'This is for the best. You'll see that in time. And if you truly want to keep this baby, we'll find a way to make it work.'

'Thank you,' she said shakily, and wiped away a tear. Knowing that her grandmother was no longer adamant that she should give up her baby for adoption did make her feel better about returning to Cornwall with her. 'At least if we can beg a lift from Mr and Mrs Fisher,' she added, making an effort to sound more cheerful, 'it won't be as uncomfortable as the train.'

Gran smiled, clearly appreciating her attempt not to be miserable all the way home. 'Why don't you go and start packing?' she suggested and gave a chuckle. 'Meanwhile, I'm going to sit down with Sheila for one last afternoon of remembering what we got up to when we were even younger than you.'

Edith trailed upstairs to pack her meagre possessions. She had smiled for her grandmother, but deep down she still felt wretched, forced to leave her new friends behind in Dagenham and return to the tiny Cornish village where she'd been born. She had left home in the first place because she couldn't bear the gossip. Now, she was returning pregnant and unmarried, and their nasty digs would hurt a thousand times more.

Gran was right though. If Percy had cared even the tiniest bit about her, he would have written a letter to her by now. He must have forgotten her name as soon as he left Cornwall. So she would have to raise this child without him, and with a war coming too.

The future seemed cold and bleak. But she was determined to do whatever was best for her unborn baby, even if her heart was breaking.

'Here we are at last,' Mr Fisher announced, glancing in his rear-view mirror as he slowed into the village of Penmarrey just after eight-thirty in the evening. His blue eyes twinkled at Edith in the mirror. 'Home sweet home. Now, whereabouts is your house, Mrs Treloar?'

Seated beside her in the back of his comfortable Ford Eight, Edith's grandmother leant forward to direct him through the lanes. Edith glanced apprehensively out at familiar landmarks, basking in the soft golden light of a Cornish sunset. There was the church with its quaint steeple, the Green Dragon public house, which the owner swore had stood in this village since medieval times, the village shop, and the tiny bakery where she had worked alongside her father since leaving school, now shut up for the day.

It all seemed so peaceful and idyllic, just as she remembered it; a far cry from the busy, impersonal streets of Dagenham that she'd left behind early that morning. Yet it was impossible to smile and be happy to be home again. How could she forget how horrible life had been before she left Penmarrey, with all those rumours about her and Percy swirling about? The worst moment came as they passed the house where Susan Teague still lived with her parents, only a few minutes' walk from her grandmother's home. Thankfully, the front door was closed and there was no sign of Susan in the generous side garden with its fruit-laden apple trees, though she caught sight of Mr Teague in his white beekeeper's garb tending to his beehives. All the same, she knew it couldn't be long before she came face to face with her former friend, maybe at the shop or walking about the village, and the thought was daunting. What on earth would she say? Though perhaps it would be better to look the other way and preserve a dignified silence.

As the car drew up outside the pretty, rose-swathed villa owned by her grandmother, where she and her father had lived since her mum's tragic death, a tall, broad-chested figure strode out to the garden gate.

Tears sprang to her eyes, and she fumbled to push open the car door.

'Dad!' Edith squealed and ran towards him.

Her father lifted and swung her around, laughing. 'Hello, peanut!'

She was thrilled by this warm welcome, hoping it meant she had been forgiven for past sins. Her father had not taken it well when he'd discovered his daughter at the heart of local gossip. The day before she'd left, he'd barely spoken a word to her, though he had handed her an envelope containing a small amount of money, explaining that it was to help her until she could find work.

Edith's grandmother was being helped out of the car by Mr Fisher. She had been looking relieved to be home, but her eyes bulged when she saw what her son was doing. 'Do be careful, Randolph!' she exclaimed. 'You don't want to hurt her.'

'I'm all right,' Edith insisted, and then caught her father's baffled look. With a sinking heart, she realised that he didn't know the awful truth yet. Gran had obviously not told him about the baby, despite having dashed off a quick note to let him know they would be returning together.

To hide her feelings, Edith turned quickly to shake Mr Fisher's hand and give Betsy a friendly hug, hoping she wouldn't think her too cheeky. 'Thank you so much for driving us home,' she told them, helping Mr Fisher with the luggage in the boot compartment. 'It was very kind of you both to let us tag along.'

'Indeed it was,' her grandmother agreed, adding warmly, 'Would you and Mrs Fisher like to come inside for a cup of tea? Or even some supper?'

Betsy Fisher had not spoken much on their long journey from Dagenham to the Penzance area, but no doubt she was still feeling the loss of her baby keenly. Remembering how unhappy she had looked during their outing to Ilford, Edith hoped the poor woman would soon feel happier and start looking ahead again. Though she could guess exactly how devastating it would feel to lose a pregnancy, especially now she knew how much she wanted to keep her own baby. It would not be something anyone could easily get over.

Now Betsy gave them a wan smile, her shoulders hunched. 'Thank you, but it's getting late and we need to reach my aunt's house before dusk.'

'Yes, I'm pretty hopeless at navigating after dark,' Mr Fisher admitted with a self-deprecating laugh, and put an arm about his wife, his smile supportive. 'And Betsy's tired after the long drive. Probably best if we get her to the farm pronto.'

'Of course. Though you must come and visit us while you're down here, Betsy. I can show you around Penzance, if you like.' Edith handed her grandmother's travelling bag to her father. 'Oh, this is my dad, by the way,' she told the couple, belatedly remembering to introduce him. 'Dad, this is Mr and Mrs Fisher. Mrs Fisher is the daughter of Gran's old school friend, Mrs Hopkins.'

They exchanged a few more pleasantries, and then Mr and Mrs Fisher headed off again into the westerly glow of the setting sun.

Edith's father gave her another hug. 'It's good to have you home, my dear,' he said fondly, and then glanced down at her figure rather more dubiously. 'Though it looks like you need fresh air and exercise. You've put on a little weight in Dagenham.'

Edith bit her lip, blushing.

'I'll go inside and make us something to eat,' her grandmother muttered and limped up the path to the front door. It was clear that she expected Edith to admit her embarrassing situation on her own . . .

Holding a bag in his hand as well as under one arm, her dad watched her go as he held the garden gate open for Edith. He was looking confused. 'Your grandmother seems out of sorts. Is her bad hip troubling her again? Or have I said something wrong?'

Oh dear . . .

'Dad,' Edith began shakily, trying to be brave, though she felt far from it, 'there's something I need to tell you.'

CHAPTER THIRTEEN

Only a few weeks after accepting her offer on the caff, Ron threw a farewell party for his friends and regular customers, and then departed, leaving Sheila just a few scribbled notes on how to understand his accounting and ordering books. She'd almost not gone to work that first day after Ron had left, terrified by the idea of being her own boss and giving the orders instead of taking them. She'd also feared what people might say, now the caff was being run by a woman on her own. Thankfully, the regulars had turned up as usual for their cooked breakfasts and afternoon tea and cakes, and nobody had complained at seeing Sheila behind the counter instead of Ron. Though, due to being short-handed, and having to do all the cooking and serving herself those first few days, a few had grumbled over the extra-long waiting time on hot meals.

Still, there'd been Judith's kindness to cheer her up, in bed with a bad head cold but sending in her grandson with a card and bunch of flowers on her first day to wish her 'Good luck!' and Constable Hobbs had made a habit of stopping by most days to say hello, checking that none of them awful Blackshirts were still making trouble for her. To her relief though, those bullies seemed to have slunk away into the shadows since that incident at the park, some of their mates having been arrested for the attack on poor Betsy.

Making an offer for the caff, dealing with the bank and the solicitors and the endless bleedin' paperwork, had left Sheila quaking in her boots. She'd never done anything like that before, and she'd thought at first that Betsy, at least, would be there for her throughout the transition. Betsy was an experienced waitress, and a dutiful daughter, and she'd always been there to back her mum when times were difficult. So the discovery that her eldest had not only been caught shoplifting but had been sent away for a few months' rest in the country on doctor's orders had been shocking. She felt nothing but sympathy for her daughter, who had clearly been left in a state by her dad's death and the loss of her baby. But the timing of her daughter's departure for Cornwall had been awkward, leaving her alone and unsupported at a time when she would dearly have loved Betsy by her side.

Ernest had also gone to Cornwall with Betsy, at least for a week or two to see her settled on Maggie's farm. But when he came back, Sheila knew he would be working at the plant as usual. So she could not rely on him for much help. Lily might be able to work some weekends to earn a little pocket money but Alice was too easily lost in a book to remember her duties. It was a shame that Edith had been forced to go home. It seemed the customers had grown accustomed to her lively, humorous presence about the place. Although none had so far admitted to missing Ron, a few had remarked on Edith's absence with regret. Put on the spot by Mr Archer,

Sheila had told a fib, saying the girl's gran had been taken ill, so she'd been asked to return to Cornwall.

She had at least procured the services of a new cook. Gordon had recently been let go from a busy restaurant in Ilford, mainly for using uncouth language and drinking while on duty. Weighing up the needs of her kitchen against this dodgy behaviour, she'd agreed to give him a month's trial, and within a few days felt sure she'd made the right decision. Gordon might be a diamond in the rough, with unkempt black hair, a crooked nose – broken twice during pub brawls, he had admitted without shame – and a shuffling gait that indicated a busted knee too, but his cooking was excellent, and he had a cheeky way about him that she liked. With his help, she was managing the caff with just the two of them, but it was a stretch.

Her excitement at finding a new cook had worn thin though when she found herself at the sharp end of sorting out a new menu that worked to his strengths and ordering fresh ingredients for the kitchen. Then there were the more difficult tasks that Ron had always handled, such as paying wages, totting up the daily takings, dealing with awkward customers and the local business guild, and making sure the caff opened up at seven o'clock sharp every morning and was locked again by late afternoon. She'd even had to deal with a new insurance policy, and hadn't known how to answer even half the questions asked of her. Henry had always dealt with insurance and legal matters like that and, to be honest, most of it left her head spinning. But she struggled on, trying to make sure she kept a strict account of everything coming in and going out of the business at least, to avoid problems with the taxman later.

'Gawd blimey . . . I never knew there'd be so much paperwork involved in running a caff,' she complained to Violet, dropping her head in her hands one night. 'I don't think I can keep this up. It's going to kill me.'

'I've never known you shrink from a challenge before, Mum,' her youngest daughter exclaimed, clearly surprised. 'If I ever said that about my own work, you'd tear a strip off me, tell me to buck my ideas up and stop whinging.' At Sheila's sharp glance, she'd grinned. 'Oh, I'm not suggesting that *you're* whinging. But I do know you can manage that caff with one hand tied behind your back.'

'Well, maybe you're right.' Sheila was flattered. 'But it's bloomin' hard work, dealing with all the things Ron used to do, *on top* of dealing with customers, carrying out orders, and even pitching in with the washing-up too. I need an extra pair of hands.' She groaned. 'Though three or four pairs would be better.'

'Ron managed with only one or two staff.'

Sheila pulled a face. 'Yes, and he'd been running the place for years. I'm so wet behind the ears, I might as well be swimming the bleedin' Channel.'

'I've not been happy at the factory for a while now,' Violet mused, looking thoughtful. 'Most of the blokes there are all right but a few keep asking me out and won't take no for an answer, and I'm just not interested in men at the moment. How about if I were to give up my job and come work at the caff with you?'

'Oh, love . . . Are you sure?' Sheila had been feeling so lonely of late. More than anything she wanted to have her daughter by her side, waiting on customers while Gordon cooked the food, and she prepared the orders and kept everything spick and span. But not if it meant Violet ruining her job prospects for the future.

Violet shrugged. 'You're me mum,' she said, looking embarrassed. 'Of course I'll help you out.'

So Violet stepped into her older sister's shoes without complaint, and Sheila was deeply grateful to her, aware that the meagre pay packet she could offer wasn't even close to what Vi had been earning at the factory.

One Saturday, Sheila stood over a family of squabbling youngsters and their harassed-looking mum as the kids argued over what to order for lunch, while Violet cleared the dirty tables and did a stack of washing-up. Through the open hatch into the kitchen, she could see – and hear – her new cook, Gordon, who was whistling a sea shanty as he fried a panful of whiting in batter, to be served with scraps and a pickled egg to Mr Archer, who loved to drop the scraps under the table for his old dog.

'May I suggest our Saturday special?' Sheila said to the mother, pointing to the chalkboard above the counter. 'Whiting and chipped potatoes with either gherkins or a pickled egg.' She winked at the youngest child. 'My cook can do you some tasty scraps o' batter too, if you're partial.'

Violet, who was not the best washer-upper in the world, fumbled a wet plate and dropped it. Mr Archer chuckled and made his usual joke about them needing to sack the juggler. Gordon peered through the hatch and gave Violet a grin. 'Don't worry, love . . . Plenty more where that came from,' he told her.

'Drop any more of them, Vi, and the next one'll be coming out of your pay,' Sheila called tartly.

'Two whiting specials, please, divided over three plates,

and with a bowl of scraps for the little one,' the woman decided at last, having counted the coins in her purse, and then turned to remonstrate with her eldest. 'And you can stop hitting your sister!'

The caff door jangled just as Sheila was handing their fish order through the hatch for Gordon to deal with. It was her friend Judith, laden down with bags as always.

'Hello, love,' Sheila said warmly, moving to greet her. 'I've not seen you since Henry's funeral. Thank you for the flowers. I hope you're over your head cold.'

'Bless you, yes. I would have come sooner to congratulate you on taking over from Ron . . . But my daughter fell sick, and I stayed home to nurse her and look after the grandkids.' Judith gave her a sympathetic smile. 'How are *you* though, my dearest Sheila? It was such a wonderful wake for your husband, thank you for inviting me. And so many mourners . . . Your Henry will be sadly missed.'

'Yes, every day is a struggle,' Sheila admitted, swallowing hard. 'But what can you do, eh? Can't stay in bed all day, bawling your eyes out. So here I am, doing me job and putting on a smile.'

'And such a lovely smile too.' Judith beamed at her. She was wearing a bright pink head scarf knotted at the nape of her neck, and a deep blue cotton dress that hugged her generous hips. A vast striped canvas bag hung in the crook of her elbow, bulging with shopping, and she opened this with a twinkle in her eye. 'Now, I have something for you. I hope you don't mind.'

Sheila was astonished. 'For me?'

'A special recipe that my grandmother and great-grandmother used to make back in Jamaica. I remember watching them cook it when I was just a little girl, with the palm trees blowing in the wind and the scent of mimosa. Ah, those were the days,' she said wistfully. 'And this recipe... Whenever I make this dish, the taste takes me straight back to Kingston. I know you're going to love it too.' She handed over a folded sheet of paper. 'It's Jamaican rice and peas.'

Gratefully, Sheila unfolded the recipe and read it briefly. 'Oh, Judith, this sounds delicious.'

'You might not be able to find all the ingredients. Though you can use beans instead of peas. And if you can't find fresh coconut milk, tinned is better than nothing,' Judith laughed. 'It's a good hearty family meal, just right for when everyone is gathered around the table in the evenings. Let me know how you get on with it.'

'I know a bloke down the market who can get me some of these ingredients, don't you fret.'

'It's the least I can do.' Judith took her usual table, glancing nervously out of the window. 'Have you had any more trouble from those young men . . . What are they called again?'

'The Blackshirts?'

'That's right, Blackshirts. Hitler supporters. Though I can't for the life of me understand why they haven't been banned. Why, there's hardly anyone with a good word to say about Hitler except that lot. They've attacked my son, you know, and even my young grandson, right in the street. And nobody does anything about it. I suppose they're afraid to speak up. Or maybe they think us Jamaicans aren't worth bothering about.' She shook her head in disgust. 'Anyway, when I heard what happened to your daughter Betsy, I couldn't believe it . . . Those thugs put her in the hospital?' Judith shuddered. 'That's downright wicked.'

Sheila nodded. 'But at least the ones who hurt Betsy have been arrested. Same as them who knocked my Henry down and killed him.' Sheila sank down at the table opposite her friend, knowing some justice had been done but feeling miserable all the same. 'Only, the police say it's not against the law for them to be marching and carrying their banners,' she added in a low, disapproving voice. 'Not so long as they don't wear that horrible uniform.'

Judith's dark eyes had widened with outrage. '*Not* against the law?' she repeated. 'I never heard the like. Why, all the newsreels say we're on the brink of war with Germany.' Judith gave a sudden sob. 'Oh, Sheila . . . Do you think that's right? Are we going to war?'

'I can't see how else we can get Hitler to stop trying to take over the whole of Europe. If we don't take a stand here in Britain, give it six months, maybe a year, and him and his jackboot soldier boys will be jumping in boats or flying across the Channel to invade us.' Sheila shook her head. 'I never thought I'd see this 'appening again . . . Another war in Europe? It ain't right. You'd think we'd all have learnt a lesson after last time. But them Nazis won't listen to reason. Not with men like Hitler running the show.' She heaved a deep sigh. 'Well, not much you and I can do about it. Your usual order, is it?'

'Thank you, yes.'

'I won't be a jiffy, love.' Sheila got up with an effort. 'As you can see, I've got Violet helping me out these days. And Gordon in the kitchen. He'll be ever so pleased to see this recipe. I'll take it to him now.'

Judith turned an amazed face in her direction. 'You're planning to give my old recipe *to your cook*?'

'Why not? Sounds like it would make a tasty special of the week. You don't mind, do you? Or is it a family secret?'

'Lord, no. But surely you won't really be asking him to make a Jamaican dish for your customers?' Judith burst into laughter, her whole body shaking with amusement. 'I can't imagine their faces when they see it on the specials board.'

'Be good for them to try something different,' Sheila told her stubbornly, and hurried off to fetch her friend her usual serving of thick buttered toast with a mug of tea.

She showed the recipe to Gordon, who nodded, agreeable to the suggestion despite the unusual ingredients. 'Looks good. I'll cook whatever you pay me to cook,' he said, and shoved the recipe in his pocket. 'I'll give it a try next week.'

'You're a star, Gordon,' Sheila told him, already fond of the man who had stepped so ably into Ron's larger-than-life shoes. Not only was he a good cook, he never pulled a face or gave her any lip, as some men in his line of work might well have done, finding themselves taking orders from a woman.

He came out to snatch a quick cuppa between orders and, having finished her meal, Judith sat with him chatting about how to prepare the dish. Violet was mopping the floor after a child had thrown up, no doubt having eaten too much and bothered by the summer heat. Schools had just broken up for the long holiday and there were kids everywhere.

Half listening to Judith's detailed instructions, Sheila carried out half an order of hot drinks for ten very thirsty workmen who'd popped in for a tea break while digging the street. She turned briskly on her way back for the rest, only to find Judith coming towards her with a tray of steaming drinks in her hands.

'Goodness. Are them the other teas and coffees for these gents?'

'Violet was busy, so I thought I'd give you a hand.' Judith nodded, handing over the tray with an embarrassed look. 'I hope I'm not treading on your toes.'

'Bless you, no danger of that.' Sheila grinned at the woman. 'Maybe I should be offering you a job.'

'I did used to work at a large hotel in Kingston, when I was about Edith's age. A long time ago now though.' Judith's beaming smile swept the caff. 'Where is Edith? Her day off, is it?'

'She's gone back to Cornwall.' Feeling awkward, Sheila took the tray of drinks over to the workmen. 'Her gran needed her to go home,' she added, and hurriedly began wiping down the table Judith had been using.

'So it wasn't because she was in the family way?' Judith murmured and smiled when Sheila turned to stare at her. 'Ah, you thought I hadn't noticed? But it was plain as the nose on your face. Well, I'm glad she's home with her grandmother. Home is the best place for a girl in that situation.' Judith nodded wisely. 'I'd best get on, Sheila. Still plenty to do today. Lovely seeing you.'

Sheila waved goodbye and turned to find Violet leaning on her mop, deep in conversation with young Fred, one of their new regulars, a skinny lad with slicked-back fair hair and a big smile.

She stopped, taken aback.

Fred, who was seventeen, had been born with a club foot that made it painful for him to walk far, so that he tended to limp and drag his right foot. Not willing to let that hold him back, ever since leaving school he'd worked a vegetable barrow in the nearby market with his dad. He often came into the caff with his dad after they'd closed up the barrow, for a bite to eat or a cuppa, but more recently Sheila had noticed him hanging about the caff on his own, not ordering anything, just chatting to Violet. Now, seeing the way Fred was twisting his cloth cap nervously in his hands while stammering something to her daughter, she guessed what drew him back here, time and again. He had a crush on Violet, poor boy. Much good it would do him, for her daughter was ten years older than him and never looked twice at anyone these days.

'Hello, Fred,' she interrupted chattily, on her way behind the counter with an armful of dirty plates. 'How's your dad?'

'Very well, thank you, Mrs Hopkins. Still fretting himself to death over Herr Hitler though.' With a muttered word of thanks to Violet, Fred collected the sandwich she'd wrapped in brown paper to take away for his lunch. 'It don't matter me telling him everything will be all right. Dad's got it in his head that he'll never see me again.'

'Sorry? *Never see you again?*' Violet repeated, her brows tugging together as she looked up from her mopping, baffled.

'Dad's worried that if there's a war, I'll be called up once I turn eighteen, and then get myself killed on the battlefield,' Fred admitted, looking embarrassed.

Sheila couldn't blame his father for being worried. She'd thought much the same about Ernest, for either he'd be considered an enemy, being part German, and locked up, or the government would demand that he enlisted straightaway, for his skills in translation. But given the boy's disability, she didn't think it likely he'd be called on to fight.

Gordon came out of the kitchen. 'There's plenty will be

happy to go and fight the Hun, if need be,' he said gruffly, though his look was sympathetic as he eyed the lad's heavy, custom-made right boot. 'But they'll send seasoned soldiers first. Not . . . Not boys.'

Fred flushed and shuffled his feet. 'I'll be eighteen soon and I don't care what my dad says. Anyway, I ain't no coward.'

'Nobody said you were,' Violet pointed out, putting away her mop.

'I'm ready for military training too,' Fred went on defiantly, 'when my time comes. My cousin Ed just turned eighteen and he got his papers through to do his basic last month. He's got a lazy eye and they took him, no questions asked. If he can do it, so can I.' The young barrow boy thrust up his chin and slapped his cap back on his head. 'I've shot rabbits before too, so I know how to handle a rifle.'

'It's one thing shooting rabbits, lad, and quite another shooting a man.' Gordon collected a container of eggs from under the counter and went back into the kitchen, whistling.

'Let's hope it don't come to that, eh?' Sheila said briskly. Her heart ached at the thought of boys going off to war, knowing that some would never come home again. She'd been at school with lads who'd bravely gone off to fight the Boers and were then conscripted again for the Great War. The knowledge that all them lads who'd survived fighting in South Africa, only to end up buried somewhere in the fields of France fifteen years later . . . it didn't bear thinking about. 'You missed a bit there, Violet. Best get the mop out again and have another go.' She gave Fred a nod as Violet turned away for the mop and bucket. 'Enjoy your lunch, son.'

Fred hesitated, his eager gaze on Violet. But when she failed to look his way, he gave up and slowly headed off. On the threshold, he stopped to hold the door open for the two Miss Cohens, spinster sisters in their seventies who were much respected in the Jewish community and had lived in Dagenham for the past two decades, elderly aunts to a lively family of nieces and nephews and great-nieces and great-nephews. The two ladies smiled at him fondly and he grinned back, exchanging a few words with them before leaving.

Sheila shook her head, watching Fred lope off down the street. 'He won't get called up to fight if there's a war. Not with a club foot. All the same, I daresay he'll find something useful to do. Fred's that kind of lad. Dependable, determined . . .' She studied her daughter thoughtfully. 'And he's got a crush on you, my girl.'

'I know,' Violet said simply.

Sheila sighed. 'Tell me to mind my own business, love, but when do you think you might start courting again? It's been a couple of years now since . . . Well, you know.'

'Don't be daft, Mum.' Violet mopped the floor, swabbing like her life depended on it. 'I'm not interested in anything like that. I lost Leonard, and that's that.'

Sheila raised her brows but said nothing to this, turning to welcome the Cohen sisters with a friendly smile. 'How are you today, ladies? Good news, your favourite table's free. I suppose word must have gone around that you was coming in. Let's get you comfortable, eh?' She gave them a wink, and the two elderly sisters laughed and nodded, following her to their preferred table under the wall clock.

Sheila turned to ask Violet to bring over the menus, her manner bright and breezy. But secretly she was thinking that enough time had passed since Leonard's death, and her youngest daughter ought to start living her life again. It wasn't as though she'd been married to the unfortunate young man, after all. Besides, with another war on the horizon, everyone needed to seize a little happiness while they could.

Violet wasn't yet ready to listen to common sense though, and perhaps she never would be. Perhaps she'd end up like the Cohen sisters, a kindly spinster aunt to Lily and Alice, and maybe a great-aunt to their children too, until her dying day.

But Sheila knew from last time around that war had the power to change everything. Even the most stubborn hearts and minds . . .

CHAPTER FOURTEEN

'Oh, what a paradise!' Betsy said to her husband the morning after they'd arrived at Aunt Margaret's farm, set on a hillside in rural Cornwall. She and Ernest stood side by side in the farmyard, breathing in the fresh country air. To one side, the sea was a glittering blue ribbon, to the other peaceful green fields stretched away as far as the eye could see. 'Blimey, I can smell salt . . . How amazing to live so close to the sea that you can smell it. My aunt and uncle are so lucky.'

'Hmm . . . There are other things I can smell,' Ernest murmured, wrinkling his nose, 'and they're not quite so pleasant. But yes, a paradise.' He looked at her searchingly. 'I wish I could stay with you, Betsy. But I can't get the time off work. It was hard enough asking for the time to bring you down here and stay a few days to see you settled. Things are so tough at the plant right now.' His eyes were troubled. 'It's the prospect of war. Everyone is so agitated, not sure what to expect.'

'Can you blame them?' Betsy shivered.

'Not at all, but it doesn't make life any easier when people are living in fear.' He put an arm about her, holding her close. 'I know you've been afraid too. I wish I could take that fear away from you. But, to tell you the truth, I'm a little afraid too.'

'Oh, Ernest!'

'But there are blessings to count. We still have each other, and we have two wonderful daughters. And I love you.'

Betsy gazed up at him gratefully. He always knew the right thing to say. 'Even after all the trouble I've caused you?'

'Trouble?'

'That stupid incident with the earrings . . .' She felt so ashamed and embarrassed, she hung her head. 'I still don't understand what happened.'

'You made a mistake. People make mistakes. The mistakes are not what's important. The important thing is to set things right.' Ernest shook his head. 'All you can do is live with the consequences and work towards a better future.'

'Then that's what I'll do,' she whispered. 'I . . . I want to be happy again.'

'And you will be, I promise.' He raised his head, once more breathing in the country air. 'Ah, this place is so easy on the eye. And you'll soon grow accustomed to the, erm, more interesting aromas of the countryside.' He grinned. 'Plus, I'm hoping you'll soon settle in here. Your Aunt Maggie is not the friendliest woman in the world, but still less formidable than I remembered.'

Her mouth tightened, remembering how her aunt and uncle had greeted them the night before, clearly unhappy at being disturbed so late in the evening. The room she was sharing with Ernest was cramped and musty, and the window looked out over some kind of muck pile. It was hard not to think the decision to accommodate them there had been deliberate.

But beggars couldn't be choosers, and she was genuinely grateful to her aunt for having agreed to house her at such short notice. All the same, it was clear she was not completely welcome, and also that things were not wonderful between her aunt and uncle.

'I wish she hadn't married Stanley,' she whispered, though the farmer had gone out early onto the land and was nowhere in sight. 'He seemed like such a charmer in the beginning. But now I think he's rather horrid.' Betsy pulled a face, admitting, 'I didn't like the way he looked at me as we were going up the stairs last night.'

Ernest blinked. 'What you mean?'

'Oh, it was probably nothing,' she said hurriedly, not wanting to cause a row between him and her uncle. 'I was just tired, that's all. And he had every right to be annoyed at us rolling in at such a late hour.' She stretched up to kiss him on the lips, smiling. 'I don't want you to worry about me. Like you say, I'll soon settle in. Anyway, the girls need you back at home. They can't have both parents absent for weeks . . . And by the time I come home, I'll be back to my old self.'

'I'll hold you to that,' he said. 'Meanwhile, I promised that we'd have a few days' holiday before I head back to Dagenham, and I meant it. So, what would you like to do first? Visit the beach? Porthcurno is that way,' he said, pointing further along the coast, 'or we could drive back the way we came, and pay a proper visit to Penzance. There were some interesting little shops in the centre, and I rather liked the look of St Michael's Mount . . . Not that I had much time to admire it as we drove past.'

'It looks like something out of an old Cornish folktale,' she agreed enthusiastically, 'like the ones Mum used to read me and Violet when we were kids. I'd love to see the castle up close. Though,' she added thoughtfully, 'Maggie says the beach at Porthcurno is perfect for swimming . . . White sands, she says, and often deserted. Do you know, I can't remember the last time I spent the day on a beach?'

'Southend-on-Sea, three years ago, with Lily and Alice. Though you only paddled up to your knees, as I recall.'

'While you swam and splashed about with the girls,' she agreed, laughing. 'Gawd, yes, I remember. Though Porthcurno sounds nothing like Southend.'

'No, thank goodness. No deafening brass bands, or endless amusement arcades and fish and chip shops and ice cream sellers.' He smiled. 'Cornwall seems a very different place . . . It feels as though we've stepped back in time.'

'I wish we could,' she admitted wistfully.

He nodded seriously. 'We've had some difficult days lately, and there may be even harder times ahead, if the BBC bulletins are to be believed. But we're going to make it, Betsy,' he insisted, taking her hand. 'You and I and the girls. We will deal with whatever happens and come through this stronger, I promise you.'

'How can you promise such a thing?' she cried, pulling away from him. 'If this country goes to war with Germany . . .'

Her husband took a deep breath and closed his eyes but was smiling again a moment later when he reopened them. 'I know it feels impossible right now, love. But I have to believe that everything is going to be all right. If I didn't, I would probably go mad.'

'Like me, you mean?' The question had been spoken lightly but she half meant it.

'You are *not* mad, Betsy. It's the world that's mad, not you.'

'I wish I could believe that.' She hugged herself, wishing she could feel properly happy again. But there was something deep inside that kept her cold and numb, like she had a block of ice for a heart these days. 'Anyway, if that's true, how does a person live in a world that's mad?'

'By taking each day as it comes and enjoying the good times. Talking of which . . . *Eeny . . . meeny . . . miny . . . moe!*' Ernest said, pretending to choose between destinations using the old nursery rhyme. He seized her hand and began to pull her back towards the farmhouse, chuckling at her protests. 'No, come along, Mrs Fisher. I've decided where to start our holiday, and I need you to beg your aunt for a picnic basket and a rug. We're going to Porthcurno Beach.'

Ernest drove the big Ford cautiously along narrow winding Cornish lanes, since banked hedgerows on either side made it impossible to see if anyone was coming the other way. The verges were all bright with swathes of tall, feathery grasses and dancing summer flowers. Thankfully, the coastal route seemed deserted except for a few farmers. Once, they met a flock of sheep coming the other way, being ushered between fields by a toothless shepherd with a crook in hand and two slinking dogs to nip at any stragglers. They also passed a hay wain, the driver having kindly pulled in to let them pass, and witnessed a horse-drawn plough turning soil in the fields, which enchanted Betsy. She had stared after it, while a chugging tractor had Ernest's head turning with professional interest. The car slipped gracefully through shaded, tree-lined hollows and splashed through a shallow ford before climbing again, the road running briefly alongside the sea itself.

'Oh, Ernest, look!' Betsy clasped her hands together, the sight of all that smooth endless blue water leaving her breathless. 'How different it is from Dagenham. I wish we could live here with the girls. They'd love it so much.'

'Yes, but unfortunately I know nothing about either farming or fishery, and I'm afraid those are the two key professions out here in the sticks.'

'Penzance is a town. Maybe there's a garage there that could do with a brilliant mechanic. Or even a salesman. People buy cars in Cornwall, don't they?'

'True, but what about the girls? If you brought them down here, they'd end up marrying farmers, most likely.' He drummed long fingers on the steering wheel, studying the road ahead. 'Nothing wrong with that, of course. We need farmers. But I suspect Lily enjoys her shopping trips rather too much to be happy buried alive in the middle of nowhere. As for Alice . . .' He smiled indulgently; Alice was his favourite, even though he tried to hide that for Lily's sake. 'My little bookworm could have a glittering career ahead if she studies hard enough. And I'm not sure Cornwall would be the best place for her to shine.'

Betsy was surprised. 'Alice is a clever girl, I grant you. But a *career*? What kind of career?'

He shrugged. 'She could do anything, frankly. My father's side of the family were all academics back in Germany, and she seems to have inherited their brains. All I'm certain of is that Alice deserves the very best libraries and teachers we can afford, and a quiet provincial town like Penzance, beautiful though it is, is unlikely to be able to furnish them.

Even less so if we settled out here in open farmland, miles from anywhere.' He grimaced. 'I've often thought that maybe if I made a push to earn more money, I could find her a good private tutor. Improve her chances of a better life. If we lived here, that would never happen.'

Catching a note of self-accusation in his voice, Betsy said urgently, 'You're a good father and an excellent provider, Ernest. The girls and I have never wanted for anything.'

But as soon as those words were out, Betsy felt silent, staring at the passing countryside in sudden trepidation, reminded of the sapphire earrings she'd somehow pocketed in Ilford.

She knew she hadn't taken them because she'd wanted them, or even because she felt aggrieved at not being able to afford such expensive jewellery. She still suffered a slight shock whenever she thought of that day, for it was a mystery to her why she had done it at all. But she had the impression that Ernest had not discounted those as motives, that he suspected her of wishing they had more money for silly trinkets like those earrings. It wasn't true, of course. But if he did fear that, and blamed himself for her moment of madness, it was all her own fault.

The thought plunged her back into depression, all the brightness and colour drained from the world. She stared at dark looming trees and oppressive, endless fields. She was nothing but a burden to her husband. And now she'd abandoned her children.

To her relief, Ernest did not appear to have noticed her abrupt shift in mood. 'Here we are . . . Porthcurno.' He pumped the brakes with alarm as they sailed rather too fast down a steep hill into the village. They looked about for signage to the beach. It was a tiny, sleepy place, barely a soul in sight, just a solitary sheep that wandered across the road, bleating mournfully.

'I wonder if that sheep knows where the beach is,' Ernest murmured, slowing to a crawl as it passed in front of the Ford's bonnet.

'Stop, please! There's a village shop.' Betsy felt an urgent need to escape before he noticed the tears in her eyes and started asking questions. She waited impatiently until he'd pulled into the side of the road, then jumped out of the car, her head turned away as she rummaged for her purse in her handbag. 'Erm, I'll check if they have any bottles of pop to go with our picnic. Unless you'd prefer beer?'

He shook his head. 'Pop is fine. And while you're in there, ask the way to Porthcurno Beach. The sea looks to be just over that crest, so I imagine we can walk from here.' He got out too and opened the boot to retrieve the picnic basket and rug Maggie had lent them.

The door to the shop was propped open, no doubt due to the heat. Betsy wandered inside, amused by how dark and old-fashioned the decor was, with dusty wooden shelving and ancient, cracked signs advertising brands that had long since gone out of business. She doubted the place had been refurbished for twenty years or more. But there was a display of lemonade and ginger beer bottles, and punnets of dark red cherries stacked by the antique till, each punnet labelled Postbridge Farm, no doubt a local farmer's produce. The cherries looked delicious.

As she carried two lemonade bottles to the counter, she picked up a punnet of cherries too, and popped a ripe ruby-red fruit into her mouth on impulse while waiting to be served.

'I saw that, Missy,' a rough voice said from the depths of the shop.

She jumped, staring around in amazement. 'Sorry?' A large, shambling man, shirtsleeves rolled up to his elbows, came out of the shadows, his bright eyes fixed on her face. Shame-faced, she spat the cherry stone out into her hand and pushed it into her pocket. 'I was planning to pay for them. The cherries, I mean. They just looked so bloomin' good, I couldn't resist. I weren't stealing, honest.'

His grin was lopsided. 'Not from around these parts, are you? That be a London accent.' He nodded, looking her up and down. 'Summer visitor, I daresay.'

Betsy took a deep breath, relieved that the shopkeeper didn't seem genuinely annoyed. In her current fragile state, it might have been the last straw. One of those men whose bark is worse than his bite, she thought.

'Close enough. I've come down from Dagenham. That's a little way east of London.' She smiled shyly. 'I'm staying at my aunt's farm. It's a few miles back along the road to Penzance. Margaret and Stanley Chellew, do you know them?'

'Everyone hereabouts knows the Chellews.' He wasn't smiling anymore though, she noticed.

Disheartened, she fumbled to open her purse. 'What do I owe you? Oh, and which way is the beach, please? We couldn't see any signs.'

'That's because there aren't any signs.' His belly shook as he laughed. 'Our best-kept secret, that beach is. Besides, it's used by the telegraph men, and they don't much like folk going down there.'

'Telegraph men?' She was confused.

'Porthcurno Beach is where all them undersea cables come in. They were first laid in Victoria's reign, back in my granddaddy's day, to run messages between Britain and India, using Morse code. These days they carry telegraphs from all over the world.' He nodded at her amazement. 'Eastern House is where they pick up the messages and send 'em on to London. You'll see it on your way to the beach. Yes, and the telegraph hut where they wind in the cables . . .'

'Goodness, I had no idea.'

He gave her a rambling explanation of how to find the right path to the beach, which she found hard to follow but was too embarrassed to ask him to repeat the directions.

'I'm Arnie, miss,' he told her, handing over the change. 'Mr Arnold Newton.'

'I'm *Mrs* Fisher,' she said in return, too awkward to add her first name, and hoped he wouldn't think her standoffish. 'It was nice to meet you, Mr Newton. Thank you so much for the directions.'

'You can thank me when you've found the beach,' he said, laughing again. 'Most folk can't manage it and come back to ask again.'

She readily believed him. Hurrying back out into bright sunshine though, she was relieved to see her husband studying a pocketbook map of the area that he'd bought on the way through Bodmin.

'Cherries? You clever wife, you know how I adore them.' He popped a shiny red cherry into his mouth and chomped absentmindedly. 'Now, I could be wrong,' he said indistinctly, 'but from this map, I think it's best to cut across this field here, keeping to the footpath, and we should eventually meet the path to the beach.'

'That about tallies with what the shopkeeper told me. Though it's hard to be sure,' she admitted, feeling foolish, 'as I could barely understand one word in three, his accent was so strong.'

He tucked the bottles of lemonade into the picnic basket, covered them with the rug, settled his hat on his head, and nodded her to follow him. 'This will be an adventure – that much I know.'

She told him what Mr Newton had explained about the underwater cables and the telegraph hut, and he listened with fascination. 'How marvellous. I wonder if we would be allowed to look inside the hut.' Then he frowned. 'No, best not.'

'You can always ask.'

'A man with a German name and the hint of an accent, asking to look at a site of sensitive British infrastructure on the eve of war?' He shook his head. 'I'd rather not be arrested.'

'I hadn't thought of that.' She felt nervous. 'Should we go elsewhere, do you think?'

'No, I'm sure it will be fine.' Ernest took her hand. 'Please don't worry, *Liebling*. I'm sorry I mentioned it. I didn't mean to upset you.'

It was certainly an adventure, Betsy thought, but the beach itself was well worth the difficult terrain. The path down to the beach was overgrown with nettles and brambles for much of the way, though forked into a rather better-kept path, marked *Private*, that led to the telegraph cable hut, situated slightly higher up. They kept heading down, until at last, under full sun, they clambered down a narrow gully through sandy rocks and came out onto hot white sands with an emerald sea glittering ahead of them, empty to the horizon.

They stood speechless on the sands for a few minutes, hand in hand, just blinking at the brightness. Then Ernest picked out a spot further along the shore, where some rocks provided a little shade from the relentless heat, and they set off, their shoes soon heavy with sand, the noonday sun beating down on their shoulders.

'This is a very special place.' Ernest looked around at the sea and high cliffs with a delighted smile. 'You're right, it would be *wonderful* to live here.'

'But impractical?'

He laughed, nodding. 'Quite impossible, yes. But perfect for a summer holiday. The girls would love this beach, certainly. We must save up and bring them to Cornwall next year.'

His smile faded though, and he said no more about that, preoccupied with spreading out the rug under the rocks for them to sit on. Betsy said nothing but knew what he was thinking. There was a war coming, and nobody knew what the world would look like in another year . . .

When the time came for Ernest to return to Dagenham, a few days later, Betsy thought her heart would break. She clung to her husband for as long as she could. Then let him go and said urgently, 'Give my love to the girls. I love you so much, Ernie . . . I'm going to miss you. I wish you didn't have to go. You will tell the girls I love them, won't you?'

'Of course I will,' he told her with obvious difficulty, then kissed her briefly on the lips and climbed into the car. 'I will see you in a month or two. Whenever you're better.' He started the engine and drove away, an intense look on his face. At the farm gates, he raised a hand in farewell before pulling out onto the road.

She couldn't see the big Ford above the high hedgerows, but listened to the engine note with tears in her eyes until all she could hear was birdsong and the lowing of cattle.

She felt lost and alone now he was gone. And she ached to see her kids again. But she couldn't risk going home before she was 'better', as Ernest had put it. So this must be her home for now.

Back inside the farmhouse, Maggie was kneading bread dough in the warm kitchen. She looked up, sharp-eyed, as Betsy stumbled in. 'Don't you fret, love, we'll soon have you back to your old self. And them girls of yours will be fine with Vi and your mum to look after them.' She slapped the soft slab of dough over in a cloud of flour and begun pressing her knuckles deep in the other side. 'What you need is to take your mind off things. You'll enjoy learning how to milk a cow.'

'Sorry?'

'Stanley will show you how to do the trick come milking time. Then there are chickens to feed and the coop to clean out, and I've been wanting to get all the rugs taken outside and beaten while this dry weather holds. Now you're here, you can help me, for it's hard, filthy work for one person alone.'

Betsy was stunned by this. But she had offered to help her aunt out with a few chores in exchange for her bed and board, so she could hardly say no . . .

'I . . . I've never milked a cow. Are they dangerous?'

'Bless you, no. Placid as they come, our cows.' Maggie pulled a face, pummelling the dough as though she hated it. 'So long as you don't get between a cow and a wall, you should be fine. And don't go upsetting them in the field, for a herd can turn funny with a stranger.' Noticing Betsy's horrified silence, she shook her head. 'Don't worry, you'll learn. Can you cook? Because I need to work on the farm account books, and I never get the time, what with cooking and cleaning every day for his lordship.'

Betsy got the impression she was about to become their live-in maid. But she didn't want to upset her aunt, so she said meekly, 'I'll do whatever jobs you need me to do, Aunt Maggie. I'm ever so grateful to you and Uncle Stanley for taking me in.'

'Hmm,' was all her aunt said, before pointing to a stack of linen that needed ironing and showing her where the iron and board were kept.

That night, Betsy woke with a start to find herself wet and shivering, standing alone in the rainy dark, outside in the farmyard. She could hear the whisper of the sea and the rough cry of a wild animal somewhere in the distance. A fox?

She was barefoot and wearing her nightie, she realised.

A dog was barking inside the house behind her. Then the door to the farmhouse was flung open and Uncle Stanley stood on the threshold, a lamp in hand, dog by his side.

'Be quiet!' he told the animal, who instantly subsided. He held aloft the lamp and peered out at her, the light spilling over dirty cobbles. 'What in God's name are you doing out there, girl? Get inside out of the rain, you foolish woman.' He turned to shout over his shoulder, 'It's your bloody niece, standing out in the yard in just her nightie.'

Betsy did not know what she was doing there, so couldn't explain herself. She turned hurriedly, hurting her bare feet on the cobbles, and began to pick her way carefully across the yard.

Maggie came out in a raincoat and wellington boots. 'Good gracious, I've never seen the like,' she exclaimed, tutting and helping her inside. While her husband locked up the house again, she fetched a towel so Betsy could dry herself. 'It's gone two in the morning. Whatever were you thinking, going outside in all that rain?'

'I . . . I don't know,' Betsy admitted, shamefaced. 'I'm ever so sorry I woke you and Uncle Stanley.'

'It was the dog barking that woke us. Going mad, he was.'

Stanley stamped back upstairs to bed, shooting Betsy a furious look from under bushy brows. 'Aye, and he's not the only one who's mad.'

Betsy didn't know what to say. As a child, she'd had a few episodes of sleepwalking, usually after some minor upset. But never since she'd grown up.

The next day, her aunt insisted on calling the local GP to visit her. Dr Martin was a handsome, fair-haired man of about thirty, who examined her and took a brief account of her medical history before declaring her fit and well. Physically, at least. 'Somnambulance is more to do with the mind than the body,' he told her, and studied the tablets her Dagenham GP had given her. 'These might be causing your problem, but if you need to take them in order to sleep, it's probably best to keep doing so.'

'So, there's nothing I can do to prevent another episode?'

Dr Martin seemed to catch the tremor in her voice, for he smiled and patted her hand reassuringly. She had told him in a cursory fashion about her 'funny turns' in recent months and how she'd been told to stay in the country until she felt less nervous about everyday life. 'It's unlikely to happen again, Mrs Fisher. A reaction to being here alone, I daresay. Maybe give it a few more days before you start worrying.'

'I'm already worried,' she admitted with a shaky laugh.

'Well . . .' He rubbed his chin, studying her thoughtfully. 'Frankly, I'm not convinced there's anything wrong with you that a few weeks of rest and relaxation won't fix. But I have a few medical case studies on anxiety that might prove useful . . . I'll look them up and see if there's any other suggestions I can make to help you.'

'Would you? That would be marvellous, thank you.'

Betsy walked out to his car with him and, after exchanging a few pleasantries about the fine weather, waved the doctor goodbye before returning to the farmhouse.

As Betsy stepped back inside, her aunt immediately stopped sweeping the hallway.

'You were a mite too friendly with that young man,' she told her with a disapproving air. 'Dr Martin's a single man, you know. And you're a married woman. It's not right to be giving him the come-on like that. What would your husband say if he could see you, eh?'

Betsy stared at her, speechless.

CHAPTER FIFTEEN

Edith's father had been horrified to learn that she was pregnant. Horrified and bemused.

'Expecting *a baby*?' he'd repeated blankly, glancing from his mother to his daughter as though for clarification. 'How is this possible? Are you sure you're not mistaken?'

Gran had rolled her eyes and looked pointedly at Edith.

Wringing her hands in dismay, Edith had stammered, 'You remember that young man, Percy . . . The gossip that went around the village before I left? Those awful things that Susan Teague was saying about us?' Seeing his brows tug together, his face darkening, she had finished in a rush, 'I'm afraid it was all true, Father.'

He seemed stunned. 'Are you talking about the Canadian boy?'

'Percy Grigg, yes.'

'Good God. But you told us those were just malicious rumours, that there was no truth in any of it.' His face had turned a deep, alarming red.

'I know. I'm sorry.'

'And all the while, you and that boy . . .' he'd spluttered, his chest heaving. 'Why, that little . . .' And he'd called Percy something that had left Edith cringing, while Gran clapped her hands over her ears, protesting at his language. 'Wait until I get my hands on him; he'll wish he'd never been born.' Then his face had changed, horror in his eyes. 'But young Grigg went back to . . . to Canada with his family. He's thousands of miles away. How on earth can this be sorted out in time? I can't have my daughter giving birth to an illegitimate child. It's simply unheard of.'

'Well, quite,' Gran had agreed calmly. 'The boy will have to come back from Canada and marry her, that's all.'

Edith had been miserable at the way nobody was consulting her on the topic. She was the one in trouble, after all. 'But what if Percy doesn't want to m-marry me?'

'I don't give a damn what that degenerate young fellow wants,' her father had thundered. 'He'll come back and marry you with a good grace. Or he'll have me to answer to.' He'd glared at his mother. 'You knew about this?'

'Only after Edith wrote to me.'

'So that's why you went to Dagenham.' His flush deepened. 'You told me it was to comfort your friend Sheila, who'd just been widowed, and attend her husband's funeral.'

'Which I did,' her grandmother insisted.

'But you knew about this baby. And you didn't tell me.' Edith's father turned, his accusing stare fixed on Edith now instead. 'Nor did you.'

'I thought Gran would tell you.'

'Yes, I see.' His lips tightened. 'In other words, I didn't merit being told personally. I suppose you just assumed the news would filter through to me eventually. As though I were nobody of any importance, rather than your *father*.' And he'd stalked away, shutting himself in his study for the rest of the evening.

Left guilty and in turmoil, Edith had spent a troubled night in the little bedroom she'd occupied since early childhood. On the one hand, it was good to be home again where everything was familiar and she felt safe, no longer fearing what would happen once she could no longer support herself. But her father's reaction to her news had left her despondent. She had made a mistake in not writing to tell him about the baby; she saw that now. But he seemed angry out of all proportion to her mistake in only writing to Gran . . . To live under the same roof with someone who seemed almost to hate her was a torture she could not endure for long. Yet what other option was there?

Seeing her so unhappy, Gran whisked Edith into Penzance the next day to buy 'some loose-fitting clothes' as she tactfully put it.

Edith had always disdained dresses, preferring to wear fitted skirts with smart blouses and sweaters. But those were no longer practical, the waistbands on her skirts already uncomfortably tight, and her bump clearly visible when viewed side-on. The only viable alternative were now the shapeless, tent-like dresses that her grandmother held up against her figure in every dress shop they visited, making her try them on in the privacy of a changing room to check there was 'room to grow'. The thought of it left her feeling very low.

'Couldn't I try making my own dresses?' Edith suggested, grimacing at the ugly dresses.

'You could, of course. But I seem to recall you're not

terribly handy with a Singer. And I refuse to waste hours of my life over such nonsense myself. I had enough of sewing seams and letting down hems when I was first married and we were watching the pennies.'

'Mrs Hopkins' daughter Betsy makes her own clothes.'

'Bully for her,' Gran said with a shrug, paying for their purchases. 'Trust me, you'll thank me later, when you can barely fit into anything,' she murmured in Edith's ear as they left the last shop on the high street, laden down with stylish paper bags. 'Besides, that green and yellow striped dress was really very fetching on you.'

'It made me look like an armchair,' Edith grumbled.

'Well, at least it didn't make you look pregnant,' Gran whispered, and took her arm. 'Now, after all our hard work,' she added more loudly, 'I think we deserve tea and cake, don't you?'

They stopped at a teashop near the harbour, a cosy place with Victorian-style décor and copper pots and pans hanging from the wall. It was very busy, but they found a corner table that had just been vacated by an elderly couple. Briskly, her grandmother summoned a passing waitress and ordered afternoon tea for two. Edith smiled up at the waitress, recalling how much fun it was to work in a busy café, constantly buzzing about with an order pad in hand and chatting to customers, but the woman looked straight through her before disappearing without a word.

'I know this must feel like the end of the world,' her grandmother said, noting Edith's dejected expression. 'But you aren't the first young woman to find herself in this predicament, and you won't be the last.' The afternoon tea arrived promptly on a beautiful, tiered plate display and she helped herself to a sandwich. 'I've already sent a note round to your young man's cousin but had no reply yet. However, I believe he's been away in Bristol on business for a few weeks, so that may explain it. Either that or he's still sulking that his father left one of their larger properties to Percy's father. Well, I shall send him another note and be more forthright this time. If that doesn't work, we'll have to visit them in person and hope to find someone in.'

'But you said we should be discreet.'

'This *is* being discreet,' her gran said tartly. 'But it's important that we discover Percy's address in Canada sooner rather than later, don't you agree?'

Having finished the cucumber sandwich she'd been eating, Rosalyn generously laced a scone with strawberry jam, adding a dollop of cream afterwards in the proper Cornish way, and bit into it.

'Mmm, heavenly,' she said dreamily. 'Your father's scones are always miraculous, of course. But these are pretty good too.' She stopped and frowned, staring at Edith's empty plate. 'You're not eating, dearest. Take a sandwich at least. You need to keep your strength up now. Two to feed, and all that.'

Edith's eyes widened in horror. 'Hush,' she hissed, glancing hurriedly about the busy teashop in case of eavesdroppers.

Thankfully, the place was packed with shoppers escaping the summer shower now tapping against the windows, and the buzz of conversation was so loud it was unlikely that anyone could have overheard.

All the same, she felt uneasy at the thought of discussing such private business in public. Their village was only a short way from Penzance, and it was more than likely that her grandmother would be recognised while they were in town. The last thing she needed was more gossip.

'Can we try to avoid discussing that particular topic except when we're alone together at home?' she asked in a low voice, leaning across the table.

'Very well.' Her grandmother topped up the teapot from the hot water jug. 'Though the time for such subterfuge will soon be over. Which is why it's so important for us to communicate with that young man of yours as soon as possible. You're not going to be able to pass that bump off for much longer as the result of having indulged in too many cakes. Especially when you're barely eating enough to keep a sparrow alive.'

Edith flushed unhappily, and nibbled at the edge of a sandwich. 'Perhaps the best thing would be for me to get on a boat to Canada and find him myself,' she muttered, appalled by the thought of having to flee British shores but unsure how else to deal with the situation.

'But what would you do if, having reached Canada safely and run this boy to ground, he then refused to marry you? You'd be in an even worse fix then. And much further along,' Gran whispered back significantly, 'given the time it takes for the passage from Britain.'

Edith's chin sunk onto her chest. 'I should save everyone the bother of sorting this out and just chuck myself in the sea right now.'

'Good grief.' Gran selected a heavily iced fairy cake and placed it on her plate. 'That's enough self-pity, Edith. Now, eat that cake and drink up your tea, or we shall miss the bus home.'

She tucked into her own fairy cake with alacrity, but her

sharp eyes continued to study Edith until they had paid the bill and were on their way back to the bus stop.

'I do wish you'd try to smile more, Edith. Your father and I only have your best interests at heart. You realise that, I hope?'

Wretchedly, Edith agreed that she did, but it was still hard not to feel as though the world were against her. She'd made one stupid reckless mistake, and her whole life had been turned upside down by it.

'Your father hasn't told you yet, has he?' her grandmother said as they walked, still watching her closely.

They had reached the bus stop, where a small crowd was gathering, most laden down with shopping bags, also waiting for the bus out of town. Thankfully, it had stopped raining, and the wet roads shone with sunlight.

Her heart stuttered with fright as Edith recognised three of the girls at the bus stop. Susan Teague, who'd been behind all the nasty rumours flying about the village before she left for Dagenham, and her two younger minions, Lizzie and Hermione.

Lizzie was at least sixteen and must have left school that summer, while her younger sister Hermione was only fourteen and sporting a brace. But Susan herself was nineteen, almost Edith's own age. They'd been thick as thieves for a time at school, happy to chat about boys and fashion as they strolled home from the bus stop, until a row had blown up out of nowhere over Stephen, a boy they'd both fancied. Neither of them had ever gone on a date with him, and indeed Stephen had moved to Bristol in search of work after leaving school, never to return to the village. But Susan had always insisted that Edith had deliberately been putting out lures to the boy, to ruin her chances.

Since then, they had barely spoken, and Susan had made friends instead with Lizzie and Hermione, whose home backed onto hers, despite the age difference. But no doubt she preferred friends who were too meek and inexperienced to stand up to her bullying ways . . . Now all three were looking in her direction with fascinated amusement, particularly Susan, whose bright blue stare was intimidating.

'I'm sorry, Gran, what . . . what did you say?'

Gran had also seen her tormentors. She deliberately linked her arm with Edith's. 'I said, your father has clearly not told you *his* news yet. Otherwise, I'm sure you would have mentioned it by now. Though I imagine your announcement put everything else out of his mind.'

They were standing at the end of the queue for the bus, out of earshot of those three girls, so long as they kept their voices down. Edith turned a wondering face towards her grandmother. 'His news?' she repeated in a whisper. 'I don't know what you're talking about. What kind of news?'

'That dreadful man!' The older woman tutted loudly. 'Before I went to bed last night, I told him to speak to you first thing in the morning. You know I never get up for breakfast if I can avoid it, so I couldn't check that he'd obeyed my instructions. But I had hoped he would have given you the news before we went out shopping, at least.'

'Gran, you're worrying me now . . . Please tell me what this is about.'

Rosalyn glanced cautiously towards the three girls, and then murmured in her ear, 'It's top secret, that's what it is. Your father is going away and I'm not sure when he'll be back. You see, he's been asked to return to service. Because of this business with Hitler, you understand.'

'Return to service?' Edith repeated in a whisper, staring at her without understanding. '*Hitler*?' Then it hit her, and she gasped, her chest tightening. 'You mean . . . He's been told to *enlist*? But nothing's been said on the wireless. We're not at war yet. And it must be twenty years since he last wore a uniform.' She was breathless, her lips numb. 'Tell me you're joking.'

'I'm sorry, my dear, but I'm deadly serious.' Her gran gave her a quick hug, no doubt seeing her distress. 'I wish he'd told you himself. It's too bad of him. Most likely, he didn't want to risk upsetting you, so put off discussing it.' She patted Edith's hand. 'Try to stay calm. It's not as bad as it sounds. He won't be going off to fight the Hun himself. Do you recall that he was a skilled pilot in the Great War?'

'Of course.' Edith had heard all his wartime stories.

'Well, he's been called back to train young pilots. He won't be expected to fly any missions himself. Or so he told me.'

Edith tried to dampen down her fears . . . She was not sure what she would do if she lost her father on top of everything else. 'But this is all so sudden, Gran.' She struggled to collect her thoughts. 'Where is he being sent to train these pilots?'

'Not so far away that he can't visit occasionally, but too far for him to live at home. So it'll just be you and me for now. Apparently, the training camp is hidden away at an air base in the middle of Cornwall, somewhere between Truro and Bodmin. Of course, it's all hush-hush, so he won't be more specific. But that's always the way,' her grandmother confided, arching her brows, 'when men start playing soldier boys. He and your grandfather were much the same last time around.'

The bus came chuntering along and they climbed aboard, deliberately seating themselves far away from the three girls who'd made Edith's life such a misery after Percy had left the village. But she could hear them whispering the whole way back to the village, and whenever she glanced around, they were staring at her with malevolent smiles.

She could guess what they were talking about. Susan had seen her out with Percy several times and had come to call just before Percy left for Canada. Glowing and rapturously in love, Edith had forgotten their petty squabble as schoolgirls and foolishly confided in Susan that she and Percy had feelings for each other . . . But it was clear that Susan had not forgotten and was still seeking revenge for the boy she thought Edith had been after too. Somehow, she'd spotted them as they went into Penmarrey Woods on their last evening together, carrying a tell-tale blanket to lie on, and had made it her mission to let everyone in the village know just what a *slut* Edith Treloar was.

Her nerves churning, Edith sat up straight and dragged the two sides of her cardigan together, hoping it would conceal the slight bulge where the baby was beginning to show. The last thing she needed was yet more scandal. Though, as her grandmother had pointed out in Dagenham, it would be impossible to keep this baby a secret forever.

Back home, she found her father in the study that had belonged to his own late father, seated in a deep armchair with their cat Tabitha on his knee. The small room smelled of pipe smoke, though the pipe lay unlit on the table beside him.

As she knocked on the door and peered around it, her dad looked up from the flight training manual he'd been reading. 'Yes? Bringing me a cup of tea, are you? Thank you, Edith, that's very welcome.'

His manner was stiff, so she guessed he had still not forgiven her for hiding her pregnancy for so long. Her apology at breakfast that morning, and her stumbling explanation that she hadn't known for quite some time herself, had not made much difference. To his mind, he was the first person she ought to have come to with such important information. Instead, she had confided in her grandmother, and yet neither of them had informed him about the baby until her return home from Dagenham. This had left him so offended, he had barely replied to her at breakfast . . . Which perhaps explained why he, in turn, hadn't told her his own news.

She set his cup beside him, along with a plate of his favourite biscuits.

'I managed to find some nice dresses in town,' she began awkwardly, and then could not hold back her indignation any longer. 'Dad, when were you going to tell me that you've been recalled by the Royal Air Force? This training camp sounds awfully dangerous. Surely you're too old to be going up in an aeroplane?' All her worries came out in a rush. 'I mean, you're *forty-two*. I've heard you say often enough that flying planes is a young man's game. I can't believe you agreed to go.' She stared at him in exasperation.

'I see your grandmother has been busy, telling you all my personal business.' But he looked uncomfortable, straightening up and putting aside his training manual. The tabby cat leapt off his lap with an accusatory look, and jumped up onto the window seat instead. '*Agreed*? Let me assure you, I didn't have much choice in the matter. When my country needs me, I must answer the call. It's that simple.'

Her father set his pipe between his teeth and lit it, fumbling with the matches. 'Besides, forty-two isn't so very old, and I doubt that I'll be flying much. Working on the ground, that's how it was described to me.' He puffed on his pipe, his head wreathed in fragrant smoke. 'Teaching young recruits what I know about aerial warfare. Frankly, it's an honour to be asked.' He paused. 'Though I suspect they're short of trainers. New camps are being set up at bases all around the country, by all accounts, and they need to be staffed by experienced men.'

Edith hugged herself, a hollow feeling inside. At least that tallied with what her grandmother had said. But she was still unhappy to think that he was leaving her at such a delicate time.

'I see,' she said reluctantly. 'And when are you leaving?'

'Quite soon, I'm afraid. Perhaps as soon as the end of this week. My bags are already packed. I'm just waiting for the final orders.'

Without meaning to, Edith burst into tears.

Her father stared at her in horror, then banged out his pipe into the glass ashtray, leaving the tobacco smouldering, and got up to put an arm about her. 'There, there . . . Please don't cry, Edith. You know I can't stand tears.' He gave her a hug. 'I won't be gone long. Maybe a few months. It all depends on how long this wretched war lasts.'

'Is it definite, then?' She sniffed, fumbling for her hanky. 'There's no doubt that we're going to war with Germany? I thought the politicians were trying to sort things out.

Everyone's been saying in Dagenham that there might be a diplomatic solution. That it won't come to outright war.'

He pulled a face. 'A fool's hope, my dear. I wish I had better news for you. But the plain fact is, there's no diplomatic solution for someone like Hitler. He's not interested in sitting around a table with politicians, hashing out a peace plan. He wants to . . . to *conquer*!' He clenched his fist and shook it, as though imitating Herr Hitler's aggression. 'We can't hope to fob off a Napoleon like him with a few paltry offers of land here and there. He wants it all.' He sighed. 'No, the only way to stop the Nazi onslaught is to declare war. And that, I imagine, is what our government intends to do.'

She dabbed at her eyes unhappily. 'But what am I going to do without you, Dad? I've got this . . . this awful situation to deal with. And you won't be here to help me.'

'I know it must feel like the worst possible timing. But there's nothing that can be done. You'll just have to make the best of it. Besides, I'm not sure what possible help I could be in your present difficulty. Your grandmother is a sensible woman and experienced in such things. She'll see you through.' He stopped, floundering as he tried to avoid being too explicit about babies and so on. Any talk of women's issues always made him uneasy. 'If only your mother was still alive . . . But there's no point wishing for what we can't have, eh?'

'Oh, Daddy!' She burst into fresh tears.

He waited in silence until she'd calmed down, patting her in a clumsy but reassuring manner. Then he went to the mantelpiece and brought down the framed photograph that sat there, studying it for a moment before holding it out to her.

'I remember the day this photograph was taken,' he said with a nostalgic smile. 'My friend Barnie snapped it with his Box Brownie. It was so windy along the prom at Penzance, your mother lost her hat, and I had to chase after it . . . twice!'

She smiled through her tears, nodding. It was one of her own favourite photographs of him and her mother, taken while they were still young and courting. Her mother looked elegant and slender, smiling under a wide-brimmed hat. The black and white photograph couldn't do justice to her vibrant red hair, of course, which Edith had inherited. They were walking along the seafront, arm in arm, and her father looked so young, he was barely recognisable as the man that stood before her now, all that dark hair laced with silver streaks.

Chuckling fondly, he glanced from the photograph to her. 'You look so like her sometimes, Edith. It brings everything back when you smile. So, please keep smiling and don't cry. Your mother wouldn't have wanted you to be unhappy. Yes, you're in a bit of a pickle . . . But your grandmother and I discussed your future last night, and we both think giving this baby up for adoption would be the best thing for you overall. If that dreadful young man can't be brought to marry you, there's no reason for you to have your life ruined by an illegitimate child.' Her father had spoken awkwardly, in a gruff voice, as though aware the suggestion would not be welcome. Nonetheless, she could tell he meant to side with his mother and try to force her into handing her baby over to a stranger, probably as soon as the poor little thing was born. No doubt he had her best interests at heart. But that didn't make it any easier to hear.

Edith glared at him, her tears forgotten. 'I already told

Gran, I have no intention of giving up this baby. It's mine!' She shook her head when he started to speak again. 'No, I'm serious. This is my baby, Dad, and no one is going to take it away from me.'

She would have stormed from the room, furious at his interference, but he called her back urgently. 'Edith, please don't go, not like that . . . If you absolutely must keep this baby, then we won't stand in your way.' She could hear how much of an effort it took for him to make that concession, his voice strained with emotion. 'I'll do what I can for you, even come home for a quick visit whenever possible, but I can't refuse this posting. Those young pilots need me too. They can fly, yes. They've all read the training manuals. But can they engage the enemy and not only survive, but also win the encounter?' His brow was furrowed. 'You've heard me talk about my time in the Great War often enough. I don't like to boast about having been decorated, but . . . Perhaps my old war stories could serve a purpose here. Extra training from an experienced wartime pilot could mean the difference for them between life and death. You do understand, don't you?'

Edith drew a deep breath, trying to calm down. She felt reassured that her father would not force her to give up her baby. He could be forceful in his opinions sometimes, that was all. It had taken all her willpower to stand up against him just now. But she knew his heart was in the right place.

'Of course I understand,' she agreed. 'You want to do your duty.'

'Precisely.'

'But if you're right and war is declared, there's no saying when you might be allowed to come home, even for a "quick visit". Nobody knows how long a war will last once it's started,' she pointed out unhappily. 'So you might not be here when . . . when the baby . . .' She couldn't go on.

He put the photograph back on the mantelpiece, grimacing. 'You're right, of course. I may not be here when the time comes. But your grandmother will, and she won't let you down.' He paused. 'Besides, with any luck, we might be able to get in contact with your young man in Canada and get you married before that happens.'

She managed a faint smile, nodding, though she knew there was little chance of that.

'Meanwhile,' her father went on reluctantly, his hands in his pockets, a frown lurking on his face, 'there's something else you should know. Before I found out about your, erm, condition, I had been hoping you might be persuaded to come home and run the bakery for me while I'm away.'

'Sorry?'

'I'm having to close it while I'm on secondment to the air force, which means letting young Jack go.' Jack was the lad who helped out at the bakery, the son of a local artist. Edith vaguely remembered him from school as a friendly, polite boy. Being three years his senior though, she had not spoken to him very often. 'He's keen enough, and I've taught him a fair amount, but not enough to be chief baker. I know the lad relies on that money to get by though, so it's been a hard decision. But now you're back, perhaps you . . . ?' He left the question unfinished.

She was shocked, realising what he was asking. 'You want *me* to run the bakery after you've gone? Oh no, absolutely not. Gran says I'll be showing soon. People would notice and then the gossip would start all over again.' She shook her head, her voice rising. 'I won't be able to show my face in the village once it's obvious I'm expecting; surely you realise that?'

Her father looked troubled. 'Yes, of course. That does change things.'

'I'm sorry.'

'My regulars will be so disappointed. Some of them positively rely on my specialist bread, especially the artisan work I was teaching you before you left. The traditional harvest loaves and so on . . . There's the village shop, of course, but they can't provide anything like our range.' He ran a hand across his furrowed brow, clearly fretting. 'I wish I knew what to do for the best. Even if the bakery is only closed for a few months, I doubt those customers would come back once it reopens. People forget so quickly . . . It's important to keep the place going.'

Edith heard the plea in his voice and took a deep breath. 'I could step in for a few weeks,' she conceded, though reluctantly. 'But only while I get Jack fully trained up to take over from me.' When his brow lightened, she added hastily, 'I won't be able to make *all* the artisan cakes and breads, mind,' she pointed out. 'And I couldn't promise to open the bakery every single day. I get so easily tired these days.'

'But you're willing to give it a try? That's marvellous, thank you, Edith.' He was smiling again. 'Perhaps you could open the bakery three mornings a week while I'm away, and only sell a small selection of our most popular items. Does that sound possible?'

She couldn't see a way around it, or not without saying an outright no. And she could hardly accuse her father of refusing to help her if she then refused to help *him*.

'Yes, very well.'

'I knew you'd come through for me.' Looking pleased, her father put an arm about her shoulders and gave her another quick hug. 'I'm sorry I won't be here when you need me most. But when duty calls . . . Besides, running the bakery may take your mind off . . . off your troubles.' He glanced doubtfully at her tummy. 'For what it's worth, I still can't tell. And I doubt most people will be able to. Not yet, at any rate.' He smiled. 'Thank you, peanut.'

She was amused that he still used his pet name for her. 'Thank you too,' she replied shyly, 'for not being furious and throwing me out when you found out about the baby.'

His eyes flew wide. '*Throw you out?* My own daughter? As if I ever would . . .' He stuck out his chin. 'You make me sound like a complete ogre.'

'Well,' she said diplomatically, after a short pause, 'I don't want to be rude, but you have your moments, Dad.'

CHAPTER SIXTEEN

With a weary sigh, Sheila turned the Open sign over to Closed and began wiping down the tables, ready for going home. The door jangled behind her again.

'We're closed,' she called wearily over her shoulder. To her relief though, it wasn't someone looking to place a last order, but her friend Judith, bustling in with a casserole dish under her arm. 'Hello, Judith, how are you, love?'

'I brought you something new to try,' Judith said in her deep, rolling voice. 'It might be a little spicy for you but if you add extra tomatoes when you're heating it up, that should help.'

'For me? That's kind of you, Judith.' Sheila beamed, touched by her friend's generosity. Judith had brought her several home-cooked dishes over the last few weeks, in an effort, Sheila guessed, to lighten her workload after Henry's death. 'I do love them recipes you bring me. And Gordon enjoys making 'em. I've been putting a couple on the specials board. We've not had many takers but those who try them say they're delicious.'

Judith laughed. 'Not everybody likes the same thing. I'm just happy to have an excuse to share some of my Jamaican recipes.'

The door jangled again, and they both looked round, surprised.

It was a small group of lads, jostling in the doorway, staring at them in a hostile way. They weren't wearing the usual get-up, but Sheila recognised them as part of that awful Blackshirts gang. The government had passed an Act of Parliament a few years back to ban political groups from wearing an actual uniform, but she noticed how it hadn't stopped these youths from dressing all in black, or marching up and down with flags and placards, and generally making a nuisance of themselves. Though they were all sporting armbands now, she realised with a sinking heart, no doubt in place of a uniform. The armband displayed a white symbol on a blue background. A lightning flash?

'We're closed,' Sheila said sharply, turning to face them with her chin up. She regretted having let Gordon go early that day. Even Violet had gone home, to check the girls were safely home from playing with friends, as school had broken up for the summer hols and Ernest would be working late. Now she was all alone in the caff with nobody to back her up if things turned unpleasant. Except for Judith, of course. But she was a friend and a customer, and Sheila would have been horrified to see her hurt.

'We don't want your bleedin' food,' one of the bigger lads replied, jeering at her. 'We want a word with that Kraut son-in-law of yours, Ernst Fisher.'

The deliberate use of Ernest's German first name made her stiffen. 'I told you, the caff's closed. You need to leave, or else.' Sheila took a threatening step towards them, though inwardly she was quaking and confused. What on earth could these lads want with Ernest?

'Oh, I'm terrified now.' As the other boys snickered, the largest lad came swaggering into the caff, and she could see that he was wearing cruel-looking knuckle dusters, like he was eager for a fight. Sheila had the impression he didn't entirely know why or who he wanted to fight. Whatever it took to make him feel bigger and better than the other young men, she guessed. 'We only want to know why a German fella like him ain't supporting Mr Mosley and Herr Hitler. It's not like he's British, is it?'

'Ernest is just as British as you and me,' Sheila told him defiantly.

The boy started towards her.

'Don't you come any closer,' she warned him, alarmed.

'Or what?' The lad kicked one of the chairs and it fell with a loud clatter, knocking another chair down with it. He kept coming, stopping right in front of her. 'All right, let's talk about the British. Because we've seen the kind of people you let into your caff . . . Blacks, Jews, all sorts.'

'I beg your pardon?' Sheila was horrified, glancing apologetically over her shoulder at Judith. 'Get out, the lot of you. Before I call the police.'

'The police don't bother us, missus. Let 'em come. What we need in this country is fascism and a strong leader like what they've got in Germany. That's the only way to set us free from the inefficiency of the ruling classes, see?' He pulled a tatty booklet from his pocket and waved it at her. 'That's what Oswald Mosley says in this pamphlet, and he's had a proper education . . . He knows what he's talking about.'

Proudly, he tapped his armband with the lightning symbol. 'That's why I joined his group . . . The British Union of Fascists. Because someone has to make a stand against this weak government of ours, before we're all dragged into a war we can't win.'

Sheila stared at him, her skin creeping.

Before she could gather her shocked thoughts, Judith stirred beside her, then launched forward, clapping her hands as though shooing away noisy magpies. 'Go away, get out . . . You're not welcome here. You heard the lady. This café is closed and you need to leave. Or we'll call the police, and *they* can deal with you.'

The other boys moved back to the doorway in surprise, but the big lad refused to budge. His vicious eyes raked Judith from head to toe. 'And what makes you think anyone was talking to you, eh? You don't even belong in this country. You're the one who needs to get out,' he added threateningly, lifting his fist towards her, knuckle duster glinting. 'Not us.'

But Sheila had heard enough, her temper soaring. Snatching up the broom from behind the counter, she flew at them. 'Don't you speak to my friend like that! Get out of my caff, you filthy little toads!' She brandished the broom at the leader, as though planning to sweep him out of her way. 'Go home and play with your placards and your pamphlets. Nobody's interested in your bloomin' fascism here.' She thought of Henry, run down and killed by idiots like these, and raised her broom higher, breathless with fury. 'You destroy peoples' lives, that's all you lot do . . . Well, I won't stand for it anymore. I won't bloomin' stand for it, do you hear?'

Thankfully, Judith dragged her back before she could

clobber the biggest lad with her broom. But he and his friends were already tumbling out onto the street, shouting and cursing, the door jangling violently.

'Come on, Turnbull,' one of them yelled at the leader.

The big lad – presumably Turnbull – wheeled around, his face flushed and angry. He spat deliberately on the mopped floor at her feet. 'Don't think you've seen the last of us,' he snarled. 'And if someone was to put another brick through your window . . . Well, you'll only have yourself to blame, speaking to us like that. You need to work out whose side you're on, Mrs Hopkins, before Herr Hitler comes calling. Because we're putting your name on our list now.' And with that enigmatic threat, he turned and ran after his disappearing friends.

Sheila cast aside her broom, and dashed forward to lock the door before sinking into a chair. Her legs were unsteady, her heart thumping. 'Them blasted boys! I swear, they'll be the death of me. Putting my name on their list indeed. Oh, I don't know what the world's coming to . . . And where's a policeman when you need one, eh? Put another brick through my window? I'll have the law on that young man if he does. Nasty little—' She stopped herself from swearing just in time, seeing Judith's shocked expression. 'Sorry, love.'

'No need to apologise, Sheila. I'm just glad you're not hurt.' Judith came over to put a steadying hand on her shoulder. The gesture was intended to be reassuring, but Sheila felt her friend trembling, and realised with a jolt how close they had both come to being attacked by those brutes. 'These are frightening times,' Judith went on unhappily, 'and nobody could blame you for getting upset. Frankly, I don't know what the world's coming to either. Some days it feels as though people are losing their minds, they say such terrible things . . . But thank you for standing up for me, my friend.'

'You're welcome, love. And you *do* belong here, so don't pay no attention to brainless thugs like them, repeating what that Mosley fella says without understanding a blessed word of it.' Sheila jumped up and gave Judith a brisk hug. 'Well, I'd better tidy up these fallen chairs. Place looks a right mess now.'

She was smiling bravely, but inwardly she was scared and wished that Henry was still alive. Her husband would have known what to do for the best, who to call about their behaviour. The police, of course. But them nasty lads hadn't done anything particularly violent or illegal, except say a few menacing things . . . She was the one who'd flown at them with a broom. For all she knew, Constable Hobbs might nod sympathetically and write it all down in his little pocketbook, but then do absolutely nothing about it. Or worse, claim she was to blame for having lost her temper with them.

Once she felt less shaky, she thanked Judith for her support and for the casserole she'd so kindly brought, and insisted she leave by the back entrance, in case the Blackshirt thugs were still hanging about outside the front. Once she was alone, Sheila locked up the caff, pocketed the takings, put the spicy-smelling dish into a wicker basket, and slipped out of the back door too.

But she was brought up short by the sight of a lad lurking in the back alley behind the row of shops. He was wearing one of the British Union of Fascists armbands too, though he pulled it off and stuffed it into a pocket at first sight of her.

'Don't be scared, missus,' the boy said, shuffling towards

her. He was tall and skinny with short dark hair, but didn't seem to be armed and his manner wasn't threatening. All the same, she eyed him warily as he went on gruffly, 'I'm sorry about Turnbull and them other lads. I hang around with them, but it ain't what it looks like.' He took off his cap. 'My name's Peter Short . . . And the thing is, I just want to say sorry.'

Frowning, Sheila put down her wicker basket, locked the back door to the caff and pocketed the key. 'Sorry for making a blasted nuisance of yourself?'

'No,' he said, surprising her. 'Sorry for what happened to your husband.'

She looked round at him sharply. 'What do you know about that?'

'More than you, I reckon. Fletcher and his dad were arrested for murder, but it weren't just them involved that night . . .' Peter Short glanced up and down the street, fear in his narrow, pinched face. 'I came to your house a few weeks back, looking for Mr Fisher. I spoke to that girl what used to work in the caff with you, only she's gone away now. Edith, is it?'

Sheila felt vulnerable, talking to one of the Blackshirts in a deserted back alley. If he decided to attack her, there was nobody she could call for help . . .

'Why did you want to speak to Mr Fisher?' she demanded, hands on her hips, not wanting him to realise how nervous she was. 'Trying to turn him into a fascist, I daresay, like you and them other young thugs. But there ain't no point. Ernest's a good man; he'll never do it.'

'You don't understand, missus. It ain't nothing like that, I swear.' He checked over his shoulder again, then whispered, 'Will you give him a message from me?'

'Eh?'

'Tell him, I'll be in the park down the road, seven o'clock tonight. Near the rose gardens. There's something he needs to know.' Peter Short backed away, staring at her. 'Will you tell him, missus?'

'Now, listen here, you little—' she began to bluster, but the boy had already turned and fled.

Sheila walked home briskly, mulling over what had happened, but none the wiser by the time she reached the house. Her feet were aching after a full day at the caff and she wanted nothing more than to be sitting down with a cup of tea and listening to the wireless. In her absence, Violet had already made supper for the girls, who were chattering cheerfully about their day as they tucked into a simple meal of cheese on toast with a cup of milk. Their school having broken up for the summer holidays, they'd spent the afternoon at a friend's house, sunbathing in the back garden and having a wonderful time, by the sound of it. Though Alice told her in disgusted tones that Lily had spent most of the afternoon reading fashion magazines and gossiping about boys with her friend Kathy, while Alice herself had helped the girl's mother weed a flower bed.

Alice looked a bit mucky, with a streak of dirt on her cheek, but Lily was clean and presentable as usual. Sheila eyed both her young granddaughters with pleasure though. She doted on them both, messy or not.

'When's your dad coming to pick you up, love?' Sheila asked her eldest granddaughter, trying to sound casual.

'About seven o'clock? He had a late meeting at the plant today.' Lily pointed to a vase of fresh flowers on the kitchen windowsill. 'Kathy's parents have ever such a lovely garden, Gran. Her mum said we could take those flowers to brighten up the kitchen.'

'As a thank you for my help with the weeding,' Alice pointed out.

Sheila bent to sniff them. 'Oh, how lovely . . . You must be sure to thank her for us. I often wish we'd been able to afford a house with a garden ourselves. Your mum and dad are ever so lucky to have got one of them new houses on the Becontree Estate. They're all so posh with such wonderful big gardens. Though I daresay your grandpa would have complained if I'd made him mow the lawn every weekend.' She chuckled at the thought, though with a tinge of sadness, for she dearly wished Henry was still with them. She could just picture him now, sitting at the table, waiting for his dinner . . .

Henry would have sent those horrid boys off with a flea in their ear, for sure. Instead, she was learning to face such terrors herself, and she didn't like it.

'Dad always grumbles about mowing the lawn too,' Alice chimed in.

'Yes, and he hasn't done it since Mum went away,' Lily said, with evident disapproval. 'The grass in the back garden is almost up to our ankles.'

'Oh dearie me.' Violet, who was making a fresh pot of tea, gave a bark of laughter. 'While the cat's away, the mice will play.'

Sheila stifled a smile too. 'Your dad's a very busy man,' she reminded her granddaughters. 'I expect he's had too much work to be bothered with the gardening. Anyway, you're old enough now to mow the lawn yourself, Lily. Why don't you offer to do it for him?' She winked. 'There might be a few pennies in it for you.'

Alice and Lily glanced at each other, then Alice said swiftly, 'I'll do it.' She was always keen to make extra pocket money by helping out around the house and garden. 'I've watched him mowing, I know how it's done. And Lily hates getting all sweaty, in case the boys call her smelly. Don't you, Lily?' she asked innocently.

Lily glared at her sister without replying.

'What on earth have you brought home from the caff this time, Mum?' Violet demanded, wrinkling her nose as she took Sheila's wicker basket and sniffed its contents. 'Blimey, it smells a bit spicy.'

'More of Judith's traditional Jamaican cooking,' Sheila explained, taking out the casserole dish and placing it directly in the oven to heat up. 'I expect there's enough for two, if you'd like to share it with me.'

'No, thanks.' Violet grinned, and the girls chuckled along with her. 'I'm happy with cheese on toast, same as the girls.'

Ernest came in about an hour later, looking tired. He stood in the doorway, his hat in his hand, and smiled at his daughters squabbling at the kitchen table over a game of snakes and ladders like a couple of ten-year-olds. Violet had told them not to be so childish, suggesting cards instead. But Sheila had chivvied her away and let the girls continue with their game. Gawd knows, she'd thought, the poor lambs would need to grow up fast enough if war broke out . . . And with their mum gone away, and all the horrid changes in the world, no doubt they were taking a little comfort from playing a game that reminded them of childhood and simpler times.

'Sorry to interrupt your fun, but it's time to go home, girls,' Ernest told them with an apologetic smile. 'Have you thanked your grandmother for cooking you supper?'

'No,' Violet replied shortly, putting down the newspaper she'd been reading. 'Because I made their supper, not Mum. She was too late coming home from the caff.'

Sheila met her son-in-law's surprised look and turned away, taking her empty tea mug to the sink. She wondered whether she should mention what that boy had said. After all, he might have wanted her to pass on that message to lure Ernest alone to the park that evening so he and his mates could clobber him.

'It seems we were both late leaving work tonight, Sheila,' Ernest said, his gaze on her face. 'Is everything all right?'

'Fine and dandy, thank you.' Sheila picked up the old knitting she'd been unravelling and carried it past him into the living room, adding, 'But I would like a quick word before you take the girls home, if you've got a minute.'

'Of course. Girls, you've got five more minutes to finish your game. And, Alice, please wash your face when you're done. I'm not taking you home looking like you've been kissing a garden gnome.' Leaving the girls giggling, Ernest followed her into the living room and pushed the door shut, studying her intently. 'What is it, Sheila? What's happened?'

Briefly, she told him about the young lad who had lain in wait for her outside the caff, repeating exactly what he'd said. 'Only promise me you won't go. What if it's some kind of ambush? They're a nasty lot and probably want to get you alone so they can give you a good kicking. Besides which,' she said practically, 'you'd have to drive there after taking

Alice and Lily home, and you won't want to leave the girls on their own at that time of the evening.'

'No,' he agreed, frowning. 'But it's not such a great distance to the park from *here*.' He checked his wristwatch. 'It's almost seven o'clock. Maybe I could leave the girls with you a little longer while I walk over there and meet this Peter Short?'

'Oh, Ernie, do you really think you should?' Sheila didn't like the sound of him going alone. 'It might be dangerous.'

'I doubt it. It's been a warm day. The park doesn't close until dusk and there'll still be plenty of people about. Besides, you said this boy has already called at the house here, trying to find me. I shouldn't imagine his friends are subtle enough to come up with a plan like that, especially when they know where I work and could simply follow me home one night.'

'But why on earth would he want to speak to you alone?'

'There's only one way to find out, isn't there?' Ernest said coolly. He put his hat back on, stopping only to say through the half-open kitchen door, 'Girls, I need to nip out again for half an hour. So you've got time for another game of snakes and ladders after all.'

Then he left the house.

'And I'm going too,' Sheila called airily through the kitchen door. 'Back soon. Vi, don't let my dinner burn, there's a love . . .'

Sheila grabbed her hat and coat, and was out the front door after him before Violet had even finished protesting. She had already lost Henry to those vile Blackshirts. There was no way she was losing her son-in-law too.

'Hang on a tick,' she called out, catching up with Ernest. He turned in surprise, already halfway across the road. 'It's a lovely evening for a walk and I need to stretch my legs. So I might as well come too.'

'Stretch your legs? But you must have been on your feet all day.' Ernest's brow furrowed.

'True, but I'd like to see what they've done to the pub down the road. Renovations, I heard. Fancy new paint job, Gordon told me.' She linked her arm with her son-in-law's. 'Can't miss that.'

He looked at her without smiling. 'Sheila, I know what you're doing. But you can't come with me. It's not safe.'

'You said it was safe.'

'I said it wouldn't be dangerous. That's not the same as *safe*.'

'No, but it's six of one and half a dozen of the other,' she said flatly. 'Either way, we'll get there too late if you don't quit bellyaching and get your skates on. That Peter Short will have scarpered and then you'll never know what he wanted.'

Ernest stared at her for a moment, then shook his head. 'Very well,' he said grudgingly. 'You may come with me. But you must let me do all the talking.'

She shrugged. 'I wouldn't know what to say anyway.'

'And once we're in the park, I shall need you to find a bench where you can sit and wait until I've finished talking to this young fellow. Though it will need to be a good distance away,' he mused.

'But I won't be able to hear a single blessed word he says...' Sheila caught his sideways frown and sighed. 'All right, keep your hair on. I'll sit on a bench and talk to the ducks.'

'There are no ducks in that park. It's not like the big park in Ilford. It doesn't have any water features,' corrected Ernest.

'Then I'll talk to meself!' She rolled her eyes. 'Blimey, are you like this with Betsy?'

'No,' he said calmly, 'but your daughter doesn't insist on going with me to dangerous meetings with political dissidents.'

'You said it wasn't dangerous,' she pointed out.

Taking a deep breath, Ernest gazed up into the fading blue of the summer sky. 'Shall we just enjoy our evening stroll,' he murmured, as they began to walk towards the park together, 'and maybe not . . . *talk* anymore?'

Bright-eyed, glad that he wasn't going to send her home again, she mimed locking her lips and throwing away the key.

Ernest laughed reluctantly. 'My dear Sheila,' he said, 'Henry used to tell me you were a difficult woman, and I could never understand why. But now I see that he grossly understated the matter.'

When they reached the small local park, Ernest directed her to a bench and she sat there, feeling a little foolish for having insisted she came along. A few minutes later, Sheila spotted the boy from the caff and signalled to Ernest that he was approaching. The two moved into the rose garden at the centre of the park. She watched them, glancing about nervously for any signs of trouble, but saw nobody was paying any attention. After about ten minutes, they shook hands and parted. Ernest came back towards her. To her surprise, he was whistling between his teeth and looking almost pleased.

'Well, what did he say?' she demanded, agog with curiosity.

'Let's head home,' he said, not answering her question.

They set off back to the house, Sheila glancing at him

from time to time. 'This is driving me mad,' she whispered at last. 'Why did that lad want to talk to you?'

'If I tell you, you must promise never to tell anyone else. Even Betsy.'

She stared. 'Why?' Then tutted when he arched his brows and said nothing. 'Oh, very well. Mum's the word.'

'He had some information about the men who arranged to have me and Henry run over.' Ernest saw her look and added quickly, 'Not the two the police already arrested, but other members of the group behind them. The decision-makers, let's say. Peter Short didn't want to tell the police what he knew, in case they arrested him too.'

'Can you trust him?'

'I think so. The lad felt guilty about what happened to Henry, as well he might. He's aware that war with Germany is coming, and he's had a change of heart. Wants to fight for Britain if it comes to a war, not against her.'

'So, what now? You'll tell the police?'

Ernest pulled a face. 'Actually, I promised him that I wouldn't. He's got a younger brother who's still involved in that gang. He needs some time to get the two of them away first. Besides, the local police would only go blundering in . . .'

'I don't understand. Don't you want them arrested?'

'Yes, but the right people need to be apprehended and locked up. The ringleaders, not just the foot soldiers. That means no police . . . Or not yet anyway. We don't want them knowing that we're on to them.' He looked thoughtful. 'I heard about an old dissident German academic who's been helping the British government uncover networks of enemy sympathisers. An intelligence agent, I suppose you would call him. Herr Schmidt is his name. I'll try to contact him.'

He smiled at her astonished look. 'He just happened to be at university with my father.'

'Oh, I see.' Sheila didn't entirely see, but knew she could trust him to do the right thing. 'Well, at least you didn't get a kicking.'

He glanced at her, surprise in his face. 'Is that why you insisted on coming with me tonight? Because you feared I might be attacked by Blackshirts?'

'Something like that.'

He thought about this for a moment, then asked, 'And how would you have saved me from this "kicking"? Leapt in and hit them with your hat, perhaps?'

'I'll have you know, I gave them Blackshirts at the caff quite a seeing-to with my broom earlier,' she exclaimed, looking flustered. 'Or I would have done, if they hadn't scarpered.'

'A broom, eh? I expect they were terrified.'

'You know, once upon a time, men were respectful and polite to their mothers-in-law.'

'Ah yes,' he said smoothly, his smile apologetic, 'but alas, I was not alive in Victorian times. Unlike your good self.'

'Why, you . . .'

But she was smiling too. Despite his comments, Ernest seemed secretly impressed by his mother-in-law's desire to shield him from harm, even if it was a bit unlikely that she could have done anything other than shriek like a banshee at any attackers, and Sheila rather fancied that his gentle ribbing was just his way of saying, 'thank you'.

He was a good man, was Ernest, she thought with a sudden burst of affection. A bit eccentric at times, but smart and dependable with it. Henry had often boasted of knowing everyone in the local area. But she suspected her son-in-law knew the *right* people.

Come the war, Britain would need all the men like Ernest they could get.

By the time they reached the house, the girls were tired and bored, having been ready to leave for ages. As they were saying goodbye to Sheila and Violet in the kitchen, Lily bit her lip and exclaimed, 'Oops, I almost forgot . . . This letter arrived for you after you'd left for work this morning, Daddy.' And she took an envelope from her bag and handed it to her father. 'It's postmarked Cornwall. But it's not Mummy's handwriting.'

Sheila caught a glimpse of the address on the envelope as he used a paper knife to open it. 'That's my sister's hand,' she said, filled with sudden foreboding. 'Why on earth is she writing to you though, Ernest?'

He read the short letter briefly and then pushed it into his jacket pocket. 'Get in the car, girls,' he said without expression, and handed Lily the keys. 'I'll be out in a moment.'

'I'm going for a bath,' Violet said, barely suppressing a yawn, and headed up the stairs. 'Night, Ernie.'

'Goodnight, Violet.' He waited until she had gone and then turned to Sheila with a grim face. 'Your sister writes to say that Betsy . . . That is, she suggests that my wife . . .' He stopped, swallowing.

Sheila was frantic with worry. 'That Betsy . . . *what*? Spit it out, for gawd's sake!'

'That she's having an affair with a young doctor,' Ernest ground out. 'Martin, his name is. She doesn't say so in as many words, but it's clear what she's trying to insinuate.'

Shocked, Sheila sought for words to reassure him. 'Maggie often likes to . . . to make mischief where there is none,' she insisted. Indeed, as his reply sank in, she began to feel quite angry on her daughter's behalf. 'If you ask me, you should just ignore her. What a spiteful letter . . . I expect Betsy's had a few appointments to see the doctor, and my sister's imagination is running riot, that's all. Besides, she's barely been down there five minutes.'

'True,' Ernest admitted. 'But when I left her, Betsy was in a very fragile state. Highly suggestible.' His face hardened. 'Some men might find it easy to take advantage of a woman in such a vulnerable condition. I'm not saying she is having an affair . . . But perhaps she might be tempted, if we are apart for too long a time.'

'Maybe this doctor does find her attractive, but there's no way my girl would do anything to encourage him,' Sheila told him straight. She knew her daughter, and she was not the sort to be unfaithful. Even if, as Ernest said, she hadn't been herself lately. Betsy was a very attractive woman and had often caught men's attention without trying. But that wasn't her fault.

'What are you going to do?' she whispered when he didn't reply, not wanting Violet to overhear them. Her youngest daughter would only worry if she knew something was wrong in Cornwall.

'I'm going to have to drive down there and see how she is,' Ernest said reluctantly. 'I can't simply ignore her aunt's letter. Betsy may be worse than she was when I left Cornwall. She may need me more than ever.' He looked away, exasperation in his face. 'But damn it . . . I must contact that German academic first. We're talking about men who stand in opposition to everything we hold dear. Once war is declared, the government will need to know who those men are, for all our sakes. Or they could end up working against us.'

'When will you leave, then?'

'I'll try to speak to Herr Schmidt in the next couple of days, and then I'll leave for Cornwall after that.'

Sheila nodded, thinking swiftly. 'Violet can look after the girls. She won't mind, not when it's this important. And I'll find someone to pitch in at the caff while I'm gone.' She chewed on her lip. 'I have someone in mind already . . . But she may not agree.'

His troubled gaze had come back to her face. 'Excuse me?'

'I know who I can get to look after the caff while I'm gone.' Ernest looked at her agog, so she added firmly, 'I'm coming with you to Cornwall.'

'Now, listen—'

'No,' she interrupted, 'you listen to me, Ernest Fisher. You're going down there for Betsy, all well and good. But I need to see my sister. It's about time I had proper words with Maggie. And not just about that bloomin' malicious letter she sent you. She didn't come up to Dagenham for your and Betsy's anniversary do, even though we asked her several times. Yes, and offered to put her up for free too. And she sent that miserable little card for my Henry's funeral instead of making the effort to come in person to pay her respects. And, if you ask me, she only agreed to have Betsy to stay in return for using her as a bleedin' servant on the farm, reading between the lines of my daughter's last letter.' She shook her head, determined to sort things out with Maggie once and for all. 'No, I'm going with you to have words with Maggie, and that's all there is to it.'

'And I don't suppose there's any chance of my changing your mind?' Before she could respond, Ernest held up a hand. 'No, please don't bite my head off. If you insist on accompanying me, once again I can't stop you.' He paused. 'Well, I could . . . But I value my health too much to make the attempt.'

'So I can pack a bag, then?'

'Pack whatever you wish. I look forward to your company, my dear Sheila. And the inevitable sandwiches.' Her son-in-law gave her a crooked smile. 'What an entertaining journey this will be, for sure.'

CHAPTER SEVENTEEN

It smelled appalling in the cowshed. Betsy wrinkled her nose but didn't dare say anything, not while her uncle was explaining the milking process to her. Stanley had already snapped her head off for not paying proper attention – once after leaving a gate open, which she had since learnt was an offence second only to murder on a farm. Her mother could be irascible at times, but she'd never met someone with such a nasty temper as her uncle and felt quite nervous around him. So she put up with the stinking, straw-laced mud her boots were sinking into – assuming it was mud – and smiled whenever he looked her way, hoping to stay on his good side.

'Now, did you follow all that? Because I haven't got all day to stand about explaining how to milk a cow. I've got a farm to run.' Her uncle scowled. 'Well? Say something, girl!'

She was hardly a girl. She was a grown woman with two children. But she swallowed her indignation and said hurriedly, 'Yes, Uncle Stanley. I'll soon get the hang of it.'

He nodded to the milking stool in her hand and jerked

his head towards the cow he'd brought forward into the stall for milking. 'Go on, then.'

She swallowed, suddenly apprehensive. 'I'm worried she might kick me.'

'Sometimes they kick out,' he agreed, and she thought she saw malice behind his smile. 'And sometimes they back into you and squash you flat. But mostly they'll just look at you like you're an idiot if you don't get it right. So set down the stool and get yourself in position, like I showed you.' He placed a metal pail under the cow's heavy, milk-swollen udders. 'Get milking.'

Horribly nervous, Betsy seated herself gingerly on the low, three-legged milking stool, leant forward between the cows' legs to where the udder hung down, seized one teat in each hand, and squeezed.

Nothing happened.

'Oh, come on, please . . .' she muttered and squeezed again, this time as hard as she could. The cow shifted, looked round at her accusingly, and its massive stomach heaved. Betsy recoiled, releasing the udder, and almost fell backwards off the stool. 'Gawd help me!'

Stanley grabbed her before she could land on her backside in the mud and hauled her back up onto the stool. 'What did I tell you? The cow knows when you don't have a clue what you're doing. You need to show her who's boss.' His hands remained around her middle even now she was seated, and he said low in her ear, making her shudder, 'Now, grab hold of them udders . . . And give 'em a good firm *squeeze*.' And as he said this, his own rough hands groped upwards as though to squeeze her chest too.

But Betsy flailed her arms and shot to her feet, almost

stumbling again, and her uncle released her at once, stepping back with an angry oath. 'Watch what you're doing, you clumsy so-and-so!'

She sat back down, arms over her chest, glowering. There was a tense silence in the cowshed. She was in half a mind to march out of there and tell her aunt what he'd just done . . .

'What are you waiting for?' he growled, standing over her. 'Them cows won't milk themselves.'

Swallowing her fury, Betsy stayed where she was. She was alone with him in the cowshed, she reminded herself, and Maggie was no doubt hard at work in the farmhouse. He employed a few men about the place, but they were mostly out in the fields all day, cutting back hedges and mending fences. There was unlikely to be anyone within earshot if she called for help. It wasn't fair, but she had to be sensible and not push him into a corner by accusing him. Men who felt cornered could be dangerous and unpredictable.

Taking a deep breath, she squeezed again, rather more gently this time, trying to imagine milk coming out . . .

And it did!

'Oh, I've done it!' She repeated the movement, more thin milk spraying into the tin pail below. Relief flooded her.

'Hmm, not bad,' he grunted. 'Now keep going. I'll be back in a few minutes.' And he squelched out of the milking shed.

As soon as he was out of sight, Betsy let go of the cow and slumped forward, her thoughts whirling in confusion. Had Stanley really intended to grab her breasts? Or had she imagined it?

It was so hard to know what to do. While not a blood relative, he was still her uncle, for goodness' sake. But she hardly felt she could confront him over something that she'd only *suspected* he was about to do, but that hadn't in fact happened. And, if she did accuse him only for her aunt to not believe her . . . she could end up being thrown out on her ear, hundreds of miles from home with no means to get back.

No, she needed to stay on this farm, just a few more weeks, until that nice Dr Martin said she was better, or at least until Ernest came to fetch her home. Which meant keeping quiet about what her horrible uncle had done, and making sure she was never alone with him again. Though how she could manage that, she had no idea.

She carried on milking, getting into a pleasing rhythm. Then the cow swished her tail, glancing round again, an ironic look in her eye. 'I'm doing the best I can,' Betsy told her, and then realised what the issue was. There was no more milk to be had. Not from this cow, at any rate. 'Erm, Uncle Stanley,' she called out, unsure what to do. 'I think this one's empty.'

He came back in a moment later, and took away the metal pail. 'I've seen worse on a first attempt,' he rumbled, glancing down at the milk she'd collected so far. 'We'll make a milkmaid of you yet, girl.' He thrust it back at her as he led that cow away.

Betsy forced herself to smile and not chuck the milk pail at his head.

A few days later, on a warm, sunny afternoon, Betsy was sweeping out the chicken coop on her aunt's orders when she heard a car horn beep and looked up to see the doctor's car bouncing slowly down the long, stony drive to the farm. She found herself smiling. This was the fourth time Dr

Martin had dropped into the farm to check on her, and she was beginning to look forward to his brief visits. It made such a change, talking to someone other than her rigid and disapproving aunt and uncle.

Embarrassed by her filthy condition, she chucked down her cleaning equipment and dashed inside. In the kitchen, she washed her hands and face at the sink, and then quickly knotted a clean headscarf over her fair hair, which needed washing and probably still had dust in it from the coop.

'Such vanity,' her aunt said scathingly, watching from the kitchen doorway. 'All this for a doctor? I've never seen the like.'

Betsy set her teeth, finding it hard to reply without snapping. 'Washing my hands after cleaning out the chicken coop is not *vanity*, Aunt Maggie. It's necessary for hygiene. And I don't want to look a mess either. What would that say about the state of my health?'

Hurriedly drying her hands, she went back outside to find the doctor exchanging a few words with Stanley, who was just heading into an adjacent field on his tractor. As she approached, her uncle fired up the tractor engine and chugged away, Stanley raising a hand in farewell without saying a word to her, much to her relief. Her uncle had barely spoken two words to her since that day in the cowshed, in fact, and had set one of his farmhands to help with the milking instead. A guilty conscience? she wondered bitterly.

She smiled at the doctor. 'Hello,' she said shyly. 'Have you come to see me again? I'm feeling much better.'

'Hello, yes, I did come to see you.' Dr Martin grinned, shaking her hand. 'And I'm very glad to hear that you're improving.' His gaze wandered down the old skirt she was wearing, and widened in surprise, no doubt at the mucky stains from the coop. 'Erm, good to see you've been keeping busy.'

Betsy gave a reluctant laugh. 'My aunt set me to clean out the bloomin' chicken coop . . . I've never had to deal with so much filth in my life. I'm sorry, I must look a state.'

'Not at all,' he said politely. 'Look, I can't stay long. I was passing and thought I should check how you are and if you need any further medication. But if you're fine—'

'Hang on.' Hearing a noise, Betsy looked round to see her aunt watching them from the doorway. She turned to the doctor, her smile strained. 'That's very kind of you, and yes, I do need a chat. But shall we take a little walk? I don't want to be overheard.'

Dr Martin had followed her gaze and now gave her a wry smile. 'Of course. Perfectly understandable.'

They walked across the farmyard and into the field, which was empty at present, the cows having been moved for the summer to the top pasture. The grass smelled sweet and fresh, and there were birds singing overhead. In the distance, the sea was a bright blue glitter under cloudless skies. A perfect summer's day, she thought, and wished she could enjoy it more. But one thing was missing from this beautiful landscape, and that was her husband.

Betsy sunk her hands into the pockets of her dress, turning to face him. 'The nightmares have stopped. And no more sleepwalking, thank gawd. But if I'm honest, I still don't feel completely myself. Ever since I lost the baby, I've felt . . . well, empty inside.' The words struck deep and she drew a sharp intake of breath, then let it go slowly, struggling to keep the distress out of her face. She didn't want the doctor to think she still wasn't able to cope with everyday life. She was getting better, she felt sure. It was taking longer than she'd hoped, that was all. 'Does that make sense?'

'You're the best judge of what makes sense.' Dr Martin's look was sympathetic. 'This isn't a physical illness, remember. It's true that your body is recovering from the unfortunate miscarriage you suffered. But the real issue is up here.' He tapped his head. 'In other words, I can only rely on what you tell me, and any symptoms you describe. You say you're sleeping peacefully and not wandering at night anymore. But how do you feel when you get up in the mornings? Full of energy or still somewhat lethargic, as you told me last time we spoke?'

She tried her best to outline her morning routine – how she often woke with a sense of dread and had to force herself out of bed. But the right words wouldn't come until she admitted in a rush, 'Though that's not because I lost the baby . . . It's because of *them*.'

He frowned. 'Your aunt and uncle?'

Betsy bit her lip. 'I shouldn't say anything . . .' She turned away. 'It's ungrateful. They're putting me up for free.'

'Is something wrong?'

She hesitated, staring down at the sweet springing grass underfoot through blurred vision. There were tears in her eyes, she realised with embarrassment. 'My aunt can be a bit rude,' she muttered. 'But that's all right, I can handle her. It's my uncle what scares me. He's a bit . . . handy.'

The doctor looked shocked. 'You mean, he touches you?'

'Oh gawd!' She buried her face in her hands, flushed and unhappy. 'Sorry, no . . . I can't say things like that about me own family. It ain't right.'

He hesitated. 'I could contact the police, if you wish.'

Her eyes flew wide and she stared up at him. 'The coppers? No bleedin' fear!' She shook her head frantically, wishing now that she'd kept her mouth shut. The thought of police officers arriving at the farm to question her uncle left her cold with dread. He would deny it, of course, and everyone would look at her accusingly. Her aunt would call her a liar and throw her out. It would cause such a rift in the family too . . . 'It was nothing. I'm sure me uncle didn't mean nothing by it.' Her eyes pleaded with his. 'You need to forget what I said. *Please*?'

'Very well,' he said after a moment's hesitation, clearly reluctant to let it drop. 'But if you ever need to talk to someone, Betsy, I'm a good listener. And if you don't want your uncle to see us talking, I have offices in Penzance that you could visit.' He gave her his card. 'I won't charge extra for my time, I promise.'

'Thank you,' she said with heartfelt relief, pocketing the card. 'You've been so kind, so helpful.'

'I'm a doctor. It's what I do.'

'I'm still grateful.' Impulsively, she touched his arm. They were standing very close, and the sun was behind him, full in her eyes. Head bent, she looked up at him shyly, blinking away teardrops on her lashes. 'Not all doctors are the same. I've met some right nasty so-and-sos in white coats. Take it from me, you're one of the good ones.'

There was a silence, and then Dr Martin cleared his throat, running a hand through floppy blond hair in a gesture that reminded her abruptly of her husband. 'Mrs Fisher,' he began, though he had recently started to address her as Betsy on occasion, 'I'm glad that I've been able to help you. But I should make it clear that . . . That is, I'm sorry if I've given you any inadvertent signals that this is anything other than a doctor–patient relationship.'

Heat flooded her cheeks, and she inhaled sharply, realising too late what he was thinking. 'Oh Lord . . . You've got the wrong end of the stick. I weren't trying to . . .' The word *seduce* leapt into her mind, and she banished it with horror, shaking her head. 'I'm a happily married woman, Doctor. I just wanted to say a proper thank you, that's all.' She folded her arms, hugging herself so tightly she could hardly breathe. 'Now I've said it.'

He jiggled his coins and keys in his trouser pockets, swaying back and forth as he considered her. 'I see,' he said after a short hesitation. 'Then I apologise. I misunderstood what you meant and should never have said any of that. Can you forgive me, Mrs Fisher?'

The way he kept repeating her married name and title was deliberate, she felt sure. She blenched, wishing there was a deep, dark hole nearby that she could sink into and never come out of.

'Of course,' she rushed out, 'it don't matter at all. Gawd, I can't believe I put my foot in it so bad.'

'Not at all,' he said smoothly. 'We won't say any more about it.' His arm shot out and he studied his wristwatch, frowning. 'Goodness, is that the time? I'm going to be late for my next house call. If you'll excuse me?'

She walked back with him to his car, feeling ridiculous. She thought perhaps she ought to return to the farmhouse, but Maggie was still staring at them through the kitchen window, and she didn't want to go back inside until the flush in her cheeks had receded.

Dr Martin got into his car and wound the window down, looking round at her. 'You're sure you don't need help with that other business?'

He meant her uncle, she realised. 'No, thank you,' she told him firmly. 'Please do me a favour and forget what I said, all right?'

'Very well. And any further medication?'

She shook her head, smiling at his persistence. 'Honestly, you've been a diamond. I don't need nothing. Gawd bless you.'

He gave her a smiling wave and drove away. She stood a moment, staring after the doctor as he pulled slowly out of the farm gates, and wished all those stupid words unsaid. She could barely think of the way she'd touched his arm, which he had misinterpreted so badly, without cringing.

Shame churned in her stomach. Thank goodness he hadn't been interested. Some men might have taken her smile and friendly touch as a come-on. Then she would have been in trouble.

A car must have passed the doctor's on the narrow, bumpy track to the farm, for she heard another horn beep, and the slowing of an engine. Then a large car turned through the farm gates, the windscreen catching the sun.

'Blimey, who's this now?' Betsy turned with a sinking heart to stare at the new arrival, shielding herself from the dazzling sun with a hand over her eyes.

She recognised the big Ford before she saw the driver. Her heart seemed to stop and then start again with a jolt. Betsy stumbled forward, mouthing her husband's name, and then saw that he was not alone in the car. Her mother was seated beside him, waving out of the window.

Betsy stood rooted in astonished silence. As Ernest pulled up beside Stanley's old van, she looked in vain for her children in the back seats. But they hadn't brought the girls.

That flash of happiness at the sight of her husband turned instantly to fear. Had something awful happened? Why on earth had Ernest returned to Cornwall before she'd written to tell him she was better? And why would he have brought her *mother* with him, of all people?

He was an easy-going man and had always got on well with her mum, but it was a long journey from Dagenham to Cornwall, and to have sat beside his chatty mother-in-law the whole way . . .

'Ernest, love . . .' She leant into his open window to kiss him and glowed when his hand came up to cup her cheek. 'I'm so happy to see you. But why are you here? What's happened? Where are the girls?' She stared past him at her mother. 'Mum . . . Blimey, when I saw you in the car, I couldn't believe my eyes. What in gawd's name are you doing here?'

Her mother, who was looking flushed and tired, gave her a big beaming smile. 'I've come to see my sister,' she said firmly, and got out of the car, a bulging straw bag in her hand. 'I ain't seen her in years, nor Stanley neither. So Ernest and I decided we'd motor down and see how you were.' She came round the car and kissed Betsy on the cheek while Ernest was getting his suitcase out of the boot. 'Aw, love, you're looking so much better. You've gone all brown from the sun.'

'Yes, I'm much better, thanks.' Betsy pushed away the embarrassing memory of what had just happened with the doctor. 'Are you sure everything's all right, Ernie? Nothing wrong with the girls? You didn't bring them.'

'We didn't think there'd be room at the farm for all of us. Besides, we're only staying a day or two.' Ernest gave her a direct look. 'The thing is, I'm hoping you're ready to come back with us to Dagenham.'

Betsy didn't know what to say. Was she ready? She didn't think so. Thankfully, she was saved from answering that by her aunt.

Maggie had come out to stare at the new arrivals too, a dripping sink plunger in hand. Her mouth fell open as she recognised them, and she exclaimed 'Sheila?' and then stood in shocked silence as her sister hurried over to give her a warm hug and peck on the cheek.

Sheila began to explain all over again why she'd come down to Cornwall, and at last Maggie found her voice again.

'There's no room for you,' she said flatly. 'Ernest can share with his wife but I don't know where I'll put you.'

'I ain't proud. I'll sleep on the sofa,' Sheila insisted. 'It's only for a couple of nights, anyway.'

Maggie looked horrified. 'The sofa? It's not big enough for you.'

'Excuse me?' Her sister looked offended.

'Your feet will be dangling off the end. Besides, Stanley wouldn't like it. Having you camped out in our sitting room, where he likes to listen to the wireless of an evening?' Maggie pursed her lips. 'I'd have to tidy up the box room for you.'

'Good idea. I'll give you a hand,' Sheila said promptly, and ushered her sister into the farmhouse, glancing back at Betsy and Ernest with a significant look.

When the farmhouse door had closed behind them, Betsy turned to Ernest. 'What is it, love? What's my mum not saying?' she demanded breathlessly, sure that some dreadful calamity had brought him. 'And please don't tell me you're only here to bring my mum to visit her sister, because she can't stand Aunt Maggie, so I know that's a whopper. Tell me the truth, for gawd's sake.'

Ernest studied her in silence for a moment, then put down his suitcase and pushed his hands into his trouser pockets. She'd never seen him look so forbidding, and it scared her. What on earth had happened?

'I had a letter from your aunt,' he told her softly. 'She wrote that you were having an affair with a doctor down here. Dr Martin?' As a horrified flush spread across her cheeks again, and she stared back at him in anguish, he nodded. 'I see. Was that him we just passed in his car, leaving the farm?'

'Yes, but . . .' She gulped. 'It's not what it looks like, honest. Dr Martin just called by to check how I was doing, that's all . . .' Her voice tailed off at the look in his eyes.

'All the way down to Cornwall, I've been telling myself that Maggie must have been imagining things. Spreading malicious rumours and hoping to put a wedge between us, for her own twisted ends. Your mother insisted that she was often the same when they were girls. But now I see there's no smoke without fire.'

'Ernest, no! There's no fire at all. Or smoke. It's all make-believe.' Betsy clapped her hands to her hot cheeks. 'My aunt had no business to write to you. No bleedin' business at all! Yes, Dr Martin's a very nice man but he's never laid a finger on me. And I've never wanted him to, neither.' Fury rose inside her as she considered the gulf between the polite, friendly young doctor and her lecherous uncle. Part of her wanted to leap into a complaint about Stanley's groping ways instead. But instinct told her not to go down that route. Not right now, when Ernest was in such an emotional state and might lash out at the older man. Maybe later, when they were both calmer and a long, long way from Cornwall . . . 'Oh, I could slap Aunt Maggie. Imagine writing such vicious lies to my husband.'

'Yes.' He looked away across the fields, and she saw his throat swallow convulsively. 'And imagine if I were the sort of husband who took such gossip seriously.'

Terrified of losing him, she placed a trembling hand on his chest. 'It ain't true, Ernie. I swear it on my life. On my grandmother's grave. There ain't nothing between me and Dr Martin. It's a load of old codswallop. I'm so sorry you've taken time off work and driven all the way down here just because of . . . of my aunt and her meddling nonsense.'

Ernest's sharp blue gaze swung back to meet hers, and she stared back at him intensely. At that, he caught her up in his arms, muttering against her cheek, 'The truth is, I didn't only come because of your aunt's letter. I came because I love you and couldn't live without you any longer. I . . . I didn't want to believe what she wrote . . . and I didn't, not deep down inside. But it turns out I'm every bit as insecure as the next man. I decided at once that I had to see you in person, to make sure. But it was just an excuse to give up this pretence that I'm coping on my own.' He kissed her passionately before pressing his cheek against hers, his eyes closed. 'I'm still every bit as madly in love with you as I was when you agreed to be my wife, Betsy. No man could ever love a woman more than I love you. Even if I'd found you *kissing* another man, I might've punched his lights out . . . But then I would have begged you on my knees to come back to me. That's how much I love you.'

She wept for joy, clinging onto him, never wanting them to be apart again. 'Ernie, I could never look twice at another man. Not with a husband like you. I've been lonely down here in Cornwall, yes. But not *that* lonely. Blimey, I'd have to be stark raving mad to throw away a man as wonderful as you. You're the best husband any woman ever had, and you're the best father too.' She held his face in her hands and kissed him on the lips. 'I love you to bits, Ernest Fisher, and don't you ever forget it again.'

Smiling, Betsy waited for him to collect his hat from the car, and pick up his suitcase, and then they walked together to the farmhouse.

Ernest's arm was about her waist, her head resting on his shoulder. She had felt so shaky and uncertain of herself only that morning. But now, with her husband there, knowing that he supported her no matter what, the world was suddenly right again.

'I know I said I was hoping you could travel back with me and Sheila. But if you're not well enough, then you must stay.' He sounded hesitant. 'You came here for peace and quiet, and to shake off your nerves. I don't want to bully you into leaving Cornwall before you're ready.'

'I want to go home.'

'Very well, I'm glad then.' He searched her face, and she guessed there must have been something in her voice that had given her away. 'But is something wrong?'

Behind them, she could hear the tractor chugging back across the field. Her Uncle Stanley on his way home. Heat flared as she recalled again that awful moment in the cowshed, his hands about her . . .

Although not easily roused to anger, she knew Ernest had

it in him to defend those he loved if goaded to it, even with his fists, and she feared what might happen if he learnt what her uncle had done. And yes, she still had no doubt that, if openly accused, Stanley would try to wriggle out of it, maybe even pin the blame on her instead, say she'd been giving him the glad eye . . . Her instinct to play it safe won over her desire to see Stanley squirm. Besides, she hated arguments, and there would be one hell of a row if she blurted out the truth.

'No,' she said huskily, distracting her husband with another kiss. 'I just miss home so bad. Cornwall's lovely . . . A paradise on earth. But when you're lonely, what's the use of paradise, eh?' She hugged him. 'No, I'm feeling much better now, and I'd like to go home to Dagenham and be with you and the girls.'

'Then so you shall, love.' But as Ernest glanced back at the approaching tractor, she caught a shadow in his face, almost as though he'd half guessed why she was so eager to leave. He didn't mention her uncle though, merely said, 'I wish I could be bringing you home in better times. The world is changing, and not for the better.'

'You're talking about war? You think it's definitely going to happen?'

He nodded slowly. 'I had to meet someone before I could leave for Cornwall. A German academic who knew my father back in the old days. I can't explain it exactly, but . . .' He paused, frowning. 'He's going to help the powers-that-be to weed out subversive elements in London and the East End. Dissidents, agitators . . . Traitors, to be blunt. The sort of men who sympathise with Hitler and might be persuaded to betray their country because of that.'

'How awful.' She didn't understand though. 'But how are *you* involved?'

'It's a long story, and not entirely mine to tell.' Tenderly, he took her hand. 'What I can share with you, my love, is what Sheila already knows, which is that a young man called Peter Short, one of the Blackshirts back home, got an attack of conscience a few days ago. He approached me through your mother with some information that needed to be taken to the right people. It felt genuine, so I tracked down Herr Schmidt and he's now talking to his contacts in the British government about it.'

'*Through my mother?*' she echoed, amazed.

'I know.' He grinned at her disbelief. 'Best you let her explain in her own words. It's a long drive home anyway, and I'm sure Sheila will talk for the entire journey, just as she did on the way down.' Ernest gave a short laugh. 'Ask her about her fighting skills with a broom. I wouldn't want to be an enemy sympathiser who got on her wrong side, I can tell you.'

She chuckled and shook her head. Her *mum*, talking secretly to Blackshirts? And what on earth was that about a broom? As usual, she couldn't tell if her husband was joking or not, but she didn't much care either way. She was just so happy that they were together again, and she was going home . . .

CHAPTER EIGHTEEN

It was agonising to stand at the garden gate as her father left for his Royal Air Force posting in mid-Cornwall. But Edith had promised she wouldn't cry, knowing how much he hated 'weeping women,' as he put it, so she waited stoically until his car was out of sight before bursting into tears.

'I'm going to miss him so much,' she sobbed as her grandmother led her gently indoors. 'Now it's just the two of us.'

'You say that as though it's a bad thing,' Rosalyn remarked, closing the front door with a heartfelt sigh. 'I love my son very much, of course. But you and I will do very well together, with no need for a man about the house. I still recall the Great War, when women had to do men's work as well as their own. We managed then, and we'll do the same again if there's another war, which unfortunately does seem likely. Besides,' she added briskly, 'we're *both* going to be kept too busy this summer to have much time for tears.'

Edith stared at her. '*Both* of us?'

'You have a bakery to stock and run,' her grandmother

pointed out calmly, taking pen and paper from her writing desk, 'and I have a young Canadian to track down. I thought it best to say nothing until your father had left. You know what he's been like. But this came in the post yesterday.' And she held up a folded sheet of paper.

Hurriedly, Edith sat up, her tears forgotten. 'From P-Percy?' she blurted out, her heart thumping.

Her grandmother arched a delicate brow at her. 'No, my dear. Not from Percy. Do please try to be sensible... I would hardly need to track him down if he'd already written, would I?'

'I suppose not,' Edith admitted, deflated. She took the sheet her grandmother was offering her, unfolded it with a sinking heart, and saw that it was indeed a letter. But from whom, if not Percy?

Squinting down at the messily scrawled signature, she pulled a face. 'Who on earth is it from? I can't read the name... Patrick something?' She gasped, eyes widening. 'But that's Percy's cousin's name. Oh, I say, how splendid.' But on rapidly scanning the rest of the letter, she slumped back onto the window seat, horribly disappointed. 'Oh no!'

'My thoughts exactly.' Her grandmother put pen to paper and began to compose her own letter. 'It's all rather unsatisfactory. But at least his cousin has enclosed their home address in Canada. So I've decided to write to your young man myself and hope for a reply before the baby is born. That's the best we can do for the time being.'

Edith reread the letter several times. They hadn't explained to Percy's cousin why they needed to contact him, hoping to keep the pregnancy a secret for as long as possible. But that meant Patrick hadn't bothered to hurry, no doubt thinking she was simply a lovesick girl left behind after a holiday romance. His cousin claimed he hadn't heard from the other half of the family since they sailed from England. Although he'd eventually bestirred himself to send an international telegram from the Penzance Telegraph Office, asking Percy to write to Edith, the belated reply he received from one of Percy's neighbours was that the family were not at home.

Patrick had no further information to give them about his cousin. He apologised for not calling at the house in person, but said he was only at home for a day or two before heading back out on business again.

'Oh my goodness. Not at home? What does it mean, Grandma? But they left Cornwall several months ago. What can have happened to delay their return?' A cold horror struck her and she swallowed hard. 'They were sailing back to Quebec in a huge ocean liner, Percy said . . . Surely it couldn't have *sunk*?'

'I'm fairly confident that a disaster of that magnitude would have made the newspapers, dearest.' Gran all but rolled her eyes.

'Yes, of course. Sorry, I'm just panicking.' Edith forced herself to shake off that awful vision of Percy and his family sinking beneath cold black waves . . .

'It's far more likely that they decided to make a detour,' her grandmother pointed out, 'perhaps to visit someone or simply do some sightseeing. Canada is an enormous country in comparison with ours; perhaps they decided to become better acquainted with it while travelling home.'

Edith jumped up and paced the room, Patrick's letter in hand, too restless to stay seated. All she could think about was finding Percy and making sure he was safe and well.

'I expect you're right,' she agreed unhappily, 'but it's so frustrating, not knowing for sure. I mean, Percy could be *anywhere*, and he has no idea about what's happened. Nothing about what I've been through, about the baby, all the gossip in the village, or Dad having to leave us and go off training pilots. I wrote to him once after he first left, but before any of that had happened . . . And then I stupidly tore up his address and threw it away. But I'm sure if he knew *everything*—' She caught her grandmother's ironic eye and subsided, reluctantly handing back the letter containing Percy's precious address in Canada. 'Though if they have taken a detour,' she added, thinking aloud, 'they must return home eventually. To find our letters waiting for them.'

Her grandmother thought for a moment. 'I suppose we could send a telegram like this Patrick fellow did. But it's hardly the most discreet mode of communication. After all, what could one possibly put that wouldn't instantly alert everyone who read it to your most private business? *Edith pregnant STOP Come back STOP Marriage required STOP.*'

'Oh.'

'"Oh", indeed.' Her grandmother gave a hollow laugh and resumed writing her letter. 'But you must write to your young man too, dearest. If he's going to be persuaded to turn around and sail back to England to wed you, which is rather a startling demand from a girl he only knew for a few weeks, I'm afraid a letter from your doting grandmother may not be enough to sway him.' She smiled around at Edith encouragingly. 'It's *you* he'll want to hear from. Not me.'

Edith beamed. 'Of course I shall write to Percy as well, Grandma. I have so much to tell him . . .'

Gratefully, she bent to kiss her grandmother on the

forehead, then dashed upstairs to the privacy of her bedroom, already mentally composing the most poignant love letter any young man ever received.

It was just after dawn the next morning when Edith opened up the bakery, as her father had always done, and began heating the ovens ready for that day's batch of loaves and pastries. Her father had taken a few days before leaving to take her through how everything was done. He'd even shown her a few tricks of the trade that she hadn't yet acquired, especially when it came to the specialist breads she might be required to bake for local festivals, such as the farmers' Harvest Supper.

She had taken copious notes, but she'd been baking bread with him for so many years now, and watching as a young child long before that, the new information had already become embedded in her head. It felt like second nature now to wait for the ovens to reach the correct temperature while uncovering the doughs she'd kneaded the night before and preparing the baking trays. It was odd though to be alone at this task. She missed the witty banter of her father as he worked, often discussing local characters and who had said what to whom in the shop the previous day.

As the August sunlight grew stronger, she wondered what her dad was doing. Perhaps he was thinking of her too, opening up the bakery on her own for the first time. She found herself damp-eyed, swallowing a lump in her throat.

'Oh, Dad,' she said, sighing as she wiped down the shelves and counter. 'I hope I do you proud.'

But she was afraid she might make a fool of herself instead.

Jack propped his bicycle against the wall outside and came shuffling into the shop just as Edith was checking the till float. 'Hello,' he said with an awkward smile, bending in the doorway to unfasten the bicycle clips that protected his trouser legs while cycling. He was a well-built boy with a shock of fair hair that looked as though he'd cut it himself with a pair of blunt scissors. 'Did you get the first loaves into the ovens on time this morning? I've been worrying all the way here in case you were late.'

'Use your nose.' Edith grinned as the boy sniffed the air before visibly relaxing. The smell of freshly baked bread was wafting through from the bakehouse room and filling the shop with its pleasant, savoury aroma, answering his question for him. She glanced at the wall clock and pulled a face. 'Talking of which, it's time to get the second batch out of the ovens. The first batch must have cooled by now.' She hesitated. 'Could you wash your hands, please, and arrange them on the shelves?'

It took some courage to give young Jack orders. But, as her father had reminded her before leaving, she was the boss in his absence.

'It's almost eight o'clock,' she added significantly. 'I'll be opening the shop soon.'

'Righty-oh,' he agreed, and he cheerfully headed through into the adjacent bakehouse room to do her bidding.

She sagged with relief. She felt foolish now for having worried about his reaction. But Jack had been taken on as apprentice baker after Edith had left for Dagenham, so it would have been natural for his nose to be put out of joint by her unexpected return and promotion to head baker.

All the same, she heard Jack whistling as he donned his white work apron and cap, and couldn't hold back a smile, sensing that her dreaded first day on the job might be trouble-free, after all.

Edith served the first wave of customers with ease. These were mainly the older generation in the village, those who were habitually up early and preferred fresh bread at breakfast. Most seemed genuinely pleased to see her again, and nobody commented on her new girth. Perhaps they hadn't noticed, she thought hopefully. Or more likely were too polite to comment.

She was just beginning to feel comfortable in her new role when she looked around with a smile to greet her next customer, and realised with a shock that it was Susan Teague, her archnemesis in the village. The girl whose mean gossip had forced her to flee . . .

'G-Good morning,' she stammered, her mouth dry, her palms oddly clammy as she met Susan's malevolent blue gaze. 'What can I g-get you?'

'Edith . . .' Susan heaved a satisfied sigh. 'So it is you. You know, I couldn't believe my eyes the other day when I saw you and your grandmother on the bus. We all thought you'd gone away. For good, everyone said. Yet here you are, back in the village again, just like a bad penny.'

Susan folded her arms over her chest, looking her up and down. Thankfully, the counter was between them, but it wasn't high enough to hide the tell-tale rounding of Edith's belly. Not from such cool, observant eyes as Susan's, at any rate.

'Goodness,' she went on slowly, 'Lizzie was right. She insisted on the bus that you were looking rather . . . erm . . . *larger* than when you left. I didn't really notice myself. But now that I look at you . . .' She tilted her head to one side with fake sympathy. 'What happened? Did they overfeed you in London?'

'I wasn't in London. I was in D-Dagenham. I was working in a c-café there.' Edith didn't know why she was even bothering to answer the wretched girl's questions. Except there were now other customers in the shop, listening with fascination as they waited to be served.

If only she could get rid of her tormentor. 'Did you need some bread, Susan? Or perhaps some of our p-pastries? They're all fresh baked today.'

She flushed, acutely aware of the stammering and stuttering in her voice and hating herself for being so nervous. Her private life was none of this rude girl's concern. But she also knew that Susan loved to gossip, and that people often listened to her.

'I brought a list from my mother.' Susan pushed a slip of paper across the counter, her intent gaze on Edith's middle. 'Your father usually puts it on the slate for us.' She frowned, leaning forward. 'You know, Edith, only a good friend would tell you this,' she went on, her tone conspiratorial, 'but you need to lose some weight. You're looking positively *rotund* these days. I mean, a person could be forgiven for thinking you were in an *interesting condition*, let's say.' And she tittered behind her hand.

Edith stood frozen in horror, staring from Susan's smirk to the shocked expressions of the other customers. She felt trapped, unable to ignore her taunts, and not even in a position to flee. She was the baker now. And this girl, however hateful, was a customer.

'I'll bag up her order for you, Miss Edith,' Jack said briskly, snatching up the list from the counter. He began to select loaves and pastries with a practised hand. 'I think the third batch is ready to come out of the ovens now, but I thought

I should wait for your say-so. You are head baker now, after all.'

Coming back to life with a rush, Edith muttered, 'Yes, thank you, quite right.' And she took the opportunity to make the escape that he'd offered her. She hurried into the bakehouse, pushed the door to behind her and sank to the floor, her hot face buried in her hands.

Edith knew she couldn't hide in the bakehouse forever. Eventually, she removed the last batch of loaves from the ovens, thankful that at least they had not burnt while she had been recovering her composure, and turned off the heat. Out in the shop, she could hear Jack dealing competently and politely with the remaining customers.

She checked each loaf as she turned them out, tapping the base to be sure there were no soggy pockets of dough inside, reassured by the hollow sound of well-cooked bread. She was suddenly glad she'd decided with her father that the shop would only be open from eight-thirty until early afternoon while he was away, at least to start. Ordinarily, he would do a second batch of baking for late afternoon. But it was better for her to start off in a modest way than risk losing customers' goodwill by being unable to produce breads to the same high quality as he would have done.

'Miss?' Jack came knocking at the door. She didn't answer, still feeling too bruised to see anyone. He stuck his head around the door. 'Miss Edith . . . Sorry to disturb you, but there's someone here to see you.'

'Susan again. Or one of her friends, perhaps?' She slid the last well-browned loaf onto the cooling tray. 'Well, you can tell Susan that Miss Edith isn't available to see anyone. For the foreseeable future, in fact. And if she doesn't like it, she can stick it in her pipe and smoke it!'

A familiar male voice said from the other side of the door, 'That's a pity . . . And after I've come so far to see you too.'

Edith spun around with a gasp and wrenched open the door. Percy stood there, as handsome and debonair as she remembered, a flickering smile on his lips as he met her bewildered gaze.

'P-Percy?' she stammered.

He took a step towards her, holding out his arms. 'Edith, my darling,' he said deeply.

'Oh, you've come at last!' She dashed into his arms, sobbing with joy.

Jack slipped away and closed the door, leaving the two of them alone in the bakehouse. It was stiflingly hot in there, given the sunny day, but all Edith could think about was how ecstatic she suddenly felt.

'I take it you're not going to turn me away, then?' he asked, looking down at her with a twinkle in his eye. 'Unlike Susan and her friends? Who is this Susan anyway, and why does she smoke a pipe?'

'Nobody . . . I mean, she's just an idiot who loves gossiping about me,' she explained, and then realised she hadn't told him *why* Susan had been gossiping. Because then she would have to tell him about the baby.

But she couldn't yet. She'd only just got him back. She just gazed up at him, drinking in his wonderful presence, her lips moving but no words coming out. Perhaps once he knew the awful truth, he would turn right around and leave England again.

'I suppose you're wondering what I'm doing here,' he said

hesitantly, misinterpreting her silence. 'The truth is, I was utterly miserable all the way back to Canada. It's a damn long voyage, and several times I thought I might chuck myself overboard. And all because of you.'

'*Me*?' She couldn't believe her ears.

'Yes, and try as I might, I couldn't get you out of my head. That night we spent together—'

'Hush!' She made sure the door was shut and then leant against it for good measure. 'There might be someone in the shop. Let's not give the villagers any more ammunition for gossip.'

'Yes, sorry.' He flushed. 'I've rehearsed this speech maybe a dozen times and I'm still managing to make a hash of it.' He took a deep breath. 'Anyway, we toured Quebec, took in some sights, then travelled home by train. My parents thought it might take my mind off you to see more of Canada, I suppose. But I was still so wretched once we got home, I couldn't settle back to my studies at university. In the end, I told my parents that I was coming back here to ask you to marry me, and nothing they could say would stop me. So then they knew it was serious.'

'You want to . . . to *marry* me?' she whispered, her heart thumping.

'If you'll have me, yes.' When she said nothing, too dumbfounded to reply, he went on almost sternly, 'I came back to England to tell you that I'm madly in love with you. So, if you say no, you don't want to marry me, I shall accept it. Nothing else I can do. But I might as well give up all hope of *ever* being happy.' A muscle twitched in his jaw. 'So, Edith, there it is. My future happiness is in your hands.'

'Goodness gracious.' She clapped a hand to her mouth,

shaking her head in astonished disbelief. 'I . . . I won't say no. I mean, I say *yes*. Because I love you too.'

He stared. 'You do?'

'Of course . . . In fact, Gran and I have been trying to get hold of you for weeks,' she admitted breathlessly. 'But I was so determined to forget all about you after you'd left for Canada that I . . . Well, I'm ashamed to say I tore up your address. Which meant there was no way to write to you, and your blasted cousin has barely been at home this whole time, so we couldn't get your address from him either.'

Beaming, Percy picked up and swung her around, Edith squealing with laughter. 'So you do want to marry me? Good heavens . . . That's what I call a miracle. My parents told me I was raving, you know. They were so convinced that I'd lost my marbles, they tried to stop me leaving the house at first. Called the doctor out to me. He said there was nothing *wrong* with me . . . I was just head over heels in love.'

Feeling safe in his arms, she smiled up into his beautiful face, memorising every line of his chiselled jaw and strong chin. 'That's exactly how I feel too. Crazy . . . but crazy about *you*.'

He grinned his understanding. 'My parents were so worried in case you said no when I got here, they came with me so I wouldn't be alone. I've left them unpacking at my cousin's house. I promised I'd go back and tell them what you said straightaway. I think they're all prepared for the worst. Won't they be relieved now?' He laughed, kissing her on the lips. 'You know, Patrick told us that he'd sent a telegram to Canada, asking me to contact you. Well, we never got it. But that's probably because we were already on our way back by then. And the blasted ship seemed to take forever . . .

What an adventure, eh?' He held her close. 'You know, you're so much softer and curvier than I remembered. But even more beautiful.'

Trembling in his arms, Edith screwed up her courage to admit why she was so much *curvier than he remembered*. 'Percy, darling, I do absolutely want to marry you, but there's something I need to tell you first.'

In faltering words, she explained that she was expecting his child, and how it had taken her several months to realise what was happening to her body. His eyes widened and his smile disappeared, replaced by a look of shock, and for an awful moment she thought he was going to change his mind and not marry her after all.

'You . . . You're not angry with me, are you?' she asked.

'Angry with you?' He stood taller and shook his head. 'Gosh darn it, it's the most wonderful thing I ever heard in my life. I was rather worried that my parents might still try to talk us out of it, you see. They keep arguing that we've barely known each other five minutes, and even said your father might try to forbid us too. He didn't take to me much, did he, your dad? But now, with a baby on the way . . . Well, it's just perfect. Of course we'll be married.'

'Yes, my father knows about the baby and insisted that we tell you the whole thing. He's had to go away . . . but I'm sure he'll come back for the wedding.' She almost sagged in relief. A wedding. Her and Percy, together in time to have the baby. All her troubles were nearly over. Those nasty village girls could say what they liked now . . . She would soon be a married woman and beyond their reproach. 'I've been so scared, Percy. I didn't know what to do or how to find you. And the baby's just been getting bigger and bigger . . .'

Tenderly, he stroked her hair, his muscular arms holding her close. 'You don't need to be afraid anymore, Edith. I don't care what either of our families have to say about it. We're going to be married and start a family of our own, and nobody can stop us.' He hesitated, looking troubled at last. 'The only thing is, I don't have a job yet . . . I'm still studying. So we'll need to hang on their coat tails a little while longer, I'm afraid. Just until I've found work and can earn enough to buy our own home. I've a fancy to be a journalist, if I can find a good newspaper to take me on. So, where should we live once we're husband and wife? Here with your family or in Canada with mine?'

Edith stared up at him. Emigrating to Canada with him had never even occurred to her. Leave behind her father and grandmother? With a war coming?

'I don't know,' she said faintly. 'But whatever we decide, let's get the wedding over with first, shall we?'

CHAPTER NINETEEN

Sheila was awoken early, startled by the sound of a cockerel crowing. She rolled over in bed and groped for her husband, finding only empty space. For a few befuddled seconds, she wondered where on earth Henry could have gone . . .

Then she remembered and pressed her face into the pillow with a mournful groan. Henry was gone. And she had been left to muddle along somehow without him.

Drowsily, her limbs still aching from the long car journey the day before, Sheila clambered out of her camp bed with much creaking, her joints making almost as much noise as the rackety old bed itself, and threaded her way unsteadily between dusty crates and bric-a-brac to the narrow, green-tinged window of her sister's box room.

Dragging aside the thin yellow curtains, she bent to peer outside. She'd rubbed a porthole on the dirty glass yesterday afternoon with a hanky, and through this she could see the cockerel who'd woken her, perched triumphant on a low wall above the cobbled farmyard, surrounded by busily pecking hens. If she'd needed confirmation that she was no longer in Dagenham, that sight provided it, along with a hazy vista of green and gold fields and the sea glittering in the distance.

She didn't know the area around her sister's farm very well. They had grown up in the same tiny village where Rosalyn and Edith lived, not far from Penzance. Though Penmarrey couldn't be as tiny as it had been in her youth, she thought, given they now had a bakery there as well as a village shop. It would be marvellous to see the old place again while she was here. But she rather suspected that Ernest planned to return to Dagenham as soon as possible.

Sheila couldn't blame the poor man for that. She'd been so relieved yesterday to see the couple holding hands and smiling at each other, showing no signs of bitterness or reproach as she'd feared. All the way down to Cornwall, she'd been half afraid their marriage would be on the rocks if Ernest thought his wife had been unfaithful. But she'd spoken briefly with Betsy around bedtime, not to accuse her but to find out the truth, and her daughter had insisted angrily that Maggie's tales were nothing but nonsense.

Furious, Sheila had almost gone to have it out with Maggie there and then, but had swallowed her fury. She knew Stanley's hot temper of old and had no wish to cause a ruckus late at night.

Nonetheless, she fully intended to have words with her lying sister before she left. It was clear that Maggie's love of stirring up trouble where none existed had not lessened with the years . . .

Feeling no need to hurry, Sheila washed and dressed slowly, choosing a pale blue, short-sleeved summer frock that she'd bought shortly after Henry's funeral but had never worn. It nipped in nicely at the waist, or what passed for her waist these days, in a fashionable style that made her look ten years younger. She gave a satisfied little twirl before putting on her sandals, feeling quite the thing.

'Oh, Henry . . . If you were here with me now, whatever would you say?' she murmured to the mirror, pinning up her wayward silvery locks and applying red lipstick. She pulled a face at herself. 'Probably . . . *Blimey, you old tart!*' Someone knocked loudly at the bedroom door, and she jumped, staring round. 'Yes?'

'Sheila,' her sister said gruffly through the door, 'when you've finished talking to yourself, breakfast's ready, in case you were ever planning on joining us.'

Sheila pursed her lips at this sarcasm but hurried downstairs after her sister to find her daughter and son-in-law already seated at the table.

'Sorry I'm late down,' she told them guiltily, 'but I overslept. All the travelling must have worn me out.' There was no sign of Stanley, but farmers were always up early, so he was probably already out and about. Maggie placed a plate of eggs, bacon and mushrooms in front of her. 'Thanks, Maggie, love. That smells tasty.' She buttered two slices of toasted bread from the rack, suddenly ravenous. 'This is lovely . . . It's so nice not to have to cook, ain't it, Betsy?' she asked, grinning across the table at her daughter.

'I did offer to help,' Betsy said quickly, smiling up at her aunt, who was wiping her hands on her apron. 'But Aunt Margaret wouldn't let me.'

'You're a guest,' Maggie said sourly.

'Oh, Maggie don't like people in her kitchen,' Sheila said at the same time, and tucked into her food.

'We're very grateful to you, Maggie, for putting us up with

so little notice,' Ernest said, finishing his breakfast. 'But don't worry, we won't trespass on your hospitality a moment longer than necessary. In fact, I'd like to take my wife back to Dagenham as soon as possible. Once she's had time to pack her case, that is.'

Betsy glanced nervously at her husband but didn't contradict him.

Maggie said nothing.

With a mouthful of egg and bacon, it took Sheila a moment to respond to his announcement, but as soon as she was able, she said in a forthright manner, 'Ernie, would you mind awfully putting that off until tomorrow, or maybe the day after? It was ever such a long drive yesterday, and I don't think I can do it all over again today. I'm sorry to be a nuisance, love, but you know what us old folk are like.' She could tell by his expression that he didn't believe a word of what she was saying. But she kept smiling in a winning fashion, just as she'd always done with Henry when he was being difficult. 'Besides, now I'm down here, I fancy a visit to the old house where Maggie and I were born and grew up. It weren't exactly the Ritz . . . In fact, it was little better than a hovel,' she told Betsy, who was looking fascinated, 'but we didn't know that when we were kids, and I've fond memories of the place, all the same.'

Her sister, who had sat down with her own breakfast, stared at her, speechless.

Sheila appealed to her. 'Maggie, wouldn't it be nice to go back to Penmarrey together and take a proper poke around? I told you about Edith last night. Lovely girl. Rosalyn's granddaughter.' She paused. 'You said you remembered Rosalyn, didn't you?'

'I remember Rosalyn,' Maggie agreed shortly, and started

to eat, scraping her knife and fork on the plate rather more noisily than Sheila thought strictly necessary.

'Well, I thought it would be a lovely idea to pop over to Penmarrey today and visit Rosalyn, and find out how Edith's been doing since she got home, if my son-in-law will agree to run us over there in the car.'

Ernest looked at Betsy and then raised his brows, almost as though his wife had spoken. 'Nothing would give me more pleasure, Sheila,' he said with only the slightest hesitation, though she got the feeling he meant the absolute opposite. 'Betsy and I can drop you off for an hour or two, and drive into Penzance. It would be nice to have lunch there, just the two of us.' And he smiled intimately at his wife, as though they were newlyweds.

'I'm not going,' Maggie said curtly. 'I'm too busy.'

Once Ernest and Betsy had gone upstairs to prepare for their outing, Sheila stacked together the dirty breakfast plates. 'I'm washing up,' she told her sister firmly, and saw Maggie's lips tighten. Ignoring her, she strode through into her sister's domain, not giving her a chance to say no. 'I thought we could have a chat while I'm doing the dishes. There are a few things I need to say to you.'

'Oh yes?' Her sister leant against the kitchen wall, her arms folded. Her expression was already hostile, and Sheila hadn't said a blessed word yet.

Undaunted, Sheila scraped the plates into the metal pail by the door and thrust them into the sink for washing. There was only an old-fashioned pump over the sink, and she worked this a few times until water came spurting through. It was warm, no doubt because of the hot weather.

'Sorry we dropped in on you unannounced last night,' she began, fishing around in the water for the knives and forks and giving them a good rub with a wet cloth. 'But Ernest was determined to come straight down from Dagenham after he'd read your letter.' When her sister said nothing, Sheila turned and fixed her with a stern eye. 'That was a work of mischief, Maggie. What did you mean by sending such a thing to my son-in-law? Betsy herself told me there was nothing in it . . . Though even if it were true, it ain't your place to go tittle-tattling about my daughter, thank you very much.'

With a burst of fiery temper, she added, unable to stop herself, 'And how dare you and Stanley not come up to give Henry a proper send-off? You could have come on your own if Stanley was too busy. Do you have any idea how I felt, my own sister not even there? It's one thing to miss Betsy and Ernest's anniversary do, but your own brother-in-law's *funeral*?'

Flushed, Maggie stirred at last. 'I couldn't come, and I told you why at the time. I sent a card. I'm sorry you lost Henry. But the farm isn't doing well, and Stanley couldn't leave, not in the middle of summer, and I didn't want to travel all that way on the train on my own. Besides, we couldn't afford it.' She straightened, her face hardening. 'No doubt you're made of money now Henry's dead and buried. But Stanley and me, we might as well be beggars. We live hand to mouth on this farm.'

Noisily, Sheila sloshed water over the plates, trembling with rage at her sister's mealy-mouthed excuses. '*Made of money*? You must be joking. The insurance payout helped me buy the caff, it's true. But it left nothing over.' She regretted having told Maggie about the life insurance money and how she'd used it to better her life. It was obvious her sister had taken this news badly. They'd always been quite competitive as kids, but now they were adults, it just felt petty. Especially as she only had the money because her husband had been killed. Didn't Maggie have any *shame*? 'And I've taken precious time away from work to come down here and give you a piece of my mind over that spiteful letter. As for Betsy... I don't know what you and Stanley have been doing to her, because she won't say a word. But I know my daughter, and I can see she ain't happy.'

'Accusations now, is it?' Maggie glared at her, hands on hips. 'Your daughter arrived here in a state, and if she's still not fixed, that's nothing to do with us. We didn't make her unhappy... We fed her and put her up, like you asked.'

'And made her toil on the farm? Oh yes, Betsy told me about having to milk them bloomin' cows.'

'This isn't a charity, Sheila. Why shouldn't she work in return for bed and board?' Maggie tried to shoo her away from the sink. 'Go on, leave off washing up. I can finish it. Go out gallivanting about the countryside with your daughter and son-in-law. I'm not coming with you, thanks.' Maggie was petulant now. 'I remember where we grew up, and it weren't nowhere special. I'll stay here and do some hard work. Though I doubt you even know what hard work is anymore, being your own boss and all.'

'You think washing up is hard work?' Sheila lowered the last dripping plate onto the draining board. 'You don't know you're born, Margaret Chellew. Nothing to do all day but feed the hens and sweep the floor. Some of us have a proper job.'

'I'd say you've been working too hard at your "proper job",' Maggie countered, a spot of red burning on each cheek. 'And it shows.'

'And what is that supposed to mean?'

'It means you look old before your time. Maybe you should give up running that caff of yours. Before it kills you.'

'Old before my time?' Sheila echoed.

'Take a look in the mirror. All those wrinkles . . . And as for that clinging dress and the red lipstick . . .' Her sister tossed back her hair. 'Mutton dressed as lamb, that's what you are.'

'*Mutton dressed as . . .* ? Gawd blimey.' Gasping in outrage, Sheila shook her dripping hands, spraying her sister with water and soap suds. 'Oops, I'm sorry. Did I get you wet? What a bloomin' shame.' And she stormed out without waiting for a response.

Upstairs, Sheila glanced at herself in the dressing table mirror a second time. She was flushed with temper, her eyes bright, chest heaving . . .

'Mutton dressed as lamb, indeed,' she muttered, but couldn't help wondering if perhaps the red lipstick had been a mistake. It was a younger woman's colour. But it was the only lipstick she owned. A present from Betsy last Christmas.

'Oh, you'll do, my girl,' she told herself, shaking off her sister's criticism with an angry laugh. 'You'll be knocking on for sixty soon. You don't need her approval.' And she grabbed up her summer hat and made her way back downstairs, hearing Ernest and Betsy waiting in the hall below.

Maggie was nowhere to be seen. But since she'd made it clear she wasn't coming out with them on this trip down nostalgia lane, there was no reason to wait for her. All the same, Sheila glanced at the closed kitchen door and hesitated. Perhaps she'd been too hard on her sister. Maggie had sent that card of condolence for the mantelpiece, and written a comfortable letter too the following week, saying how much she'd always liked Henry. But that wasn't the same as turning up for his funeral, was it?

Still, even if it meant putting up with her sister's daggers at dinner tonight, Sheila had at least aired the grievances she'd been nursing, and that was the important thing.

'Everything all right, Sheila?' Ernest asked, frowning. Betsy too was looking worried. It was clear the couple had heard her and Maggie rattling back and forth at each other in the kitchen.

'Never better,' Sheila declared, and jammed her hat down on her hair with a determined smile. 'Off we go, then. A whole day to explore old haunts. What a lark, eh?'

Sheila had been too tired and grumpy the evening before to do much more than stare wearily at the Cornish landscape they were passing through. Now though, refreshed by a good night's sleep, and feeling lighter after having given Maggie a much-deserved piece of her mind, she sat squeezed up beside them on the generous front bench seat of Ernest's Ford Eight and peered out at every landmark, exclaiming every so often with fascinated pleasure, 'Oh, will you look at that?'

'This taking you back, Mum?' Betsy asked, sounding amused.

'I'll say . . . Gawd, what a lovely little Cornish cottage.' Sheila craned her neck to get a better view of the tiny, white-washed cottage nestled beside a reed-thick stream. 'Did you see the thatch work on that, Ernest? Two lovebirds made of straw above the doorway. Eighteenth century, I wouldn't be surprised.'

'More likely seventeenth century,' Ernest remarked, slowing to look back at the quaint cottage before driving on. 'Hmm, a peaceful spot.'

'Blimey, look over there!' Sheila pointed across fields of shimmering green to where the sea lay, a deep idyllic blue, barely rippled by a wave on this hot, still summer's day. 'That looks like an old fishing boat. Gone out after Cornish sardines, perhaps? I swear, we ate fish three times a week in the season when Maggie and I were nippers.' She smiled, able to feel nostalgic at last, now her fury over her sister's spiteful letter had blown itself out. 'My cousin married a Penzance fisherman, you know. She was much older than me, mind. Must be in her seventies now, if she's still alive. We lost touch years ago. Dad never liked that side of the family. Betsy, do you remember? Poor Dad . . . He done his best by us though. That's all you can ever do, eh?'

Betsy threw a sympathetic smile over her shoulder. 'You and Dad did your best for us too, Mum. I never wanted for nothing, and I never heard Violet complain either.'

'That's kind of you to say so, love. But I know you and Vi sometimes went without, and that's the truth.'

Sheila sighed, recalling some difficult days during her thirties when Henry had fallen ill with a serious lung disorder after pneumonia and couldn't work for nearly six months. She'd taken on a cleaning job and some seamstressing where she could, but those had been lean times indeed.

'Lily and Alice are lucky to have such a good earner for a father,' she added, though Ernest was intent on the road ahead. 'This lovely new car, and that nice big house of yours . . . I would have thought I'd died and gone to heaven to be living somewhere so fancy as you, back when I was your age.'

'This is the place,' Ernest said, pointing to the village sign for Penmarrey. 'Edith's grandmother's house is that way. Whereabouts did you used to live, Sheila? Let's see if we can find it.'

Eagerly, Sheila leant forward and directed him through the village, though falteringly at first. It had been so many decades since she and her parents had moved to Dagenham to start a new life there, leaving Maggie behind to marry her first husband. Her voice choked as she recognised the pub on the corner where her dad had often gone drinking after work, and a friend's house where she used to go visiting. They'd moved into Penzance since then, according to Rosalyn. The charming row of rabbit hutches she remembered had gone, replaced by a dismal lean-to shed. And other changes made her struggle to recognise the tiny lane until almost too late . . .

'Down there!' Wildly, she thrust out an arm to point, overcome by emotion, and Ernest ducked. 'Turn right.'

'But we can't . . . There's no room for a car!' Betsy exclaimed, gripping her seat in horror.

Ernest merely grinned and turned down the narrow lane between high, bushy banks. The hedgerows bristled with the same wildflowers she remembered from her youth, when walking home from the local school with Maggie. These days the school was for primary age only, older pupils being sent by bus into Penzance.

They began to pass a row of familiar terraced cottages,

some of the gardens heavily overgrown. 'This is it . . . We lived there, on the end of the row,' she told Betsy excitedly, and then gasped as she saw what had been done to her childhood home. 'Gawd, what a mess! Why, they've dug up the front flower beds.' Where her mother had toiled for hours over her beloved roses and cottage garden favourites, a rackety-looking old vehicle was parked on a dirt track leading to the front door. 'And all for somewhere to park their bloomin' car.'

'Thus modern life,' Ernest murmured, coming to a halt beside the final cottage. '*Sunflowers*,' he read from the painted sign on the cottage wall. 'Rather ironic, given the lack of a garden. Is that what it was called in your day, Sheila?'

'No,' she grumbled, feeling unhappy. 'It was plain Number Five, Miners Row. They used to dig for tin hereabouts, back in Georgian times. That's when they built the cottages, to house the workers. By our day though, tin mining had dried up, the whole row had been bought by the local squire, and I think he rented the cottages out to anyone who could afford 'em.'

They sat for a moment, looking at the squat eighteenth-century cottage with its vanished front garden where she and Maggie had once played barefoot in the sun.

'Mum?' Betsy glanced at her, hesitant. 'Do you want to get out for a proper look?'

But Sheila shook her head. 'No, love, I've seen enough,' she muttered, pushing aside her disappointment with an effort.

Things changed over the years, didn't they? People grew old and died. It was ridiculous to get upset over a few missing flower beds and a silly house name, she told herself firmly.

'Let's drop in on Rosalyn and Edith, eh?' She managed a smile. 'Edith said her dad runs a little bakery in the village. It can't be hard to find in a place this size. Maybe they sell Cornish pasties. We could buy some to take back to Maggie's for tea tonight.'

'Good idea . . . I'd enjoy a Cornish pasty.' Ernest turned the big Ford with surprising ease in the narrow lane, and drove slowly on towards the centre of the village, with Sheila squinting back at her childhood home until it was out of sight . . .

The bakery was indeed easy to find. They parked near the village duckpond with its shady hanging willows and strolled across the green to the shop and nearby bakery, both converted from old Cornish houses with high gabled, slate-tiled roofs. To Sheila's relief, the bakery door was propped open, so it was clearly still open, despite it being almost lunchtime.

There was some commotion inside. Laughter, raised voices . . .

'Hello?' Sheila said, bustling inside out of the bright sunshine, keen to be distracted after a difficult morning.

She could smell fresh loaves and pastry, the smell mouthwatering . . . And there was Edith herself, pretty in a summer frock, pristine white baker's apron wrapped about her thickening waist, her face wreathed in smiles. A fresh-faced, sun-browned young man had his arm about her shoulder, and she was gazing up at him with undisguised love and happiness.

Never had Edith looked as carefree and full of joy, and it did Sheila's old heart good to see her so changed.

'Goodness . . . Is that you, Mrs Hopkins?' Edith turned to stare, her expression stunned. 'What are you doing here?'

'I came down with Ernest, love. We're taking Betsy back to Dagenham.' Betsy came in behind her, hand in hand with Ernest, both nodding to Edith. 'How are you?' She hesitated, looking at the young man's proud smile. 'And who's this?' Though she already felt sure she knew the answer and couldn't be happier for the young couple.

Blushing, Edith said shyly, 'You remember I told you about Percy Grigg from Canada? Well, this is him. And he's my fiancé now . . . Oh, Mrs Hopkins, Betsy . . . We're going to be married!'

CHAPTER TWENTY

Betsy wound down the car window to wave goodbye to her mum, and then sat back as Ernest drove out of the village, heading for the coast. 'You don't mind having to come back for Mum later, do you? She seemed so keen on having lunch with Rosalyn and Edith, I didn't want to drag her all the way to Penzance with us.' She still couldn't quite believe that Ernest had come down to Cornwall thinking she'd been unfaithful in his absence, yet still determined to win her back if possible. His generosity of spirit made her love him more than ever. What a wonderful husband he was, she thought, smiling at him warmly. 'I wish the girls were here with us, but the truth is, I can't wait to explore Penzance with just the two of us. It's such a hot day too . . . What do you say to paddling in the sea after lunch?'

'Will it involve removing my shoes and socks?'

'That's the general idea. You'll need to roll your trouser legs up a little way too,' she pointed out, laughing, 'unless you want to get them wet.'

'Salt water and tweed don't mix,' Ernest said firmly. 'I'll definitely roll them up, and keep hold of them while I paddle, even if I look ridiculous doing so.'

'I love you, Ernie,' she said, touching his arm. 'You know that, don't you?'

'Of course.' He smiled at her, but she caught a slight hesitation in his manner. 'I love you too, *Liebchen*.'

Worried by that look in his face, which she'd thought their lovemaking yesterday had banished, Betsy gripped her hands in her lap, looking out of the window. But she was unable to enjoy the beautiful rolling green countryside as the big car bowled effortlessly along the main road towards Penzance and the coast.

'Darling, is . . . is something the matter?' she asked eventually, fearing his answer.

'Not at all,' he said, again with the smooth reassuring smile. But it didn't quite reach his eyes and convince her.

'Ernie, please . . .'

He drove for a while without speaking, but she could see him thinking, always so clever, always working out every angle. 'This doctor . . .' he began, glancing at her sideways, 'was there ever a moment when you were interested in him? I know you said there wasn't, but perhaps you were taken off guard yesterday, and felt you couldn't be entirely truthful with me.'

'No,' she insisted, hot-cheeked. 'I told you, he's a very nice man. The kind of man we might be friends with back home. But that's as far as it goes.'

He nodded, seeming to accept that. But a moment later, he said, 'I wish I could meet him, all the same.'

'Why?' Because he wants to make sure, she thought,

frightened that he didn't believe her and perhaps would never trust her again, despite his reassurances.

'I would like to thank him, that's all. For looking after my wife so well.' He gazed at the road ahead. 'After all, if it wasn't for this Dr Martin, I might have found you too unwell to come back home with me.'

She hoped that was the truth, and it wasn't because he still doubted her. But there seemed nothing else to say, so she quelled her nerves and tried to enjoy the picturesque landscape. She didn't know when she might see anything as beautiful again once they were back in Dagenham, much as she loved her dear old hometown.

On reaching Penzance, they drove slowly out along the coast to admire the impressive white stone turrets and towers on the beautiful St Michael's Mount. The medieval castle was bathed in sunlight and cut off from the mainland by high tide, a few rowboats heading to and fro with passengers. They sat together on a grassy verge and watched as the sea sparkled under the sun like a million diamonds, and for a while Betsy felt her troubles drifting away on the water's ebb.

Ernest was right, she told herself. She did feel well enough to go home, though it wasn't the kindly Dr Martin who had cured her of the blues. Rather, she'd cured herself by realising, as the days passed, how much harder and colder everyday life was without her husband and children around her. Her aunt had been so mean at times, and she wasn't sure she would ever forgive her for writing so maliciously to Ernest over nothing, and Uncle Stanley was a creep with wandering hands . . .

She couldn't wait to get home and kiss her darling Lily

and Alice, to sleep in her own comfortable bed again, and wake to find Ernest beside her every morning. She belonged with her own family, for better or worse. Although the deep sorrow over her lost baby and Dad's tragic death hadn't left her, and the constant threat of impending war still brought nightmares, she knew now that she would better cope with those trials at home, surrounded by those who loved her. Cornwall was an idyllic place, but it was only people who could comfort and console her, not a landscape.

They lunched at a cosy spot near the harbour in Penzance, a discreet French bistro, which would not have been out of place in London, as Ernest commented when he first saw it from across the street, before raising his brows at the menu posted in the window.

'Are you sure we can afford a posh place like this?' Betsy hesitated on the threshold, anxious.

Ernest took her hand. 'We need to enjoy life while we still can. Come on . . .' And he pulled her inside, grinning at her shocked expression.

They ordered *coq au vin* to share and sat watching the passers-by and the busy harbour below. She couldn't remember the last time they'd been out dining together like this; not since their courtship days, she suspected. As they waited for their meal, they chatted over a small glass of wine about country life and how much the girls would enjoy a summer holiday in Cornwall.

'Though Mum would insist on coming with us,' Betsy pointed out when Ernest spoke enthusiastically about the places they could visit, amused by the thought of him spending several weeks cooped up in a car with his mother-in-law as well as his two daughters. 'She seems to have enjoyed returning to her roots, have you noticed?'

Ernie shrugged, not as horrified by this prospect as she'd expected. 'Your mother did grow up around here,' he said, 'and of course she must come with us if we take a holiday in Cornwall.' He toyed with his wine glass, staring down towards the harbour, his look faraway. 'Sheila is all alone now. She has Violet, of course. But she's a widow now, and that changes things. We must make allowances for her loneliness, and make sure we don't shut her out.'

Betsy readily agreed, but his words stirred a rawness inside her. She sucked in her breath, overwhelmed by the memory of that terrible night when she'd lost her dad and almost her husband too.

He reached across the table and took her hand. 'We're going to make it, you and I.' He held her gaze. 'Yes?'

She nodded jerkily, smiling at him through a sheen of tears. 'Yes, of course we will,' she whispered, though there was doubt in her heart.

A ruckus outside on the street made Betsy turn her head, staring through the bistro windows, hung with dainty, Breton-style lace nets. There were men walking past, loud and swaggering. But it was their uniforms rather than their noise that struck her. 'Oh,' she said bleakly, glancing across at Ernest. 'Soldiers. It's silly of me, maybe . . . But I didn't expect to see any down here in Cornwall.'

He too was looking their way, his expression grim. The soldiers were walking in a tight group, laughing and chatting, smart in their army uniforms. Most weren't young but in their late twenties and thirties, she noticed, watching them pass. Others in the street had also turned to look at them, perhaps also making the same connections as her. Soldiers would likely become a commonplace sight on their streets if war was declared . . .

'Every region has its regiments,' Ernest murmured, also studying them. 'Cornwall is no exception. Those are professional soldiers, by the look of them. All this recent talk of war . . . They must be itching to see some action at last. And they'll have it soon enough, from what the newspapers have been saying this past week.'

He got up to retrieve a daily newspaper, abandoned on an adjacent table, and showed her the front page.

HITLER REJECTS PEACE PROPOSALS, one headline shouted in large block capitals, above a grainy photograph of soldiers training, along with the chilling caption: *British troops on high alert*.

'I wish Britain didn't have to get involved in what's going on abroad. I hate it so much,' she moaned, but hurriedly fell silent when the waiter appeared with their delicious-smelling *coq au vin*. She didn't want to be thought unpatriotic. When the man had gone, she met her husband's shrewd gaze. 'You do understand what I mean, don't you, Ernest? It's not because I think Hitler is right or anything stupid like that. It's only that—'

'You don't want men like that to die,' he supplied softly.

She nodded. 'I don't want anyone to die.'

'Unfortunately, *Liebling*, people are already dying. Those who oppose Herr Hitler or belong to the wrong ethnicity for his tastes.' He kept his voice low, perhaps aware that his slight German accent might cause consternation among the other diners. 'Britain must intervene. Or this country will be next on his list.'

'I know you're right. It's just all so horrible and frightening.' She began to eat her *coq au vin* but couldn't enjoy the rich sauce or the chicken that melted off the bones. It might as well have been sawdust in her mouth. 'If there *is* a war, what will happen to us, Ernie? And to our girls? You told me to trust that everything would be all right. And I want to. But you might be called up and become a soldier like them. Or arrested for being . . . being a foreigner.' She choked on the words, unable to continue.

He was listening calmly, eating while she spoke. 'All of that could happen, yes. But going to war against Germany is the only course of action left to Britain. Or the government might as well surrender these islands to Hitler right now and prepare to be slaughtered.'

She stared, wide-eyed. '*Slaughtered*? Oh, Ernie, you can't mean it. You really think it would be as bad as *that*?'

'Letting the Nazis get the upper hand would be worse than you can possibly imagine. Hitler would love to add Britain to his roster of conquests. And he would happily kill anyone who tries to resist, or who doesn't fit his model of the perfect Germanic citizen. That's why it was so important that I spoke to Herr Schmidt about those Blackshirts before driving down to collect you,' he added, lowering his voice, 'or I would never have delayed my departure.'

Betsy met his sombre gaze. 'Then it has to be war?'

'It has to be war,' he agreed, but gave her a lopsided smile. 'However, it's not all doom and gloom, my love. Difficult days define us in a way that easy days never can. And I'm convinced that Britain will rise to the challenge. As will our own family.' Ernest lifted his glass of wine in a toast, his eyes locked smilingly to hers. 'To *this sceptr'd isle* . . . And to my beautiful wife and daughters, whom I intend to protect with my life.'

This announcement horrified and frightened her, but she forced a smile to her lips and lifted her own glass in a toast too. 'To my loving husband,' she said faintly. 'And to better peace talks.'

Ernest drank but shook his head as he put down his glass. 'Ah, my love, I wish peace talks would work. Then we could come down here with your mother and the girls next summer, and have a wonderful time camping in the fields or staying in some quaint bed and breakfast. But the time for such hope is over. From now on, we need to face reality.'

'Reality?' she stammered.

'I'm afraid so,' he agreed, a sadness in his face that made her want to cry, for he was so rarely unhappy. 'It's impossible to keep pretending that everything is going to be fine. That we can make plans for the future and expect to keep them. The truth is, we'll soon be at war with Germany, this war will be bloodier than the last one . . . and none of our lives will ever be the same again.'

When they returned to the farm later that afternoon, Sheila excitedly telling them all she had discovered about Edith's young Canadian fiancé, Betsy was startled to see the doctor's car parked outside the farmhouse.

She sat up, chewing anxiously on a fingernail, not even caring that it would ruin her varnish. Whatever was the doctor doing there?

As Ernest pulled through the gate, she saw Dr Martin coming out of the house with Maggie in tow. Her aunt was busily chatting away while he listened, a sombre look on his face. But they both turned at the sound of the car approaching, a quick smile lighting up Dr Martin's face when he saw who it was.

Betsy's tummy churned with nerves, fearing a confrontation between her husband and the doctor. She climbed out, swiftly followed by her mum.

Despite her haste, Ernest was already standing in front of the bonnet by the time she shut the passenger door. He was gazing steadily towards the young, fair-haired doctor. 'Dr Martin, I presume?' he asked, an ironic look on his face.

'That's him, yes,' she admitted. 'He must have come to check on me. But there was no need. And I daresay Aunt Maggie has been telling him how I'm better and will be leaving soon.' She hoped that was all her aunt had been saying, at any rate. Not stirring up yet more trouble where none had previously existed. 'Let's go inside, Ernest. The doctor won't want to stop and chat . . . He's always in a hurry to finish his rounds,' she fibbed.

But Ernest paid no attention, walking towards the other man, his hand outstretched. 'Hello,' he said smoothly, 'you must be Dr Martin. I'm Ernest Fisher, Betsy's husband. I've come to fetch her home.' He paused, as they shook hands. 'You have no objections, I take it? I hear you've been treating my wife during her stay here.'

Dr Martin was looking her husband up and down while Ernest studied the doctor closely in return. 'Yes, that's right. No objections whatsoever. In fact, I'm delighted to hear she's feeling well enough to return home.' His smiling, uncomplicated gaze shifted to Betsy's face. 'Hello again, Mrs Fisher. I must say, you're looking much improved today. Your husband is to thank for that though, I expect.' He was smiling, apparently oblivious to Ernest's tension. 'I'll be sorry not to see you again. But very glad that you're on the mend.'

'Yes, thanks for everything, Doc.' Betsy came forward falteringly to shake his hand. She was deeply aware of her mother listening behind them, and her aunt's beady-eyed stare drilling into them both too. Their silent judgement infuriated her. She had done nothing wrong, except perhaps develop a friendly relationship with a man who wasn't her husband. Yet she felt guilty, nonetheless. He was quite attractive . . .

'I couldn't have done it without you. The state I was in when I first come down here, and then the sleepwalking . . . You've been a friendly face while I've been in Cornwall.' She risked a glance at Maggie as she said this, feeling a throb of resentment at the way she'd been treated. 'I'm very grateful for your help.'

'You're welcome, Mrs Fisher.' The doctor hesitated, smiling past Betsy. 'Ah, but this must be your mother. Mrs Chellew has just been telling me how her sister had come down to visit her as well. It's very good to meet you, Mrs Hopkins.' And he shook hands with Sheila as well, who began telling the poor man about how beautiful the Cornish landscape was and how lucky he was to be living there, while he struggled to get a word in sideways.

Stanley had come out of the farmhouse, arms folded, a hard look on his face. He hadn't said much to anyone since Ernest had arrived, but Betsy had caught his gaze on her from time to time, a warning look in those unpleasant eyes. She knew what that look meant. *Don't tell your husband what I did, or else.*

Now more than ever she wouldn't say a word about what

happened in the cowshed. She had no intention of spoiling whatever precious time she had left with Ernest before war was declared and he signed up to fight. What would be the point? *Least said, soonest mended*, as her mum would say. Though she would certainly have private words with her aunt before leaving the farm. The bleedin' cheek of that woman, writing ugly whoppers to her husband back home, knowing how much trouble it might cause between them. There was enough bad blood between the two halves of the family as it was. There was no need to go creating more.

For a brief moment, Betsy wondered if Aunt Maggie had done it deliberately, in the hope of getting her niece off the farm. That certainly made better sense than trying to stir up anger and bitterness for no reason. Maggie could hardly have missed the way Stanley had kept staring at Betsy and must have guessed her husband's lecherous ways could not be contained forever.

Ernest had not moved while Sheila continued to witter on about Cornwall, and now interrupted his mother-in-law, saying, 'My apologies, Sheila, if I could butt in for a moment . . . ? Doctor, since I'll be taking your patient off your hands tomorrow, how much do I owe you for her treatment?'

Dr Martin shook his head, turning to him with that pleasant smile again. 'Nothing whatsoever, Mr Fisher. Your wife already paid me herself.'

To Betsy's alarm, her husband's smile became fixed. 'Is that so?' He seemed to be speaking through his teeth.

Unable to bear this a moment longer, Betsy grabbed her mother's arm and began to drag her into the farmhouse. 'Come on, Mum,' she muttered, 'I want to start packing. Will you help me? Goodbye, Dr Martin,' she threw over her shoulder. 'Thank you again.' Betsy hurried past Stanley without looking at him, reaching the safety of the shady farmhouse with relief.

She hoped she was imagining Ernest's grim mood. But it was soon clear she wasn't. Even as she headed into the farmhouse, Maggie and Stanley following them inside, she overheard the doctor saying with obvious embarrassment, 'Look here, old man, if you're thinking what I *think* you're thinking, then you're barking up the wrong tree.'

Maggie bustled away, muttering something about soaking a ham, and Stanley shuffled after her, his face averted.

'I'm going to pack my case,' Betsy declared, heading upstairs.

'Me too, love.' Her mum followed her, stopping to glance through the door into Betsy's room. 'Blow me, your room's nicer than mine,' she said, pulling a face as she came right inside and peered around. 'Though that ain't saying much. My room's the size of a rabbit hutch and full of rubbish too. And I'm sleeping on a camp bed like a soldier. I keep expecting to hear a trumpet at dawn, instead of that noisy bloomin' cockerel crowing at all hours.'

Betsy, already folding clothes neatly into the suitcase Ernest had brought with him, had to chuckle at this. But her laughter soon died as she thought of her husband asking the doctor for a word in private. 'Oh, Mum . . . Why does life have to be so complicated?'

'I don't know, love. But if you ever find out, tell me.'

'I never looked twice at Dr Martin.'

'Of course you didn't.' Her mum pursed her lips. 'My sister's always been a spiteful so-and-so. But she got worse after she married that Stanley Chellew,' she added in a whisper. 'Still, I expect being married to that beast for longer than five minutes would turn most women sour. In fact, I'm surprised his customers don't send back their churns, saying his cows' milk is on the turn.' They both snorted with laughter, though quietly, in case the two downstairs heard them. 'Anyway, your Ernie knows it was all pure nonsense. Just your aunt's usual poison pen . . . So don't you fret, love.'

Betsy managed a smile but couldn't feel as confident. All she could think about was what the two men were saying to each other outside . . .

Reaching for her bag of dirty laundry, she stiffened. Ernest was coming up the stairs with a heavy tread. Her mum shot Betsy a keen look, then made for the door. 'I'll go and start packing me own stuff,' she said, with rare tact. 'Though it'll only take two minutes. I barely brought anything but a nightie and me toothbrush. But perhaps Maggie will need a hand downstairs, peeling the veg for supper.' She passed Ernest in the doorway. 'Everything dandy, Ernie?'

To Betsy's relief, her husband was smiling, and not between his teeth anymore. 'Never better, Sheila. See you later.' He closed the bedroom door firmly after her and turned to Betsy, holding out his arms. 'Come here, darling.' She went to him, and he held her close, pressing his stubbled cheek against hers. 'Can you forgive me? I'm a jealous dog. I don't mean to be, but sometimes a fellow can't help it.'

'Of course I forgive you.' Though she wasn't sure what she was meant to be forgiving him for. 'But whatever did you say to the doctor?' She swallowed. 'And what did *he* say to you?'

Ernest gave a low laugh, which surprised her. 'Let's put it

like this, I don't think I ever had anything to worry about from your Dr Martin.' When she looked up at him wonderingly, he added softly, 'Between you and me, he told me I was quite wrong if I thought there was something going on between the two of you. There was nothing explicit said, understandably given the circumstances, but I got the gist of it. You see, our dear doctor isn't particularly interested in the ladies.'

Betsy wrinkled her brow, confused. 'Sorry? What do you mean?'

'You know what I mean.'

Her eyes widened slowly as she realised the hidden significance of his remark. 'Oh!'

'Oh, indeed.' He laughed at her dumbfounded expression. 'I, on the other hand, am very interested in the ladies. Though only in one *special* lady these days.' He kissed her deeply, and her arms locked about his neck in warm, drowsy satisfaction. Eventually, he murmured in her ear, 'Darling, shall we lie down for an hour or two? Your aunt told me supper wouldn't be ready until six, and I'm sure nobody will miss us.'

Relieved beyond words that everything seemed right between them again, she melted against her husband, smiling.

'Yes, please, Ernest.'

CHAPTER TWENTY-ONE

Early one morning in the last week of August, Edith woke before her alarm clock had gone off and rolled over with a little difficulty, her large tummy hampering her somewhat. Though that was hardly surprising, she thought with a sigh, rubbing a hand over her belly where it ached and tightened in a now familiar way. One of the local team of doctors had been called out recently to examine her following a nasty spasm, and had pronounced her about six months gone, give or take a week, but in excellent health overall. She just wished these awkward pains would stop . . .

To Edith's relief, Dr Martin hadn't seemed shocked to discover that his young patient was not a married lady but had smiled instead and merely wished her and her fiancé well when Percy, waiting anxiously downstairs, had explained that their wedding day was to be the very next weekend.

And this was the day itself.

Her wedding day.

What a strange thought, though a happy one. She would soon be a married woman and on her honeymoon. Though the honeymoon was a mere two days in a hotel in Southampton before they boarded a ship bound for Canada as Mr and Mrs Grigg. The travel documents had all been acquired, and she had received the new passport with her married name, which would only become legally valid once the wedding had taken place. Thankfully, there had been no need for a visa to travel to Canada, it being part of the British Commonwealth, And once there, their marriage certificate should be enough to allow her the right to stay indefinitely.

Her heart thumping with excitement, Edith clambered out of bed and padded across to check on the weather. There was a lively breeze shaking the trees in her grandmother's garden, but no sign of clouds on the horizon to spoil the day. The sky was already a deep, peaceful blue as far as the eye could see, and the sill was warm to the touch as she leant forward to throw open the window.

'Ouch!' Leaning forward had not been wise, she realised. It had set off that odd pain again . . . She winced, rubbing her tummy more forcefully. 'Goodness, that doesn't feel right.' Anxiously, she pulled on her housecoat and hurried along the landing to knock on her grandmother's door. 'Grandma, are you awake?'

'Of course I'm awake.' Her grandmother pulled open the door, already dressed, her hair neatly combed. 'I've been awake since dawn, worrying about all the thousand things that could go wrong today.' She stopped, her eyes narrowing on Edith's worried face. 'My dear? What is it? You're not unwell, I hope?'

'It . . . It's the baby, I think.' Edith rubbed her tummy where she'd felt that pain again, the one that kept irking her when she least expected it. Though sometimes it shifted and surprised her. 'I don't know what it is, exactly . . . But it's the most uncomfortable thing. At first it was a horrid bubbly sensation like indigestion, or bad tummy ache. So I ignored it because pregnant ladies get indigestion all the time, don't they? Only it's getting more and more uncomfortable, Grandma, and I . . . I think something's wrong,' she ended in a frantic whisper.

'Oh, my dear.' Her grandmother hesitated, looking thoughtful. 'May I?' She was reaching out to Edith's tummy.

Edith nodded, close to tears.

'Where did you feel this pain last?' When Edith guided her hand to the right spot, her grandmother pressed lightly on her pronounced bump, and the spasm-like pain came again. Only when Edith sucked in her breath, making a face, her grandmother surprised her by merely chuckling. 'There's nothing wrong, dearest. That's your baby kicking.'

Edith stared at her. 'K-Kicking?'

'Good gracious, you didn't realise what that was?' Her grandmother's smile died when Edith stood trembling and uncertain. 'But of course you didn't. How could you know? I should have explained . . . You see, babies kick in the womb. What you've been feeling is perfectly natural and will only get stronger as the weeks pass. Indeed, if you ever go even a day or two without feeling that little bumping sensation, you should call a doctor.'

'I feel like such a fool. All this time, I thought it was indigestion.'

Tentatively, Edith put a hand on the spot where she instinctively guessed the bumping pain would come next and within a few seconds felt again the nudge of a foot or perhaps a tiny hand coming to meet hers.

'Oh!' She gasped and then laughed, meeting her grandmother's amused gaze with joy in her heart. 'You're right, Grandma. It's my baby! Oh, I can't wait to tell Percy.' She beamed. It wasn't in fact painful, she thought, merely a little uncomfortable and surprising. 'And I suppose it knows I'm here, and that I'm talking about him or her, and that's why he or she is *kicking*.'

'Yes, dearest, of course the baby knows,' her grandmother agreed, and gave her a quick peck on the cheek. 'Now, hurry away and wash before breakfast. Then we must arrange your beautiful hair with summer flowers and get you dressed ready to walk to the church with your father.' She smiled fondly at her granddaughter. 'You don't want to be late for your own wedding, surely?'

'No, Grandma,' she said obediently, but couldn't resist adding, just a little impatiently, 'Though I wish so much that I could tell if it's a boy or a girl. How does anyone bear *not knowing* for all these months? And having to knit everything in white and lemon and lilac, just in case you guess wrong? It's intolerable.'

'It certainly is. Now, hurry up. Your father's downstairs too. We had breakfast together an hour ago. I've never seen him so agitated.'

'Agitated?' Edith, who had been heading back to her room, turned in alarm. 'That's not like him. Has something happened?'

'No, dearest. He's just never been the father of the bride before, and I think he's worried that everything will go horribly wrong. That you'll change your mind halfway down the aisle—'

'Never!' Edith declared passionately.

'Yes, that was always unlikely. But it is possible that the vicar's bicycle will have a flat tyre and he'll be late getting to the church, as he was when poor Emily Flannery married that lawyer from Penzance. And last night, though admittedly after several glasses of wine, your father did rather naughtily suggest,' her grandmother added, a mischievous smile on her lips, 'that Percy himself might get cold feet and not turn up to marry you.'

Edith merely grinned and shook her head, filled with a pulsing glow of happiness that seemed to start with her kicking baby and spread all the way out to the tips of her fingers. 'Well, I can't speak for the vicar and his rusty old bicycle . . . But Percy will be waiting at the altar for me when we get to the church, of that I'm certain.' She laughed, returning to her bedroom. 'Or he'll have me to answer to.'

When she reached the church, walking beside her father in his smart RAF uniform, who had been granted leave from the training base for a bare forty-eight hours, she found a small crowd of villagers gathered outside the lych-gate. She knew the villagers often gathered outside the parish church even for weddings they were not planning to attend, just to see the bride in her finery and maybe throw a little rice or rose petals after the ceremony. Yet somehow she had never expected anyone to turn out for *her* wedding . . . Let alone so many.

Surprised, she halted and glanced around at her grandmother, who was leaning on her cane as she followed at a slower pace. 'Grandma, all these people . . . They're not here to see me, are they?'

'Of course they are, my dear,' she said with a reassuring

smile, catching up with them. 'People love a bride. The dress, the flowers, the veil . . . Go on, don't disappoint them.'

But Edith hesitated, still uncertain. Her specially designed wedding dress, despite all its fussy frills and flowing Empire-style line, could not disguise the fact that this particular bride was expecting a baby.

'Courage, Edith,' her father murmured, taking her hand and placing it on his arm. His gaze sought hers. 'We'll do this together, yes?'

With a firm nod, her courage rising, she continued on her way, passing under the old porched lych-gate where she and her friends had often played on rainy days as youngsters. She remembered those days now, the sun rising bright in the sky on her wedding morning, and wished that she had not let those early friendships fade away as she got older. Perhaps if she hadn't fallen out with Susan, for instance, and had felt able to confide in her properly from the beginning, as a trusted and beloved friend, she might not have fled the village for Dagenham, and her condition would have been discovered earlier. Then she and Percy might even have been married before now. But in her loneliness after he'd returned to Canada, she'd been too ashamed by the rumours to stay and confront Susan. Because of Edith's own naivety, not taking enough care to be discreet, Susan had chanced to see them together on Percy's last evening in Cornwall, hand in hand, two lovers going into the woods together . . . And she hadn't seen them returning. That one night together had been enough to condemn her.

She tried to walk with her head held high, a bride's happy smile on her face. But it was so difficult, every step a purgatory . . .

Then, to her dismay, Susan Teague was there among the crowd, her pinched face glaring at Edith from behind her mother and sister, who by contrast seemed happy to be there.

Foolishly, she wished that Violet Hopkins, with her brave determination to overcome grief, could have been there to be a bridesmaid and lend her some much-needed strength. Or that kindly Mrs Hopkins, still smiling despite losing her beloved husband, and Betsy and Ernest, who had suffered a cruel loss and come through stronger, could have stayed a while longer in Cornwall to see her married. But of course they all had their own complicated lives back in Dagenham, and she must follow her own path now.

So, not having dared ask anyone in the village to be part of the bridal party, she had only her father and grandmother for company.

The Hopkinses and the Fishers had sent a joint telegram though, which had arrived just after breakfast as she was being helped into her wedding dress. A telegram of congratulations, wishing her and Percy all the best in their married life together. Reading it had made her cry for joy. They had known each other such a short time, but already she felt part of their family.

Yet, even as she locked eyes with Susan, her steps faltered again, and her courage slipped a little . . .

Then Lizzie and Hermione, Susan's slavish younger followers, dashed out in front of the bridal party.

Shocked, Edith stopped dead, not sure what to expect, and her father stopped too, staring at the two girls from under bushy brows.

But Hermione merely held out a pristine white hanky, embroidered with an H, nodding at her to take it. 'Something new *and* borrowed,' she whispered before darting away again with a muttered, 'Don't forget to give it back later.'

Lizzie grinned and handed her a dried, pressed cornflower, its blue flowers still vibrant. 'Something old *and* blue.' Then, with a wink, she followed her friend back into the crowd, calling back over her shoulder, 'You look beautiful, by the way.'

Edith stood frozen and utterly bewildered, Hermione's hanky in one hand and Lizzie's blue cornflower in the other.

'Push the hanky up your sleeve, Edith,' her grandmother instructed her calmly, though with a twinkle in her eye, 'and as for that dried cornflower . . .' Stepping forward, she arranged it artfully in Edith's red hair. 'There, perfect.'

'A blue flower? With my red hair?' Edith spluttered. 'Why on earth . . . ?'

'Dear child, you remember the old bridal rhyme,' her grandmother told her, arching a brow even as she smiled.

'Ah, of course!' Her father slapped his knee, laughing out loud. 'The four things every bride needs for good luck on her wedding day.'

'Of course, the old rhyme,' said Edith, feeling silly for not having recalled it before. '*Something old, Something new, Something borrowed, Something blue.* But are they allowed to be doubled up?'

'Oh, for goodness' sake, don't you know anything?' demanded Susan, stepping out from behind her mother. 'Of course you're allowed to double up.' She pointed to the hanky, now dangling out of the puffed sleeve of Edith's wedding dress. 'But mind, that's one of Hermione's brand-new hankies. Her mother just embroidered a fresh set for her. So she's expecting it back after the ceremony, remember. It has to be *borrowed*.'

'And preferably returned *unused*,' Hermione added from the crowd, and everyone laughed.

'Though it is a wedding,' Susan's mother pointed out, 'and everyone's a watering pot at a wedding, so Hermione should expect to get it back *damp*, at least.'

'And Lizzie's given you a cornflower,' Susan went on doggedly, ignoring these interruptions. 'It was dried and pressed between the pages of a book because it bloomed a few weeks back, so it's old. But it's also blue.'

'Susan picked the cornflower bloom herself,' Lizzie stuck in hurriedly, ignoring her friend's furious look, 'as soon as she met Percy at the bakery and realised you two were getting hitched.'

Susan folded her arms, a flush in her cheeks. 'It's a beautiful flower,' she muttered, 'for a beautiful bride.'

Edith stared at the three of them in astonishment, from Lizzie and Hermione's glowing faces to Susan's clearly penitent expression. Susan Teague. Her chief tormentor. Her oldest friend. *A beautiful flower for a beautiful bride*. And her heart swelled with unexpected joy and forgiveness. Yes, perhaps Susan had said some dreadful things and made her life a misery. And she'd certainly had no right to gossip like that behind her back, and especially not to call her a . . . a *slut*. Just remembering that word caused her pain. But looking into Susan's eyes, seeing the guilt and hesitation there, Edith felt sure there must have been a reason for her to behave so cruelly . . . And perhaps she might have discovered that reason if she had spoken to Susan directly instead of running away and trying to pretend none of it had ever happened.

'Thank you,' she said huskily, and smiled at the three girls, but especially at Susan. 'That's awfully kind of you. The truth is, you took me by surprise just now . . . I'd forgotten about that old wedding rhyme, and you're right, I'm not wearing anything old, new, borrowed *or* blue that I know of . . . At least,' she added with a sudden realisation, 'Grandma did lend me her antique pearl necklace for today, which is technically both old *and* borrowed—'

'No, darling, it's not a loan. It's a gift. A wedding gift for my granddaughter,' Gran interrupted, adding sheepishly, 'Though yes to the old part. It's Victorian. Your grandfather bought it for me as an engagement present. I'm sure he would have been thrilled to see you wearing it on your wedding day.' Her smile was misty. 'And maybe one day you can hand it on to your own daughter or granddaughter.'

'Thank you, Grandma,' Edith whispered, touching the necklace with tears in her eyes. She swallowed hard against the lump in her throat, determined not to become a watering pot herself and be forced to use Hermione's handkerchief before she'd even got into the church. 'As for these other things, it was so thoughtful of you,' she said, smiling round at them all. 'I'll never forget it.'

She took a step forward but Susan had not moved and was standing right in front of her, arms folded, blocking her path to the church.

Edith looked at her apprehensively, not sure what to expect.

'Could we talk later? You and me . . . and maybe Percy too?' Susan asked in a low voice. 'After the wedding, I mean?'

'Erm, if you like.' Taken aback by this request, Edith was relieved when Susan finally stepped aside, and she was able to take her father's arm again, continuing on towards the church. But the sight of the vicar hovering in the church doorway made her forget everything except the most important thing of all. She was getting married today . . . and to the love of her life. Edith stopped dead at the thought, her heart thumping wildly, so overwhelmed by emotion that she couldn't even think or speak, let alone walk.

'Dearest,' her grandmother murmured from behind her, 'you haven't forgotten that your bridegroom is waiting for you inside, and most likely having a heart attack by now, the length of time it's taking you to get into the church . . .'

'Oh yes,' Edith gushed, laughing and crying at the same time, and somehow managed to drop her bridal bouquet.

Urgently, someone pressed the bouquet back into her hands. Fresh green, white, cream, and soft salmon-pink flowers, wrapped in silk.

Her grandmother fumbled with the lace veil, drawing it down over Edith's face. 'A little old-fashioned these days, a veil, but wonderfully mysterious,' she whispered. 'There, now you're ready.'

'Oh, Grandma,' Edith gasped.

'I know, dearest. It all feels too much. But you'll get through the ceremony, trust me, and everything will be marvellous.' Her grandmother embraced her warmly. 'Now, let me get to my seat first, and then wait for the organ music. Yes?'

And with that, she slipped into the church, leaving Edith alone with her father in the hot August sunshine.

'That awful Susan was right, you know,' her father muttered as they took their places at the church door. He cleared his throat, clearly emotional too. 'You *are* beautiful, my Edith. I only wish your mother could have been here today to see you.'

Edith smiled tremulously. 'Thank you, Daddy. I wish that too.' And she felt the most tremendous kick under her ribs at those words.

This time, she knew it wasn't indigestion or something wrong with the pregnancy. It was her and Percy's baby, saying hello again. Saying, *I'm here, and I love you both*. And she put a hand to her ribs where the kick had been and patted it gently.

'I love you too,' she whispered back.

Percy was waiting for her at the altar, straight-backed and formal in his groom's suit, a white flower in his buttonhole, a smile on his lips that was only for her.

Edith paced slowly and magnificently down the aisle towards him, her father close by her side. The tears in her eyes meant she could barely see the faces of the congregation, though she could smell the rich, sweet fragrance of all the flowers her grandmother and her village friends had wreathed around every pew end and pillar in the church, and the traditional music the organist was playing thundered in her heart, as though echoing the emotions she could no longer hold back . . .

At last she was almost at his side, only a few feet away, and saw his parents and cousins smiling from the front pew, and Gran seated proudly upfront on the bride's side, nestled beside her friends, all the village ladies in their best summer finery and smart hats. Blinking away her tears, she drew back her veil on reaching her husband-to-be, even though her grandmother had suggested she should leave her face covered until the end of the ceremony. She wanted to be able to see Percy clearly and have him see her. She didn't want to miss a single second of her wedding day.

'Dearly beloved,' the vicar began, mercifully having reached the village church on time without suffering any bicycle emergencies or other hold-ups on this most important of occasions, 'we are gathered here today . . .'

Side by side before the altar, Edith and Percy looked at each other, and smiled.

CHAPTER TWENTY-TWO

It was almost the end of August and Sheila thought the caff in Dagenham had never been busier. There were men in uniform everywhere too, as retired army personnel were called back for retraining in anticipation of another war. She served them all with good humour, enjoying the men's banter as well as the extra business, but deep down she was worried. A war would mean so many changes, and she'd only just got used to the idea of running the caff as her own boss . . .

But they would be celebrating Betsy's birthday that week, just the thing to take everyone's mind off the coming war, even if it meant Sheila had been buzzing about more than usual in recent days, trying to organise a special birthday bash at the caff. Not that she begrudged the extra work, making a big fancy cake behind her daughter's back and organising her granddaughters to make secret presents for their mum. In fact, Sheila was thrilled to see her eldest daughter looking so much healthier than she had been earlier that year. The time spent down in Cornwall had done Betsy good. And she and Ernest had soon made up after that spiteful letter of Maggie's, thank goodness.

There hadn't been a single grain of truth behind her sister's malicious tale-telling, of course. Yes, the doctor had been good-looking, but it would take more than looks and a few kind words to turn her daughter's head. Ernest was a wonderful husband and father, and only an idiot would throw away a man like that for a summer fling. Betsy was no idiot, Sheila thought with satisfaction, watching her daughter deal with an awkward customer with a smile and an extra round of buttered toast.

Sheila had found a moment alone with Betsy on the way back to Dagenham to ask her why she thought her aunt had written that letter to Ernest, given it was all rubbish.

Betsy had hesitated. 'Maggie wanted shot of me,' she'd finally muttered, 'that's all I can think.'

'But why?'

Her daughter had looked embarrassed though, and refused to go into any detail. Then Sheila had remembered Stanley pressing Betsy's hand rather too fondly when saying goodbye, and how his eyes had roamed over his niece before Betsy had snatched back her hand and climbed hurriedly into the car. Had Stanley made a pass at her daughter while she was his guest at the farm? If he had, it was no wonder Maggie had been so keen to send Betsy back to Dagenham as soon as possible, even if she had to stir up trouble with Ernest to do so. It also made sense that Betsy wouldn't have said a word to anyone, not even complaining to her or Ernest. Stanley was a bully and a blusterer, but he was also a slippery customer, and Sheila had no doubt he would quickly have tried to pin any blame for wandering hands on the victim.

'I never did like that Stanley Chellew,' she'd ventured, flashing Betsy a reassuring smile. 'Well, you're on your way home now. Least said soonest mended, eh?' She'd paused. 'Though if you ever want a chat . . .'

'I'm fine, Mum,' Betsy had insisted, chin up. 'But thanks, anyway.'

And that had been that.

Violet was still working alongside her at the caff, a little brusque with the customers at times but competent enough. Now that Betsy had joined them again too, it had become a family business.

'Your dad will be looking down at us from heaven and smiling today,' she told her two girls fondly after their first day working together, her arms about their shoulders. 'Dearest Henry . . . How I miss the ol' fellow, God rest his soul. But we have to do our best, eh?'

It had been the proudest day of her life when the old sign above the door – RON'S CORNER CAFF – had been replaced with THE SINGING KETTLE, her own preferred name for the caff. A bit la-di-dah, perhaps. But the regulars seemed to approve, and with Dagenham busier than ever, she was making plenty of money to pay Gordon, Violet and Betsy good wages at last, plus a little left over for herself and a few planned renovations to the décor, assuming a declaration of war wouldn't put a sudden stop to her plans . . .

The girls piled in mid-afternoon, having finished playing at a friend's house, and danced about their mother, singing 'Happy Birthday!' at the tops of their high-pitched voices as Betsy tried to serve two bewildered customers their bacon sandwiches. 'Go and sit down, you noisy pair,' she told them, laughing. 'Yes, I know it's my birthday but I still have a job to do. Blimey, you'll get me the sack at this rate.'

'But you're her daughter . . . Gran would never sack you,' Alice exclaimed, looking astonished.

'Oh, wouldn't I?' Sheila demanded in a mock-threatening manner, emerging from the kitchen, and waved a large wooden spoon at her granddaughter. Though since she'd just been using it to stir a pan of tomato soup, it dripped all down her arm, a tomatoey splash landing on her cheek. 'Oh gawd!'

The girls fell about laughing, and even Betsy bit her lip to stop from chuckling as she hurried over to wipe soup off her mum.

Violet came out of the kitchen to ask what on earth all the ruckus was about, and was instantly accosted by Alice, who pulled a sad face and claimed to be 'starvin'', begging her aunt for a bacon sandwich of her own. Betsy intervened with a shake of her head, outraged by this request, and Alice was sent away with an apple instead to keep her quiet.

'When are we bringing out the birthday cake?' Lily asked Sheila in a low voice. She was swiftly becoming a serious young miss, her large blue eyes always watchful, and a good head on her shoulders.

'Not until closing time,' Sheila replied out of the corner of her mouth, eager for Betsy not to overhear them.

'And the presents?'

'Did you bring 'em?'

Lily nodded solemnly. 'They're in my bag. We didn't wrap them but we tied some ribbon in a bow around each present to make them look fancier.'

'Good idea, love.'

Lily was watching her mother serve a tray of hot drinks. 'Can I help? I could serve some teas and coffees.'

'No, love . . . Thank you, but what if you scalded yourself?' Sheila winked and handed her an apple too. 'Go and keep your sister company, there's a good girl. Maybe after Christmas you can start working here on a Saturday morning and earn yourself some pocket money.'

Lily's face brightened, and she ran off to sit with her younger sister, both girls soon munching cheerfully on their apples. Once they were finished, they set to work blowing up five or six brightly coloured balloons that Gordon had brought in as his contribution to the birthday party before making his excuses and heading off home. He wasn't one for birthday parties, he'd told Betsy apologetically.

Just as Violet was wiping down the tables and Sheila was cashing up, the postman pushed open the door to the caff and popped his head inside. 'Got a second-post parcel here for you, Mrs Hopkins. Marked *Fragile*.' He held up a small parcel wrapped up in brown paper and tied with string.

Surprised, because she hadn't been expecting a delivery, Sheila took the parcel from him. 'Thanks, John.'

When he'd gone, she turned the Open sign to Closed, and then carried the parcel back to the counter. The two girls buzzed about her excitedly. 'What is it, Gran? Something for the caff?'

'I've no idea,' she admitted with a grin, and sent Lily to fetch scissors. Then she cut the string and stripped off the brown paper wrapping. Inside, was a small cardboard box, which she opened to reveal something wrapped in greaseproof paper. 'But it smells bloomin' tasty.'

'Smells like cake to me,' Alice exclaimed, her eyes lighting up.

'And me,' Betsy agreed, peering into the box. 'Look, there's a note with it.'

Gingerly, Sheila fished out the folded note and opened it. 'Oh,' she said indulgently, beaming around at them all, 'it's from Edith. What a diamond she is. She's only gone and sent us a couple of slices of her and Percy's wedding cake because we couldn't make it in person. Oh, and she says thank you for the telegram. It made her cry.' Sheila blinked, rereading that line, and then pulled a face. 'That don't sound too good. I'm sure we didn't mean to make her cry on her wedding day.'

'I'm sure she was just crying with joy, Mum,' Violet said, rolling her eyes.

'I hope you're right.' Sheila unwrapped the two slices of heavily iced wedding cake and sniffed them appreciatively. 'Oh, how lovely . . . Fetch out some plates and forks, would you, Vi? There's no point saving it until later.' She winked at her eldest daughter. 'There's not quite enough to go round but don't worry, Betsy. Never fear . . . Violet and I baked a lovely big cake for your birthday and we'll bring it out when your Ernest gets here.'

Betsy laughed. 'I wasn't worried, Mum. If there's one thing I can count on every bloomin' birthday, it's you and Violet baking a whopping big cake for me. It's a wonder I'm not the size of a house, the amount of cake I get each year.'

'Cake is very good for you,' Sheila told her indignantly. 'It's full of eggs and butter and all sorts, ain't it, Vi?' But her youngest daughter merely laughed, handing her a fork.

Lily tugged on her sleeve. 'Gran, I'm worried that Dad's so late for the party.' She'd been watching the street outside for some time now, her keen eyes constantly checking for her father's arrival. 'I don't want him to miss out on the celebrations.'

'Bless you,' Sheila said, her heart aching at the anxious look in her granddaughter's face, 'we'll make sure we keep a piece of cake for your dad. He did say he might be a bit late, so don't fret.' When Lily stayed where she was, ignoring her, Sheila felt even more certain that the girl was fearful for her father's safety, perhaps recalling what had happened at the last big family celebration, when some villains had given Ernest a going-over on the way to his anniversary do. Concern made her add hurriedly, 'Listen, love, your Aunty Vi can put the wireless on, and we'll all have a nice knees-up while we wait, eh? If they're playing something worth dancing to, that is. We don't want none of that mouldy classical music they're always putting on. Violins and so on.'

Violet turned the wireless on, and although at first it was just two men droning on about Hitler and the peace talks, eventually a nice tune came on, and the two girls held hands and danced in the middle of the caff, kicking their feet up and giggling. Sheila watched this with satisfaction, glad to have taken Lily's mind off her troubles.

She and Violet sat down eventually with a cuppa and a sliver of wedding cake each, which was surprisingly tasty after being stuck in a box for who knows how long.

'This icing is perfect.' Violet made an appreciative noise. 'And the fruitcake – so moist and rich!'

'Her dad is a baker, love. I expect he taught her how to make an iced fruitcake when she was knee-high to a grasshopper. So you'd expect it to be bloomin' good, wouldn't you? Of course, this must have been made for the bakery originally, because it takes weeks to make a good one like this . . . You need to let the cake mature before you can ice it.' Sheila had to admit that it was the best fruitcake she'd ever eaten though. 'Edith made some amazing cakes when she was working at the caff, didn't she? It's a pity she couldn't have stayed longer. I remember one day, she baked a great big—'

The door jangled, and they all looked round.

'Daddy! Daddy!' Alice ran towards her father and threw her arms about him so violently that he staggered backwards, chuckling. 'You'll never guess what . . . Edith sent us slices of her wedding cake in the post, all the way from Cornwall. Gran says it's the best ever, though she's already scoffed hers down. But we saved a bit for you, Dad. You like fruitcake, don't you?'

'I love *all* cakes,' Ernest said solemnly, picking his youngest daughter up and swinging her round so that she squealed with laughter. 'But is there squash, too? It's so hot out there . . . I'm parched and need to drink something cool straightaway.'

'I'll pour you a cup of orange squash,' Lily said promptly, and slipped away into the caff kitchen.

'I'm glad you're here, Dad,' Alice told him with a burst of enthusiasm. 'Because Mum's got a birthday cake as well. Gran and Aunty Vi made it for her specially, and they're going to put candles on it and everything. *Two* cakes in one party. That's what I call smashin' . . .' She sat down and began chasing crumbs of wedding cake around her plate.

Ernest ruffled his daughter's hair and then came towards them with a serious expression. 'Ladies.' He chucked a folded newspaper onto the table between them. 'What a day.'

'What's happened, darling?' Looking worried, Betsy got up to kiss him on the cheek.

'Happy birthday, *Liebling*. I'm sorry I'm so late.' He kissed his wife and held her close. But he wasn't smiling. 'It's this damn war,' he admitted, glancing at Sheila. 'Peace negotiations have completely collapsed. The newspapers expect an announcement from the government at any moment. We need to brace ourselves for what's next. It's not going to be pleasant, I'm afraid.'

Sheila resolutely lifted her chin and refused to look at the newspaper headlines. She'd read a few in recent days, passing the corner newsstand on her work to open up the caff for the day, and could not feel more depressed about the way the world was going. Perhaps, she thought, if she pretended not to notice the horrors unfolding across Europe, she could stay sane. But she knew it would be impossible to look away forever.

'Here's your squash, Dad,' Lily said, and handed it to him, her serious gaze fixed on his face. 'Will . . . Will you be going away? If it's war, I mean?' Her voice cracked on the word 'war', but she took a breath and went on more steadily, 'There are girls at school who say their dads will be going away when war's declared. They want to be soldiers and fight the Germans.' Concern was etched in her face. 'Are *you* going to fight the Germans too, Dad? Even though you *are* a German?'

Ernest put his arm around his daughter and groaned. 'I won't lie to you, Lily. It's a bad situation. And nobody knows exactly what will happen once war is declared. But yes, I may have to go away, and I may eventually have to fight my own people. But that day could be a long, long way off. It may never come, in fact.' He glanced at Sheila, who was listening intently, and gave a crooked smile. 'Besides, I'm half British as well as half German. So whichever side I chose, I'd be fighting my own people.' He paused. 'To my mind, it's more a question of right and wrong. The things Hitler has been doing are clearly wrong and cannot be permitted to continue. So, if I had to become a soldier, I would consider myself fighting for what is right and leave the whole idea of country out of it for as long as possible.'

There was a strained silence, the wireless playing classical music in the background while nobody paid the least attention to it. Alice and Lily were looking dismayed, while Betsy gazed uneasily at her husband.

Unable to bear it any longer, Sheila jumped to her feet and clapped her hands. 'Gawd, what kind of birthday party is this, eh? Betsy, you're the birthday girl . . . How about a nice dance with your hubby? We ain't got no champagne, I'm sorry to say. But I did bring a bottle of my home-made gin, thinking we might enjoy a tipple together.' She winked at Alice and Lily, who were both smiling again, though more for her benefit, she was sure, than because they felt happy. 'Moonshine ain't fit for you two nippers though. You ain't old enough yet.'

'Thank goodness for that,' Ernest muttered, 'as it might have killed them.'

'I'll pretend I didn't hear that, Mr Fisher,' Sheila told him, but gave a chuckle. 'Violet, where's that plate of sandwiches Gordon made us before he left? Bring 'em out, and we'll have a proper feast. Then, if there's still nothing but this old dirge on the wireless, the girls can play the spoons while their mum and dad have a birthday dance.'

Lily's jaw dropped at this, her eyes wide with disbelief. 'Play the *spoons*?'

'When I was young,' Sheila explained, 'we didn't have the wireless. So we had to make our own entertainment. I swear on my life, my old grandaddy played the spoons like he was born to it. I'm not saying I'm as good as him, but I can teach you and Alice to do the trick.' To her relief, Lily and Alice fell about laughing at the idea, their fears forgotten for the moment. 'Oh, you don't believe me? Violet, love, fetch us a pair of large spoons. The biggest, shiniest pair you can find.'

And Sheila cracked her knuckles, puffed and panted, and then swung her arms in violent circles, pretending to be limbering up for a vigorous bout of spoon-playing.

And the girls kept laughing, shaking their heads at their silly old gran.

They passed another hour or so drinking gin, playing the spoons and dancing, and even used the now-empty box from Edith and Percy for a game of pass the parcel, a few sweets rattling inside for the eventual winner. They were just getting ready to clear the party food and drink away, and head home for the evening, when there was a rap at the door.

It was early evening and still light outside. Sheila could see a skinny man in a suit and tie, glancing up and down the street. Ernest went to the door and looked out at him. 'We're closed,' he said smoothly, 'but can I help you?'

The man had already moved on to the next premises, but came back with a ready smile. He held out a poster. 'Good evening. I work for the council, and we need to make sure everyone sees this public notice. Can you stick it in your window so passers-by can see it? Thanks for your help.' With a brisk nod, he hurried on, and Ernest came back into the caff, head bent, reading what he'd been given.

'What does it say?' Sheila asked curiously.

Ernest looked up at last, his face drawn and unhappy. 'I saw something about this in the newspapers yesterday but I didn't think it would happen so soon. It's an evacuation order.' He handed the poster to Betsy, a sombre look passing between the couple. 'The government recommends that all children living in London and the surrounding built-up areas, from four- and five-year-olds right up to school-leaving age, should be sent into the country.'

Sheila stared, aghast. 'Sent away?'

His gaze shifted to his daughters. 'It doesn't say the order is mandatory though. At this stage, it's just a suggestion. So, the girls don't have to go. Not if we don't want them to.'

Betsy stood pale and trembling, staring at her daughters as well. Standing beside her, Violet hugged her reassuringly, reading the poster over her sister's shoulder.

'You heard what Ernie said, sis,' Violet told her in a hearty voice, forcing a smile. 'It ain't mandatory.'

'Yes, but the government must be about to declare war on Germany, mustn't they? And they must think London will be bombed first.' Betsy swallowed. 'Otherwise why order a mass evacuation?'

Ernest nodded. 'That's what the politicians are afraid of, yes. But it's all guesswork at this stage. Nobody knows for sure what will happen. And until we do, we might as well keep our girls close at hand.'

'But if it ain't safe for them here . . .' Betsy glanced at Sheila, her look appealing. 'What do you think, Mum?'

'Sorry, love, don't ask me,' Sheila said hurriedly, disliking being dragged into a dispute between husband and wife, though she would personally much rather not see her two young granddaughters sent to live away from home on the government's say-so.

'I ain't going nowhere,' Lily insisted, folding her arms and glaring at her mother.

'You don't want to send us away, do you, Mum?' Alice asked in a quavering voice.

'I . . . I've got a bad feeling, that's all.' Betsy reached for Alice's hand, adding cajolingly, 'And if most of your little friends are going too, wouldn't that be fun? A few months spent in the country . . . I had a break just like that in Cornwall, to help me get better, and it was lovely. Fields everywhere, with cows and sheep and donkeys . . . What could be nicer, eh?'

'Would we be going to Cornwall too?' Alice asked hopefully.

'I doubt it,' Betsy admitted. 'Cornwall's a bit far away, love. Most likely somewhere on the Norfolk coast, the poster says . . . That's north-east of here. Near enough for us to visit you, if we can.'

Alice looked unimpressed. 'Cornwall sounds nicer.'

'Well, we haven't decided if you're going yet,' Ernest told them, and let the air noisily out of a red balloon, so that both girls chuckled at the rude noise. 'Now, who's going to help me tidy this lot away? It's been a lovely birthday party, but I expect your gran's getting tired by now and would like to go home.' And he locked gazes with his wife, who said nothing.

Sheila nudged her way through the tight-packed crowd on the busy platform, muttering, 'Excuse me,' and 'Sorry, coming through.'

Every now and then, she glanced back at Alice who was staring about herself wide-eyed, gripping a small, battered case that kept knocking against her knee, a paperback tucked under one arm, and her coat pocket bulging with an apple and sandwiches for the journey. 'You all right, love? Stay close behind me, there's a good girl. Don't worry, we're almost there . . . Here we are, carriage three. That's your carriage. And look, it's your teacher. Hello, Mr Hamilton.'

The harassed-looking teacher, ticking off a list of names, turned at her voice. 'Mrs Hopkins, there you are at last. I was beginning to lose hope. Only Alice coming with us?' He handed over a name tag with *Alice Fisher* written on it, string dangling off the end. 'That's fine, we can squeeze her in with Jemima and Fiona. Just tie that onto her jacket, would you?' He turned away, distracted by another family approaching. 'Hurry along and join your friends, Alice.'

But Alice didn't budge. She glared up at her grandmother as Sheila threaded the tag string through one of her jacket buttonholes, her expression defiant. 'I don't want to go to Norfolk,' she said through gritted teeth. 'Why can't I stay home like Lily? She's still at school but she don't need to leave Dagenham. It ain't fair!'

It broke Sheila's heart to see her young granddaughter looking so pinched and cross. But Betsy had put her foot down over the evacuation order, so that was that.

'I'm sorry, love,' she groaned. 'But it's for your own good. If German pilots drop a bomb on us here in Dagenham, at least you'll be miles away on the Norfolk coast.'

'I don't want *Lily* to get blown up though!'

'Your sister will be safe enough in the shelter with your

mum and dad, don't you fret. Your dad's already digging a good spot for the shelter at the bottom of the garden.'

'Why can't I go in the shelter too, then?' Alice demanded. 'I wouldn't take up much room. I wouldn't take any of my books down there. Just a blanket, I swear.'

Sheila hugged her young granddaughter, a sharp pain in her chest at the grief of parting. 'Now, your mum and dad explained it ten times over, so there's no need to make that face. You'll be better off in the country, like all the other youngsters. And Norfolk's not so very far away. You'll be home again before you know it, I promise.'

Alice looked unconvinced. 'Where's Mum gone?' she whispered, her lip trembling.

'She went to buy you something for the journey, love.' Sheila peered anxiously about for Betsy and eventually saw her pushing through the crowd of anxious, hanky-waving parents and older siblings. 'There she is. Betsy, over here!'

Betsy's frantic expression cleared when she caught sight of them. 'Coming, Mum,' she called back, and fought her way to their side.

The carriage doors stood wide open, kids milling about everywhere inside the train. They were all carrying suitcases and hugging stuffed toys, and wearing name tags too, like they were items of lost property. Sheila wanted to grab Alice and take the poor child home again before she could be whisked away to the depths of Norfolk. But it was no use . . . Ever since listening to the dire warnings of other mothers down their street, Betsy had been so worried about her youngest, there'd been no arguing with her.

Lily herself had put her foot down, flatly refusing to leave Dagenham, and since she was old enough at fifteen to know her own mind now, it would have been ridiculous to insist. But Alice was still young enough to be on the school's list of recommended evacuees, and Betsy had insisted that she, at least, should be sent away to Norfolk with the other kids.

Betsy bent to kiss her daughter and whisper something in her ear. Then she slipped a paper bag of sweets into her other pocket. 'Be a brave girl for me. You can write as soon as you get there. I've put a few pence in your pocket for stamps, and there's paper in your suitcase. Don't write reams and reams though, will you? Because that paper won't last forever and I'm not sure if you'll be able to buy more where you're going in Norfolk.' She hugged her daughter and then pointed to the train. 'Go on now, love. Have fun with your friends.'

Reluctantly, casting a final bitter look over her shoulder, Alice trudged off to join the other girls from her class. Together, they made their way down the railway carriage and stood crowding about the window with the other kids, all jostling each other and waving at their respective parents.

Alice lifted a hand in farewell, and Sheila gave a noisy gulp, trying not to cry. Then the train whistle blew, startling the girls, and as the train jolted and began to move, a white cloud of steam enveloped the carriage and for an awful moment, Sheila could no longer see her granddaughter.

Then the mist cleared, and they could see Alice waving madly and shouting, 'Goodbye, goodbye!' as the train chugged away. 'Give my love to Dad and Lily.'

Sheila dragged her hanky from her sleeve and waved it, shouting back, 'Have a grand old time, Alice. Enjoy the countryside.'

Then the train was gone, and all the parents turned and

shuffled away from the platform, looking dejected. Sheila knew how they felt.

Betsy was crying.

Her own eyes brimming with tears, Sheila handed her daughter the hanky. 'There you go, love. I know it's for the best. But the government shouldn't be doing this. Telling parents to part with their kids . . . It ain't natural.'

Betsy blew her nose, nodding. 'But I couldn't live with myself if a bomb fell on the house and our Alice was killed.' She swallowed, dabbing at the wet mascara under her eyes. 'The thing is, Mum, I had such a funny feeling when that council notice came through the door, telling us all how to install a shelter in the garden . . . I know it's daft but just then, I had the most awful premonition—'

'Oh, love, don't!'

'Well, Alice should be safe now, so I can rest easy again, can't I?' Betsy shook her head. 'I hate having to send her away, but what else can we do? Lily's old enough to make up her own mind about staying. But Alice . . . I know she's growing up, but she's still our baby, and Ernie dotes on her. He'd be broken-hearted if something were to happen to his little girl. No, it's best that she's gone to Norfolk with the other kids.'

Together, they walked back to the bus stop. Sheila wondered how Violet was getting on at the caff. Her youngest daughter was covering the morning shift for both of them, with Gordon working in the kitchen. No doubt the atmosphere would be tense and difficult by the time they got to work, Sheila thought wryly. Violet wasn't very good at giving orders without sounding like a sergeant major. Though if war was about to be declared, it wouldn't matter much if Gordon took umbrage at Violet's tone. He'd likely be called up for military training within a few weeks anyway . . . The thought made her dejected, wondering how on earth she'd manage without a cook. Not that she couldn't fry eggs and bacon herself if push came to shove. But there was all the stocktaking and washing-up and serving to be done too, and she couldn't be everywhere at once.

Betsy was still crying, her face buried in her hanky.

'Don't keep crying, love. You'll make your nose red.' Though Sheila wished she herself could stop sniffling too. 'Alice has always wanted to travel, ain't she? Full of spirit, that girl. She'll soon stop missing home and start enjoying herself.'

But at the back of her mind, she was uneasily aware that Alice had sometimes been bullied for being a bookworm and not interested in dolls and dresses like the other girls. Usually, her sister stuck up for her. But Alice would have to learn to stand up for herself in the country.

'Besides,' she added brightly, hoping to cheer herself up as much as Betsy, 'Alice squeezed so many bloomin' books into that suitcase, I'm amazed she could even pick it up. So she'll have plenty to read once she gets to wherever they're sending her. You know Alice ain't never happy without a book in her hand, bless her.'

'That's true.' Betsy gave a choking laugh. 'While she's got a book she can escape into, she'll be right as rain. Most likely.'

And she dragged out her hanky again and blew her nose so noisily that several passers-by stared about themselves in astonishment, perhaps wondering if it was the *Queen Mary* liner docking. Sheila almost said as much out loud, then decided her daughter likely wouldn't find the joke funny, not in her rotten mood . . .

'Oh, love,' Sheila exclaimed, and gave her daughter a hug, 'We've had a right old year, haven't we? And it don't look like things are in a blessed hurry to get much better, more's the pity,' she admitted. 'But if we stick together as a family, and keep our chins up, everything's bound to work out all right in the end, eh?'

But even as she said this out loud, Sheila sighed inwardly, casting her eyes up to heaven and hoping to goodness she was right, and there would be light at the end of the tunnel, eventually . . .

CHAPTER TWENTY-THREE

Betsy was peeling potatoes for Sunday lunch in the kitchen, gazing out at the late summer sunshine, two days after Alice had set off for Norfolk. A shout went up from the sitting room and she jumped violently and wheeled about, her heart racing. *What on earth . . . ?*

'Mum!' Lily cried, dashing to the kitchen door, a puzzle piece in her hand. All morning, she'd been trying to put together a jigsaw puzzle with her grandmother, following the picture on the box. 'There's going to be a statement from the prime minister on the Home Service. Dad says to come quickly, or you'll miss it.'

With a nervous spasm, Betsy dropped the potato she'd been peeling back into the bowl of dirty water. *A statement from the prime minister?* That could mean only one thing . . .

A chill ran through her, but she nodded mechanically and gave her daughter a smile, grabbing up a tea towel to dry her hands. 'I'll be right there, love.'

She'd been thinking about Alice while peeling the veg for lunch, wondering where her youngest was at that precise moment, and what she was doing, and whether she was happy or wanted to come home, and why on earth she'd ever thought it was a good idea for her to be evacuated. It had been two scant days since they'd waved goodbye to Alice at the train station, but they'd been the longest days of her life. Like Ernest, she was hoping that Alice would send a letter soon, eager to hear what she'd been up to since leaving home. But the poor child could hardly have settled in yet in Great Yarmouth, where she and her school had been sent.

'Betsy, where are you? The prime minister's already speaking.' It was Ernest, his voice deep and urgent.

'I'm coming,' she insisted, and hurried through into the sitting room, still drying her hands.

She arrived just in time to hear Neville Chamberlain saying in his posh, cut-glass accent that the British ambassador in Berlin had given the German government a note, saying that unless the Brits heard back from them by eleven o'clock that morning, agreeing to withdraw troops from Poland, then Britain would be at war with them.

A note? It sounded like a playground dispute. *Give Poland back or else . . .* Only the result would be war, not a trip to the headmaster.

Another chill ran through her, and she hugged herself, staring first at the clock on the mantel, which read a little after a quarter past eleven, and then at her husband, whose face was drawn in sharp lines.

'I have to tell you now,' the prime minister went on, his tone oddly matter-of-fact given the terrible importance of what he was saying, 'that no such undertaking has been received, and that consequently this country is at war with Germany.'

The broadcast went on, explaining what would happen next, and listing things they should be doing in preparation for the outbreak of war, but Betsy was no longer listening. She buried her face in her hands and sobbed. Ernest rose and put an arm about her shoulders.

Lily, still clutching the piece from the large and complicated jigsaw puzzle, asked, 'What did the prime minister mean, Dad? What's going to happen now?' There was fear in her voice and she suddenly looked much younger than her fifteen years. 'Are the Germans going to . . . to drop bombs on us?'

Betsy's mum put away the cardigan she'd been knitting for the autumn, got up and pulled Lily into a compulsive hug. 'There, there, love . . . Don't you worry about Germans and bombs and so on. Your dad's putting up a shelter in the back garden. We'll be safe enough in there. It'll all work out in the end, you'll see.' But when she gazed across at Betsy and Ernest over the girl's fair head, there were tears running down her cheeks too.

'So, it's happened at last. All this waiting, but finally we're at war with Germany,' Ernest said heavily. 'My country is at war with . . . my country.'

'Promise me you won't enlist,' Betsy whispered fiercely.

'My dear, you know I can't promise anything of the kind.'

'Hush,' her mum told them urgently, nodding to the radio. 'There's more . . . They're talking about air-raid sirens.'

As they listened in gloomy silence, the man on the Home Service demonstrated the sound of a warning siren, and explained that on hearing it, people would need to drop everything and make their way calmly to a shelter, whether private or public, and wait there until the all-clear was sounded, which he also demonstrated.

'*Calmly*,' her mum repeated with a snort. 'As though anyone could be calm listening to them awful sirens, screechin' away . . .'

'I wish our Alice was here,' Betsy said miserably. 'She's probably listening to this right now up in Norfolk. She must be so afraid, and none of her family are with her.'

'Poor poppet,' her mum agreed, her eyes shiny.

'Alice is a brave girl. She'll cope. And she has her friends around her; don't forget that.' Ernest shook out a clean handkerchief and gently dried Betsy's tears with it. 'Trust me, she's better off where she is.'

Betsy could only hope he was right, so glad of his unruffled strength and common sense in this awful moment.

Yes, Alice would probably be well taken care of in Norfolk. But her fears for him were undiminished. She crossed her fingers behind her back, anxiety tightening her chest, hoping against hope that only younger men would be called to enlist. Ernest was over forty now, surely too old to be serving his country? But that hope faded as the news presenter now spoke of how government ministers were already planning to rush through an emergency Act of Parliament that would allow them to draw on a wide age range of civilians to swell the ranks of Britain's armed forces. Ernest was listening soberly, his blond head bent towards the wireless.

He caught her looking and said, almost roughly, 'Even if I am over the age for enlistment, I *must* join up and fight. You understand that, don't you? Not to do so could be disastrous, and not just for me, but for our whole family.'

Betsy bit her lip to stop from sobbing, tears trembling in her eyes.

'Of course you must enlist,' her mum exclaimed, clapping

him on the back with grim approval. 'Blimey, we all know what folk round here would say if you didn't, you being half German. Besides which, the government would round you up and put you in a prisoner-of-war camp in two shakes of a lamb's tail. Or worse, accuse you of spying for the other side, and gawd knows what would happen *then*.' Sheila shook her head vigorously. 'No, you have to put your name down, if only for the sake of the girls.'

'Agreed.'

And now Betsy wept, unable to hold back her tears any longer. Lily stared wildly from her to Ernest, tears in her own eyes. 'Dad?' she whispered.

'Come here, dearest.' Ernest held their daughter close, their fair heads bent together. 'I'm sorry, truly I am. But there are moments in life when you must choose to take a stand, one way or the other – even if it's hard, you still have to do it.'

'Are you talking about duty?' Lily clung to her dad.

'Yes, dearest. It's my solemn duty to enlist, both to protect you and your mother, but also to defend this country, which is my homeland every bit as much as Germany ever was. I must make a choice, and defending Britain is what I choose. It's the right thing to do.'

'But *why* is it right?' Lily demanded, crying now, and Betsy knew she was afraid for her father. Mortally afraid, just as she was. They both knew deep down that he would have to fight. But knowing and accepting were two different things.

'Because we can't allow fascists like Hitler to trample over a whole people's right to live in freedom and happiness under their own flag,' he explained gently. 'And you heard Mr Chamberlain, didn't you? Since Hitler has refused to back down and has invaded Poland, Britain's only option is to declare war on Germany, to defend liberty and guard against tyranny.' He gave a deep sigh, closing his eyes briefly. 'So, here we are.'

Betsy rushed from the room, unable to listen a moment longer.

Ernest was right, of course he was. But it was so bleedin' unfair. She had fought hard to recover from her breakdown, to return to better health and come home to her family. And for what? She'd barely been home five minutes, and now she was about to lose her husband to the army. And the German war machine that was even now marching into Poland was notoriously cruel and powerful. What chance would British forces have against such a beast?

She knew there was a chance she and her daughters might never see Ernest again once he'd enlisted, and it felt as though her heart was shattering into a thousand pieces. The pain was worse than anything she had ever known, worse than coping with her father's senseless murder, or losing her unborn babies, or having to wave goodbye to dear little Alice . . .

How could she possibly bear this agony?

Betsy woke late a few days later, even though it was a Wednesday. Her mum had given her the day off to be with Ernest, who had taken a few days' leave from the plant while he put up the Anderson shelter that had finally been delivered and saw about enlisting for action. People were saying they should expect bombs to be raining down on them at any minute, now war had been declared, so everyone was in a hurry to make preparations. She herself had been buying up tinned milk and vegetables, and a few extra bags of flour, worried what would happen if the local shops were bombed or supply routes got cut off.

Her husband was no longer in bed, and she soon realised what had woken her, surprised by hammering and voices from the back garden.

Belting up her dressing gown and pushing her feet into carpet slippers, Betsy hurried downstairs and peered out the back door, which was standing open in the September sunshine.

Lily was out there too, helping her dad erect the Anderson shelter at the end of the garden. They were wedging the structure into the enormously deep hole he'd dug, following the instructions that had arrived with the shelter kit. He had promised to build steps down into the shelter next, but for now it was merely a muddy slope. Their daughter's dress and bare legs were spattered with soil, but she seemed cheerful enough, no doubt distracted from events by the messy job in hand, while her father wrestled with a curved sheet of corrugated iron, cursing liberally in a way that soon had Lily clapping her hands over her ears.

With a wan smile, Betsy filled the kettle, put it on the stove to heat, and rinsed out the teapot. Soon, she heard hammering again from the garden, and her husband's voice, begging Lily to, 'Hold it still, for goodness' sake!' The water having come to a boil, she lifted the whistling kettle off the stove, and caught the familiar tread of the postman, followed by the letterbox rattling.

Betsy peered down the hallway and sure enough, there was a small envelope lying on the mat.

She dashed forward and snatched it up. 'Thank gawd!' It

was her youngest daughter's handwriting. A messy scrawl, but more or less legible. She hadn't quite got their address right, which perhaps explained why the letter had only just arrived when Alice had insisted that she would write as soon as she arrived in Great Yarmouth.

'Ernst!' she cried, rushing outside with the letter held aloft. 'It's from Alice. Take a rest from knocking together that bloomin' shelter and let's read our daughter's letter.'

Ernest wiped a smudge of dirt from his forehead, which merely smeared it more, and leant on his spade. 'You'll be glad of this shelter when the bombs start falling,' he pointed out, but nodded. 'You can read the letter out to us while we rest. We're puffed out, aren't we, Lily?'

'I'll be happy never to dig another hole ever again,' Lily admitted, dragging herself out onto the grass.

But as Betsy tore open the envelope, eager to read Alice's letter, her husband added softly, 'Darling, remember not to call me *Ernst*, yes? You don't do it often anymore,' he added, 'but nowadays, more than ever, it's important that I fit in.'

Betsy stared at him, unfolding the letter. 'Did . . . Did I call you *Ernst*? I had no idea. Sorry, love. You were always Ernst to me when we were courting. I suppose it just slipped out . . .'. She saw Lily's confused stare, and explained, 'It was only after we got married that your dad started to go by Ernest instead.'

Lily exclaimed, 'I don't understand. Dad? I always thought your Christian name was Ernest. Now you're telling me it ain't?'

'Given what happened during the Great War, I thought it best to change my name from Ernst to Ernest, on account of it sounding more British.' Ernest took out a hanky to wipe a sheen of perspiration from his forehead, for although they were into September now, the weather was still warm and bright. 'It wasn't something you needed to know when you were little. Now you're old enough to understand.'

Lily nodded slowly, but there was still a look of consternation on her face. 'There's so much I don't know about you, Dad.'

He gave her a reassuring hug. 'One day, Lily, I'll sit down with you and Alice, and tell you all about my family back in Germany, and how my father married my mother . . . Who was English, of course. But right now, let's listen to Alice's letter, shall we?'

Betsy took a deep breath and read the letter aloud.

Dear Mum and Dad,

I am very very very unhappy here. Please come and get me straightaway. We have been stuck in a house in Great Yarmouth with two old ladies what don't know how to boil an egg. Not joking. Breakfast is toast, and nothing else. If you don't come soon, I will waste away. I will wait two days for you and then I am coming home on my own if you ain't here. I still have sixpence what Gran gave me for my birthday and if the train is more, I will hitch a lift home instead.

Love Alice

Ernest laughed, hearing this, and Betsy glared at him. 'It ain't funny,' she insisted, deeply affected by her daughter's letter. 'How can you laugh? Our Alice is unhappy. I thought she'd like being with her mates from school when she was evacuated, but this . . .' Betsy clutched the letter to her chest. 'What do you think we should do? Tell the school?'

Lily, who had decided not to return to school that autumn but to start looking for work instead, said practically, 'But what can the teachers do? Alice is in Norfolk now. That's miles away, ain't it?' She shook her head, a sceptical look in her eyes. 'Anyway, she's likely just messin' about. She won't run away. Not Alice. She'd miss her three square meals a day too much.'

'But you heard what she wrote,' Betsy exclaimed, defending her youngest. 'These old women she mentions, they're only feeding them toast. Not proper cooked meals like Alice is used to. No wonder she thinks she's wasting away, poor lamb.' Betsy sank onto the grass, suddenly weak and shaky. She wished she knew what to do. All her instincts told her to rush to Alice's side at once. But Lily was right about one thing – Norfolk was a long way away. And there was a war on now.

'This bloomin' letter was misdirected too, Ernie. Look!' She showed him the envelope with its slanted, badly scripted address. 'Alice must have written this last week when she first got there. She says she'll wait only two days; well, that was ages ago. Gawd, she might have given up on us replying by now and run away. She could be anywhere . . . Ernie, whatever are we going to do?'

Climbing laboriously out of the hole, Ernest wiped dirty hands on his overalls and reached for the letter. 'Let me read it for myself,' was all he said. He stood, head bent, to read his daughter's letter. He laughed at one point, briefly showing the letter to Lily. 'Your sister spelled it *Yarmuff* at first, see? Then crossed that out and spelt it correctly, Great Yarmouth.'

Then his smile faded as he read on, and he clucked his tongue, his look troubled. 'You're right, Betsy. This doesn't sound like Alice at all. And her handwriting is all over the place . . . She must've had some run-in with the other kids to make her this miserable.'

'She had trouble with a couple of bullies last year, didn't she? Because she's clever.' Determined now, Betsy jumped to her feet. 'Let's drive to Norfolk and rescue her. Right now. Today.'

'My darling Betsy . . .' Turning a startled gaze towards her, her husband tucked the letter into his overalls pocket. 'I know you mean well by Alice, but you're not thinking straight.'

That was the last straw. Ignoring him, Betsy turned to her eldest daughter. 'Lily,' she said firmly, 'run and wash your hands, and get some clean clothes on. You're coming with us.'

Her daughter, eyes alight with astonished excitement, glanced uncertainly at her dad, and then dashed back inside the house without a word.

Ernest took both Betsy's hands in his. '*Liebchen*, I have to go back to the office tomorrow, and Sheila will be expecting you at work too. We both have responsibilities here. Alice will be fine . . . She's just missing us.'

'*Just*?' she cried, eyes kindling at how dismissive he was being.

'I was the same at her age when I was sent off to boarding school. It can be unpleasant and frightening the first time you have to live away from home. But Alice is a level-headed girl. Once she's got over the shock of being offered only toast for breakfast,' he added with a twinkle in his eye, 'she should soon settle down and begin to enjoy herself.'

'Ernie, you didn't see her at the train station,' she whispered. 'Her poor little heart was broke. It took me and Mum ages to get her onto the platform, let alone aboard the train.' She gave a cracked laugh, remembering how they had coaxed and cajoled her to join her friends. 'I had to bribe her with sweets in the end. She didn't want to leave home.'

'That doesn't mean she's going to run away.'

A little flushed and indignant now, Betsy released her husband's hands. 'I'll go on my own, then. I'll take the train to Great Yarmouth meself, and bring our daughter home, see if I don't.' Frustrated, she turned and stalked away.

He caught up with her in the cool shade of the kitchen. 'Betsy, you're being ridiculous. You can't go.'

'And you shouldn't come indoors in muddy boots,' she snapped. 'And I don't need your bloomin' permission to leave this house.'

'I'll mop the floor. And that's not what I meant, and you know it.' Ernest hesitated. 'Given your recent illness, and now war being declared . . . It's not a good idea for you to be travelling anywhere on your own.'

She opened her eyes wide. 'Then come with me.'

'I can't,' he admitted. 'I've got an appointment this afternoon. I can't miss it.'

Taken aback, she stared at him. 'An appointment? Whatever do you mean?'

His expression was torn. 'At the armed forces recruiting office,' he told her. 'I warned you I was planning to enlist, and I can't leave it much longer or people will start saying I'm an enemy sympathiser. You must see how much danger it would put you and the girls in.'

'Enlist? Already?' Betsy pulled away from him. 'But what

if you never come back?' she choked. 'Me and the girls . . . We'll be all alone.'

Lily came thundering down the stairs, calling out excitedly, 'Mum? Dad? You'll never guess what . . . Alice is coming down the bloomin' street.'

With a sharp cry, Betsy rushed to the front door, flinging it open and stumbling down the front path. And there was Alice, trudging wearily towards them, her fair plaits dishevelled and her gait shuffling, dragging her suitcase as though it weighed a ton.

'Alice, love!' Betsy sobbed. She threw open the gate and ran down the street towards her youngest daughter, her carpet slippers clacking noisily all the way. With an effort, she pushed aside her fear over Ernest enlisting. They would likely not take him anyway, given his age. Her daughter was more important for now.

'Gawd, whatever have you done now?' She clutched Alice to her chest and squeezed her tight. 'Oh, pet . . . Please tell me you never came all the way home on your own?'

Lily, having followed her, now took Alice's suitcase from her, chiding her sister gently, 'Whatever have you been up to, you silly sausage? That letter of yours gave Mum fifty fits. She's been trying to get Dad to drive up to Norfolk to rescue you.'

Alice, released from Betsy's stranglehold, saw her father standing at the front gate, and pulled a face. 'Oops.' She heaved a sigh. 'No need now though, is there? I'm back.'

Betsy laughed, a tear running down her cheek again. But at least she was crying with joy this time. 'Yes, yes, you are.'

'Sorry if I frightened you, Mum.' Alice gave her an exhausted smile. 'I just couldn't stand it anymore. And the other kids said evacuation wasn't obligatory. That means I didn't have to stay if I didn't want to,' she finished stubbornly.

Betsy turned to her husband, so relieved to have her daughter back that she could barely speak. She could see the same emotion on Ernest's face, but he merely tapped Alice gently on the shoulder, saying, 'I suppose all's well that ends well.'

'That's Shakespeare,' Alice said promptly, perking up.

'Top of the class,' her father murmured fondly and pulled her into a hug.

Aware of the neighbours' curtains twitching, Betsy took Alice by the hand and led her firmly inside. 'Have you eaten, dear? You'll want something hot, I expect.'

'Yes, please, Mum. But *no toast*. I wouldn't mind if I never had buttered toast again in my entire life. I swear, it was all they ever gave us to eat in that 'orrid place.' Alice sat down heavily at the table, and for once Betsy didn't even remind her to wash her hands before food.

'Ungrateful pup,' Lily told her sister, tutting. 'It sounds like them ladies were doing their best.'

Alice had the grace to look embarrassed. 'They were all right,' she conceded grudgingly. 'But their cooking . . . It weren't nothing on yours, Mum. Or Gran's.' She gave an exaggerated yawn and rubbed her eyes. 'Blimey, I'm so bloomin' tired. Maybe I should have forty winks.'

Ernest sat down beside her and took his daughter's hand. 'Before you fall asleep, we all want to know how you got back home on only a sixpence?'

Alice blushed, looking guilty. 'You won't be cross?'

'Let's hear it first,' he said.

'Well, I packed me case and climbed out the window this morning before it was light. I ran down the street and kept going until I got a blister on the back of me foot . . .' She grimaced. 'It hurt so bad, I sat down by the side of the road to think. Then this big truck came along, so I stuck out my thumb. And the driver stopped. I was a bit scared, but he was a really nice man. He said he was going my way and told me to hop inside.'

'Dear heavens,' Betsy said faintly, trying not to imagine all the dreadful things that could have happened to her daughter during this escapade.

'Alice Fisher, what have I told you and Lily about accepting lifts from strangers?' her father demanded, steel in his voice.

'I know, Dad.' Alice squirmed under his glare. 'It was wrong. And I'll never do it again in my life, I swear. Only the thing is, that blister . . . I was in bloomin' agony, I couldn't have walked another step.' She kicked off her shoes under the kitchen table, groaning. 'I need some of Gran's special blister ointment.'

'This truck driver,' Lily interrupted impatiently. 'He drove you to Dagenham, did he?'

'More or less. He said my parents would be worried stiff, so he agreed to give me a lift to the outskirts of Dagenham, though it was out of his way. He couldn't drop me any closer, because he was already worried about being late, so he let me out about three miles from town. I had to walk the rest of the way.' Alice sighed. 'Well, *limp* . . . I thought I'd never get here. It was the longest walk of my life.'

Betsy was terrified at the thought of her daughter having got into a truck with a stranger. But at least she was back safe and sound. She bent and kissed her on the forehead. 'Well, you're home now, and you're not being evacuated again. Not unless the government don't give us a choice. And that's final,' she added, with a defiant glance at her husband.

Ernest nodded. 'Yes, no more Great Yar*muff*.'

Alice grinned, looking relieved.

'I'm glad you're back with us, Alice,' Ernest went on, his voice turning stern again. 'But we need to have a proper chat later about the right way to go about escaping from old ladies in Norfolk, and one that doesn't involve getting into vehicles with strange men. Is that understood?'

'Yes, Dad,' Alice said meekly.

Feeling much happier now her youngest was safe at home again, Betsy was unpacking Alice's suitcase later when she heard the click of the front door and went downstairs to find Ernest standing in the hallway, looking blankly at nothing, his hat in his hand. He had gone out to the recruiting office after lunch, claiming they would probably turn him away because of his age, being over forty now, but it was worth trying anyway.

'Well?' she asked, studying him anxiously. 'What happened? Did they turn you down?'

His gaze rose to hers, troubled. 'No, they accepted my application. I'll be getting my orders in the post, probably within the next week or two. Apparently, so many men have enlisted in the past few days, they've been struggling to find training camp places for us all.'

'Oh, Ernie, no . . .'

'I'm sorry, darling. But there's no way round it.' He looked around vaguely, listening to the silence in the house. 'Where are the girls?'

'Alice had her nap and woke up feeling much better,' she said with an effort, 'so Lily's pushing her sister round to the caff in their old go-kart, since her blister's still hurting and she wants her gran to look at it. You should have seen them when they set off, giggling like five-year-olds, Alice veering all over the place . . .' She was smiling, but there was an aching hole in her chest where her heart had been. There was so much that Ernest would miss now he had enlisted. Not just go-kart antics but birthdays and Christmas . . . Maybe more than one Christmas. 'They're not going to understand why you're going away.'

'Of course they will. Plenty of their friends will be coming to terms with their fathers leaving too. The queue at the recruiting office was out of the door . . .' He stared down at his hat, not moving. 'I'll tell them when they get home.'

'Ernest?' Worried by his stillness, she kissed him and held him close. 'What is it? Are you regretting it already?'

'No,' he said promptly, and stepped back to look at her, a frown on his handsome face. 'Absolutely not. Enlisting was the right thing to do, and I stand by the decision. The only thing is . . .' He paused, his brow furrowed.

'Yes?' she prompted him.

'After I'd passed my physical examination, they sent me along the corridor to speak to a man from a different department. I thought I'd be going into the army, but apparently not.' He hung up his hat at last, and ran a hand through floppy fair hair, slicking it back. 'It's because of my German heritage, you see.'

She was confused. 'But you said they accepted your application. They must think you're British enough to join. What did they want?'

'I don't think I can tell you.'

'Eh?'

He seemed to be struggling for the right words, then said, 'The truth is, Betsy, I was warned not to say anything, not even to you. I even had to sign some documents . . .' He pulled a face, then whispered, 'It's top secret.'

'*Top secret*?'

He smiled at her baffled expression. 'I'm afraid so, *Liebling*. All I can say is, I've joined up but it looks like I won't be doing any ordinary soldiering.' When she began to speak, he shook his head. 'No, I shouldn't even have said that. You need to forget it. And not repeat it to anyone, understand? Not even the kids. And especially not your mother.' He grimaced. 'Tell your mother, and everyone in Dagenham would know by tomorrow.'

'But know *what*?' Her heart was thumping. 'I can scarcely say a word to anyone when I ain't got the first bloomin' clue what you're talking about. Not doing any *ordinary soldiering*?' She studied him, disturbed by how mysterious he was being. 'Surely you don't mean . . . spying?'

His eyes met hers. 'All you need to know is, I'm going to do us proud, Betsy.' He kissed her on the lips, a strange light in his face. 'And I love you.'

Her heart stirred at his words.

She might not know for certain what role he'd been assigned in the coming war, but she understood what *she* needed to do, and resolved at once to do it, for better or worse. The country was at war with Germany now, and her husband had chosen to fight on Britain's side. She would need to be strong while he was away, for him and for their daughters, and that was all that mattered.

'I love you too,' she told him with sudden passionate intensity, and closed her eyes as he took her in his arms.

EPILOGUE

Edith clung to the deck railing while she peered cautiously overboard, watching the huge ocean liner plough through heavy, rolling waves below. Behind them were the green, sunlit shores of England, though she could no longer make out details like ribbons of road or clusters of buildings. Ahead of them lay open sea, and at some point in the future, at least a week from now, the Canadian coastline would appear on the horizon, an unknown and exciting place, waiting for her to discover it.

She leant back against Percy, who had insisted on standing behind her for safety, his arms locked about her growing belly. 'This is to prevent you from falling in,' he'd quipped when they'd first ventured onto the deck to watch the port of Southampton shrink into the distance. There came another fine spray of sea water on the wind, the boards now slippery with it, the air moist and salty.

'Still thinking about your grandmother?' Percy asked, his voice a rumble in her ear. 'Don't be sad, darling. Rosalyn said she would try to visit us once the baby is born, remember. Next spring, perhaps, once sailings start again after the winter ice has cleared.'

'Assuming the government will let her leave England,' Edith reminded him gloomily. 'Now that we're at war with Germany, everything's different, isn't it?'

'I suppose you're right.' There was a note of strain in his voice. 'You heard the captain though . . . War's only just been declared, so we should be safe enough crossing to Canada this week. Soon though, the waters around Britain may start getting dicier. I wouldn't want to be sailing next week.'

'Yes, it was a good idea of yours to leave so soon after the wedding.' She put a quick hand to her belly as the baby shifted position, causing a momentary spasm of discomfort. 'It's strange though,' she added, thinking of the child inside her. 'Everything changed for me even *before* Britain declared war on Germany.'

His arms held her comfortable and safe as the ship rose and fell steeply. 'You mean . . . because of the baby?'

'Yes, but other things too. It's been such a strange year.' Edith stared out to sea, mesmerised by the vast, heaving, dark blue waters that seemed to stretch on forever, rippling into the distance. 'Before I met you, Percy, I was so sure I knew what my future life would look like . . . Working with Dad in the bakery, learning the trade, helping Gran in the garden and with those church fetes she loves.' She smiled at the bittersweet memories. 'And I assumed that maybe I'd get married one day and settle down in the same village where I was born. Until I met you and fell in love,' she added softly, and felt his arms tighten about her. 'Then you left and everything went wrong, so I ran away to Dagenham.'

He made an apologetic sound in her ear. 'I'm sorry about that.'

'Don't be. It wasn't your fault any more than it was mine.'

'Maybe Susan's fault, then?'

'It was *nobody's* fault,' she told him firmly. 'Besides, I forgave Susan for those horrid things she said about me, remember?'

Though how could either of them possibly forget? It had been the most extraordinary thing, but Susan Teague had come to find Edith in her grandmother's rose garden at the wedding reception and begged a few minutes alone with the bride and groom. Edith hadn't known what to expect, glancing nervously at Percy, but had been too curious to say no. The three of them had crossed the lawn until they were out of earshot of the other wedding guests. Then Edith had turned to face her old friend, her hand locked in Percy's for support. To her amazement, Susan had stood wringing her hands, tears in her eyes. 'I wanted you to know ... I shouldn't have told anyone what I'd seen that night. I don't know what came over me, but I never meant for things to go that far,' she'd confessed. 'And afterwards, I was too stubborn to admit I'd made a mistake by blabbing my mouth off and ruining your reputation. But I can't live with the shame a moment longer. The truth is, I behaved abominably towards you, Edith ... and I'm so, so sorry.'

'But why do it in the first place?' Edith had cried, not understanding.

'Because I was jealous of you and Percy.' Seeing Edith's astonishment, Susan had nodded, dragging a hanky out of her sleeve to dab at her eyes. 'Yes, I'm sorry, it's true. Ever since we were at school and had that stupid row over Stephen,' she'd sobbed, 'I've been so afraid that I'm just not p-pretty or c-clever enough to *ever* attract a b-boyfriend.' She'd taken a shuddering breath, clearly fighting for control. 'You see, I worked so hard for years to get Stephen interested enough to ask me out, and after all that, he told me outright that it was *you* he'd fancied all along. That he'd only been friendly to me so he could get closer to you.'

'Oh, Susan!'

But she hadn't finished. 'And the worst thing, Edith, was that you weren't even interested in him. You turned him down flat, and he left the village and never came back. It felt to me like you'd just thrown Stephen away and left me heartbroken.'

'I didn't realise.'

'Then Percy came along and seemed to fall for you in ten seconds flat too.'

'Maybe not quite *ten seconds*,' Percy had murmured and then grimaced, having caught Edith's sideways look. 'Sorry, do go on.'

'I thought if I could make *you* feel bad,' Susan had admitted, shamefaced, 'it would make *me* feel better. Only I felt like hell instead. And when you came home again, I meant to say sorry at once for what I'd put you through, but didn't know how. I was just so ashamed and embarrassed, so I pretended that I didn't care about your feelings. Only I really did . . .' With a sob, Susan had wiped away the fat tears rolling down her cheek. 'It was none of my business. Not any of it. Can you forgive me?'

'Of course I can, silly,' Edith had blurted out, also crying, and thrown her arms about Susan, whom she'd feared and disliked for so long. Because she'd known that, if she couldn't forgive Susan after such a heartfelt apology, and on her wedding day too, she would never be able to forgive anyone for anything the whole rest of her life. And she'd wanted a clean start for her married life with Percy. To be a brand-new Edith, no longer afraid of what people might say about her but determined to be true to herself and her husband. The sort of young woman who could begin again in a fresh place like Canada with untold adventures waiting ahead . . .

Bringing Edith back to the present moment, Percy stroked a few tangled red strands of hair from her face as the sea breezes tore wildly about the deck. 'Yes, I remember . . . You amazed me that day. I'm not sure I would have been so forgiving.' When she didn't reply, still looking mistily out to sea, he tightened his arms about her. 'Unhappy?' he asked, his breath warm on her cheek.

'Goodness, no. Though it's true that I wish Gran could have come with us,' she admitted, aware of a deep sadness inside her at that absence. 'But she wants to stay in Penmarrey, so Dad knows there'll be someone there when he comes home at last. She says that will keep him strong during the war. And that's important. Everyone needs someone. I've got you,' she pointed out, revelling in the warmth of his strong body anchoring her to the deck. 'But who has Dad got, if not my grandmother?'

'So, in other words, you're *not* unhappy.' He paused. 'But you're not as happy as you could be?'

Edith laughed at this tortuous thinking. 'Quite the opposite, darling. I'm perfectly happy. That's what's so extraordinary.' She thought back to the timid, confused girl she'd been before she met Percy, and felt as though that had been another Edith altogether. 'You see, when I was growing up, I always thought of myself as a stay-at-home girl, a born homebody . . . I was content with the idea of never going beyond Cornwall in my whole life. But then I went to Dagenham – on my own – and now look at me!' She flung her arms wide, as he supported her from behind. 'I'm a citizen of the world.'

'Yes, and I can't wait for you to see Canada,' her husband told her, a catch in his voice. 'Or for our child to be born there.' At that moment, she felt the baby kick, right under his hand. He choked in surprise and then laughed out loud. 'Seems like somebody's keen to see Canada too. And it is the most beautiful country.' He cradled her happily. 'I promise, you'll soon fall in love with it and not miss Cornwall one little bit.'

'I fear I may always miss Cornwall,' she warned him, aware of the constant tug of home, but smiled when the baby kicked again.

It felt strange to imagine this new life growing bigger and stronger inside her, and to know that soon they would discover if this was a boy or girl, and name them accordingly, possibly after a grandmother or grandfather. Their child deserved a name that was loved, as he or she would be loved. It was also odd to realise that this child would be born in Canada and perhaps never know Cornwall and the world she had left behind . . .

Shouts disturbed her thoughts, and they both looked round in surprise. Others were glancing that way too, no longer gazing forward but back at the land they'd left behind barely half an hour before. One little boy broke away from his mother and ran helter-skelter along the wet deck, stumbling and slipping. He was pointing upwards, exclaiming excitedly, 'It's one of them new planes Dad was telling us about. A Spitfire, it's called . . . Look, they're *all* Spitfires!'

Everyone had turned to look now, craning their necks as they peered up into the soft blue-grey afternoon sky.

Sure enough, one swift, bright-winged plane buzzed past the ocean liner, as though the pilot was wishing them *Bon voyage*, and then turned to fly westward alongside the English shore, towards Cornwall. A cheer rose up from the ship as a moment later another two Spitfires appeared, their wings gleaming in the sun as they banked right to follow the other plane.

An audible sigh sounded from the crowd as the planes were lost to view through the gathering haze of sea mist.

'Smashing!' the boy exclaimed, grinning up at his mother.

Percy had released her at the first shout, turning to watch the planes intently.

She reached for his hand, keeping a tight grip on the deck railing to avoid slipping, and glanced up at her husband's face. He had still been following the path taken by the planes but glanced back at her when she spoke his name, a faraway look in his face.

'What are you thinking?' she asked softly.

'It doesn't matter.'

She didn't believe him. 'You're wishing you could pilot one of those Spitfires, aren't you? Like those young men my dad's been training at the RAF base.'

There was conflict in his face. 'I want to be there for you and the baby when it comes . . . But you're right, I do wish I could have the chance to fight.' He grinned. 'I say, weren't those Spitfires marvellous though? It must be the most incredible feeling in the world, to be up there among the clouds, like a god.' He stopped abruptly. 'But as far as I know, there's no conscription in Canada yet, and I won't enlist, not when I have all this responsibility at home. There are plenty of other young men to take to the skies in planes like that. Men without beautiful wives and babies on the way,' he added with a lopsided smile, and bent to kiss her. 'I love you so much, Mrs Grigg.'

'I love you too, Mr Grigg,' she replied shyly, and blushed when the lady with the young boy smiled at her in passing. 'Though I'm rather tired now,' she whispered, thinking of their cosy, sea-facing cabin with a curtain that pulled across the porthole, just right for a pair of drowsy newlyweds who couldn't get enough of each other's company. 'It was such a fatiguing business coming aboard, wasn't it? Passport control, waiting to be allowed across the gangplank, and then being allocated cabins . . . I could do with a lie-down before dinner.'

'A lie-down, you say?' he murmured, one brow raised. 'Sounds like a wonderful idea. Let me lead you to your boudoir, madame. It's a seven-day voyage, after all. Plenty of time for staring at the sea, and dining in the restaurants, and maybe the odd turn about the dance floor now and then.' Desire kindling in his eyes, he lifted her hand to his lips. 'We need to pace ourselves.'

'And take plenty of naps?' she suggested.

Percy grinned. 'You read my mind,' he agreed with a wink. 'You know, whoever invented the honeymoon, I could shake his hand.'

She smiled, recalling the delirious wonder of their wedding night in a fancy hotel in Southampton. 'Maybe it was a woman.'

'Oh, judging from the experience so far, I'm pretty confident it was a man.'

Edith merely laughed and shook her head. If dear Percy wished to believe that a man derived more pleasure from the honeymoon than his wife, it didn't seem worth arguing about. After all, they would have a lifetime together for her to teach him the error of his ways.

Behind them, in the misty distance, the sun had disappeared. Rainclouds had gathered instead, and it looked as though a storm was brewing over England. Glancing back at her homeland one more time, Edith caught the faint buzz of engines as the Spitfires ran training missions up and down the coast, no longer visible to those on deck, merely a gleam now and then spotted through the clouds.

She felt a pang as she thought of her grandmother in Cornwall, and her father training all those new pilots, and Mrs Hopkins and everyone at the corner café back in Dagenham. She hoped they would be safe and that she would see them again one day, for war was coming to Britain. And who knew what dangers it would bring . . .

Go back to where it all began – don't miss the first book in the glorious Cornish Girls series…

Available now in paperback, eBook and audiobook.

Follow up with some festive fun for the Cornish Girls...

Available now in paperback,
eBook and audiobook.

Enemy gunfire on Penzance beach brings the Cornish Girls rushing to the rescue…

Available now in paperback, eBook and audiobook.

Can the bonds of motherhood give them the strength they'll need to get through the war?...

Available now in paperback, eBook and audiobook.

Can love still thrive in the uncertainty of war?

Available now in paperback, eBook and audiobook.

The war is over and now the healing can begin…

Available now in paperback,
eBook and audiobook.

The world is at peace at last. Is it time for the Cornish Girls to love again?

Available now in paperback,
eBook and audiobook.